to discover. Cabot's historicals are her shining stars, and this one belongs on fans' keeper shelves."

—*RT Book Reviews*, 4 stars

"From the first page I found myself rooting for the young widow. Amanda Cabot offers a delightful read, and as I turned the pages I was swept away with a story of love, courage, and sacrifice. Recommended!"

—Tricia Goyer, bestselling author of 32 books, including *Beyond Hope's Valley*

"One thing I know to expect when I open an Amanda Cabot novel is heart. She creates characters that tug at my heart-strings, storylines that make my heart smile, and a spiritual lesson that does my heart good. Her stories are like the first sweet scents of spring—pure pleasure."

—Kim Vogel Sawyer, bestselling author of *My Heart Remembers*

WITH
AUTUMN'S
RETURN

WESTWARD WINDS · BOOK 3

WITH AUTUMN'S RETURN

A NOVEL

AMANDA CABOT

Revell

a division of Baker Publishing Group
Grand Rapids, Michigan

© 2014 by Amanda Cabot

Published by Revell
a division of Baker Publishing Group
P.O. Box 6287, Grand Rapids, MI 49516-6287
www.revellbooks.com

Printed in the United States of America

Library of Congress Cataloging-in-Publication Data
Cabot, Amanda, 1948–
    With Autumn's Return : a novel / Amanda Cabot.
        pages cm. — (Westward Winds ; #3)
    ISBN 978-0-8007-3461-9 (pbk. : alk. paper)
    1. Wyoming—History—19th century—fiction. 2. Chrisian fiction. 3. Love stories. I. Title.
PS3603.A35W58 2014
    813'.6—dc23   2013029559

14 15 16 17 18 19 20   7 6 5 4 3 2 1

For Judith B. Stumpf, my sister, my friend,
and a woman who, like the fictional Elizabeth,
is kindhearted and a skilled healer.

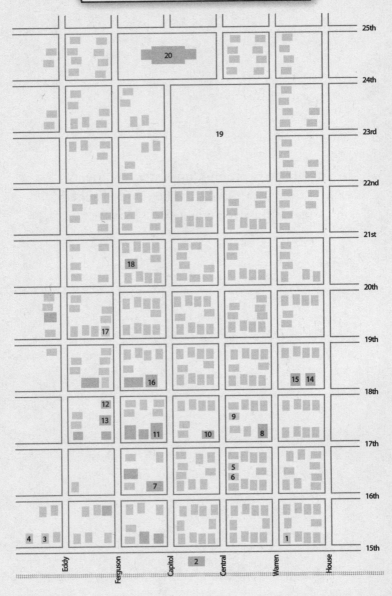

Cheyenne, Wyoming Territory 1887

1. Phoebe's Bordello
2. The Depot
3. Livery
4. Nelson's Lumberyard
5. Elizabeth's Office
6. Jason's Office and Home
7. InterOcean Hotel
8. The Cheyenne Club
9. Doc Worland's Office
10. Ellis Bakery and Confectionary
11. Opera House
12. Elizabeth and Gwen's Home
13. Harrison's Home/Landry Dry Goods
14. Chadwick Home
15. Taggert Home
16. Maple Terrace (Miriam and Richard's Home)
17. Courthouse
18. Barrett Landry's Home
19. City Park
20. The Capitol

Italics indicate fictional locations.

1

At last! Elizabeth Harding grinned as she hung the sign in the window. Thirteen black letters. Four words. A simple message. If passersby noticed the wooden placard, and she hoped they would, they would have no way of knowing what those words meant to her, that they represented the culmination of a dream that had begun when she was only seven. They didn't need to know. All they needed was the message the sign imparted.

Once she was certain the board was perfectly straight, Elizabeth took a step back, then twirled around. It was silly perhaps, and some might call it undignified to be so excited, yet she couldn't help it. Today was the first day of her new life.

Yielding to impulse, she hurried outside and studied the

sign. "The doctor is in." Yes, indeed she was. And soon she'd be treating her first patient. The advertisements she had placed in the newspaper had alerted the city's residents to her impending arrival, and today's paper announced the official opening of her medical practice. It would be only a matter of minutes before the front doorbell tinkled, signaling the presence of someone needing her care. Everything was ready. Or was it?

Assailed by the fear that she might have forgotten something, Elizabeth hurried back indoors and began studying the rooms that comprised her office. The waiting room, with its two benches and four chairs, was spotless. The potted plant that her sister had somehow kept alive through the long Cheyenne winter was carefully placed on the low table, and though sun did not yet stream through the westward-facing window, the room was bright and cheerful. There was nothing amiss here.

Elizabeth moved slowly into the room that would serve as a combination office and examination room. Although it did not boast the fancy equipment she'd seen in Eastern hospitals, it was well-appointed. She had a cleverly constructed examining table with braces that allowed her to raise either the head or the foot. She'd even asked the carpenter to build a small stool so that shorter patients or children would be able to climb onto the table. The desk and chairs were new and matched the glass-fronted cupboard that held the supply of medicines that had been delivered only yesterday. She needed nothing more here.

A quick study of the modest infirmary on the opposite side of the hallway told her everything was in place. Though she hoped few patients would need to avail themselves of it, its presence meant that Elizabeth could tend even the most seriously ill patient, and the small kitchen behind it would ensure that her basic needs as well as those of her patients would be satisfied.

Returning to the main room and sinking into the chair behind her desk, Elizabeth smiled. The sign was perfect. The office was perfect. Soon everything would be perfect, for soon she would have proof that the years of studying, of practicing, of enduring the snide remarks and blatant jeers of her male classmates were all worthwhile. Soon she would have her first patient, and then she—and the world—would know that Elizabeth Harding was a doctor, a real doctor.

Five minutes later, unable to remain seated, she wandered back to the waiting room and gazed outside, her eyes moving from bustling Central Avenue to the sky. Her sisters hadn't exaggerated when they'd claimed there was nothing that compared to the Wyoming sky. Though initially Abigail hadn't been impressed with much about the territory, even she had liked the sky, and Charlotte had been so in love with her first husband that she had declared everything about Wyoming beautiful.

Deep blue with only a tiny puff of a cumulus cloud floating by, the sky was magnificent, but even if it had been dismal and gray all the time, Elizabeth would still have chosen Cheyenne for her new home. Though it had yet to achieve statehood, Wyoming was a progressive territory. Not only had it been the first to grant women the vote, it even had women bailiffs and jury members.

Elizabeth's smile broadened as she thought of all that Wyoming had to offer. It wasn't simply the fact that both her sisters had settled here that had brought her to Cheyenne, though she was counting the months until they'd be reunited. Even more important was the knowledge that she would face no old-fashioned prejudices about women's roles. Cheyenne wasn't like the East, where Elizabeth would have had to battle for acceptance. No one here would declare that she was nothing but a glorified midwife.

She cringed at the memory of one of her classmates making that very proclamation the day they'd both graduated, Elizabeth second in her class, the scoffing classmate close to the bottom. He had been offered partnerships with several successful physicians. She had received no such offers. Instead, she'd been advised to seek a position as a midwife.

Cheyenne was different. She'd be accepted for her skills. Central Avenue, one of the city's primary north-south streets, was busy. Women strolled by, intent on their purchases. Though on another day, Elizabeth might have made a game of guessing which of them were clad in gowns Charlotte had designed, she had no interest in games today. Men walked more briskly than the women, but while a few appeared to be headed toward her office, they detoured to the office next door, frowning when they saw that it was closed. Apparently the men of Cheyenne had a greater need for an attorney than they did for a doctor.

"It's the perfect location," Charlotte had written as she described the building she'd chosen for Elizabeth's office. Her oldest sister had been living in Cheyenne, serving as one of the city's premier dressmakers, when Elizabeth had announced her intention of moving West as soon as she finished school. In typical big sister fashion, Charlotte had volunteered to select an office for her. "It'll save you time," she had declared, pointing out how long the renovations to her new husband's store were taking. "I'll have everything ready before you arrive."

The logic had been unassailable. More than most people, Charlotte knew how eager Elizabeth was to open her practice. That was why she and her husband had lent Elizabeth the money to outfit the office. Elizabeth's other sister Abigail had contributed a portion of her teacher's salary to pay for her schooling.

"There are two offices in the building," Charlotte's letter continued. "A young attorney has the other one. The best part is, he lives above his office, so you'll never be completely alone, even if you work late."

Though Elizabeth had hoped to have her residence above the office, Charlotte had been adamant that she live in Charlotte's former apartment with widow Gwen Amos and her child, at least until Charlotte and her husband returned from their extended trip East. "It'll be ideal," Charlotte insisted when she and Barrett had stopped in New York for a brief visit with Elizabeth on their way to Massachusetts. "Gwen's a wonderful cook, and you'll love little Rose. Besides, it wouldn't be seemly for you to live alone," she had added, "especially with a single man next door. I haven't met him, but I've heard that he's charming and handsome. Not as handsome as Barrett, of course."

In Charlotte's mind, no one could be more handsome than the man she'd married, but she'd made no secret of the fact that she believed both Elizabeth and Gwen needed loving husbands. That was one battle Elizabeth chose not to fight. As dearly as she loved her sisters, Elizabeth knew they would not understand that she did not care about handsome men, single or otherwise. When she'd first realized that being a

13

doctor was the plan God had made for her life, she'd had long conversations with Mama and Papa. Though they'd supported her aspirations, they'd both cautioned her that it would not be an easy life and that few men would be willing to marry a woman whose first calling was to her patients. It had not been difficult to accept that, for unlike Charlotte and Abigail, Elizabeth's dreams had never centered on a husband and children. She had come to Wyoming to heal bodies, save lives, and be the best aunt possible to Charlotte's son and any children Abigail might have. But Charlotte was in Massachusetts, getting the training she needed to open a school for the blind, and Abigail was still in Washington Territory while her husband finished his commitment to the Army.

Elizabeth stared out the front window, looking at the wagons and carriages that rolled by. Though she didn't wish ill on anyone, surely there was someone who required a physician's care. Children broke bones, and gastric distress affected people of all ages. But though the street traffic had increased, no one stopped at Elizabeth's door.

Perhaps she'd made a mistake, telling Gwen she shouldn't visit today. Elizabeth hadn't wanted to expose Gwen and her daughter to illness unnecessarily, but there appeared to be no danger of that. The only ailment they were likely to contract was boredom.

Refusing to open her watch and see how long she'd spent staring outside, Elizabeth returned to her desk and unfolded the morning newspaper. She had brought Mr. Taggert's *Telegraph* with her, planning to cut out the notice she'd placed in it, but she might as well read the news. There was nothing else to do.

"Verdict Likely Today." Elizabeth shuddered at the article that held a place of prominence on the first page. According to Gwen, the Bennett trial was the most sensational of the year. Adam Bennett, a young rancher, had been accused of killing his wife in a fit of rage. What made the trial so sensational wasn't simply the fact that murder had been committed, but the manner of death. Helen Bennett had been bludgeoned. Even in a city that had once been noted for its lawlessness, the crime was heinous, as was the thought that the man who had once promised to love and cherish Helen was responsible for her brutal death. Though he declared his innocence, Adam Bennett had been found with blood spattering his hands and clothing.

The citizens were divided in their opinion. Many agreed with Gwen that Adam Bennett was guilty, but his attorney, the man whose office adjoined Elizabeth's, claimed otherwise, staunchly defending his client's innocence. Elizabeth simply prayed that justice would prevail.

Closing the paper, she looked at the still-empty waiting room.

"Today's the day." Though Jason Nordling tried to control the enthusiasm in his voice, the glint in his client's eyes told him he'd failed. Adam Bennett's normally guileless blue eyes held a gleam that hadn't been there a minute ago. "The prosecuting attorney and I will make our closing statements," Jason continued. "Then the jury will decide."

Bennett nodded. "And by the end of the day I'll be free."

Jason looked around the small room where his meetings with his client had taken place. Though not a jail cell, it was scarcely larger, and it boasted no windows. The walls and floor were in sore need of repainting, the two chairs and table scarred. It might be fanciful, but to Jason the room always smelled of despair. No wonder Bennett was anxious to leave.

"I hope that's the case." Believing in his client's innocence, Jason had done his best to represent him. He thought he had a strong argument, but juries could be unpredictable.

"It'll happen," Bennett said with more confidence than he'd displayed during the trial. "People trust you. That's why I hired you. You can convince 'em."

"I hope so." Jason felt a surge of excitement flow through his veins. This was the reason he'd become a lawyer: to see justice done. While the three years of drafting wills, bills of sale, and articles of incorporation that had constituted his legal career thus far had paid his bills and given him a comfortable nest egg, it wasn't what he'd envisioned when he'd studied law. This trial represented everything he sought: to exonerate innocent men. "Just remember what I told you. Keep your eyes down, and no matter what happens, do not smile. You want the jury to know that you're a serious man."

Bennett nodded.

Half an hour later, Jason stood in front of the jury, carefully making eye contact with one man after another. They appeared to be listening intently, even the man who'd yawned so frequently during the various witnesses' testimony. Jason had spoken for six minutes; now it was time for his final statement.

"And so, gentlemen of the jury, you see that my client, Adam Bennett, was as much a victim as his beloved wife. We'll never know why the stranger entered the Bennett home that night, whether he was intent on robbery or something else. All we know is that Helen Bennett is dead. The prosecuting attorney has tried to convince you that her husband killed her, but we know otherwise. Helen Bennett died at the hands of an unknown assailant, leaving her husband alone in this world, bereft of the woman he loved. The prosecuting attorney told you that my client had his wife's blood all over him. We do not deny that. You heard Adam Bennett's testimony. You know that he acted as any loving husband would. He gathered his wife into his arms, trying to save her. If I had a wife and had found her covered with blood, I would have done the same. So, I venture, would you."

Jason took a deep breath, pausing long enough to let his gaze move from one juror to the next. When he was satisfied that he had their full attention, he delivered his conclusion. "Adam Bennett is no more guilty of killing Helen than you are, and so I ask you to deliver the only possible verdict: not guilty."

As the jury filed from the courtroom into the adjacent deliberation chamber, Bennett caught Jason's eye and winked. A wink? The corners of his client's mouth turned up in what appeared to be a fleeting smirk, causing a knot of alarm to settle in Jason's stomach. Something was amiss, for that was not the reaction he had expected.

It took the jury less than an hour. When they returned to the courtroom, their faces solemn, not one looked at the defendant. That was not a good sign. Jason felt his palms begin to sweat, and when he glanced at Bennett, he saw the man swallow deeply. The smirk was gone. His client was as nervous as he.

For a moment, the only sounds were the shuffling of feet and an occasional cough. The judge stared at the jury. "Have you reached your verdict?"

The foreman nodded. "We have, your honor."

"And what do you find?"

The foreman handed a folded piece of paper to the judge. Waiting until the judge opened it, he confirmed the contents. "We find the defendant, Adam Bennett, not guilty."

As the words registered, exultation rushed through Jason, brushing aside the shards of doubt that had assailed him. It was over. He'd done it. He'd won his first trial.

At his side, Bennett cheered. "I knew it!" he cried. "I knew you could do it."

Though he frowned at the outburst, the judge declared that Adam Bennett was free and banged his gavel to dismiss the trial. The courtroom erupted into pandemonium as spectators reacted to the decision. The prosecuting attorney's grim expression left no doubt of his opinion. Jason would visit him later and tell him the truth, that he'd done an outstanding job of presenting his side of the case. But first Jason needed to talk to his client. His former client.

He turned to the man who'd sat beside him for days, intending to shake his hand, but something in Bennett's expression stopped him. Gone was the innocent look that he'd seen in those light blue eyes each time they'd met. In its place, Jason saw satisfaction and something else, something he would almost call evil.

"She deserved it, you know," Bennett said, not bothering to lower his voice. "She wouldn't listen to me. The Bible says a wife needs to obey her husband. She wouldn't, and so I had to kill her."

Bile rose in Jason's throat, and for a moment he thought he might be ill. The pride he'd felt over winning his first criminal case vanished, replaced by the realization that he'd been wrong, horribly wrong. It didn't matter that he'd been duped, that his client had lied to him. The simple, brutal facts were, Adam Bennett was guilty, and thanks to Jason, he was now a free man.

"Wait," Jason said as Bennett headed for the door. Perhaps there was something he could do. Perhaps he could persuade Bennett to give himself up, to accept the sentence he deserved.

Laughter echoed off the courtroom walls. "You can't do anything to me. Nobody can." It was as if the man had read Jason's mind. "I'm not guilty. The jury said so."

And I'm a fool, Jason reflected as he gathered his papers and prepared to leave. It appeared that Mrs. Moran had been right, after all. She'd taken him aside the day he'd announced that he wanted to study the law and had advised not setting his sights so high. He should have been a farmer. He should have spent his days growing things rather than trying to serve justice. Turnips weren't guilty of anything, and wheat didn't kill innocent women. But the pride the reverend had warned Jason about had made him believe he was destined for a different life. Look how it had turned out. Instead of preserving justice, he'd defended a criminal and helped a guilty man go free. At least the reverend wasn't here to witness his son's shame. If he were, he'd be thankful that Jason had never called him pa.

"Jason," one man called as he exited the courthouse. "What do you think?"

"Did you know?" another demanded.

Jason brushed them off, not wanting to talk to anyone. He needed to compose his thoughts; he needed to come to grips with what had happened; most of all, he needed to forget that today had happened. He'd been gullible, foolish, stupid. The adjectives bounced through his mind, each stronger than the preceding.

Normally he enjoyed the five-block walk from the courthouse to his office, but nothing was normal about today. Today was the day that Jason Nordling, the man who thought he was destined to be a prominent trial attorney, set a guilty man free. *Pride goeth before destruction, and a haughty spirit before a fall.* The verse from Proverbs that the reverend had quoted so frequently reverberated in his brain. Jason had been proud that Adam Bennett had chosen him from all the attorneys in Cheyenne. He'd believed the man when he'd said that Jason was the only attorney for him. No wonder! No one else would have been so easily manipulated. Jason Nordling was a fool, an unmitigated fool.

By the time he reached his office, he wanted nothing more than to disappear through the doorway and never emerge. But as he approached the building, he noticed that the door next to his was open. This must be the new doctor's first day. Jason had seen workers entering the building as they constructed the interior rooms, and he'd seen the gold lettering that proclaimed it the office of E. M. Harding, MD, but he had not met the man. He might as well do it now. It was only neighborly. Besides, the day couldn't get any worse.

"Hey, Doc!" he called out as he walked through the doorway.

Elizabeth's breath caught as her heart began to pound. It had finally happened. Her first patient had arrived. This was what she wanted, but oddly, when she'd envisioned this moment, she had believed the first person to seek her services would be a woman. How silly. Men needed treatment as much as women, and there were more men than women in Wyoming. A patient was a patient, and this particular one was very, very welcome.

Taking a deep breath and forcing herself to walk slowly, as if this weren't the moment she'd been anticipating all day, Elizabeth entered the waiting room, her eyes making a quick assessment of her caller's condition.

"Good afternoon, sir. How can I help you?" He did not look ill. Far from it. If she had been asked to describe a man in peak health, it would have been this one. At least six feet tall, he was blessed with glossy dark brown hair, lightly tanned skin without the slightest hint of pallor or sallowness, clear brown eyes, broad shoulders, and a face that most women would find exceedingly attractive. His features were perfectly sculpted, and were it not for the square chin, he might be called beautiful rather than handsome. The chin gave him a look of determination, verging on stubbornness.

Dressed in a suit that appeared to have been tailored for him and an expensive hat held in his hand, he seemed a successful, healthy businessman. Elizabeth could not imagine why he was consulting her. Perhaps he had come on behalf of his wife, yet he exhibited none of the urgency she would have expected of a man with an ailing spouse. As she took a step closer, Elizabeth noticed that his eyes appeared filled with pain, and tiny lines had formed next to his lips. Perhaps the man was suffering from dyspepsia.

21

"I'm looking for the doctor." As if to underscore his words, he glanced at the open door to her office, as if he expected to see someone seated at the desk.

"I am the doctor," she said firmly.

"You?" A frown accompanied the question. "You're E. M. Harding, MD?"

Elizabeth tried not to bristle, though the man's attitude reminded her of her classmates. They'd given her the same incredulous look the first day. When that and their obvious disdain had not discouraged her, they'd resorted to other tactics, including attempting to sabotage her work.

"Indeed I am Dr. Harding, Elizabeth May Harding." She would not list her qualifications, for they had been clearly spelled out in the notices she had placed in the *Telegraph*. "Whom do I have the honor of addressing?"

He blinked, and Elizabeth knew there was no dust mote in his eye. The blink was an involuntary reaction, caused by his trying to accept the fact that she was not a man. When she'd worked in the hospital wards, some of her male patients had refused to let her treat them. Others had grudgingly agreed, but all had greeted her arrival with incredulity. This man was no different.

For a second, she thought he would not deign to respond, but then he said, "Jason Nordling."

Her neighbor. The handsome, charming man whose presence Charlotte claimed would keep her safe at night. The man whose defense of Adam Bennett made the front page of the paper each day. He was supposed to be in court, convincing the jury that his client was innocent. The trial might be over, but if that was the case, he certainly didn't look like a man celebrating a victory.

"It's a pleasure to meet you, Mr. Nordling." That was an exaggeration, but perhaps if Elizabeth pretended that she hadn't noticed his discomfort at discovering her identity, this encounter might improve. After all, he was her neighbor, and if there was one lesson Mama had taught her daughters, it was to be polite to neighbors. And, though Elizabeth now believed it unlikely, there was still the possibility he was a patient. "Is this a social call, or do you require my professional services?"

One eyebrow rose, as if the question amused him. "I assure you, Miss Harding, that I have no need of your professional services today, nor will I ever."

He took another step into the waiting room, his gaze moving slowly as he appeared to assess the furnishings. Elizabeth revised her initial impression. Jason Nordling wasn't simply determined or stubborn; he was arrogant. He might not choose her as his physician, but there was no reason he should deny her the courtesy of addressing her as "Doctor."

"Mr. Nordling, my name is Dr. Harding, and I assure you," she said, throwing his words back at him, "that even the healthiest of men needs a physician occasionally."

This time both eyebrows rose, and when he looked at Elizabeth, he gave the impression of looking down that perfectly chiseled nose. "If I needed a doctor, it wouldn't be you."

Elizabeth took a deep breath, trying to release her anger even as she recognized that part of that anger was directed at herself. It appeared she'd been a fool to believe that Cheyenne was different from New York City, that its citizens would accept her as a doctor, despite her gender. *You can leave now.* That was what she wanted to say to the man with the supercilious expression, but the pain she'd seen in his eyes stopped her. Her instincts told her there was more to this man than simple prejudice.

"And the reason you wouldn't consult me is . . ." Perhaps she was inviting trouble, but Elizabeth wanted to be certain she understood the cause of his disdain. Perhaps he was disturbed by something else and she was nothing more than a convenient target for his frustration.

Her hopes were dashed when he studied her, his eyes moving slowly from the top of her head to her toes in what seemed an insolent appraisal. "I'm certain you know the reason." Once again, his voice held a sarcastic note. "It's the same reason you'll find it difficult to attract other patients. Dr. Worland may be getting on in years, but he's . . ."

As she had, Jason Nordling let his voice trail off, expecting her to complete the sentence. She did. "A man."

"Precisely."

A wise woman would demand that he leave rather than subject herself to more disdain, and yet she did not. Though she had never been able to convince the other students that she was as qualified as they, Elizabeth couldn't prevent herself from hoping that this man would be different. Perhaps it was simply because today was her first day of practice, but Elizabeth could not shake the feeling that if she could change Jason Nordling's mind, it would be an important step in being accepted by the community.

"Tell me, counselor," she said, trying to keep her voice even, "have you had any experiences with a woman doctor, or are you speaking from hearsay or perhaps blind prejudice?"

His eyes narrowed, as if he were unaccustomed to being questioned. "I told you. I'm a healthy man. I've had little experience with doctors."

Elizabeth tried not to sigh. "So it is prejudice." She tipped her head to look him in the eye. Her next words were designed to provoke a reaction, and she didn't want to miss it. "I must admit that I'm surprised. I thought that as an attorney you believed that everyone was innocent until proven guilty, yet it seems that you've condemned me without any evidence or a trial. Does the principle of presumed innocence apply only to men?"

Jason Nordling's reaction was greater than she'd expected. Elizabeth had thought she might see a twinge of shame in his eyes. Instead, he flinched as if she'd struck him but kept his voice steely as he said, "Women have a designated place in society. Just like men, they have their roles, and those roles do not include practicing medicine."

Perhaps it was petty of her, wanting to prove him wrong, but Elizabeth didn't stop. Jason Nordling wasn't different. Oh, he was more handsome than her classmates, but his attitude was the same. Though Mama had warned her of the dangers of a sharp tongue, Elizabeth took a step closer, her nose twitching as she inhaled the scent of starch and soap that clung to the handsome but bigoted attorney.

"Do the roles you would consider appropriate for women include those of a wife and mother?" she asked. Had her sisters been here, they would have smiled at the deceptively soft tone Elizabeth used. They'd told her it was as distinctive as a rattlesnake's warning and that the sting that followed was as dangerous as the snake's bite.

"Of course." Jason Nordling looked at her as if she were slightly addled. Perhaps she was, to believe she could convince him of the error of his opinions.

"But practicing medicine is not."

25

"That is what I said."

He'd taken the bait. Elizabeth nodded, as if she agreed with him. When his eyes widened slightly, she continued. "Then if a child should fall and scrape his knee, his mother would be wrong to cleanse the wound and bandage it."

Jason Nordling's eyes flashed with apparent disgust. "Of course not. That's what mothers do."

Elizabeth gave him her sweetest smile. "If that is true, I don't understand your logic, counselor. Surely you understand that one aspect of practicing medicine is cleansing and bandaging wounds. You said it was all right for a mother to do that, and yet you distinctly told me that women should not practice medicine."

Lines bracketed his mouth as he frowned. "You're twisting my words."

"I don't believe so. What I believe is that your logic is twisted. Women have always been nurturers and healers. Why shouldn't they be dignified with the title 'doctor'? Furthermore, the traditional roles you seem to espouse have no place on the frontier. Women are homesteaders; they defend themselves and their families. Why, Esther Morris was even a justice of the peace. Why shouldn't women be doctors?"

The man was angry. The rigid line of his neck and the scowl that marred his handsome face were testimony to that. So was the tone of his voice when he spoke. "It's one thing to care for a child, but no man would rely on a lady doctor. I hate to disillusion you, Dr. Harding"—Jason Nordling emphasized her title—"but your practice is doomed. My advice to you is to terminate your lease on this building and head back East or wherever it is you came from."

Elizabeth took a deep breath, wanting nothing more than

to vent her fury on him, to wipe that arrogant smirk from his face.

"That, Mr. Nordling, is advice I have no intention of heeding. Furthermore, if I did want legal counsel, I assure you that you'd be the last person I'd consult."

The barb hit its target, for his face flushed ever so slightly. "At least we agree on one thing. You'd be the last person I'd want as a client." Placing his hat back on his head, he turned on his heel and headed toward the door. "Good day, Doctor."

2

Jason tossed his hat onto his desk, then shook his head. There was no point in destroying a perfectly good Stetson simply because he was angry. He retrieved the hat and placed it on the hat rack, frowning at himself. Once again he'd been wrong. When he'd left the courthouse, he hadn't thought the day could worsen, but it had. The moment he'd set foot inside Dr. Harding's office, it had gone downhill faster than a runaway stagecoach. He'd expected to spend a few minutes in casual conversation. Instead, he'd been blindsided. Someone should have warned him that his next-door neighbor was a woman. Not just a woman but a beautiful one. Not just a beautiful woman but one with a tongue as sharp as a snake's bite. E. M. Harding, MD, was as different from the eager young man Jason had expected to meet as the Wyoming prairie was from the fertile farmlands that surrounded his childhood home in Michigan. From the moment he'd walked through her door . . .

Thoughts of doors reminded Jason of his own. Though

he doubted he'd have any clients this afternoon, he turned the sign in his front window from "closed" to "open." No fancy "the doctor is in" signs for him. His was basic, unlike the beautiful doctor's. Jason frowned again, remembering his first sight of her. If he hadn't been so distressed by the aftermath of the trial, he might have noticed that the approaching footsteps were those of a woman, but he'd been so caught up in his own misery that he had paid no attention to either the softer steps or the swish of skirts. And so he'd been surprised. Shocked. It wasn't simply that he hadn't been expecting a woman; it was that Elizabeth Harding was one of the most beautiful women he'd ever seen.

Even though her light brown hair had been pulled back into a sensible coil, the curled fringe on her forehead softened her face and drew attention to her eyes. When he'd recovered from the initial shock of discovering that E. M. Harding was a woman and had drawn close enough to study her face, Jason had discovered that her eyes were blue, a clear blue that reminded him of Sloan's Lake on a sunny day. At first those eyes had been warm and welcoming, but then they'd begun to flash with anger, anger that was directed at him.

He'd done nothing more than speak the truth. It wasn't simply that men would not accept her. Everyone knew women did not have the constitution to be doctors. How would she amputate a limb? Even the formidable Mrs. Moran couldn't have done that. Jason frowned. Today of all days, he did not want to think of his father's housekeeper. He was still frowning when he heard the front door open. Pasting a welcoming smile onto his face, he walked into the waiting room, his smile becoming genuine when he recognized his visitor. If anyone could lift Jason's mood, it would be Richard Eberhardt.

"I came as soon as I heard the news," Richard said as he carefully placed his hat on the stand. The forty-year-old merchant was noted for his conservative demeanor. Unlike Jason, he'd never toss his hat in a fit of anger. A couple inches shorter than Jason's own six feet, Richard was thinner than average with medium brown hair and brown eyes. Jason had once heard someone say that Richard was so ordinary looking that it was easy to overlook him. That, Jason knew from firsthand experience, was a mistake, for the man had been blessed with a keen mind and almost unfailing business acumen. They'd first met when Richard sought legal advice, but they'd quickly become close friends. That was why Richard's absence from the courtroom had been so unexpected.

"I thought you were going to come for my closing remarks."

Richard nodded. "I had planned to, but Miriam wasn't feeling well this morning." In a move that had surprised Cheyenne society, Richard had married the former Miriam Taggert a few months ago. Though it was clear to Jason that Richard and Miriam were deeply in love, others claimed that Miriam had sold herself short, that she should have chosen a younger, more handsome man. That was nonsense, for Jason doubted anyone would care for her more than Richard.

"Did Miriam consult Dr. Worland?" Richard's wife hadn't struck Jason as one of those women who were constantly complaining about their health, and so if she was ill, it was probably something serious.

Richard shook his head. "It didn't seem that serious. It must have been something she ate, because she recovered by noon, but by then it was too late to go to the courthouse."

"I'm glad she's all right." While Miriam was not the type

of woman he planned to marry, Jason felt genuine affection for his friend's wife.

"You and me both, but Miriam's not the reason I'm here."

Jason nodded as he gestured toward the door to his office. There was no reason to remain standing in the long hallway that divided his office. The right side held a good-sized waiting room in the front with a slightly smaller library behind it. The left side of the building contained only one room: the office itself. Though narrower than the other chambers, Jason liked the long rectangular space.

"So you heard the news," he said as he closed the door behind him. He wouldn't bother asking who had told Richard. It didn't matter. "I assume you heard how Bennett fooled me."

Settling into one of the two client chairs, Richard raised an eyebrow. "That's what I believe happened." He emphasized the pronoun. "Not everyone agrees. Some think you knew he was guilty but took the case to make a name for yourself."

Jason clenched his fists, releasing them slowly. He should have expected that reaction. After all, not everyone in Cheyenne knew him personally. Those who did not had no way of knowing that he would never have accepted Adam Bennett as a client had he thought the man had murdered his wife.

"You know better than that." Too agitated to sit, Jason began to pace the room. "It's true that Bennett deserved a defense. Everyone does. But if he'd told me the truth, I wouldn't have defended him. I'd have advised him to plead guilty and accept his punishment."

Leaning back in his chair, Richard raised an eyebrow. "Do you think he would have agreed, knowing that he'd be facing a noose?"

Jason shook his head and continued his pacing. "You're

probably right. A man who'd kill his wife—especially the way he did—and then lie about it wouldn't be willing to pay the price." When he reached the far wall, Jason turned and faced Richard. "You know what bothers me even more than the fact that he lied?" It was a rhetorical question, and so Jason did not wait for a response. "Adam Bennett showed no remorse. To the contrary, he seemed proud of the fact that he'd killed Helen. If that isn't evil, I don't know what is."

The lines that formed between Richard's eyes told Jason he agreed. "That didn't sit well with a lot of folks. They don't think a murderer deserves to live."

"And they blame me."

Never one to mince words, Richard nodded. "Some do. You might want to avoid public gatherings for the next couple days. Let the hotheads cool down a bit."

"If I want to get beat up, I can always go next door." The instant the words were out of his mouth, Jason regretted them. He didn't want to think about Dr. Harding, and he most definitely did not want to talk about her.

"You've met the doctor?"

His lips tightening at the memory of their meeting, Jason said, "It was one of the less pleasant events of the day, and considering what happened with Adam Bennett, that's saying a great deal."

Richard was silent for a moment, his expression pensive as he stared at Jason. "I'm surprised. I've never met her myself, but Miriam says the doctor is charming."

"She wasn't charming to me." As memories of her sharp retorts whirled through his brain, Jason glared at Richard. "Some friend you are. You knew the doctor was a woman, but you didn't tell me."

"Didn't I? It must have slipped my mind." Richard's feigned innocence irritated Jason almost as much as the way Dr. Harding had pronounced the word "counselor" when she'd addressed him.

"A likely story."

A shrug was Richard's response. He crossed his ankles, appearing to relax. "I'm going to make up for my previous lapse," he said, his voice as smooth as Dr. Harding's skin had looked. "Miriam and I are planning a party to welcome the new doctor to Cheyenne, and—"

Jason wouldn't let him finish the sentence. "Why on earth are you doing that?" He was annoyed as much by the fact that his thoughts continued to stray to his acerbic neighbor as by Richard and Miriam's plans.

"It's simple. She's Charlotte Landry's sister."

"Barrett's wife?" Everyone in Cheyenne knew of Barrett Landry, the cattle baron whose name had been mentioned more than once as a senatorial candidate. Jason had even heard speculation that he was planning to marry Miriam Taggert at one point. That must have been idle gossip, for Richard had married Miriam and not too long afterward, Barrett had announced his engagement to a woman named Charlotte. "Barrett's wife is the doctor's sister?"

"One and the same. Before she married Barrett, most of Cheyenne's women knew her as Madame Charlotte. Her last name was Harding, though she didn't use it very often."

That explained why Jason had made no connection between Barrett's bride and E. M. Harding, MD.

"According to Miriam, Charlotte used to design gowns that outshone ones from Paris," Richard continued. "That's how they met. Miriam was one of Madame Charlotte's best customers. Then they became friends. A bit like you and me."

The story was only mildly interesting, and Jason saw no reason why Richard was recounting it. "All right. I see that there's a tenuous connection between your wife and the new doctor. I still don't understand the necessity for a party."

Richard chuckled. "You obviously don't know how women's minds work. Miriam would do anything for a friend, and so she promised Charlotte that she'd watch over her sister until Charlotte and Barrett return from the East."

"From what I've seen, Dr. Harding doesn't need anyone watching over her. That tongue of hers could cause lacerations even Doc Worland couldn't heal."

The way Richard pursed his lips told Jason he was trying to control his mirth. It wasn't amusing. Nothing about Dr. Harding was funny. "I see that Elizabeth made an impression on you," Richard said, his voice just short of a chortle.

"She did, and that impression made me regret having her as a neighbor."

Richard uncrossed his ankles, then crossed them again, as if he were planning to remain in the chair. While Jason wouldn't evict him—the man was, after all, a close friend—he wished that he would leave. This conversation had gone on far too long, venturing onto subjects that were best left untouched.

"Perhaps your encounter today was an inoculation," Richard suggested. "If so, now you're immune."

One thing was certain: it had been as painful as an injection. "That's an intriguing theory, but I have no intention of testing it. With a bit of luck, I won't have to see her again." It was a long shot, especially given the proximity of their offices, but a man could dream.

"I hate to dash your hopes," Richard said, his voice betraying no remorse, "but that won't be the case. Miriam and I expect you to attend our party."

"I'd rather be tarred and feathered."

Raising his eyebrows, Richard gave Jason a skeptical look. "I never realized you were prone to such exaggeration."

"I was not exaggerating. A man doesn't volunteer for pain, and having to be polite to Dr. Harding would be painful. Why would I do that? Life hands us enough trouble on its own."

If Richard heard him, he gave no sign. "Miriam and I are looking forward to having you as our guest."

"I'm afraid I have another commitment that evening."

"You don't even know when it is."

"True, but I'm certain I have a previous engagement, whenever it is."

"Coward!" Richard's smile took the sting from his epithet.

"That's not the worst thing I've been called, especially today." When he'd left the courthouse, Jason had heard men declaring that he was as guilty as his client. "Murderer," they'd hissed as he walked by.

Richard nodded, almost as if he'd read Jason's thoughts. "That's the reason you need to come. It's next Friday at seven. By then the uproar over Bennett's trial will have died down. It will be time for you to get back into the public eye." He rose and walked to the hallway for his hat. "Maple Terrace is too small for what Miriam has in mind, so her parents have agreed that we can use their home. Between Miriam and her mother, it seems as if half of Cheyenne has been invited." Richard settled the hat on his head. "Many of the guests could be potential clients. You need to be there."

"All right." Jason knew his acceptance sounded grudging, and it was. "Just keep me away from your guest of honor."

Laughter was Richard's only response.

"I can't believe it, Gwen." Elizabeth unpinned her hat and placed it on the bureau in the room that had once been her sister's. The apartment over Charlotte's former dress shop was modestly sized, but it boasted two bedrooms as well as a central space that served as kitchen, dining room, and parlor. Gwen and her daughter shared the bedroom overlooking Ferguson Street, while Elizabeth's room offered a view of the small backyard, a view that was blessedly free of Mr. Arrogant Nordling. For the first time, she admitted that Charlotte might have been right when she claimed it was better not to live over her office. At least here there were no reminders of her unpleasant neighbor.

"The man was insufferably rude," Elizabeth continued. "As bad as the men in my classes." Though her hands were still shaking with anger, she forced herself to take care as she removed her gloves. They had been a Christmas gift from Charlotte, and Elizabeth didn't want to damage them. "I could almost understand my classmates," she admitted. "They were angry that I'd taken a place that could have gone to one of their friends. But there was no reason for Mr. Nordling to behave the way he did." She'd obviously been mistaken in believing that what she had seen in his eyes was pain. The man was simply ornery, obstinate, and unable to admit that women were capable of far more than his narrow-minded prejudice allowed.

When Elizabeth finished recounting the litany of Jason

Nordling's rudeness, Gwen's lips tightened, giving Elizabeth the impression that she was trying to bite back her words. Finally, she said, "At least he showed you his true colors at the beginning. Not all men do."

The words echoed through Elizabeth's brain like a clanging bell. Once again she'd spoken without considering the consequences. She should have remembered the story Charlotte had told of how Gwen had believed she'd found true love, only to discover that the man she thought loved her and Rose hid a dark side.

Knowing that Gwen preferred no mention of her past, Elizabeth fixed an ironic smile on her face and attempted to lighten the discussion. "How sad that that's the only good thing we can say about Mr. Nordling." As she'd hoped, Gwen smiled. The moment had passed.

When they returned to the kitchen for Gwen to put the final touches on dinner, the heavyset woman's face lit with another smile. No one would call Gwen beautiful, but when she smiled, her light blue eyes sparkled and her cheeks grew rosy, giving her face much-needed color. For a moment, she looked almost pretty, despite her ordinary features and the extra pounds that even Charlotte's expert tailoring could not completely hide.

"I have good news," Gwen said, holding out a creamy envelope. "Miriam and Richard are planning a party in your honor next week." Her smile turned into a grin as she lifted the lid from a pot and tasted the simmering stew. "I already opened my invitation. That's how I know."

There hadn't been many parties in Elizabeth's life. Her father had put them and dancing in the same category, calling them frivolous wastes of time. As a result, neither Elizabeth nor her older sisters had learned to dance until after Papa's death. Both Charlotte and Abigail's letters had mentioned attending several parties, but Elizabeth had been too busy studying to think about social gatherings. The truth was, she was more comfortable dealing with sick and injured people than with men and women whose conversation revolved around more mundane subjects. Look at how poorly her time with Jason Nordling had turned out.

"I didn't come to Cheyenne to spend my time at parties," she told Gwen. "I ought to be treating patients." To Elizabeth's chagrin, her voice sounded as firm as Papa's had when he'd announced that his daughters should concentrate on more serious things than which ribbons matched their gowns. Though she'd loved her father, there had been times when she had wished he'd been a bit more flexible. Now it seemed she was becoming just as rigid. She couldn't let that happen, for if she did, she might lose patients the way Papa had lost congregations.

Gwen reached for a loaf of bread. "Miriam agrees with you. That's why she's having the party at her parents' house and why she invited all her friends and her parents' associates. She wants them to meet you so that when they do need a doctor, they'll think of you."

Elizabeth turned as the sound of laughter reached her ears. Though Rose had been playing quietly in the parlor, something had caught her fancy, with the result that a giggle had turned into a full-fledged laugh. Like her mother, Rose had a sunny disposition. So did Miriam Eberhardt. Though she'd only met her twice, Elizabeth understood why she'd become one of Charlotte's closest friends. Now that friendship was being extended to Elizabeth.

"I hadn't considered that." Elizabeth smiled as she added, "I suppose it's like the ads I placed in Miriam's father's paper—advertising. Charlotte told me that Miriam was responsible for most of her clientele, that once she bought a few dresses from her, her friends wanted similar gowns." Miriam had even defied her mother's edict to buy only Parisian fashions, insisting that Charlotte's were more beautiful.

Gwen looked up from the bread she was slicing. "The Taggerts are influential, and Miriam wields her own power, especially with the younger women. The party will be good for you."

"So long as I don't have to speak to Jason Nordling."

A knock on the door interrupted whatever Gwen might have said. To Elizabeth's surprise, Gwen's cheeks flushed as she called out, "Come in, Harrison. Dinner's almost ready."

The man who lived next door entered the small apartment, hanging his hat on the rack with the familiarity of someone who'd done it dozens of times before. He had. When Charlotte and Barrett had decided to go East for the summer and perhaps longer, Barrett's brother had volunteered to come to Cheyenne to oversee the expansion of Barrett's new dry goods store, and Gwen—generous Gwen—had insisted on providing meals for Harrison. Now that Elizabeth was here to serve as a chaperone, she had invited him to eat with her and Rose and Elizabeth. It was, she said, the least she could do, since Barrett was letting her live here rent-free.

"How was your first day of practice?" Harrison asked as he moved further into the apartment, settling into one of the chairs that flanked the dining table. Though he addressed the question to Elizabeth, she noticed that his eyes returned to Gwen, and he appeared to be studying her, as if memorizing each feature, while Gwen seemed to be looking in every direction other than Harrison's. How odd. Though it was true that Harrison was not a man who would warrant a second glance from a woman who cared only about physical beauty, Elizabeth did not believe Gwen judged people based on superficial appearances. Harrison's dark brown hair and blue eyes could have been striking, but they were overshadowed by the solemn expression that seemed habitual. Though she did not know the reason, other than the times when his eyes were fixed on Gwen, Harrison Landry did not appear to be a happy man.

Elizabeth was not a happy woman, at least not today. "My first day was a great success," she said, not bothering to mask her sarcasm, "unless I wanted patients. I had not a single one."

His eyes still on Gwen, Harrison shrugged. "You need to be patient."

"That's what Gwen said. The problem is, I'm not a patient person. Today seemed endless. I never had a minute to spare when I was in school, so it felt strange to have so much empty time." Once Jason Nordling appeared, boredom hadn't seemed so bad.

Gwen turned from the stove to grin at Harrison. "I told Elizabeth to enjoy being idle. Before she knows it, she'll be so busy that she'll wish for a free moment. I predict that by the time autumn returns, I'll rarely see her because she'll have so many patients."

It was an encouraging thought, except for the fact that autumn was more than three months away.

Harrison nodded, his eyes intent as he watched Gwen ladle the stew into a serving dish. "You should listen to Gwen. She's a wise woman."

Her face once again flushed, Gwen called to her daughter. "It's time to wash your hands, Rose."

The little girl who'd just turned four was a small version of her mother, with light brown hair, blue eyes, and the prettiest of smiles. Rose managed to keep her expression solemn while Gwen offered a blessing for the food, but when the stew and bread were served, she grinned and began to shovel spoonfuls of the hearty concoction into her mouth. "Good," she murmured between bites.

"Delicious as always." Elizabeth seconded the child's opinion. The speed with which Harrison emptied his bowl left no doubt that he was enjoying the food. It was only when he'd accepted a second helping that he laid down his spoon, his expression once more solemn.

"Have you ladies heard the news about the Bennett trial?" he asked.

Elizabeth shook her head. "I met Mr. Nordling this afternoon, and he didn't look happy. I assume that means the jury found Bennett guilty."

"The man is as guilty as June days are long." Harrison clenched his fist and pounded it on the table, startling Rose. "Unfortunately, the jury didn't know that."

Elizabeth wasn't surprised by Harrison's first comment. He'd been adamant in his belief that Adam Bennett had killed his wife, and she'd suspected that only a guilty verdict would satisfy him. It appeared, though, that the jury had not shared Harrison's opinion. That would explain Harrison's anger; it did not explain Jason Nordling's mood. The man should have been celebrating his victory.

Elizabeth looked up from the bread she was buttering,

fixing her eyes on Harrison. "That's why we have juries, isn't it? So they can weigh the evidence and make a decision."

A glare accompanied his response. "The jury was bamboozled. Jason Nordling gave Bennett a brilliant defense. He was so good that everyone on the jury believed him. It was only after the verdict was delivered that Bennett admitted he'd done it. Admitted?" Harrison's voice rose to little less than a shout. "He boasted. That miserable, murdering man boasted about what he'd done."

As Harrison shouted the final words, Rose began to cry.

"It's all right, sweetie." Gwen wrapped her arm around her daughter's shoulder. "Mr. Landry's not angry at you."

Her cheeks tearstained, Rose looked up at him. "You're not?"

"No, indeed." Though his voice was still harsh, Harrison appeared to be trying to modulate it. "The problem is, I don't know who riles me more—the murderer or his attorney."

Elizabeth had never met Adam Bennett, so she had no opinion of him, but she found herself disturbed by the knowledge that Jason Nordling had defended a confessed murderer. Though his arrogance and blatant bias had annoyed her, she had thought him a basically honorable man. It was true that everyone deserved a defense. Papa had been adamant about that, and yet . . . The question was, at what point had Mr. Nordling learned of his client's guilt?

An hour later, Harrison had returned to his apartment, and Elizabeth was helping Gwen wash dishes while Rose played with her doll.

"I'm afraid I made a huge mistake," Gwen said as she rinsed a bowl and handed it to Elizabeth.

Her mind still filled with the thought that an admitted

murderer was now free on the streets of Cheyenne, Elizabeth had to force herself to concentrate on what Gwen was saying. "What kind of mistake?" It seemed as if the only mistake that had been made today was in exonerating a guilty man.

"I shouldn't have invited Harrison to take his meals with us." Gwen swirled the dishcloth around another bowl, loosening the bits of dried-on stew. "It seemed like a good idea. I haven't wanted to talk about it, but I've been worried about Rose. She needs a man's influence in her life, and Harrison seemed like the answer to prayer, living so close and being Barrett's brother. Now I don't know."

"What's the problem?"

"Harrison scares Rose. She doesn't cry easily, but you saw her today." Gwen glanced over her shoulder, assuring herself that Rose was no longer crying.

"Harrison seems like a kind man." Unlike Jason Nordling. *Kind* was not a word Elizabeth associated with the attorney. He was harsh and dogmatic. Elizabeth blinked, realizing that the same words could be applied to her. She was judging Jason Nordling without knowing all the facts. He'd been upset this afternoon. That could have been because he'd just learned that his client was guilty rather than that his conscience was bothering him for defending a guilty man.

"Oh, he is kind." For a second, Elizabeth couldn't imagine what Gwen meant. Then she remembered that they were discussing Harrison Landry, not Jason Nordling. "Harrison is . . ." As Gwen pronounced his name, color rose to her cheeks, and she ducked her head, as if trying to keep Elizabeth from seeing her blush. "It's just . . ."

Placing the bowl she'd just dried on the cupboard shelf, Elizabeth darted a glance at Gwen. Though she'd known her only a few weeks, Elizabeth had never before noticed Gwen's tendency to blush. Yet tonight she'd flushed multiple times. Thinking about it, Elizabeth realized it was always when Gwen was discussing Harrison. She was acting more like a schoolgirl than a woman of one and thirty years.

"I doubt Harrison's used to being around children," Elizabeth said. "He probably doesn't realize how easily they're frightened." It was a plausible explanation, especially since Harrison had been visibly disturbed today. Who wouldn't be, given the jury's verdict?

Gwen's eyes brightened. "That's probably the reason. I hope you're right."

What Elizabeth hoped was that, if what she suspected was true and Gwen harbored tender feelings for Harrison, those feelings were reciprocated. Gwen didn't deserve to be hurt again.

3

Someone was pounding on the door. Jason glanced at the clock, his eyes widening when he realized how late he'd slept. Nine o'clock. Normally he wakened no later than seven. Of course, last night had been anything but normal. His sleep, what little of it he'd managed to get after exhaustion had overcome him and he drifted into slumber, had been disturbed by dreams. Images of Adam Bennett's gloating and Elizabeth Harding's disdain had mingled with the thought that everything had changed, and not for the better. Now this. It was probably someone wanting to tar and feather him for his role in the Bennett verdict.

As he struggled into pants and a shirt, Jason's brain registered the fact that the pounding was on the door to his residence, not the office downstairs. If he hadn't been so groggy, he would have realized that he could not hear anything that happened at the front of his office from here. Like many buildings in this part of Cheyenne, his had an outside stairway that led to his apartment on the second floor, and his bedroom was located on the back side. Though clients had never come to his apartment, it was common knowledge that he lived here. Anyone, including a maddened crowd, could be outside.

Jason flung the door open, relief flooding through him as he ushered Richard in. The relief receded a second later when the expression on his friend's face registered. Richard gave no smile of greeting, nothing more than a short grunt.

"Is something wrong?"

"That depends on your definition of wrong," Richard said as he lowered himself into one of Jason's two comfortable chairs.

The main room of the apartment was sparsely furnished. A wobbly table and two chairs met Jason's needs on the rare occasions when he cooked for himself, and since he had few guests, he'd seen no need to place more than two chairs in the parlor. This was a temporary abode. When he fulfilled his promise to his father and married, he'd buy a house for his bride and the children he hoped they'd have. In the meantime, Jason saw no need for additional furnishings.

He sank into the other chair and waited for Richard to speak. His friend inclined his head, the somber expression in his brown eyes leaving no doubt that whatever he was about to say was unpleasant. "Adam Bennett's body was found this morning. It's a good thing the sheriff recognized his belt buckle. From what I heard, there wasn't much left of his face. It seems someone decided to show him how Helen felt."

Jason closed his eyes for a second, letting the words and the images they conjured settle in his brain. "Vigilante justice." As an attorney, he abhorred the very idea. And yet, as a man, he understood the desire for revenge. Letting a confessed murderer go free was a travesty of justice.

"Any idea who's responsible?"

The brief shake of Richard's head confirmed what Jason assumed. "No one's talking. There's one good thing," Richard continued. "The uproar over your involvement seems to be dying down faster than I'd expected."

"You mean I won't be a pariah. I may still have a few clients."

"That was never in question. Tempers always cool."

Jason wondered whether Elizabeth's would. An hour later, he was still thinking about her as he headed toward the courthouse to file some papers on behalf of a client. Though the placard announced that she was in her office, there was no sign of her. Not that Jason had stared at the window. He hadn't. But if his eyes had drifted that direction while he walked by, well . . . It was nothing more than curiosity about a neighbor, not the desire to see the beautiful doctor with the light brown hair again. That woman might have hair the color of honey, but her tongue was steeped in vinegar.

It was good that he hadn't seen her, for he didn't want another tongue-lashing. But Jason had seen no sign of patients, and that was not good for the doctor. It might be only the second day that her office was open, but she couldn't last indefinitely without patients. She had rent to pay, and even though her new brother-in-law had once been one of Cheyenne's cattle baron millionaires, his fortune had been lost after the disastrous winter had killed most of the cattle. Barrett had enough expenses without trying to support Elizabeth as well.

Jason muttered beneath his breath as he crossed the street. He had no reason to worry about Elizabeth Harding. It was ridiculous to care about the woman who had tried to flay his hide. He would not, he absolutely would not, walk by her office again. He didn't want to see her; he didn't want to think about her; and he most definitely did not want to continue thinking of her as Elizabeth. That was far too familiar. She was Dr. Harding, nothing more.

Elizabeth tried to keep a smile on her face as she reached for her hat and gloves. Mama had told her daughters that if they smiled on the outside, they'd soon be smiling on the inside. Mama hadn't simply given the advice; she'd followed it. Even when she'd been in the final days of her life, suffering from the terrible wasting disease that had taken her to heaven decades before Elizabeth had been ready to lose her, Mama had smiled, and that had given Elizabeth hope. Mama had been smiling the day she'd told Elizabeth how proud she was of her and that she was convinced that being a doctor was God's plan for her. "I remember how you tried to heal every wounded animal you found," Mama had said, her voice little more than a whisper. "Soon you'll be healing people."

Not soon enough. Elizabeth hadn't been able to heal Mama. In that case, it had been a matter of knowledge. Elizabeth hadn't known enough to stop the march of Mama's illness. Now it was a matter of opportunity. Though she knew much more than she had when Mama died, Elizabeth couldn't heal people unless they came to her.

She drew her gloves over her fingers, smoothing out the wrinkles, then peered at the small mirror to assure herself that her hat was straight. It had been another day without a single patient. She hadn't even had a visitor. Elizabeth paused, debating whether to carry a parasol. A look at the stiff breeze told her this was not a day for parasols, any more than it had been a day for patients or visitors. It wasn't that she wanted to see Jason Nordling. The only reason she was thinking about him was that if he had stopped in, it would have interrupted the boredom, at least for a few minutes. Today she hadn't even had a newspaper to read.

Keeping her smile fixed, Elizabeth locked the front door behind her, then crossed Central as she headed home. The walk was less than four blocks total. If she tried very hard and smiled the entire time, perhaps when she reached the apartment, she would put her discouragement behind her and could pretend that today had been a success. Though Gwen would undoubtedly counsel patience, Elizabeth couldn't help wondering whether she had made a mistake. Charlotte had had customers the first day she'd opened her dress shop, and Elizabeth had expected the same.

Perhaps she should have remained in the East. While it was true that the only positions she'd been offered there were as a midwife, at least she would have had patients. That was more than she could say here. Still, there was something exciting about living in a city that was only twenty years old but boasted millionaires, an opera house, and a bakery and confectionary that rivaled any she had found in New York.

By the time she began to climb the stairs to the apartment, Elizabeth was feeling more optimistic than she had all day. This was God's plan; she simply needed to wait for his timing. And while she waited, she could count her blessings, including the fact that Gwen and Rose were part of her life. Elizabeth's smile faded when she heard Gwen's voice. Her normally subdued friend was shouting.

"Thank goodness. The man had it coming."

"So you approve?" Harrison's voice was equally loud, and

the exasperation that laced it told Elizabeth the argument had been going on for some time.

"Indeed I do."

Elizabeth opened the door, then stopped at the sight of Gwen and Harrison glaring at each other as if they were mortal enemies. Rose had buried her face in her mother's skirts, her fists clutching the fabric as if she feared that she would be torn away.

"What is going on?" Elizabeth demanded. "I heard you when I was only halfway up the stairs."

Her face flushed, Gwen shot Harrison another angry look. "Harrison and I were having a minor disagreement."

"It didn't sound minor to me. What's the problem?"

"Gwen approves of vigilante justice."

Elizabeth raised her eyebrows at Harrison's statement. That didn't sound like Gwen. "What do you mean?"

As she stroked Rose's head, trying to comfort her daughter, Gwen looked at Elizabeth. "You must not have heard the news. Adam Bennett is dead."

"He was killed by someone, or more than one someone, who believed in an eye for an eye," Harrison explained. "The man was battered to death."

"Oh!" Elizabeth gripped the edge of the counter, trying to quiet her nerves. Though she had heard about frontier justice, she hadn't expected to encounter it here. "I hadn't realized Cheyenne was so . . ."

Before she could complete the sentence, Harrison raised one brow. "Barbaric?" he suggested.

"The word is practical," Gwen announced. "Now no one needs to fear for their lives. Justice was served."

"Not so," Harrison countered. "As much as I deplore their decision, the justice system found Adam Bennett not guilty."

"And it was wrong." Gwen's eyes flashed with anger. "If you'd lived here as long as I have, you'd agree with me, Harrison. It's good that Adam Bennett paid for his crime."

Though Harrison's lips tightened, he made no response.

Supper was a subdued meal with both Gwen and Harrison quieter than usual. Even Rose, who normally chattered about everything, was silent, seemingly apprehensive.

When they rose from the table, Harrison turned to Elizabeth. "I almost forgot. The items your sister ordered for you have arrived."

This was the first Elizabeth had heard about an order, but something in Harrison's demeanor told her not to question it. "Shall I pick them up now?"

"I'd appreciate that. With all the confusion of construction, I might lose them otherwise." Brusquely, he thanked Gwen for the meal, then held the door open for Elizabeth.

When they reached the bottom of the stairs, Elizabeth turned to him. "Charlotte didn't order anything for me, did she?"

Looking abashed, Harrison asked, "How did you know?"

"You're a poor liar. Your lips twitch when you're not telling the truth."

"I'll have to remember that." He ran two fingers over his lips as if admonishing them not to twitch. "I wanted to talk to you without Gwen overhearing. I need your advice."

Elizabeth gestured toward his storefront. "My first advice is that you'd better give me something to take back or Gwen will realize this was all a ruse."

Unlocking the front door, Harrison nodded. "I wouldn't want that to happen."

He ushered Elizabeth into the store. Though the workers

had left for the day, the room was crowded with ladders, crates, and piles of lumber. The expansion of what had once been the Yates Dry Goods store into Charlotte's former dress shop was still far from complete. Elizabeth wrinkled her nose and tried not to sneeze at the dust that hung in the air.

"I have some nice glass vials," Harrison said as he switched on the light. "You could use them for medicines."

For her nonexistent patients. Keeping that thought to herself, Elizabeth nodded. "Thank you. Now what's bothering you?"

"I wonder what I've done to offend Gwen, besides the disagreement today. You're her friend. I hope you can tell me what's wrong. It wasn't my goal to irritate her, but I seem to have done precisely that."

And judging from the anguish Elizabeth saw in his eyes, that disturbed Harrison. Perhaps there was more to his concern than a simple desire not to offend the woman who provided his meals. Recalling Gwen's apparent attraction to him, Elizabeth hoped that was the case.

"Other than tonight, I don't believe Gwen's angry with you, but she is worried about Rose. You saw how upset Rose was last night, and you two shouting at each other today didn't help."

Harrison sighed as he reached for a box marked "glassware." "It's all my fault. I don't know much about children." He sighed again. "It's been a long time since I was one. I was the oldest of three boys, and we had no sisters, so I've had no experience with little girls."

Elizabeth was tempted to echo Harrison's sighs. It was no wonder he scared Rose. He simply didn't know any better.

"Rose seems frightened by loud voices," Elizabeth said, deliberately lowering hers. "I know it's not easy, especially when you're upset, but you might want to modulate your voice."

Harrison was silent for a moment. "My brothers used to say that I talked too much, but this is the first time I've been told I talk too loudly." He nodded. "I'll try to be quieter. It's important."

What was important, Elizabeth decided three days later, was for her to start doing something. Just sitting in her office, waiting for patients to appear, was accomplishing nothing. Gwen had warned her that it might take time but claimed that even if Cheyenne's residents weren't ready for a woman doctor yet, they soon would be. Gwen was confident. Of course, Gwen had been in a better mood for the past couple days, perhaps because Harrison seemed to be making a special effort to speak softly. Elizabeth could tell that it didn't come naturally to him. After all, the man had a booming voice. But he was trying, and though Rose was still wary, there had been no further tears. That was good.

What was not good was that Elizabeth spent her days pacing the floor of her office, wondering when the first patient would set foot inside. Her neighbor didn't have that problem. One of the disadvantages of spending time in her waiting room was that Elizabeth observed an almost constant stream of men entering Jason Nordling's office. Most stayed less than half an hour, making her wonder whether they were clients or simply people coming to talk. In either case, he wasn't bored, and he wasn't lonely.

Like hers, his days had a routine. She'd see him enter his office each morning a few minutes after she opened hers.

Toward midday he'd emerge, his step jaunty as he headed somewhere, presumably for dinner. An hour later, he'd return. And then precisely at five each afternoon, he'd lock the door to his office.

When she'd left the apartment this morning, Elizabeth had decided that this afternoon would be different. She was going to pay a visit, and if things went the way she hoped, by the end of the day she might have a partner. Though she hadn't envisioned working with another doctor, she had wakened with the realization that that was the route many of her classmates had taken. It had proven advantageous for them. Perhaps it would for her too. After all, there was more than one way to succeed, and if one thing was certain, it was that Elizabeth May Harding, MD, was going to succeed.

After tying her hat ribbons and slipping on her gloves, Elizabeth turned the sign in her front window over. Seconds later, the door firmly locked behind her, she headed north. Her destination was only a block away. Elizabeth smiled when she reached it and saw the sign in the front window. This doctor was in. That was good. Even better, she reflected as she opened the door, there were no patients waiting for him. Elizabeth's smile broadened as she considered the possibility that her lack of patients might be due to an unusually healthy population, not an unwillingness to consult a woman doctor. Keeping her smile firmly fixed, she entered Dr. Worland's office. Though she knew little about him other than the fact that he had been one of the first physicians to come to Cheyenne and that he was reputed to be a good one, she hoped he would prove amenable to her plan.

Elizabeth looked around, quickly assessing her surroundings. The building that housed Dr. Worland's office was a bit larger than hers, and so it was no surprise that the interior was larger too. Other than size, his waiting room resembled hers, with benches along one wall and a few chairs in the middle. Unlike hers, his boasted no live plants, and the front window was in need of a good cleaning.

"What can I do for you, miss?" The doctor who emerged from the interior room was older than she had expected—perhaps in his mid-fifties—with hair that had turned completely gray. Deep lines bracketed his mouth and eyes and furrowed his forehead. The crevices and the slumped shoulders told Elizabeth his life had not been an easy one, and she felt an immediate affinity with him. Life in the Harding household had not always been easy, either. Frequent moves had meant that Elizabeth's only true friends were her sisters, and a perpetual shortage of funds meant the family lacked many of the small luxuries others took for granted. Still, on the opposite side of the scale, she had been surrounded by love. Not once had she doubted either her parents' or her sisters' love for her. Elizabeth hoped that Dr. Worland had been as fortunate.

Before she could introduce herself and explain the reason for her visit, the doctor gestured toward his examination room. "I can see you're suffering from female ailments," he continued as he ushered her into the interior room. Though the furniture arrangement was different, the older doctor's examining room was remarkably similar to Elizabeth's.

"I have just the thing to cure you." He pointed toward a cabinet filled with patent medicine.

And in that moment, Elizabeth knew that her dreams of a partnership with the older doctor were nothing more than that: dreams. She wasn't certain what offended her more, his casual diagnosis of a nonexistent illness or the fact that he was prescribing bottles of what any respectable practitioner knew was of no more value than snake oil.

"Surely you don't dispense those." She took a step closer to the cabinet, frowning when she realized that he had everything from Hostetter's Celebrated Stomach Bitters, to Faith Whitcomb's Nerve Bitters and Peruna, to Brandredth's Vegetable Universal Pills. The only thing celebrated about the vile concoctions was the speed with which patients became dependent on them, for their alcohol content was far greater than whiskey.

"Of course I prescribe them to my patients." Dr. Worland's eyes narrowed in what appeared to be suspicion. "Who are you to tell me otherwise, Miss . . . ?" He let his voice trail off in an obvious request for her name.

Elizabeth complied. Though it was clear this would not be a congenial meeting of colleagues, there was no reason for him not to know her identity. "Harding," she said. "Dr. Harding."

The annoyance that she'd seen on his face when she'd questioned the patent medicines was replaced by disdain. "Ah yes. I heard there was a pretty little lady who fancied herself a doctor." Dr. Worland drew himself up to his full height, which was only an inch or two more than Elizabeth's own five and a half feet. "I'll tell you the same thing I told those busybodies: you won't last long. Folks in Cheyenne have no use for a lady doctor."

The message was the same one Jason Nordling had delivered, and it was no more welcome coming from the lips of a physician than it had been then. Less, in fact, for the doctor should know better. But he didn't. Elizabeth's hopes were dashed by the realization that Dr. Worland was as intolerant as her classmates. Intolerant and possibly incompetent.

"That's where you're wrong," she told him, her voice low but firm. "It may be that Cheyenne's residents are unaccustomed to having a woman doctor, but they'll soon discover that I have much to offer them."

The older doctor's upper lip curled, and his voice held more than a note of mockery. "You're like those young whippersnappers. You think you know more than me."

"I did not say that." Although she did know that patent medicines caused more harm than good. "I had hoped we could work together."

"You did, did you?" This time there was no ignoring the sarcasm. "Exactly what did you think you could do? I already have a gal come in to clean the bedpans."

Elizabeth had cleaned her share of bedpans. She'd scrubbed operating tables, just in case the new theories that infections were caused by dirt were true. She'd done that, but that was hardly the extent of her experience.

"I assure you that I can do more than that."

Dr. Worland shook his head, his doubt obvious. "Those are mighty brave words. Tell me, missy, did you ever have to amputate a leg?"

"I've done it."

It was clear he hadn't expected that response, and for a second, he said nothing. "Did your patient live?" he demanded.

"She did. I fitted her with a wooden leg. Now she walks with only a slight limp." That was an exaggeration. Miss Thompson's limp was more than slight, but she was walking again, and both she and her parents considered that little more than a miracle after her leg had turned gangrenous.

"Harrumph." Dr. Worland glared at Elizabeth. "Did you ever deal with typhoid?"

Elizabeth wasn't certain why she didn't leave. It was clear there would be no partnership, not even a possible sharing of professional experiences. This man's interrogation told her he wasn't interested in learning what she had done; he merely wanted to trip her up. But still, she couldn't stop herself from responding. "I have treated typhoid. Cholera, malaria, and diphtheria too. And before you ask, the mortality rate of my patients was below average."

Raised brows telegraphed his disbelief. "That's a fine story, missy. It might convince others, but I'm not so easily taken in. It's as plain to me as the nose on my face. You've got yourself some book learning. Probably some newfangled ideas too. Those won't sit well with folks out here. Folks expect the basics. Bleed 'em, blister 'em, and purge 'em."

She should have expected it, given the cabinet filled with patent medicines, and yet Elizabeth was shocked by the doctor's treatment basics. "You're joking, of course."

His eyes narrowed as he took a step closer, his expression threatening. "I most definitely am not joking. I learned my trade as a surgeon during the War Between the States. I saved plenty of men using exactly those techniques. A flighty little lady like you isn't going to convince me to change my ways."

"No Eastern doctor would resort to heroic medicine." Though she had never understood the reason for the term, the now-discredited techniques of bleeding, blistering, and purging were frequently referred to as heroic medicine. "We have much gentler and more efficacious methods of treating our patients."

His face darkening with anger, Dr. Worland jabbed a finger at Elizabeth. "You think you're smart, don't you, with that brand-new diploma and those big words? Let me tell you something, missy. You'll never be a doctor here. Go back East. There's no future for you in Cheyenne."

4

I'm glad you didn't mind coming early." Miriam Eberhardt extended both hands in greeting as Richard led Elizabeth into the large parlor that would serve as a ballroom tonight. Like Miriam, the room was dressed in its best, but Elizabeth had expected no less. As Richard had driven her east on 18th Street, he'd pointed out Maple Terrace, the building that contained five three-story town houses. Though there was no question that they were far more spacious than the apartment Elizabeth shared with Gwen, Richard claimed that his and Miriam's home at Maple Terrace was too small for entertaining. The same complaint could not be made of the Taggerts' mansion. With a tower on one corner and a turret on another, plus a large circular window over the front entry, the huge sandstone building was the most ornate on 18th east of Central Avenue.

Elizabeth smiled at both her hostess and the beautiful room. Miriam wore a grass-green silk gown that shimmered as she walked, while potted palms and arrangements of fresh flowers graced the parlor. The floor was bare, the carpet having been removed for dancing, and only a few chairs lined one wall. Though at the moment the room was virtually empty, Elizabeth knew that within an hour, it would be filled with the sights, scents, and sounds of guests. Now it was the fragrance of lilacs and the somewhat discordant sounds of musicians tuning their instruments that greeted her.

"I know some people prefer to make an entrance after the other guests have arrived," Miriam continued, nodding her perfectly coiffed blonde head to punctuate her words, "but Mama and I thought a receiving line would be the best way to introduce you to everyone. That way we'll know we haven't missed anyone."

Elizabeth smiled again. "The thought of a receiving line takes me back to my childhood. Every time we moved to a new town, there was a receiving line at the church. My sisters and I dreaded them, because it seemed that all the ladies wanted to pinch our cheeks."

"Oh, my!" Miriam laid her hands on her cheeks, as if she were imagining a pinch. Tall and slender with sparkling green eyes, Miriam might not be beautiful, but she was attractive, and her vivacious personality made it easy to understand how she'd become one of Charlotte's closest friends. "That sounds painful," Miriam said as she lowered her hands.

"It was."

"But moving had to be even worse. I hated it when we had to leave Denver because Papa decided Cheyenne needed another newspaper. I pouted for weeks and told him and Mama that they were ruining my life." She feigned a pout. "They're now quick to remind me that if I'd stayed in Denver, I'd never have met Richard." Miriam cast a fond glance at her husband, who stood a few feet away, as if unwilling to eavesdrop on their conversation.

"I'm afraid our moves weren't my parents' choice. Papa was a minister—the kindest, godliest man you could imagine—but he had very strong opinions, and they weren't always what the church fathers wanted to hear. It seemed that we'd no sooner get settled than we'd have to move again. Fortunately, I had my sisters."

They were a large part of the reason Elizabeth had chosen Cheyenne for her office. Charlotte had made it her home almost two years ago, and though she and Barrett were currently in the East with Charlotte's son, David, they expected to return before winter. Just as wonderful, by the end of the year, Abigail and her husband would settle here too. When Ethan's commitment to the Army ended, Abigail claimed they planned to raise sheep and babies, although she admitted that she expected to have most of the responsibility for the latter. "Ethan can have his smelly sheep," she'd written. "I'll take care of the babies."

"It doesn't seem fair, does it?" Miriam linked her arm with Elizabeth's and led her to one of the chairs. "We might as well rest our feet while we can," she said. "This may be our last chance until dinner is served." She shook her head, setting her delicate gold earrings to bouncing. "I don't think I'll ever understand people. Papa's strong opinions bring him more subscribers, but your father's resulted in uprooting your family."

Elizabeth wished she hadn't mentioned the moves. It hadn't been a ploy for sympathy. Unlike Abigail, who had hated the disruption, Elizabeth had considered the family's moves almost an adventure. It was only now with the perspective of adulthood that she realized how much her sisters had sheltered her. She tried to lighten the mood by grinning. "The pinched cheeks weren't that bad."

As she'd hoped, Miriam returned the grin with one of her own. "I can promise you won't have any of those tonight."

And she did not, though Richard, who must have heard more than Elizabeth had realized, pretended to pinch her cheek when he rejoined her and Miriam. "You picked an excellent location for your office," he said as he took his place at Miriam's side. "You're next door to a good friend of mine. I understand you've met Jason."

Elizabeth tried not to wince at the thought that, as one of Richard's close friends, Jason Nordling had probably received an invitation to tonight's party. It had been unrealistic to think that their paths would not cross again. Cheyenne was not a large enough city to provide anonymity. "Yes, I have met him," Elizabeth said, keeping her voice noncommittal, "but I can't take credit for choosing the location. My sister and Barrett are responsible for that."

A few minutes later, Miriam's parents descended the stairs, apologizing profusely for not having greeted Elizabeth when she arrived. "A piece of lace came loose," Mrs. Taggert said with a frown at the offending ruffle, "and it took Mary Alice eons to fix it." Though a couple inches shorter than Miriam, Amelia Taggert had the same slender build, and it was clear that Miriam had inherited her blonde hair from her. The green eyes, though, were a legacy from her father, a tall, heavyset man with graying brown hair and ordinary features. Were it not for his vividly colored eyes and the impeccably tailored clothing that announced his success, Elizabeth doubted anyone would give him a second look.

"You wouldn't have loose flounces if you bought your clothes from Elizabeth's sister," Miriam told her mother, her expression indicating that this was one subject on which the two women would never agree.

Quick to intervene, Mr. Taggert shook Elizabeth's hand. "I appreciate your placing your advertisement in the *Telegraph*. I hope the results have been what you expected."

Unwilling to admit that she had yet to treat a patient, Elizabeth merely nodded. The results had not been what she had expected, but perhaps her expectations were unrealistic. Everyone from Jason Nordling to Dr. Worland seemed to believe that was the case. But there was no time for introspection, for the guests began to arrive. As the first entered the mansion, Mrs. Taggert arranged the receiving line in the spacious foyer, placing herself at the beginning, followed by her husband, Richard, Miriam, and then Elizabeth. "We're saving the guest of honor for last," she explained. The position suited Elizabeth, reminding her of the church receiving lines where, as the youngest child, she had been the last to greet parishioners.

"Yes, I'm delighted to be living in Cheyenne," Elizabeth said more times than she could count. "Yes," she told the women who asked, "this is one of my sister's designs." Fortunately for Elizabeth, Charlotte had left most of her clothing behind, including this emerald-green silk gown. The scooped neckline highlighted the strand of tiny pearls that Mama and Papa had given Elizabeth for her eighteenth birthday, but the gown's true beauty came from the artful draping of the overskirt. Dipping below the waist in the front, it was gathered into a bustle that extended into a short train. And, though she had not planned it, the color complemented Miriam's gown, causing more than one woman to comment on how well Elizabeth and Miriam looked together.

"I can't believe how many people are here," Gwen said when she arrived with Harrison. Though she had tried to demur, he had insisted on accompanying her, claiming that he wanted a beautiful woman on his arm. Even Gwen's scoffs had not managed to hide her blushes. And the way she clung to Harrison's arm tonight reminded Elizabeth how little Gwen was accustomed to society. Her simple farming background and Army life with her husband had not prepared her for the glitter of Cheyenne's upper crust.

"You look lovely," Elizabeth said softly. "Just think of all the stories you can tell Rose tomorrow."

"Good move," Harrison murmured. "You know how to calm her. I'll take over now." He led Gwen to a small table where a formally clad man was offering guests cups of punch.

Though her throat was dry, Elizabeth knew it would be at least another half hour before she could enjoy the cool refreshment. She smiled and greeted the next guest, trying not to let her smile fade when she saw that Jason Nordling was in line. It wasn't as if she were surprised. She'd known it was probable that he'd been invited when she learned of his friendship with Richard. It wasn't as if she didn't know how to be polite. She did. And it wasn't as if she'd have to spend more than a few seconds conversing with him. There was no reason, absolutely no reason, to be bothered just because Jason Nordling was coming her way.

Looking more handsome than ever in his formal clothing, he inclined his head in a short bow as he greeted Mrs. Taggert. Whatever he said must have charmed her, for Elizabeth heard the older woman laugh. It appeared Mr. Nordling had to uphold his reputation of being charming . . . to everyone except her.

"Good evening, Dr. Harding."

Elizabeth smiled at the fact that the man who'd questioned her abilities as a physician was now addressing her as "doctor." The smile was wiped away as he continued.

"I'm glad to see you did not heed my advice." Jason Nordling took Elizabeth's extended hand. Unlike some of the men, he did not hold it beyond the accepted time, and though his lips were curved in a smile, the smile did not extend to his eyes.

"What advice was that?" she asked, keeping her own voice as sweet as she could. No matter how annoying she found this particular guest, she would not create an unpleasant scene at the party. It was only a few seconds, after all. She'd greet him, and then she'd be free of him for the rest of the evening.

Elizabeth darted a quick glance at Miriam, wondering whether the next guest was ready to proceed along the line. Unfortunately, Miriam was engaged in what appeared to be a lengthy discussion with a strikingly attractive auburn-haired woman and an older man who kept a proprietary hand on her arm. Though he appeared to be old enough to be the redhead's father, the man's expression made Elizabeth believe he was her husband. Both appeared to be well acquainted with Miriam, making Elizabeth fear she would be required to spend more time than she'd expected with the arrogant attorney.

"What advice?" Mr. Nordling raised a quizzical brow. "Surely you recall that I advised you to pack your bags and leave Cheyenne." He kept his voice low enough that it could not be overheard, making Elizabeth wonder if he was teasing or serious. She would pretend there was no question, that this was simply playful banter.

"And miss the pleasure of your company tonight?" Elizabeth hadn't realized that her voice could sound so sugary. "Why, that would have been a fate worse than death."

Before he could reply, the woman who'd been speaking to Miriam tapped Mr. Nordling on the shoulder with her fan. "Hurry, Jason. The sooner we're through this line, the sooner the dancing will start. I've saved the first and last for you." A coquettish smile accompanied her words.

"Surely your husband will want the honor of those particular sets." Though he phrased it as a suggestion, the steel in Jason Nordling's voice made it no less than a command. "I'll content myself with another one." Singular. There were undercurrents here that Elizabeth did not want to explore, but one thing was clear: the beautiful redhead and Jason Nordling were far from strangers.

Jason stepped away as Miriam intervened. "Elizabeth, I'd like you to meet Mr. and Mrs. Chadwick." She nodded at the auburn-haired woman and her escort. Though Mrs. Chadwick was as tall and slender as Miriam and dressed in a russet silk gown that highlighted her slim beauty, her husband was of average height, with the heavy build that Elizabeth associated with fighters. The gray wings at his temples left no doubt that he was considerably older than his wife, probably close to fifty, while Mrs. Chadwick appeared to be less than thirty. "Nelson is the owner of Cheyenne's finest lumber company," Miriam explained, "and Tabitha—"

Before she could complete the sentence, Nelson Chadwick interrupted. "Thank you for the compliment, Miriam. If we are the finest, a lot of the credit goes to my foreman." He gestured toward the man standing on his other side, a brown-haired man of around thirty whose hazel eyes were fixed on Tabitha Chadwick, while the lovely redhead was staring at Jason Nordling. "Let me introduce you to Oscar Miller." Nelson grinned. "Although he'll try to deny it, Oscar is one of Cheyenne's most eligible bachelors. I suspect Tabitha and I were invited simply so that he would come."

Though Mr. Miller murmured a greeting, Elizabeth noted that his eyes continued to stray to Tabitha Chadwick, and—judging from the frown that crossed his face—he was not pleased by her attention to the young attorney.

Apparently unaware of the tension among her guests, Miriam nodded at Mrs. Chadwick. "Tabitha was one of your sister's best customers—after me, that is."

Tabitha Chadwick turned back toward Miriam and Elizabeth. "Charlotte is indeed a talented seamstress. I don't know what we're going to do without her."

"Wear gowns more than once."

Tabitha gave an exaggerated shudder at Miriam's suggestion. "Never," she declared as she reached for her husband's hand. "Nelson would never allow that."

An hour later, Elizabeth's cheeks hurt, not from being pinched, for as Miriam had predicted, there had been none of that, but from the effort of smiling. She must have been introduced to a hundred people. All were polite. Most were curious. If there was one thing Elizabeth had learned by the time the reception line disbanded, it was that no one here had met a woman doctor. Though they'd said little about her profession, she had seen their puzzled expressions when they'd complimented her on her gown. Had they expected her to wear trousers and a jacket like Dr. Worland? Surely they realized that being a doctor didn't make Elizabeth less than a woman. But perhaps they did not. Even Mama had warned that Elizabeth might have to sacrifice the most fundamental aspects of her femininity, becoming a wife and mother, if she wanted to pursue her dream of being a physician.

"My feet hurt," Miriam admitted as the last of the guests made their way into the parlor. "I need to sit down before the dancing starts."

Though Elizabeth would have appreciated the rest, the sight of Gwen seated at the opposite side of the room, looking a bit forlorn, perhaps because Harrison was engrossed in what appeared to be an animated conversation with Nelson Chadwick and his foreman, led her in that direction. There had to be something she could say to boost Gwen's spirits.

Keeping a smile firmly fixed on her face, Elizabeth made her way through the crowds. Although she tried not to eavesdrop, her ears perked when she passed two middle-aged women, their expressions telling her the subject of their discussion was unpleasant.

"The man is as handsome as can be," the woman in the deep purple dress announced.

Elizabeth's curiosity was piqued as she speculated on the identity of the handsome man. In her estimation, Jason Nordling was the most handsome in the room, but perhaps the woman was referring to someone else.

Her companion, clad in a lemon-yellow gown that did not flatter her coloring and that was definitely not one of Charlotte's creations, nodded. "True, but Mama used to say 'handsome is as handsome does.' I couldn't ever trust him. I mean, what kind of man defends a murderer?"

The subject of the women's discussion was indeed Jason.

Purple Lady nodded. "You're correct. No one with any honor would do that."

"It's a matter of principle," Yellow added.

If she were prudent, Elizabeth would have continued on her way, pretending she had not heard the women discussing Jason Nordling. And yet, no matter how she felt about him personally, she could not let them malign the man who'd done nothing more than uphold the Constitution.

Elizabeth wasn't certain when her opinion had shifted. Perhaps it had occurred when she'd been so appalled by the vigilante justice that had ended Adam Bennett's life. All she knew was that she had wakened one day with the realization that, whether or not he'd known the truth of Bennett's guilt when he'd accepted him as a client, Jason Nordling had been right to defend him, for in doing so, he'd guaranteed Adam Bennett one of the rights that made America such a great country. Now these women were denying that.

"I know it's rude to interrupt," Elizabeth said as she inched her way between the two ladies, "but I couldn't help overhearing. I agree with you," she said, inclining her head toward Yellow. The woman smiled, obviously gratified by Elizabeth's approval. She wouldn't be so happy when she heard the rest. "Mr. Nordling's defense of Adam Bennett was indeed a matter of principle. I think one of the finest things our country's founding fathers did was ensure that everyone is entitled to a defense." Yellow's eyes widened. Clearly, she had not expected that. "I'm not condoning what Mr. Bennett did, and I doubt Mr. Nordling was, either," Elizabeth said, watching both women's expressions, "but I do applaud the fact that Mr. Nordling upheld the principles of the Sixth Amendment."

"I never thought of it that way," Purple admitted.

Though Yellow's lips thinned, she said nothing, and Elizabeth suspected that the conversation would resume as soon as she left.

"I saw you talking to those ladies," Gwen said when Elizabeth joined her. "They didn't look too happy with whatever you were saying."

Two dances later, Elizabeth learned just how unhappy they were when she passed by Purple and Yellow on her way to the punch bowl.

"I wouldn't have expected it of Madame Charlotte's sister," Purple said. "Charlotte is such a sweet lady, but Elizabeth . . ." She paused, searching for a word. "She's not womanly. Look at the way she argued with us. She was acting just like a man."

Yellow nodded. "One thing's for certain. Even if I were on my deathbed, I wouldn't go to her."

Elizabeth gritted her teeth. Miriam had organized this party to introduce her to the community and help her attract patients. Instead, Elizabeth had alienated at least two potential patients. And to think she'd done it in defense of Jason Nordling!

"Everyone seems to be having a good time." Miriam appeared at Elizabeth's side, a half-filled cup of punch in her hand.

"It's the loveliest party I've ever attended." Particularly if Elizabeth forgot about the way she'd offended Yellow and Purple.

"That must mean no one pinched your cheeks."

"No one even tried." Fortunately. Of course, Purple and Yellow might have had other ideas, less friendly ones than a pinch on the cheeks. Elizabeth and Miriam spoke of trivia for a few minutes until a waiter collected their now-empty cups and murmured something to Miriam.

"It's almost dinnertime," Elizabeth's hostess said. "Mama wants Richard and me to lead the procession, but first . . ." Miriam's eyes lit. "Ah, there you are, Jason." Her smile snagged him as surely as a lasso. When he was standing at her side, Miriam smiled again. "Would you escort Elizabeth in to dinner? I've seated you next to her." Without waiting for a reply, she turned toward her husband and led the way to the dining room.

Jason's lips twisted in what appeared to be an ironic smile as he bent his elbow and offered his arm to Elizabeth. Though Elizabeth expected him to follow Miriam and Richard, he held back, letting others precede them. Bending his head slightly, as if he were confiding a secret, he said, "It appears you're going to have even more of the pleasure of my company than you had anticipated."

Once again, they were playing the happy guest game. Elizabeth matched Jason's smile with one of her own, a smile dripping with simulated sweetness. "Fortunately, my mother taught me how to be polite."

His eyebrows arched. "If you were being polite the day we met, I'd hate to see you when you're rude. It's been a long time since I've had such a tongue-lashing."

"I wasn't being rude," she countered. Surely she hadn't been. Elizabeth thought back, trying to recall what she had said. Surely she had done nothing to deepen the pain or discomfort or whatever it was she had seen in his eyes that day. "I was simply being honest. You riled me, Mr. Nordling." And he was on his way to doing it again. Those arched eyebrows were designed to make her feel insignificant. Elizabeth knew it. That was the same look Charlotte used to give her when she was annoyed. Charlotte's goal had been to make

Elizabeth apologize. It hadn't worked then, and it wouldn't work now.

"Call me Jason."

"Why?"

"Why not? If we're going to have to make polite"—he threw her word back at her—"conversation for the next hour and a half, we might as well be on friendly terms."

"All right." It was a less than gracious agreement, but Elizabeth was not feeling particularly gracious. "You may call me Elizabeth."

The first rush to enter the dining room had subsided. Placing his hand on top of hers in what appeared to be a courtly gesture, Jason nodded toward the doorway. "They're expecting us."

As they entered the room, Elizabeth saw that in addition to the long table with its seating for more than two dozen, a number of smaller tables were placed around the perimeter. Still more were located in the adjoining room. The Taggerts were clearly accustomed to entertaining large groups.

"There's one thing I don't understand, Jason." It felt odd, speaking his name. While it was true that in her thoughts Elizabeth sometimes referred to him that way, this was the first time she'd pronounced his given name. "Other than not offending our hosts, why would you want to be friendly with me?" she asked. "I know you have no respect for me." And that knowledge rankled.

For a second, Jason's smile faltered. Renewing it, he shook his head. "You misunderstood. It's not a matter of respect or disrespect. I simply think you're mistaken if you believe you can succeed as a doctor."

"Because I'm a woman."

He shook his head. "Because the citizens of Wyoming aren't ready for a woman doctor."

"That's not what you said before."

A spark of what appeared to be pain lit his eyes, and in that instant Elizabeth suspected she'd misjudged him. Her parents had warned her that she was too quick to judge. Perhaps she had done that again, believing Jason Nordling to be arrogant and rude. Whether or not he'd known of his client's guilt when he'd undertaken his defense, the trial and its aftermath had to have been difficult.

It was as if he'd heard her thoughts. "That was one of the worst days of my life," Jason admitted. "I was angry and frustrated, and I took it out on you." He dipped his head so that his lips were closer to her ears. "I'm sorry. Can we start over?"

Elizabeth smiled, and for the first time, the smile she directed at Jason Nordling was genuine. "I'd like that."

"Then shall we find our seats, Elizabeth?"

She was thankful they had had the chance to talk before dinner, because once they were seated at the middle of the long table, there was little opportunity. Tabitha Chadwick, on Jason's left, monopolized the conversation. Every time he turned to speak to Elizabeth, Tabitha would put her hand on his arm and interrupt, ignoring the glares her husband shot from the opposite side of the table. It didn't seem to matter that Jason's replies were monosyllabic. Tabitha kept talking and laughing, her eyes sparkling with animation, her lips curving into what Elizabeth would have called a sultry smile.

"She's trying to make Nelson jealous," Oscar Miller, who sat at Elizabeth's right, explained as he tipped his soup bowl to catch the last spoonful of consommé. When they'd first been seated, Oscar had given Elizabeth a perfunctory greeting, then devoted himself to the woman on his right, but when Tabitha's actions had left Elizabeth without a partner, he'd proven a gentleman and had tried to include Elizabeth in his conversation. Now, however, he'd turned ever so slightly and was addressing her directly.

"Why would she want to do that?"

Oscar's hazel eyes narrowed, and his lips tightened. "Because then Nelson will buy her an expensive trinket. Mr. Mullen has a diamond bracelet that Tabitha wants. Nelson told her she'd have to wait until Christmas, so this is her revenge. She's flirting with Jason to get her way."

Perhaps she had led a sheltered life, but Elizabeth had never encountered so brazen a woman. It was bad enough that Tabitha was trying to manipulate her husband, but openly flirting with another man when she was married—that was beyond Elizabeth's experience. Oh, it was true that there had been unfaithful couples in several congregations where Papa had served, but they had tried to keep their liaisons secret. This seemed far worse, for Tabitha's actions could only humiliate her husband. All for a diamond bracelet.

"You look skeptical." Oscar buttered a piece of bread as he spoke. "Trust me, it's true. I spend enough time with both Chadwicks to know what's happening. Now, if you want to get Jason's attention, pretend you're hanging on my every word."

"I don't want Jason's attention."

"Don't you?"

Dinner seemed interminable. Though normally he would have enjoyed the numerous courses of delicious food, today Jason had only one thought: escape. Short of being rude and creating a scene that would cause Nelson more pain, there was no way to stop Tabitha from monopolizing him. Those coy looks and the way she leaned toward him, moving so that he'd have to be blind not to notice her décolletage, were invitations to a game Jason had no desire to play.

Keeping his eyes fixed on his plate, as if the succulent beef were the most fascinating thing he'd ever seen, he tried to ignore the way Tabitha pressed her leg against his. She was beautiful. There was no doubt of that. But so was Elizabeth Harding. The difference was, Elizabeth's beauty was softer, and she made no aggressive moves. It was almost as if she were unaware of her beauty. Jason thought that unlikely. Women were always aware of their effect on others. If they lacked beauty, they found other ways to be noticed. And yet, Elizabeth seemed different. Tonight had shown him that.

She was more opinionated than any other woman he'd ever met, and she might slice a man's skin with her sharp tongue if she disagreed with him, but Jason doubted she'd ever be petty, and he knew to the very marrow of his bones that if she were married, she would give her husband the love, honor, and fidelity he deserved. Elizabeth Harding was unusual and intriguing, and he wanted to learn more about her. Much more.

They'd gotten off to a rough start, but that didn't mean they had to remain adversaries. "Blessed are the peacemakers: for they shall be called the children of God." Jason could hear the reverend reciting that verse along with the rest of the Beatitudes. Jason wasn't naturally a peacemaker. He knew that. But he had been speaking the truth when he told Elizabeth he wanted them to have a new beginning. There was no reason to wait.

Though Tabitha was in the middle of a sentence, Jason turned to his right and faced Elizabeth. "May I have the pleasure of escorting you home this evening?"

5

Elizabeth wasn't certain why she'd agreed. The truth was, she had been surprised by Jason's suggestion. It was also true that she'd been impressed by his apology earlier in the evening and had found herself looking forward to sharing dinner conversation with him. It had been disappointing—decidedly disappointing—that Tabitha had dominated the table talk and kept Elizabeth from learning more about Jason, but that didn't explain why she had accepted his invitation so quickly. Whatever the reason, she had, and here she was, sitting next to him in his comfortable carriage.

The sun had set, but the June air was still warm enough that she was in no hurry to return home. Jason, it appeared, felt the same, for instead of continuing down 18th Street to Ferguson, following the most direct route from the Taggerts' mansion to Elizabeth's modest apartment, he had turned north on Warren Avenue, apparently heading for City Park.

"Did you enjoy the party?"

Elizabeth nodded. "For the most part." She wouldn't mention her discussion with Purple and Yellow and their reaction. There was no reason for him to know that the two busybodies did not trust him, especially since it was unlikely they'd seek his professional services. "The evening was pleasant, but I doubt it accomplished Miriam's objective."

Jason slowed the horse and turned to look at Elizabeth. "What did she hope to accomplish other than introducing you to half the population of Cheyenne?"

His exaggeration made Elizabeth smile. She was still smiling as she said, "Miriam thought that if people met me, they'd be convinced I was a good doctor."

Jason's chuckle made Elizabeth bristle. Though she'd thought they had begun to forge a friendship, she was obviously mistaken, for here he was, laughing at the thought that she was a competent physician.

"I'm sorry," he said, his voice sounding contrite. "I wasn't laughing at you. Not at all. I simply found it amusing that Miriam used the same tactic on you that Richard did on me. I'm not a great partygoer, but Richard convinced me it was important that I attend this one because it would get me back into the public eye and show people I'm not a monster, even if I did defend Adam Bennett."

Elizabeth's eyes widened. "You didn't want to come, either?"

As the carriage moved slowly up Warren, Jason shook his head. "I know gatherings like Richard and Miriam's are important—one of my professors claimed they were essential for attracting new clients—but I don't enjoy them. Somehow, it seems almost dishonest, trying to charm people so they'll hire me as their attorney."

This time it was Elizabeth who chuckled. "I felt the same way until I convinced myself it was no worse than putting an announcement in the paper." She was silent for a moment, gazing at the stars sprinkled across the sky. Though Cheyenne had streetlights, there were far fewer than in New York, so the sky appeared darker, the stars brighter than in her former home.

"Does it work?" she asked. "Do parties like this bring in clients or, in my case, patients?"

Jason shrugged. "It's not always that easy. I certainly didn't have clients lining the street waiting to consult me the first month I opened my practice." He let out a self-deprecating laugh. "I still don't, although I have enough to pay my rent. There are a number of very wealthy men in Cheyenne, but I'm not one of them."

The honesty of his admission touched Elizabeth's heart, for she suspected that most men would have exaggerated their financial situation.

"I never expected to become wealthy," she told Jason. If there was one lesson her parents had taught, it was that money did not bring happiness. Her sisters' lives had proven that. Charlotte's first husband had made decisions with tragic consequences, all because he wanted riches, while Barrett, her second husband, claimed that he'd found true love and happiness only after he'd lost his fortune. And though Abigail's husband had given up a vast inheritance, believing a distant cousin deserved it more than he, Elizabeth doubted anyone could be happier than Abigail and Ethan.

"You're a wise woman not to expect riches." Jason tugged the reins, slowing the horse again. "It took me about three months to become established here. If you're fortunate and the women of Cheyenne accept you, I'd say that by the time autumn returns, you should have a good number of patients."

Autumn. Jason was the second person to suggest it would take that long. "I hate the thought of waiting."

"I know." Coming from another man, the words might have been nothing more than a platitude, but Elizabeth sensed Jason's sincerity. "It's difficult to be patient when you've spent so much time preparing, but there's no easy answer."

"I know." She repeated his words. "I wish you were wrong, but I know you're not. Everyone warned me this would not be easy."

As Jason shifted on the seat, the scent of his soap teased Elizabeth's nostrils.

"If you knew it would be difficult, why did you decide to become a physician?"

Elizabeth took a deep breath, almost as startled by the question as she had been by Jason's invitation to drive her home. Unlike her classmates, who had scoffed as they demanded why she thought she had the ability to become a doctor, he had asked what had driven her to her decision. That was a far different question. No one outside her family knew the story, but Elizabeth found herself wanting to share her reasons with Jason.

"It probably sounds silly, but it started when I found a wounded bird. One of our neighbors' cats caught it and ripped the poor thing's wing." Though she kept her voice even, Elizabeth had never forgotten the anguish she'd felt that day, and even now, she could feel her heart contract as she remembered the bird's distress. "I scared the cat away, but then I didn't know what to do. I couldn't bear watching the bird try to flap its wing, even though it couldn't fly."

"Did you heal it?"

Elizabeth shook her head. "I tried, but all I accomplished

was frightening it even more. It died in my hands." And no matter how many tears she had shed or how many prayers she had lifted to heaven, nothing had brought the sparrow back to life.

"How old were you?"

Once again, Jason sounded as though he really cared. This was the first time a man had taken a genuine interest in her calling. Not even Ethan and Barrett, her brothers-in-law, had made more than polite inquiries about her classes.

"I was seven."

"Ouch." Starlight provided enough illumination for Elizabeth to see Jason's wince. "Even a small hurt is magnified at that age."

It was odd. No one had ever said that, and yet it was true. She'd been young enough to grieve but not old enough to know that she'd done the best she could. "I had better luck as I grew older. I was ten when the local doctor showed me how to splint my dog's broken leg. When he was able to walk without a limp, I knew that healing wounds was what I wanted to do with my life." And here she was, fourteen years later, a diploma in her hand. "What about you? What made you decide to be an attorney?"

"My father's housekeeper." They had reached the four-block expanse of City Park. Slowing the horse even more, Jason began to guide the carriage around the perimeter. At this time of night, there were no pedestrians, but a few coaches had entered the curving paths of the park itself. "Mrs. Moran was always ordering me around," he said, his voice sharp with remembered anger. "If I protested or asked why, she'd say it was the law. Eventually I decided to find out what the law really said. Before I knew it, I was hooked."

How different Jason's upbringing had been from hers. Though her parents had always been in control, Elizabeth could not recall them issuing orders without explaining why they were needed. Sensing that the housekeeper's dictatorial ways still bothered him, Elizabeth sought a way to make Jason laugh. "Hooked?" she asked. "Like a trout?"

"Exactly."

"So the law is a worm?"

Jason's chuckle became a full-fledged laugh. "I should have known you'd have a memorable retort. Is that what they taught you in medical school, how to make people laugh?"

"Hardly." There had been precious little laughter in her classes. "That's from having two older sisters. They were always bigger than me, so I tried to outwit them."

"Did it work?"

"Not very often," Elizabeth admitted. "They were, after all, still older than me, so they had a lot of ways to outsmart me. I tried, though."

"I had no chance with Mrs. Moran. My father made it clear that when he wasn't around, she was in charge, and she never let me forget it."

As the sliver of a moon skirted beneath a passing cloud, Elizabeth considered Jason's statement. It sounded as though his childhood had been lonely. Though she suspected she knew the answer, she felt compelled to ask, "Do you have any siblings?"

The evening was dark, but not so dark that Elizabeth could not see Jason's expression. His lips curved into a grimace. "My mother died when I was born, and my father never re-married. When I was old enough to understand, he told me that Mrs. Moran had set her cap for him, but he wouldn't dishonor my mother's memory by marrying someone he didn't love."

And Mrs. Moran had taken out her frustration on Jason. Elizabeth closed her eyes, searching for something amusing to say to lift his spirits, but try though she might, she could find nothing.

"I'm sorry," she said. "Everyone deserves to be loved."

"You don't need to pity me. My father loved me in his own way, and the experience taught me a lesson. No matter what I have to do, my children will not be raised by a housekeeper. They'll have a mother with them every hour of the day and night. They'll never be left alone."

Though he said nothing more, Elizabeth's imagination conjured the image of a small boy in the throes of a nightmare, waking and having no one to comfort him. Poor Jason.

"Have you been to the park before?" Jason asked as he turned the carriage toward the center. The message was clear: there would be no further discussion of his childhood tonight.

"Not at night." Though the park was beautiful during the day, moonlight gave it a special allure. The curving roads seemed mysterious, and were she so inclined, Elizabeth would have called them romantic. But tonight was not a night for romance. Tonight was business, a night for developing relationships with potential patients.

She settled back on the seat, trying to relax while her mind whirled at the realization that the evening hadn't turned out the way she had expected. She might not have gained any patients, might instead have alienated several, but she had accomplished at least one thing. Not only had she and Jason forged a truce, but she was beginning to believe she'd been mistaken about him. In the time they'd been together, she had seen his arrogance disappear, falling away like a butterfly's chrysalis, revealing a man with surprising vulnerabilities as well as fundamental strengths. Though she knew her sister would crow with triumph were Elizabeth to admit it, Charlotte had been right. Jason was charming.

Count to ten. Nelson Chadwick clenched his fists, knowing that counting to ten or even to ten thousand would not dissipate the anger that surged through him. What he wanted was to wipe the smirk off his wife's face. He'd said nothing while they were at the Taggerts', for he had no intention of creating a scene that would be reported to every busybody in Cheyenne. He'd kept his lips pressed firmly together as they'd driven home, but now that they were inside the house that Tabitha had made over to suit her, he could no longer remain silent.

"How could you behave like that?" he demanded, anger coloring his words and turning his voice harsh as he closed the door to the small parlor behind them. Though he doubted the servants had any illusions about the state of his marriage, there was no point in exposing them to the sordid details, even though the generous salaries he paid would ensure their silence. His staff was loyal; his wife was not.

"Like what?" The smile that accompanied Tabitha's seemingly innocent question was the sweet one that had fooled him at the beginning. It fooled him no longer.

"Like a slut." He spat the words. "You're my wife, Tabitha. I expect you to remember that and act accordingly."

Her eyes narrowed slightly, and her smile faded. "I danced the first dance with you. What more did you want? You were out of breath by the end of it. I did you a favor by letting you sit down."

As she turned, Nelson grabbed her arm. "The only reason you danced with me was because Jason had the sense to refuse you. Give him credit. He's not simply my attorney; he's a wise man."

Ironically, it had been Jason, the man she had tried to seduce this evening, who had cautioned him when he'd begun courting Tabitha. "She's so much younger," Jason had said, his voice as calm as if he were discussing nothing more important than the weather. "Are you certain she's the right one for you?" But Nelson had refused to listen. It had seemed like a miracle that beautiful, young Tabitha Barclay loved him. Who was he to question miracles? Now he knew the truth. It had been no miracle, simply cunning on her part.

"Jason's handsome too." The smirk had returned to Tabitha's face.

Nelson tightened his grip on her arm. Though he'd never hit a woman, he felt an almost irresistible urge to slap her smirk away. "This has got to stop right now. I will not tolerate any more of your flirting. I've given you everything you wanted, and even though the only part of our wedding vows that you heard was the part about 'for richer,' you owe me something in return."

Wincing as she tried to pull her arm away, Tabitha glared at him. "What did you have in mind?"

"Respect!" He wouldn't ask for love, for he knew that was impossible. Tabitha did not love him; she never had. After observing her for the five years of their marriage, Nelson wasn't certain she was capable of loving anyone other than herself. Respect was different. She owed him that much.

He glared at the face he'd once thought so beautiful. "When you're in public, you will conduct yourself in a manner becoming to your position as my wife. You will not flirt with Jason Nordling or anyone else. You will not humiliate me."

Tabitha's eyes filled with fury. "Or what? Will you kill me like Adam Bennett did his wife?"

The urge to wrap his hands around her throat grew stronger. "Don't tempt me, Tabitha, and don't forget that without my money, you'd be nothing more than a common shopgirl."

"I wish I'd never married you." Her lips curved with scorn as she jerked her arm from his grip.

Nelson nodded. "For once we agree on something."

If it hadn't been completely out of character for her friend, Elizabeth would have said that normally cheerful Gwen was sulking. She'd burned the eggs, and the toast was barely warmed. More alarming, she'd snapped at Rose, leaving the child with a bewildered expression. Though Elizabeth had wakened filled with pleasant memories of the previous evening, it appeared that Gwen had not.

By the time Elizabeth returned, Gwen had been in her room with the light extinguished, giving Elizabeth no opportunity to ask about her friend's experience. This morning Gwen had deflected each of Elizabeth's questions about the party, leaving little doubt that it was the cause of her ill humor.

Elizabeth waited until breakfast was over and Rose was playing with her doll before she broached the subject again. "What's wrong, Gwen? And don't pretend that nothing's bothering you."

Pursed lips were the only response.

"C'mon, Gwen. Why are you so unhappy?"

Gwen poured herself another cup of coffee, making a pro-duction out of reaching for the sugar bowl. When she spoke, her words were little more than a mumble. "I shouldn't have gone to the party."

"Why not?" To the best of Elizabeth's knowledge, no one had snubbed her, and other than the time he'd spoken to a few men, Harrison had not left her side. "I thought you enjoyed it. Almost every time I looked at you, you were smiling."

Gwen stirred another spoonful of sugar into her coffee. "I wasn't smiling on the inside. Seeing everyone there reminded me of all the things I'll never be: smart and pretty and thin. I'm hopeless." She took a sip of coffee, frowning as she put the cup back on its saucer. "Look at me, Elizabeth. I'm a failure. The only thing I want is for Rose to have a father, but how will I attract one when I'm fat and ugly? No man will marry a woman like me."

Something had triggered Gwen's bout of self-pity, but Elizabeth doubted she would learn the cause. The only thing she could do was try to convince Gwen she was mistaken. "You're not ugly, and you're not fat." Admittedly, Gwen was a bit heavy, but not dangerously so. And some men, or so Elizabeth had heard, preferred women with extra meat on their bones.

"You don't have to lie." Gwen drained her coffee and poured herself another cup. "I know what I look like. No man would give me a second glance."

"I think you're mistaken. It seems to me that Harrison has given you more than a second glance. If you ask me, he's interested in you."

"Hah!" Gwen spat the word. "Harrison's interested in me all right. That was clear last night. He told me I was a better cook than the Taggerts' fancy French chef. Don't you see, Elizabeth? I'm the woman who feeds him, nothing more." And before Elizabeth could respond, Gwen burst into tears.

6

I need your advice."

Jason ushered Nelson Chadwick into his office, wondering if it was his imagination or whether the man had aged since he'd seen him. It had been only a couple days since the party at the Taggert mansion, but the lines on Nelson's face seemed more deeply etched, and Jason didn't recall so many gray strands in his hair.

"Advice is why you're paying me," he said as lightly as he could. Despite Nelson's somewhat haggard look, Jason was glad to see him. He'd been afraid that their first meeting since Richard's party might have been awkward because of Tabitha's behavior. Jason had found it embarrassing. He could only imagine how Nelson felt. The woman's overtures had been blatant, far more than the mild flirtation some women enjoyed. Uncertain whether he should say something or wait for Nelson to mention it, Jason decided on silence. The truth was, even if he were interested in Tabitha—which he was not—he would never have accepted her offers. Not only did Jason not trifle with married women, but she was the wife of a client. That made Tabitha doubly off limits. The fact that he was here this morning suggested that Nelson knew that.

Settling into the chair behind his desk, Jason pulled out a piece of paper and prepared to take notes. "What can I do for you?"

"I believe it's time to expand the lumber company."

"That makes sense. I've heard that your business is good." A smile of satisfaction lit Nelson's face. "We have more work than we can handle, especially with the capitol and the depot under construction. It's making people realize that Cheyenne is a great place to live."

"It is." Jason had certainly found that to be true. With the exception of the Bennett case, his time in Cheyenne had been both pleasant and profitable. Unlike Elizabeth's. While she had seemed to recognize the truth in his statement that it took a while to establish a practice, he imagined that she had hoped that Richard's party would bring her at least one patient. So far, it had not, and that had to be discouraging.

Jason hoped she would not be so disheartened that she'd leave, for though he had not expected it, he'd found himself replaying his conversation with Elizabeth and wishing for the opportunity to continue it. No other woman had lingered in his memory the way she did, and he . . . Wrenching his errant thoughts back to his client, Jason scribbled a note on the sheet of paper. *Invite her to supper.* With a frown, Jason crossed out the words, carefully inscribing *Chadwick Lumber Expansion.*

"The problem is, expansion is expensive. We'd need more equipment as well as additional space." Nelson pursed his lips and shook his head slightly as he continued. "I thought it might be time to offer shares in the company."

Jason made another note. "And become a corporation."

"Exactly. What do you think?"

"You've probably already considered this, but in exchange for the money you'd raise, you'd be giving up some control. You'd have to establish a board of directors, and you'd be responsible to the shareholders."

Nelson nodded. "My plan was to keep a controlling block. I intend to hold 51 percent of the stock."

"That's wise. You're the current owner and the founder; you ought to retain control." Jason scribbled a few notes on his pad before he looked up. "It shouldn't take me more than a couple days to draft the papers for you."

Most clients would have been happy, but Nelson appeared concerned. "There's a problem. Even though he knows how important this is to us, Oscar is reluctant to expand at all if it means bringing in investors."

"Did he say why?"

Nelson's face reddened. "He told me he was worried about what would happen if I should die. You know the terms of my will. Tabitha inherits the business, but Oscar is guaranteed his position for as long as he wants it. I think he's afraid he could be voted out of the company if I wasn't there." The veins on Nelson's hands protruded as he gripped the chair arms. "I told Oscar I wasn't planning to enter the pearly gates any time soon, but he's adamant. He barely listened to my arguments, just told me he'd leave if I incorporated. That's why I need your help. Do you have any suggestions?"

"That depends on how valuable Oscar is to you."

"Very. He handles all the workers, and there's no one who

does that better. More than that, he's loyal." Nelson relaxed his grip on the chair arms as he leaned forward to emphasize his words. "I have to admit that I wasn't happy when Tabitha insisted that I hire him. I doubted he could do the job, but Oscar has proven to be the best employee anyone could ask for. I couldn't run the company without him."

Jason scribbled a few notes, then looked up at Nelson. "You could leave him a portion of the company. Maybe not your full share, but enough that he'd have a say in running it."

"But he wouldn't have full control."

"No." Unless he married Tabitha or could convince her to let him vote her shares along with his.

Jason tried not to frown at the thought of Oscar and Tabitha together. He'd witnessed Tabitha's flirtations with her husband's foreman on too many occasions to think Tabitha would be unwilling to marry Oscar if she found herself widowed. The question was whether Oscar was enamored with Tabitha. That was not a question Jason would raise. "Let's see what else we can come up with."

They were discussing alternative approaches to convincing Oscar when a shadow darkened the front window. Nelson turned and grinned. "It looks like the lady doctor has a visitor."

Like Nelson, Jason had recognized the woman. "I imagine Miriam's here as a friend, not a patient. It seems to me that the people of Cheyenne aren't yet convinced that women are cut out to be doctors."

His grin fading, Nelson gripped the chair arms again. "Some aren't cut out to be wives, either."

"Miriam! What a nice surprise." Elizabeth hurried across the waiting room to greet her friend. "Would you like some coffee? I keep a pot going." She wouldn't add that the primary reason was that the caffeine helped her stay awake during the long, boring days.

"No, thank you." For the first time in their acquaintance, Miriam appeared uneasy. Normally she was the picture of poise and elegance, but this afternoon her smile seemed forced and she clasped her hands together as if to keep them from trembling. "I'm here as a patient," she said softly.

Elizabeth tried to mask her surprise. "What's wrong?"

Miriam shook her head. "Nothing. Unless I'm mistaken, something is very, very right. I believe I'm going to have a baby, and I want you to attend me."

A shiver of delight made its way up Elizabeth's spine. She had her first patient and for the best of all reasons. "Come into my office." She gestured toward the next room. "Let's see if I can confirm your diagnosis." Ten minutes later, Miriam climbed down from the examining table, her face sober as she looked at Elizabeth. Her own heart pounding with excitement, Elizabeth smiled. "Your diagnosis was correct. By the middle of January, you and Richard should have your first son or daughter."

"And you'll be there?"

The hesitation in Miriam's voice surprised Elizabeth. While her colleagues had disparaged female ailments as figments of women's imagination and claimed that childbirth should be relegated to midwives, Elizabeth believed women deserved the same level of care as men. Childbirth was often routine, but when it was not, a physician's skill could mean the difference between life and death. "As my mother used to say, I wouldn't miss it for all the tea in China."

A smile wreathed Miriam's slender face. "I'm so glad. Mama doesn't speak of it very often, but I know she had a difficult time when I was born. That's why I'm an only child." Miriam clasped her hands so tightly that her knuckles whitened and her face grew pale. Concerned, Elizabeth led her patient to one of the chairs in front of her desk and took the other.

"Mama said she almost died," Miriam continued, "and she claims it was the midwife's fault. She won't tell me what happened, just that it was a ghastly experience, but as soon as Richard and I were married, she insisted that I needed to have Dr. Worland attend me when I was with child."

Miriam wrinkled her nose as if she smelled something unpleasant. "You know how determined Mama can be. Richard says she only wants the best for me, but that's not Dr. Worland. I think he's a scary old man. The medicine he gave me made me sicker, and he even tried to put leeches on me when I was a child." A shudder accompanied Miriam's words. "I screamed so much that Papa sent him away. Oh, Doctor, I hate leeches!"

"So do I." Elizabeth had been warned about leeches and purges her first month of medical school. "Modern doctors don't use them, especially for a woman who's expecting a child." Elizabeth gestured at the cabinets that lined one wall of the room. "You can look around if you like, but I assure you that I have no leeches."

A smile once more lighting her face, Miriam nodded. "I knew you wouldn't. Pastor Saylor always said God has perfect timing, and you're the proof that he does. He sent you to Cheyenne just when I needed you."

When Miriam left half an hour later, Elizabeth was still

beaming with happiness. What a wonderful day! She had her first patient, and despite Miriam's fears, she had seen no reason why that patient would have a difficult delivery. Miriam and her minister were correct. God did have perfect timing. He'd known that Elizabeth was becoming discouraged, that she feared she would never be accepted as a physician, and he'd sent Miriam to her. What a wonderful day!

She was humming when the doorbell rang again.

"You sound happy," Jason announced as she greeted him.

"I am. I have my first patient."

"Miriam Eberhardt?"

Elizabeth blinked, momentarily surprised that he'd known about Miriam's visit. How silly of her. "I should have known you'd see her." After all, she saw most of the clients who entered Jason's office.

He nodded. "There are few secrets in Cheyenne, especially among neighbors."

Afterwards, Elizabeth couldn't imagine what had caused her to blurt out the question. Perhaps it was because she was so happy that she wasn't thinking clearly. Perhaps it was because the question had haunted her for days. All she knew was that she heard herself saying, "There is one secret. Did you know Adam Bennett had killed his wife when you took on his case?" The instant the words left her lips, Elizabeth regretted them. How gauche of her. She'd put Jason in a difficult position, all because her curiosity had overruled her common sense.

"You don't mince words, do you?" To her surprise, he didn't sound angry, simply a bit startled.

"I'm so sorry, Jason. Sometimes my tongue runs away with itself. I had no right to ask that."

"Yes, you did. We're friends, or at least I'd like to think we are, and friends don't keep secrets from each other."

"Thank you for not being annoyed with me. And thank you, too, for counting me as one of your friends." Elizabeth liked the idea that she and Jason were friends. Her first patient and a new friend. It was indeed a good day.

His expression serious, Jason said, "To answer your question, no, I didn't know my client was guilty until he announced it in the courtroom. He swore he was innocent every time we met, and I believed him."

Though Elizabeth's heart soared with the knowledge that Jason had not knowingly helped exonerate a killer, his lips twisted into a grimace. "I never thought I was gullible, but the evidence seems to say otherwise."

She was the one who'd introduced the painful subject. There had to be a way she could provide at least a bit of comfort. Elizabeth led the way into her waiting room and took a seat on one of the benches, indicating that Jason should sit next to her. "You had no way of knowing Adam Bennett was a liar," she said as firmly as she could.

Jason shrugged. "I keep thinking I should have."

Elizabeth turned slightly so she was facing Jason. His eyes were solemn, and his chin looked more square than normal, as if he were clenching his jaw. "How could you know? My father used to say that only God sees inside our hearts."

A short nod acknowledged her words. "He sounds like a wise man." Jason appeared to relax. "Perhaps I'll meet your parents someday. With both you and your sister settling here, I imagine they're eager to see Cheyenne."

Elizabeth had tried but failed to picture her parents in Wyoming. Neither one had been west of Lake Champlain, a fact

Papa had once announced with pride. They were both Vermonters to the core, and though they'd been nurturing parents, she doubted they would have approved their daughters' move West.

Rather than try to explain all that to Jason, Elizabeth said, "Papa died half a dozen years ago. My mother never really recovered from that or from being forced to leave the parsonage. She died less than two years later."

"I'm sorry. I can't imagine that it's ever easy to lose a parent. I know it was difficult for me when my father died." Jason shifted on the bench, seemingly searching for a comfortable position. When he looked back at Elizabeth, his expression reflected curiosity. "You mentioned a parsonage. Was your father a minister?"

She nodded. "You sound surprised."

"I am. I didn't realize that we had more in common than sharing this building. My father was a minister too."

Though his tone was matter-of-fact, Elizabeth realized she'd been given a key to Jason. More than many, she now understood what his childhood had been like. It was no wonder Mrs. Moran had raised him. If Jason's father had been like hers, he had been so busy with his parishioners that he had little time to spend with his son and had probably been unaware of how unkind the woman he trusted to care for Jason was. Elizabeth had been fortunate, for she'd had Mama and her sisters, but Jason had had no one other than the housekeeper. No wonder he had such strong opinions about how children should be raised.

The room was crowded, filled with large bodies, loud voices, and the smells of tobacco, Macassar oil, and perfume. Young women, and some who were no longer so young, smiled at the men who lined the bar, standing closer than a society matron would feel proper. Phoebe Simcoe laughed at the thought of a society matron setting foot inside her front door. If one did, she'd probably swoon either from the sight of all the flesh bared for men's ogling eyes or the glimpse of one of her neighbors—perhaps even her husband—doing the ogling. It would serve her right. Proper women weren't supposed to know that places like Phoebe's existed, and they most definitely were not supposed to visit. So far, none had.

Phoebe's smile widened at the realization that the room was more crowded than usual for a Monday. Perhaps that was because Friday had been quieter than normal. The Taggert/Eberhardt party had kept a number of Phoebe's regular patrons occupied. Tonight they were making up for lost time.

She walked slowly around the room, greeting the men, ensuring that each one had the girl he preferred. Though the sun had yet to set, the room was dark, thanks to the velvet draperies that were never opened after noon. The men who visited expected Phoebe to protect their privacy. That was why, although the building had a front door, the clientele normally entered through the side, where a large lilac bush blocked views from the street.

"It's good to see you, Alfred," Phoebe said as she approached a tall, thin cowboy who spent most of his pay here. "Sheila's occupied right now, but I know she'll be pleased that you came. Can I offer you another whiskey while you wait?"

One of the things that set Phoebe's establishment apart from others was that she did not charge men for anything other than the girls' favors. The whiskey and refreshments that she provided were free to anyone who visited, whether or not they chose to go upstairs with one of the girls. Almost everyone did. Phoebe's rates might be double that of other bordellos in Cheyenne, but the men did not complain. They claimed that the entertainment was worth the cost.

She greeted another patron, but though she kept her eyes fixed on him, her senses alerted her to the opening of the door. Casually, she looked up. It was as she had hoped. He was here, his brown eyes brightening when she gave a short nod. A second later, he was gone.

It took the better part of a quarter hour for Phoebe to finish making the rounds of the front room. Though she chafed at the delay, she knew he would not mind. The last time she'd been late, he'd insisted that he understood. And he did. She knew that. It was simply that she disliked the idea of his being alone. The man came here for companionship. He deserved it.

Phoebe left the front room, moving as casually as if she had nothing on her mind other than replenishing the supply of plates, but once she was in the hallway, she moved quickly to her private quarters. While the girls' rooms were on the second story of the building, she'd turned half of the first floor into her own lodging. There were only two entrances to Phoebe's boudoir, an interior one and one that opened onto the alley behind the building. Both were always locked.

Gripping the key in her left hand and sliding it into the lock, she opened the door and walked into her sitting room. He was there, lounging on the settee that he'd once told her was one of the most uncomfortable pieces of furniture ever invented.

"Good evening, Nelson." For the first time all evening, her enthusiasm was genuine. Nelson Chadwick was one of the few men she entertained and the only one she'd given a key to her rooms. Though she would never admit it to anyone, especially not him, Nelson was the only man she considered more than a customer. "This is a pleasant surprise. I didn't expect you tonight." Although she had hoped that, since he'd been occupied on Friday, he would find a way to visit her early this week, Phoebe was wise enough to know that it was not always easy for a man to leave his wife.

He rose, opening his arms to her. "I had to come. I couldn't stay away another hour."

Phoebe moved into his embrace, laying her cheek next to his for a moment. His ragged breathing and the rapid beating of his heart alarmed her, but she dared say nothing. Nelson would hate knowing he'd shown any sign of weakness. Slowly, as if nothing were amiss, Phoebe drew back and placed her hands on his shoulders, beginning to remove his coat. Nelson wasn't normally this impatient, but there was no knowing what torture that wife of his had put him through.

Though Phoebe had never met Tabitha Chadwick, she'd seen her around town, making eyes at anything that wore pants and had a well-endowed wallet. And though Nelson had never complained, Phoebe had heard enough gossip to know that Tabitha was happy to take his money but refused to give him the one thing his money couldn't buy: a child.

"Not tonight." Nelson took her hands in his, removing them from his shoulders. "Tonight all I want is to talk. My life is a shambles, and I don't know what to do."

It was worse than she had feared. Phoebe wrapped her arms around his waist and drew him closer to her. "It'll be all right, Nelson," she crooned, more alarmed than she would ever admit. Nelson had always impressed her with his strength, both physical and emotional. Something was very, very wrong if he was admitting to weakness. "You'll fix it. I know you will."

"I don't know what to do," he repeated.

Phoebe closed her eyes and pressed her lips together, lest her words escape. Now was not the time to tell him that the only way he'd get his life back on track was to mend his relationship with Tabitha and that it might take a miracle to do that. Nelson didn't believe in miracles.

7

ood to see you, Harrison." Jason extended his hand to
the older man who had just entered his office. Though
Harrison admitted to having celebrated thirty-six birthdays,
a mere eight more than Jason, to Jason he seemed almost as
old as Cyrus Taggert and Nelson Chadwick, men in their
late forties. Jason wasn't certain why Harrison appeared old
unless it was the fact that his expression was normally solemn, almost dour. Though there was a physical resemblance
between Harrison and Barrett Landry, Barrett had always
struck Jason as the more optimistic of the two.

"I hope this is a social call. I'd hate to think you were
having problems with the store." It had surprised Jason that
Barrett had not remained in Cheyenne while his dry goods
store was being renovated and expanded into what had once
been Charlotte's dress shop, but Barrett had claimed there
was no one he trusted more than Harrison. "He'll do a better job than I could," Barrett had confided when he'd hired

Jason to draft the documents that authorized Harrison to act on his behalf.

Harrison shook his head. "You're wrong on both counts," he said as he followed Jason across the hall into his office. "This is not a social call, and the expansion of the store is on schedule. When it's finished, Landry's Dry Goods will be the finest shop of its kind in the capital city. Of course, I don't mind admitting that I still can't believe Barrett wants to spend the rest of his life as a shopkeeper. When we were growing up, he claimed he hated the family store."

Barrett had told Jason a similar story, relating how what might have seemed like a coincidence to others had been God's way of offering him a new direction for his life. "Barrett's an adult now." Jason waited until Harrison was settled into a chair before he took the one behind his desk. "People change."

Harrison nodded. "You can say that again. I don't suppose everyone changes, but it sure seems the Landry brothers do. That's the reason I'm here. I'm hoping to buy a ranch, and I wanted to be certain you'd handle the details for me."

Though Harrison had never struck Jason as a joking man, he wondered if he was pulling his leg. Surely he and Barrett weren't planning to swap roles, with Harrison taking over the now-failing ranch and Barrett opening his own dry goods store.

"A ranch in Wyoming?"

"That's right."

"But Barrett claimed you didn't like the territory."

"People change. When I left, I discovered there were aspects of Wyoming I could not forget." The gleam in Harrison's eye puzzled Jason. Few men of his acquaintance were that enthusiastic about cattle.

"So you want me to help you purchase a ranch of your own. Are you certain that's wise?"

"Hiring you?" When Harrison's lips curved into a mocking smile, Jason realized he'd been wrong about Barrett Landry's brother. The man had a humorous side. "I think so. Even though some folks are still upset about the Bennett case, I trust you."

"Thank you." For the confidence, not for reminding Jason of the worst day of his career. "That wasn't what I meant." And he suspected Harrison knew that. "I'll be glad to help you with the legalities, but are you sure you want to go into cattle ranching? Barrett's not the only one who lost his fortune this year. You'd be hard-pressed to find a cattle baron who's happy." The combination of overgrazing, a dry summer, and the worst winter in decades had destroyed many ranchers' dreams, resulting in foreclosures and bankruptcies.

"I'm not that foolish." Harrison's grin told Jason he was enjoying his confusion. "Besides, I'm not especially fond of cows. And yes," Harrison said, his grin widening, "Barrett informed me that the correct term is 'cattle.' I want no part of critters that moo. I'll take horses any day. That's what I want to raise. They're beautiful creatures, and I believe there's a market for them here."

Horses. That would explain his excitement. It was easier to be enthusiastic about horses than cattle. "There's definitely a market. Between Cheyenne's growing population and the Army's needs, you should have no trouble selling good horse-flesh." And Jason had no doubt that Harrison intended to raise first-rate horses. "It's an excellent plan."

The older man nodded, but his smile faded. "The ranch and the horses will be easy. It's the third part of my plan that worries me."

"What's that?"

"A wife." Harrison rose and walked to the window, leaving his back to Jason. "Two years ago the thought didn't bother me in the slightest, but now I hate the idea of living alone."

Jason tried to mask his surprise. "Have you told Barrett? He once claimed you were a confirmed bachelor." Of course, Barrett also believed his brother disliked Wyoming.

"I never told Barrett about her."

"Her?" That explained the gleam in Harrison's eye. Good for Harrison. "It sounds as if you've settled on someone. Do I know her?"

Harrison nodded and returned to the chair he'd vacated only a minute before. "You've met her. It's Mrs. Amos. Gwen." He closed his eyes and leaned his head against the chair back as he let the words tumble out. "She caught my eye the last time I was out here. At the time, she was keeping company with another man. I've been accused of being a lot of things, but one thing I'm not is a poacher. When I saw the lay of the land, I did the only thing I could and went back to Pennsylvania. But when I heard the other fellow was gone, I jumped at the chance to come back. Problem is, now that I'm here, I'm not sure it's such a good idea, even though I can't get her out of my mind."

Jason felt a moment of deep affinity with his client, for he suffered from the same problem. No matter how he tried, he couldn't stop thinking of Elizabeth. Thoughts of her intruded at the most inconvenient times, like when he was supposed to be counseling a client. Memories of her smile and her acerbic tongue lingered, making Jason eager to see her again and capture new memories. Like Harrison with Gwen Amos, Jason couldn't get Elizabeth out of his mind. Unlike

Harrison, he had no intention—absolutely no intention—of marrying the woman.

"Why did you even try to forget her?" Jason had good reasons for not entertaining notions of marrying Elizabeth Harding but knew of no reason Harrison could not pursue Gwen.

"Because of her daughter. I scare the child." Harrison clenched his fist, and for a moment Jason thought he might pound it on the desk. Instead, he slowly straightened his fingers, frowning all the while. "Can you imagine any woman wanting to marry a man who frightens her child? I don't mean to. It's just that I don't know how to act around a little girl." He raised his head, his eyes locking with Jason's. "Do you have any suggestions?"

Jason was silent for a moment, considering what had to be the most unusual request for advice he'd received. He shook his head slowly. "That's not a subject they taught in law school. The only thing I can think of is to practice on some other little girls. There'd be less at stake with them."

"That's not a bad idea. Problem is, I don't know any children other than Rose."

"I don't either." Jason's clients were grown men who did not bring their children to his office. While he saw small children at church, he had no dealings with them and, though he wouldn't admit it to Harrison, he had always considered them an exotic species. Like the elephants he'd seen in a circus, they were something to be enjoyed at a distance.

"So you can't help me." It was a statement, not a question.

Jason started to nod, then stopped. "My father would tell you to pray."

Harrison snorted. "I can hear God laughing when he hears

that prayer. 'Dear Lord, please send a couple little children my way.' Hah!"

"Try it. You might be surprised at the results."

Harrison leaned forward, his blue eyes serious. "I hope you're not planning to charge me for that advice."

"I was not."

"Good. Then I'll give you some of mine. Don't wait as long as I did to find yourself a wife." Harrison's wink said he was enjoying this. "You never know, the right girl might be waiting for you next door."

Highly unlikely. Elizabeth wasn't waiting for a husband, and if Jason were looking for a wife, it wouldn't be a lady doctor. He wanted a woman who'd put his children and their happiness before everything else, not one whose patients would be her greatest concern. Elizabeth was a fine woman, an intriguing woman, but she was not the kind of woman Jason would marry.

The air had begun to warm, with each day a bit hotter than the previous. This morning as the three of them had walked toward Elizabeth's office, Rose seemingly content to stay at her mother's side, Gwen had explained that that's the way it always was. By the end of July, Cheyenne would be experiencing the heat of summer. Today was pleasantly warm, the perfect weather for the Independence Day parade. When they arrived, Elizabeth brought a bench from the waiting room and installed it on the boardwalk in front of her office. In all likelihood, they would stand while the parade passed, but as they were waiting for it to begin, she and Gwen would have a comfortable seat. Rose had other ideas.

"Horses!" The little girl pointed toward the wagon decked with red, white, and blue bunting that made its way along 16th Street.

"Yes, sweetie," Gwen said, trying to restrain her daughter's exuberance, "you'll see horses today. Now stay close to Mama."

"Don't wanna."

"Then we'll go home."

Though a stubborn expression settled on Rose's face, she moved to the spot her mother had indicated, right in front of the bench.

"This was a good idea," Harrison said as he joined them. "We'll have a fine view from here." Refusing the offer of a seat, he stood next to the bench. Perhaps it was Elizabeth's imagination, but it appeared that the view Harrison enjoyed was of Gwen, not the parade route. Though Gwen kept a sharp eye on her daughter, her face flushed each time her gaze flitted to Harrison. Elizabeth bit back a smile at the sight of her friends' obvious infatuation.

Like most of Cheyenne's residents, Gwen had dressed for the occasion, donning a blue dress with white trim. A red sash completed the patriotic ensemble. Harrison followed tradition and had placed a red, white, and blue ribbon over his hatband, while Elizabeth turned her ordinary navy skirt and white blouse into holiday garb by carrying one of her sister's white parasols that sported red and blue artificial flowers on its perimeter and patriotic ribbons twining around its handle. Only Rose had a new outfit, a bright blue skirt with a red gingham shirtwaist, and tricolored ribbons tying the ends of her braids.

"When Gwen described the parade route, I thought we

should come here so we get to see the marchers before they're tired," Elizabeth told Harrison. The marchers and floats would assemble near the train depot, then proceed up Central Avenue to City Park. After circling the park and passing by the site of the future capitol building, they would return south on Capitol Avenue, or what many residents still called Hill Street. In preparation for the cornerstone laying, the city fathers had decided to rename Hill to honor the capitol, but since it had been less than two months, the new name had yet to take hold.

As the crowds began to gather, Elizabeth looked around, wondering where Jason was. Like hers, his office was closed for the day, but he had told her that he always watched the parade.

"Looking for someone?" Harrison asked. The twinkle in his eye told Elizabeth he'd seen the way she had been scanning the crowds. It was silly to be so flustered, but Elizabeth felt color rise to her cheeks. She was as bad as Gwen, blushing like a schoolgirl. Gwen was looking for a husband; Elizabeth was not. Still, there was no reason to lie.

"I wonder where Jason is," she admitted.

"Maybe at the depot. Some people like to watch the beginning of the parade." Harrison pulled out his watch and snapped it open. "It should have started two minutes ago."

Though she could not see the new building from here, Elizabeth turned in the direction of the depot and saw Jason round the corner from 15th Street. Although normally he walked quickly, today he strolled along the west side of Central, perhaps because that was the sunny side where most of the paradegoers were gathered, stopping to talk to people along the way. A few greeted him warmly, but Elizabeth's heart sank when she saw that many were curt, and a few turned away from him in obvious shunning. Though she could not hear any of the words that were exchanged, she had no trouble reading one woman's lips. "I don't trust him," she said as she yanked her husband's arm and drew him away from Jason. Elizabeth couldn't let that continue.

"Excuse me for a moment," she said to Gwen and Harrison as she rose. A second later, she was crossing the street toward Jason. When she reached him, she placed a hand on his arm, smiling when she saw that in addition to his tricolored hatband, Jason wore a red tie with his white shirt and dark blue suit. He was a walking patriot, a man anyone could trust, despite anything those women might say.

"We've been waiting for you," Elizabeth said, making certain her voice carried to the women who'd turned their backs. "Did you forget that you were going to watch the parade with us?" There had been no such agreement, but Elizabeth refused to consider her statement a lie. She was helping a friend. She had been shunned enough to know that, no matter how brave a face you put on, it hurt. The only things that helped were friendly overtures. "Let's go." As Jason nodded briefly, Elizabeth added, "Afterwards, I hope you'll join us for a picnic in the backyard at home." It was odd to realize that the apartment where her sister had once lived had become home so quickly.

"Thank you, but . . ."

As they crossed the street, Elizabeth tightened her grip on his arm. "I wish you'd accept both invitations. I was feeling a bit like a third wheel. Gwen and Harrison don't need me." Especially today when they appeared so enamored of each other. If she were occupied with someone else, Gwen and Harrison could devote themselves to each other. "You'd be doing me a favor."

Jason shook his head. "You're the one who's doing me a favor. I'm certain you saw that I was receiving a less than cordial reception."

Elizabeth wouldn't deny it, but she would clarify what she saw. "I noticed that it was women who gave you the cold shoulder. The men seemed more welcoming."

Jason paused in the middle of the street as a boy rolled his hoop in front of them. "I noticed that too. I'm not sure why it was true, but it was."

"It's good news, since most of your clients are men. I suspect their wives don't have a lot of influence when they're choosing an attorney."

Jason chuckled. "I can't believe my ears. You—a woman who's been outspoken about women's abilities—are saying that?" When Elizabeth nodded, he grinned. "Not to change the subject too much, but I noticed several women leaving your office this week. I hope they were patients."

"They were. It's been slower than I'd hoped, but I am treating a few patients."

"So you're not planning to leave Cheyenne."

Elizabeth looked up, startled by the suggestion. "I never considered that."

"I'm glad." His smile warmed her more than the July sun. "I wouldn't want to lose my neighbor." He paused. "And my friend."

Pleasure welled up inside Elizabeth, threatening to overflow. It was amazing how good it felt to be with Jason. When they reached the others, while Jason shook Harrison's hand and greeted Rose, Elizabeth told Gwen what she'd done.

Gwen's smile was instantaneous. "What a good idea. Rose seems to like him." She gestured with her head.

112

Elizabeth turned in the direction Gwen had indicated and saw Jason kneeling next to Rose. He whispered something in her ear, and when she giggled her assent, he lifted her into his arms and placed her on his shoulders.

"Horsey!" Rose cried, tugging at imaginary reins. "Horsey."

Though Elizabeth smiled, she heard Harrison snort and saw that he was glaring at Jason's back. "I wonder what's bothering him."

Gwen shrugged. "I have no idea. I don't think I'll ever understand how that man's mind works. One day he's friendly, the next he's aloof." She gave Elizabeth a crooked smile. "And they call us flighty. Men are worse. I tell you, Elizabeth, sometimes I think we'd be better off without them."

She was beautiful. Jason took a deep breath, trying to calm the sudden racing of his pulse. It was ridiculous. He was a grown man, not a schoolboy. This was not the first time he'd seen a beautiful woman. And it certainly wasn't the first time he'd seen Elizabeth. But the sight of her descending the steps took his breath away. Perhaps it was the sky blue dress she was wearing and the knowledge that it was the same shade as her eyes. Perhaps it was the way the skirt draped, hinting at slender legs and ankles. Perhaps it was nothing more than the way the sun highlighted her hair, making it appear as if she had a halo. Jason didn't know the cause. All he knew was the effect. He was standing beside his carriage, feeling as awkward as a boy sparking his first girl.

"I could have walked," Elizabeth said when she'd arranged her skirts on the seat. "It's less than four blocks."

But then he wouldn't have had the pleasure of holding

her hand as he helped her into the carriage. Jason shook his head. "Richard would have had me drummed out of town. When he invited me, he insisted I accompany you."

It hadn't taken much persuasion. At the time Richard had issued the invitation to the Cheyenne Club's annual reception, Jason had found it ironic that he, whose role in exonerating Adam Bennett had caused the city's residents to reconsider his standing as an attorney, was being asked to escort the woman who'd yet to be accepted as a physician. They'd be two pariahs, he'd thought. But after the kindness she'd showered on him during the Independence Day parade and afterwards, when she'd treated him like part of her family, Jason realized he didn't care what others thought. He enjoyed Elizabeth's company and looked forward to their time together.

"I thank you, and so does Harrison. He was so miffed that Gwen wasn't invited that he announced he wouldn't darken the doors of the Cheyenne Club if he were paid to go. But I know that if you hadn't offered to drive me, he would have swallowed his pride and accepted the invitation, just so I'd have an escort."

Elizabeth leaned forward slightly as they approached the club that many in the city considered to be the epitome of the social ladder. Situated on the northwest corner of 17th Street and Warren Avenue, it was an imposing building, and its members included the wealthiest and most prominent citizens of not only Cheyenne itself but the surrounding territory.

With its mansard roof, wraparound porch, and the large central tower that loomed over 17th Street, the Cheyenne Club was one of the dominant buildings in this part of the city. Elizabeth had probably walked by it numerous times as she'd explored her new home, but Jason was certain she had never seen it looking like this. The porches were draped with large U.S. flags, creating a sheltered verandah, and the sparkle of incandescent lights beckoned visitors to stroll around the perimeter of the club for a few minutes before they entered the building itself.

"I'm curious to see the inside," Elizabeth admitted as they took their second turn around the verandah, greeting and being greeted by members and other guests. "Charlotte told me so many stories about it."

One more circuit, and then he'd take her indoors. Though he wouldn't tell her, Jason didn't share Elizabeth's enthusiasm for the interior. Oh, it was an impressive building all right. But once they were inside, there would be no reason for her to keep her hand on his arm. Most likely, they'd be separated, at least until dinner was served. No matter how elegant the interior, without Elizabeth at his side, it would lose its luster.

"Charlotte probably told you that this is the most exclusive place in the city," Jason said as they rounded the corner. "Even though many of its members have fallen on hard times, the annual reception is the biggest social event of the summer."

Elizabeth shot him a mischievous smile. "Even bigger than our Independence Day picnic?"

Jason returned the smile as memories of the second meal they'd shared rushed back, flooding him with pleasure. "Bigger, but not necessarily better." The backyard of Elizabeth's home had been decorated with a single flag, not the dozens that lined the club's verandah, and the food had been simple picnic fare: fried chicken legs, biscuits with strawberry preserves, dried apple pie. But, though less ostentatious, Jason knew that the picnic he had shared with her would prove to be far more memorable than tonight's banquet.

She chuckled. "Spoken like a lawyer. You choose your words carefully."

"That's true. I do. So consider this." He lowered his voice so that he was practically whispering. "I'd rather be back in your yard."

Her chuckle turned into a full-fledged laugh.

When they entered the building itself, Jason's concern that he and Elizabeth would be separated was realized. Once Miriam and Richard greeted them, two of Jason's most important clients approached him, asking to speak with him. He turned to Elizabeth, hoping she understood that he couldn't offend the men. "I have a couple things to attend to."

She nodded. "Don't worry. I can keep myself occupied until dinner is served."

The conversation with his clients took longer than he'd expected, and it was a full half hour later when Jason reentered the hallway and heard the booming voice.

"I tell you, the world is changing and not for the better."

Jason frowned as he recognized the speaker. Doc Worland. What was the old windbag talking about now? Jason moved to the doorway and looked around. There, on the opposite side of the room, surrounded by a group of men, Doc Worland was holding court. He continued to speak, his words slightly slurred as if he'd imbibed a bit too much whiskey. "What kind of world is it where women think they can be doctors?" he demanded. "I tell you, they don't have what it takes."

Though the parlor had been filled with conversation, a sudden silence greeted the doctor's words. Jason heard the sound of heels tapping on the floor. Feminine heels. He entered the parlor and watched as Elizabeth approached the older doctor. The crowd parted, much as Jason imagined the Red Sea had parted, allowing her to face her adversary.

"That's a very provocative assertion you've made, Dr. Worland." Elizabeth's voice was cool but clear enough to be heard in every corner of the room. "Would you mind explaining why you believe that to be true?"

"Look, missy. I don't have to answer to you or anyone." Doc waved a finger under her nose. If it was supposed to intimidate her, it didn't succeed. If anything, it caused Elizabeth to stiffen her spine. That and the heels on her shoes brought her to almost the same height as Doc.

"So what you alleged before, that women don't have—I believe your term was 'what it takes'—is simply your opinion and not a proven fact."

The man's face flushed, although whether with anger or the effects of whiskey, Jason wasn't certain. "I didn't say that. Everyone knows it's true."

"Not everyone," Elizabeth retorted, her voice as sweet as the strawberry preserves she'd served three days ago. "I don't know that to be a fact. Please explain it to me."

Guests moved closer, circling the two physicians like vultures over a carcass.

"All right, missy. You asked for it." Doc thrust his shoulders back, as if trying to increase his height. "Women aren't smart enough and they're not strong enough to be doctors."

Jason bit the inside of his cheek to keep from smiling as he remembered his first encounter with Elizabeth. He'd been as belligerent as Doc, but it hadn't stopped Elizabeth from pointing out the errors in his logic. There was no reason to think she'd be kinder to Doc merely because he was her elder.

"Those are interesting claims, but I'm afraid they're not

based on facts." When Doc glared at her, Elizabeth continued. "Let's start with intelligence. Would you agree that if a man were accepted at one of the country's most illustrious medical schools, that would be proof of his intellect?"

"Of course." When Doc began to relax, Jason felt a twinge of sympathy for the man. Doc didn't know Elizabeth or he would have realized she was only beginning.

"Did you know that a woman needs to be in the top 10 percent of all applicants just to be accepted in the same school?" she demanded. "Wouldn't that seem to indicate that a woman has to be smarter than 90 percent of her male colleagues?"

His face reddening, Doc ran a hand through his hair. "You're trying to trick me."

"No, Doctor, I'm not." Though he was visibly angry, Elizabeth kept her voice as cool as a January morning. "I simply wanted to demonstrate the fallacy of your thinking."

"You think you're smart," he sputtered.

"I don't *think* I'm smart, Doctor Worland. I *know* I am. Shall I tell you how I know that? You told me I was. You said that being admitted to medical school was proof of a person's intelligence. I was admitted to medical school. Furthermore, I graduated." She paused for a second, letting her words echo throughout the room before she gave him a sweet smile. "Did you?"

The blood drained from Doc's face, and for a second Jason wondered if he'd respond. Though he'd never questioned the doctor's credentials, judging from Elizabeth's question and Doc's reaction, she knew more about the man than most of his patients.

"Missy, I'll have you know that I served in the Army during the War Between the States."

"Yes, you did," she said, her expression remaining calm, though Jason had seen her flinch when the older doctor had called her missy. "I admire you for your service, but you didn't answer my question. Did you or did you not complete medical school?"

The blood that had fled Doc's face returned, flushing his cheeks, while a vein in his forehead began to throb. "I know more than you'll ever learn," he shouted. "That's all that matters."

"Perhaps it is," she conceded, "but if my life were at stake, I would like to know that my doctor had the benefit of expert training."

"The war was all the training I needed. Everyone knows I'm the best doctor in Cheyenne."

Doc stormed from the room, heading for the bar that had been set up in the adjoining parlor. In his wake, Jason looked at the guests who remained. Though many of them appeared entertained by the argument, several of them, notably women, wore pensive expressions. Jason didn't claim to be a mind reader, but he suspected that the women were having second thoughts about Doc. Until tonight, he had been the acknowledged premier physician in the city. Now? Now Jason wasn't so certain.

The points Elizabeth had made were valid. Even more, they'd been eloquent, and eloquence, Jason knew, was often what convinced people. His law professors had stressed that while it was critical to have the law itself on your side, it was equally important to be able to communicate that law and its implications to jurors. Elizabeth had been both articulate and convincing. Patients might not be lining up outside her office when she opened it tomorrow morning, but he imagined that many of the people who'd been here tonight would think twice before consulting Doc again.

As he made his way to Elizabeth's side, Jason grinned. How fortunate for him that she hadn't decided to be an attorney, for if she had, between her clear thinking and her gift for oratory, he had no doubt that she would have given him a run for his money.

8

Rose deserved a treat. Perhaps it was only because the morning had been so boring that the thought kept floating through Elizabeth's brain. She had cleaned her office, not that it had needed cleaning. She'd organized her books, not that they'd needed organizing. Now she was wearing a groove in the floor, pacing the length of the hall. The only good thing she could say about that was that it kept her blood flowing. But while she'd paced, she'd thought of the little girl who'd been such a good friend to Elizabeth's nephew. Charlotte had told her how Rose had befriended her son, not seeming to be bothered by the boy's blindness. She'd also mentioned how much Rose enjoyed sweets and that her favorites were the ones Mr. Ellis sold at his confectionary. Perfect. Elizabeth would get a bit of fresh air, and Rose would have a treat for supper.

After locking the door, Elizabeth headed north on Central, smiling as she realized that this was one of the most beautiful days of the summer. With only the lightest of breezes to stir the air, it was warm, yet the dry heat was refreshing. And there was no doubt that the brilliant blue sky with a few lazy cumulus clouds drifting across it was magnificent. If the poets hadn't already celebrated the beauty of a Wyoming sky, they should.

Though it was only a block away, Elizabeth had not been inside the Ellis Bakery and Confectionary, but she had heard that the breads and pastries were as renowned as the candies. Perhaps she'd buy a small cake for Jason. Elizabeth knew that he rarely ate at home, claiming that he was the world's second worst cook. The award for absolute worst went to Mrs. Moran, or so he alleged. It had been little more than a casual comment made the day he'd stopped by to say hello and had found Elizabeth reheating some stew. When his stomach had growled, she had offered to share her lunch with him. It had been one of those times when they'd spoken of a dozen different things, yet only one memory lingered. The more she heard, the more Elizabeth realized that Jason's childhood had been far different from hers. He might not have faced financial privation as her family had on numerous occasions, but he'd lacked the warm, loving environment that had more than compensated for hand-me-down clothing and watery soups.

Elizabeth doubted that watery soup had ever been part of Jason's life, and it certainly wasn't now when he took most of his meals in restaurants. But perhaps even fine restaurant food became ordinary if eaten too often. That must have been the reason he'd seemed to savor the stew she'd shared with him and why Jason claimed he preferred her backyard picnic to the banquet at the Cheyenne Club.

Fried chicken and cold biscuits couldn't compare to the succulent beef, oyster pudding, and the flaming dessert that the club had provided. That dinner had been delicious, once Elizabeth's temper had cooled and she'd stopped seething over Dr. Worland's prejudice. The truth was, his diatribe had been no different from what she'd endured in school, and, unlike her classmates' taunts, her discussion with Dr. Worland had wrought at least one benefit: a few more women had come to her office. Some of them had been at the club that night. Others said they'd heard what had happened. All had announced that they wanted a doctor who was fully trained. It was a start. Thanks to her new patients and indirectly to Dr. Worland's hostility, she had enough money to splurge on cakes and candies.

When she reached the corner of 17th Street, Elizabeth paused, waiting for a wagon to pass before she crossed Central. From here she could see her destination. Three wide windows topped with generous transom windows gave it an appearance of elegance, and the steady stream of customers left no doubt of its popularity. As she watched, a woman exited the confectionary. Fashionably dressed in a black walking suit and gloves, with a black-trimmed bonnet, the blonde appeared to be a couple inches shorter than Elizabeth. Though her clothing made Elizabeth suspect that she was a widow emerging from deepest mourning, the almost imperial tilt of her head proclaimed her confidence. Perhaps it was that confidence that caused her to stumble. Elizabeth didn't know. All she knew was that one second the woman was walking, the next she lay crumpled on the boardwalk.

Picking up her skirts, Elizabeth rushed across the street. "Are you all right?"

The woman attempted to rise, then shook her head as her leg gave way. "I'm afraid I twisted my ankle." Elizabeth noted that although the woman's grammar was correct, her voice did not have the cultured tone Elizabeth would have expected, given the fine clothing. "It appears that this is not my lucky day," the woman said.

Elizabeth crouched next to her. Judging from the woman's inability to put any weight on the ankle, she suspected the injury was more serious than a simple strain or sprain. "Let's get you to my office, and then we'll see how lucky or unlucky you are." A confused expression greeted her words. "Oh, I'm sorry. I should have introduced myself. I'm Elizabeth Harding. Dr. Harding."

The woman nodded. "That's right. I heard folks say there was a lady doctor in town." She attempted to stand again, then grimaced as she sank back onto the boardwalk. "I appreciate your offer, ma'am, but I can't go to your office. It wouldn't be proper."

"Why ever not?" Surely this woman didn't agree with Dr. Worland that females could not be effective physicians.

The woman's blue eyes clouded. "I'm Phoebe Simcoe."

If Elizabeth was expected to recognize the name, she did not. "I'm pleased to meet you, Mrs. Simcoe. Now if you'll try not to put any weight on your injured ankle, I think we can get you to my office."

"But you shouldn't . . ."

Elizabeth shook her head. "Arguing will not help your ankle. I can, but I need the instruments in my office. Be careful. I'm going to lift you up." Sliding her arms around Phoebe Simcoe's waist, Elizabeth drew her to her feet. Though she appeared slender, Mrs. Simcoe was no lightweight. Elizabeth wished

Dr. Worland were here to watch her. He'd no longer question her strength if he realized she'd just lifted her own weight.

"Don't hurry," she said as Phoebe clung to her. "I don't want to do any more damage to that ankle." It took longer than Elizabeth had expected to get her patient to her office, and both women sighed with relief when Phoebe was safely ensconced on the examining table. "This may hurt a bit," Elizabeth said as she unfastened Phoebe's high-button shoe. As she had feared, the ankle was badly swollen. A gentle touch confirmed her fears. "You've fractured your ankle, Mrs. Simcoe. Fortunately, it's not a compound fracture. Once I put it in a plaster cast, it should heal properly."

Phoebe clenched her fists as Elizabeth touched the swollen appendage. "How long will it take to heal?"

"Six weeks, if you're careful. You'll need a crutch to keep the weight off it."

"Six weeks!" Phoebe shook her head. "The fellas will laugh at that."

It was not the reaction Elizabeth had expected. Patients frequently groused at how long it took for bones to heal, but few laughed. Though she hated to deliver what might sound like a lecture, Elizabeth needed her patient to understand the gravity of her injury. "A broken ankle is not a laughing matter. Ankles are complex joints, and a fracture can be very serious. You were lucky, Mrs. Simcoe."

The blonde whom Elizabeth guessed to be around thirty appeared thoughtful. "Maybe I was lucky, after all. You were there right when I needed you. I doubt any other woman in the city would have helped me."

Again, it was an unexpected reaction. Elizabeth reached for a bandage. "Another woman might not have been able to set your ankle, but I'm sure she would have helped you." Another woman might have taken Mrs. Simcoe to Dr. Worland. His office was slightly closer than Elizabeth's, and he was, as he had announced at the Cheyenne Club, the most prominent physician in the city.

A hint of amusement filled Phoebe Simcoe's blue eyes. "You don't know who I am, do you?"

"You told me you were Phoebe Simcoe. Your clothing makes me believe that you're a widow."

"That's true," she said as Elizabeth began to wrap her ankle. "Mr. Simcoe has been gone for almost ten years. Most folks here just call me Phoebe. That's the name of my business: Phoebe's."

Though Elizabeth wracked her brain, she could recall no stores by that name. "I'm sorry, but . . ."

Phoebe chuckled. "You haven't been here very long, have you?"

"A bit less than a month."

"And you probably haven't had much reason to frequent 15th Street. That's where my business is. On the northeast corner of 15th and Warren." She looked down at her ankle. "I run a bordello, Dr. Harding. That's why the good women of Cheyenne pretend I don't exist."

If Phoebe Simcoe expected her to be shocked, she was mistaken. While Phoebe was the first madam she had met, Elizabeth was well aware of the existence of bordellos, the women who lived there, and the men who frequented them. Papa had preached many a sermon deploring the circumstances that led women to brothels at the same time that he reminded his congregation how Jesus forgave that very sin. Elizabeth would not judge Phoebe.

"Then I'm doubly glad I decided to go to Mr. Ellis's today. You needed a doctor, and I needed a patient. The women of Cheyenne may admit my existence, but so far they're not lining up in the streets, waiting for me to treat them." Elizabeth bit her lip, wishing she could retract the words. She should never have told Phoebe Simcoe—or any of her patients—how small her practice was. "Forgive me," she said. "I didn't mean to burden you with my tale."

Phoebe's eyes narrowed, and she was silent for a moment. Then, nodding briskly, she asked, "How would you like a dozen patients? My girls need a doctor. They don't like it, but I insist on monthly checkups. Doc Worland performs them, and they like that even less. He lectures them most every time he comes, and he's rougher than he needs to be."

While it would be unprofessional to agree, Phoebe's description was consistent with Elizabeth's impression of the older doctor. She felt a moment of elation at the realization that, not only would she be gaining more patients, but she would be able to make those patients' lives a bit easier. "I'd be honored to treat your girls."

"You'd need to come to my place."

"That's fine. I make house calls."

Phoebe held out her hand, gripping Elizabeth's firmly. "Thank you, Doctor. It seems this was my lucky day, after all."

Dust and rubble. It was everywhere. Harrison tried not to frown, but if there was one thing he disliked, it was disorder, and that was rampant. Oh, the workers claimed they were following his plan. Most days he knew they were. They had demolished the wall between what was once Mr. Yates's dry goods store and Charlotte Harding's fancy dress shop, the one with the French name that Harrison never did learn to pronounce. The result would be a large, well-lit store with plenty of space for the goods Barrett planned to carry. Right now, it was an unmitigated mess, just like Harrison's life.

He had made no progress with Rose. No matter what he tried, she still shied from him. Before Independence Day, he had consoled himself with the thought that she was wary of all men, but seeing her with Jason had destroyed that illusion. Rose had giggled and laughed as she played with Jason. There was no doubt about it: Harrison was the only man she distrusted.

He stuffed his hands in his pockets and walked toward the front door. Once he'd assigned the tasks, he had little to do. If he tried to help, all he did was get in the workers' way, and that delayed progress. Barrett would not be happy if he and Charlotte returned to discover that the store renovation was incomplete. That was why Harrison had a schedule, not just for the store, but for his life. And, unfortunately, the life plan was not going well.

Perhaps he should take Jason's advice about Rose. It was good—one part, anyway. Practicing with other girls made sense, but the problem remained that Harrison didn't know any other little girls. The other part of Jason's advice was just plain silly. Pray. God had more important things to worry about than providing Harrison with a little girl who'd teach him what other little girls liked.

Wincing at the seemingly endless sound of hammers and saws, Harrison shook his head. Perhaps it wouldn't hurt to try. He wouldn't pronounce the words aloud, of course, but thinking them couldn't hurt, could it? Gaining Rose's trust was important, and it wasn't as if he had any other ideas. He had nothing to lose and maybe, just maybe, everything to gain.

Turning away from the workers, Harrison faced the front window, closed his eyes, and sent a prayer heavenward. When he opened his eyes, he blinked, certain he was mistaken. It couldn't be. But it was. Two little girls stood outside the window, their noses pressed to the glass.

"Well, young ladies, who are you?" he asked as he stepped outside. He wouldn't call them answered prayers, even though that was exactly what they were. Though the bright sunshine caused him to squint, the girls' eyes were wide with innocence. Harrison was no judge of ages, but since they were of different heights, he guessed that one was a year or two older than the other. Both had big brown eyes and dark brown hair gathered into uneven braids.

"I'm Rebecca," the taller girl said, "and she's Rachel."

All right. They had names, and they hadn't run away shrieking with fear the instant they saw him. That was good, but where was their mother? What little Harrison knew about young girls included the fact that they did not wander the streets of Cheyenne unaccompanied. "Aren't you supposed to be with your mother?"

It was the wrong question. Tears welled in the shorter one's eyes, while the older one frowned. "She's gone," Rebecca told him. "Our ma went to heaven."

"Pa said it would be a long time until we saw her again," the younger girl added.

"I see." What Harrison saw was that he was going to need

lots more practice if he had any chance of charming Rose. He'd asked two questions. The first had been innocuous, but now the girls were close to crying. He'd have to try harder. "I saw you at the window. What were you looking at?" Surely there wasn't anything wrong with that question.

"We heard hammers." Not surprisingly, it was Rebecca, the older one, who answered. "We thought they might be building a stairway."

That was one thing that was not included in the building renovation. Barrett had seen no need for an interior staircase. "There are already two on the outside," Harrison said, pointing to the one that led to his apartment. A matching stairway on the opposite side of the building led to the apartment Gwen and Rose shared with Elizabeth Harding.

"We saw that, but it only goes to the second floor." Rachel's expression said that Harrison should realize how inadequate that was. He did not. "We were looking for a stairway to heaven."

The pain that clenched Harrison's heart made him gasp. There was no reason to ask why the girls wanted a stairway that stretched all the way to heaven. "I'm sorry," he said as softly as he could, "but we're not building a staircase."

Though Rebecca appeared stoic, Rachel began to sob. "I wanna see Ma again."

He'd thought it couldn't get worse, but it had. "Does she have a handkerchief?" he asked Rebecca as the tears rolled down Rachel's cheeks.

"She always loses it." Rebecca dug into her pocket and withdrew a large square of calico. "You can use mine. You gotta hold it to her nose, cuz she's not very good at blowing."

And so Harrison found himself kneeling on the boardwalk,

holding a brightly colored piece of calico to a little girl's nose as a tall man clutching a baby to his chest raced toward him.

"There you are!" the man cried when he reached the girls. Clad in denim and boots, with a Stetson perched on his dark brown hair, the man would have resembled many other men in the city were it not for his distracted expression. "I thought I'd lost you," he told the girls. When Rebecca and Rachel looked up, their eyes filled with confusion, he turned toward Harrison. "What were they doing here?"

Harrison mopped the last tears from Rachel's face and returned the handkerchief to Rebecca. "It appears they were looking for a stairway to heaven."

The way the man's lips tightened told Harrison he was struggling for composure. "I should never have read them the story about Jacob and the ladder. Now they want me to build one so they can visit their mother."

Harrison rose. As he'd thought, the young father topped him by a few inches. "I'm sorry for your loss. It looks as if you have your hands full."

"You can say that again." The baby in the man's arms began to fuss, causing him to slide one of his fingers between her lips. When she started to suck, he turned back to Harrison. "The woman who's been caring for the girls during the day came down with diphtheria. I'm on my own now." He looked at the two girls who had returned to staring into the store, as if they didn't believe Harrison's story of no stairway. "It's not too bad at home, but I needed to buy a few things in town and, well . . . You saw what happened. I turned my back for a second, and these two were gone." He nodded at the baby in his arms. "If Ruby could walk, she'd probably have gone with her sisters."

Harrison's heart ached almost as much as it had when he'd heard the girls talking about their special staircase. "Is there anything I can do to help?" He could probably do the man's shopping for him.

The man's eyes brightened. "Would you watch these two while I go down the street to Myers Dry Goods? I need some clothes for them."

Harrison wished Barrett's new stock had arrived. If it had, he could help the man without having to look after two young girls. "You'd trust me with your daughters, Mr. . . . ." He let his voice trail off.

"Granger. Kevin Granger."

"I'm Harrison Landry."

"Barrett Landry's brother? I heard he bought this store from Mr. Yates."

"Exactly. Barrett's expanding it. When it's finished, it'll be the most modern dry goods store in town."

Kevin Granger nodded. "I promise to do all my shopping there if you'll just help me out today."

"I wish I could, but I don't know anything about little girls. All I did was ask a couple questions, and I got tears."

Kevin shook his head slowly. "It wasn't you. Rachel cries a lot. I'd be much obliged if you'd help me."

Though he suspected he was making a mistake by agreeing, Harrison could not forget that he'd prayed for this opportunity. It would be the worst kind of ingratitude to toss aside God's gift.

"What do I do?"

The tall man's face brightened. "It's easy. You ask them."

It wasn't as easy as Kevin claimed, but when Harrison learned that Rebecca and Rachel liked to skip rope, he found a rope inside the store and held one end, helping one girl twirl it while the other jumped. When Rachel and Rebecca tired of that, he learned that they enjoyed singing and found himself joining in childhood ditties. It took less than an hour, but by the time Kevin returned, Harrison was more tired than if he'd spent the entire day at heavy labor.

"Can we come back, Pa?" Rebecca asked as they left the backyard. "I like Mr. Landry."

"Me too," Rachel chorused.

Kevin grinned. "See, I told you it was easy."

Jason wasn't certain what surprised him more, the fact that Elizabeth was carrying a package that appeared to have come from Mr. Ellis's bakery or that she looked a bit like the Cheshire cat, her smile so wide that it urged a man to return it. "Good afternoon," he said. "Something smells delicious."

Though he hadn't thought it possible, her smile broadened. "I brought you a spice cake."

One day when they'd had little else to discuss, he had mentioned that was his favorite, never thinking she'd remember. But she had, for here she was in his office, holding out a box of mouth-watering cake. "Is this all for me?"

Elizabeth nodded. "If you like. I thought you might share a piece with me, though. You see, I'm celebrating the addition of a dozen new patients."

That explained the grin. "Twelve patients in one day is wonderful."

He took the cake from her and gestured toward his library. Though the table there was designed for poring over multiple books, it could do double duty as a dining table. As soon as he'd heard Elizabeth's story, he'd run upstairs and grab a knife and a couple forks and plates.

"Tell me about it." He hadn't seen that many women entering her office. In fact, he hadn't seen any patients, but that could be because he'd spent an hour in here where the only window overlooked the alley.

"The way it got started wasn't wonderful," she admitted. "A woman fell and broke her ankle outside Mr. Ellis's store. Fortunately, I saw her and was able to help. I'm sorry about her injury, but I'm certainly not sorry about the new patients, especially since I'll be calling on them regularly."

Though he knew it wasn't impossible that twelve people in Cheyenne would have picked this day to consult Elizabeth and that they all would require periodic treatment, something about it sounded odd to Jason. "Do you mind my asking who these new patients are?"

The Cheshire cat grin faded, replaced by an expression that seemed almost wary. "I haven't met them yet, but they work at Phoebe Simcoe's establishment. She's the woman who broke her ankle."

"What?" Jason couldn't hold back his cry of surprise. "You're going to treat whores?"

"I'll be treating women who need a doctor." Elizabeth's voice was cool, her expression so strained that Jason knew he'd made a mistake. Still, he couldn't let her continue on that path without warning her. They were friends, and friends were honest with each other, even when the news was painful.

Using the tone his professors claimed was most effective in convincing reluctant juries, Jason said, "I know you want more patients, but I think you're making a mistake. You've just started winning over the women, and this will set you back. Word spreads quickly in Cheyenne—you know that—and when it does, no decent women will want you to treat them."

She wasn't convinced. He could see that. Her lips thinning, Elizabeth shook her head. "I understand that Dr. Worland used to attend Phoebe's girls. From what I gathered, his visits there didn't hurt his practice."

"That's different."

"Because he's a man?"

Jason nodded slowly. There was no point in dissembling. "You may not like it, but you know there's a difference. You've said it yourself. Women have to be smarter than men to be accepted at medical college, and now that you've graduated, everyone expects you to be more competent, more upstanding, and better in every way than your male colleagues." When she started to bristle, Jason added, "It's like being a minister's child. You're held to a higher standard."

"That doesn't make it right."

"I didn't say it did." Jason had hated the way his father's parishioners scrutinized his every move, complaining over the slightest infraction when it was Jason's fault but ignoring it when one of his friends was responsible.

Elizabeth's eyes flashed the way they had the day he'd met her, her heightened color telling Jason how much this discussion irritated her. "I'm not condoning Phoebe's life-style or that of her girls. It's deplorable that any woman is forced to sell her body. But I took an oath to heal, and that's what I plan to do. Phoebe's girls need my care as much as—perhaps more than—what you call the decent women of Cheyenne."

"Principles are fine," he said softly, hoping to diffuse her anger, "but you need to be practical too. Don't do something that will hurt your career."

"This won't."

Jason could only hope she was right.

9

Elizabeth wasn't certain what to expect when she went to the bordello. When she'd thought about it, she'd envisioned a building painted flamboyant colors. At the very least, she'd thought it would be tawdry. But had she not seen the discreet sign next to the front door, she would have walked by the two-story brick building with the lace- and velvet-covered windows. There was nothing distinctive about it other than its size. While it wasn't as large or as ornate as the cattle barons' mansions that lined Ferguson and the streets near the Cheyenne Club, it was more than average sized. It had to be to accommodate a dozen women and half a dozen servants. Although unpretentious, all it needed was a wide front porch, and it would have appeared to be home to a large family.

As Elizabeth climbed the steps to the small stoop by the front door, she reflected that the absence of a porch was deliberate. While she had waited for her cast to dry, Phoebe had spoken of the building she called home, saying she hadn't bothered with an architect but had had it built to her specifications. Undoubtedly Phoebe had realized that no one would use a porch. She had told Elizabeth that, unlike some madams, she chose not to put her girls on display. Furthermore, it was unlikely visitors would want to advertise their presence by sitting on the porch. According to Gwen, Phoebe catered to the most influential members of Cheyenne's society. Perhaps that was why she referred to it as a bordello rather than a whorehouse. The term wasn't important. What was was that the building housed the majority of Elizabeth's patients.

Gripping her bag, she tried not to frown. No matter what Jason had said, treating Phoebe's girls was the right thing to do. They needed medical care, and they deserved to be treated with respect, regardless of how they earned their living. The frown she'd tried to repress settled on her face as she remembered Jason's expression the day she'd told him she would be treating these women. Just when she thought she understood him, he did something unexpected.

While she hadn't believed he would be overjoyed by the idea, Elizabeth hadn't realized he'd be so adamant about her treating Phoebe's girls. Had it been another man, she might have believed that he was one of Phoebe's customers and feared she'd discover that, but Elizabeth was convinced Jason did not frequent Phoebe's or any of what Mama referred to as houses of ill repute. Elizabeth couldn't explain how she knew, but she was certain Jason would not pay for a woman's favors. It wasn't simply that as a minister's son he would have heard numerous sermons about the evils of fornication. Those sermons might have influenced him, but they weren't the only reason he wouldn't visit Phoebe. Though he and Elizabeth disagreed on some things, fundamentally, Jason was a man of honor, and that honor would not allow him to demean a woman.

That thought—no, Elizabeth corrected herself, that knowledge—chased away her frown. Jason had disagreed with her decision to treat Phoebe's girls, but the reason had nothing to do with him. It was because he feared Elizabeth would hurt her chances for acceptance as a physician, and he'd wanted to protect her. How sweet!

Her smile as wide as the Wyoming prairie, Elizabeth knocked on the door. A few seconds later, she was escorted into what would have been called a parlor in another house. Elizabeth wasn't certain what term applied here. Like an ordinary parlor, it was furnished with comfortable seating, a few small tables and lamps. Like an ordinary parlor, it boasted a thick carpet. Unlike an ordinary parlor, it had a second door to the outside, perhaps so that patrons could enter without attracting attention, and unlike an ordinary parlor, the paintings that hung on the walls brought a blush to Elizabeth's cheeks. Portraits of women wearing only scraps of cloth artfully draped over their bodies looked down from each of the walls.

"I see I've shocked you," Phoebe said as she made her way into the room.

Grateful to have something less controversial to look at, Elizabeth focused her attention on the woman who'd invited her here. Though she was dressed in the unrelieved black that she'd worn the day she broke her ankle, today her hair was gathered into a simple chignon rather than the elaborate coiffure she'd sported that day. What held Elizabeth's attention was her awkwardness with the crutch. It had been almost a week since Elizabeth had prescribed it for her. By now she should have become accustomed to it.

"I'd say I was startled rather than shocked. The truth is, I'm more concerned about your ankle than your artwork." Elizabeth pointed toward the crutch. "You're still having trouble with it."

Phoebe nodded her agreement. "I can't seem to get the hang of it. I was hoping you could show me what I'm doing wrong. First, I want you to meet my girls. Girls!"

They must have assembled in the long hallway that extended from the front to the back of the house, for they entered the parlor as soon as they heard Phoebe's command. Like the exterior of the house, they were not what Elizabeth had expected. They wore no face paint, and their hair was neatly braided. The only clues to their profession were the unnatural shade of some of the girls' hair and the elaborately trimmed wrappers they wore. Though as modest as the wrappers Elizabeth owned, these had more ruffles and lace than she'd ever seen. Even Charlotte's fanciest creations were plain compared to this.

As the girls filed into the room and perched on the various chairs, Phoebe inclined her head toward Elizabeth. "This is Dr. Harding. As I told you this morning, she's going to replace Doc Worland."

A round of cheers greeted her words and warmed Elizabeth's heart, confirming her belief that she had made the right decision in treating these women. "Thank you. I want to assure you that I'll do my best to keep you healthy."

Elizabeth looked around the room, noting that several of the girls appeared to be no more than sixteen or seventeen years old, while others were in their middle thirties. What they all had in common were their eyes. There was a quiet resignation in them that told Elizabeth they knew there was no hope of changing their lives. But, though her heart ached for them, Elizabeth could not set them on different paths. All she could do was tend to their medical needs.

She gave the girls a smile, hoping they'd realize she was their ally. "I also want to assure you that whatever you tell me will be kept in confidence."

"Except from me." Phoebe's voice filled the room, and though no one said a word, Elizabeth saw several of them wince.

"Even from you, ma'am," she said firmly. "What I learn will be kept confidential. That is my responsibility as a physician."

"But Doc Worland . . ."

Though she hated to contradict Phoebe, particularly in front of her girls, Elizabeth could not back down. "I am not Dr. Worland. I can compromise on many things, but patient confidentiality is not one of them."

For a long moment, Phoebe said nothing, merely stared at Elizabeth as if expecting her to flinch. At last, she nodded. "All right. I'll find out sooner or later, anyway." She gestured toward the girls. "They'll wait for you upstairs in their rooms. You might as well start with me. This ankle's itching something awful."

As the girls climbed the staircase, Phoebe led the way down the hallway. Elizabeth saw a large dining room on the right, behind the parlor, but the wall on the left was unbroken except by one door at the very end. Pulling a key from her pocket, Phoebe unlocked that door.

"These are my private quarters," she said as she led the way into a sumptuously furnished sitting room. Like the parlor,

Phoebe's boudoir had a second entrance, this one leading outside. Opposite the entrance, an open door revealed a bed-chamber. There were no portraits of scantily clad women here. Instead, the walls boasted delicate watercolors of European scenes. Elizabeth recognized the Roman Colosseum and Paris's Notre Dame Cathedral but couldn't identify the bridge.

"It's the Bridge of Sighs in Venice," Phoebe said as she sank onto a horsehair settee. "I keep the pictures to remind me that there's a world outside of this house." Though there was a wistfulness in her voice that made Elizabeth think Phoebe regretted her choice of profession, she would say nothing. She was here as a physician, not as a judge or even an advisor.

"I noticed that you're left-handed," Elizabeth said, gesturing to the hand that still held the key. "I hadn't realized that before. It's no wonder you're having difficulty with the crutch." To keep the weight off her injured ankle, Phoebe had to manipulate the crutch with her right arm and hand, and since that was her nondominant side, it was awkward. "Perhaps you should try a cane instead. I can have one delivered this afternoon."

Phoebe wrinkled her nose. "Go ahead. It can't be any worse." She was silent while Elizabeth inspected her ankle, but when Elizabeth declared it was healing well and that the itching was normal, Phoebe gave Elizabeth her most persuasive smile. "Are you sure you won't tell me what you learn from the girls?"

Elizabeth suspected this was the reason Phoebe had asked to be first. She wanted another chance to persuade Elizabeth. "I can only tell you if it's something that might endanger the others. I've heard there have been a few cases of diphtheria in the area. If one of your girls contracted it, you would need to know so that you could quarantine her."

Phoebe's lips thinned. "None of them have diphtheria."

They did not. As she completed the last of her examinations three hours later, Elizabeth suspected Phoebe might have preferred diphtheria.

"Are you going to tell her?" Sheila Kerrigan asked when Elizabeth confirmed her diagnosis. The petite brunette had classic black Irish coloring, with hair so dark a brown it was almost black and deep blue eyes. In the lilting voice that betrayed her origins, she told Elizabeth she was twenty-two years old and had been in Cheyenne little more than a year. "Sure and it's different from Ireland," she said with a grin. "There are no soft days here." Soft, she explained, meant a day when the rain fell as a mist. So far, Elizabeth had seen no days of rain, soft or otherwise. And what she saw now was a young woman in a difficult situation.

"I said I wouldn't tell Phoebe, and I won't. Of course," she added, watching Sheila's expression carefully, "you won't be able to hide it forever."

The pretty brunette clenched her fists. "She'll want me to get rid of it. That's what happened when Annie got caught."

Elizabeth wasn't surprised. As deplorable as it was, she suspected that was the normal practice when a girl "got caught," as Sheila had phrased it. "You can probably hide your condition for another month or six weeks," she told Sheila, "but I'd suggest you not wait. It'll only get harder. If you'd like, I'll go with you when you tell Phoebe."

Her eyes widening with surprise, Sheila tipped her head to one side. "Would you?"

"Of course." Five minutes later, Elizabeth knocked on the door to Phoebe's sitting room and found the madam sitting with her leg propped on an ottoman. "Sheila has something she needs to tell you."

"Something tells me I'm not going to like it." Phoebe gestured toward the two chairs opposite the settee. "What is it, girl?"

The harsh tone made Sheila flinch, but she straightened her shoulders as she sat. "It's good news for me. Dr. Harding confirmed that I'm going to have a baby." The smile Sheila gave Elizabeth faded when she saw Phoebe's eyes narrow and spots of color rise to her cheeks. Though Phoebe's reaction was what Elizabeth had expected, she was surprised by its intensity.

"Good news?" Her face contorting with anger, Phoebe spat the words. "That's just about the worst news you could have brought me." She fixed her gaze on Elizabeth. "Will you help her get rid of it?"

"I can't." It wasn't what Phoebe wanted to hear, but it was the only answer Elizabeth could give. "Even if Sheila wanted that, I took the Hippocratic oath, and that—"

Phoebe interrupted, glaring at the petite brunette. "You can't want this baby. It'll ruin everything."

"I do want it." Sheila's eyes darkened. "I watched my mam bury three little ones. I'm not going to bury mine."

"How are you going to earn a living? You won't be able to entertain anyone when you're as big as a horse."

"I'll find a way. There has to be one."

Phoebe scoffed. "You're fooling yourself if you think anyone will hire you. The only thing you're fit for is working here, and the bun you've got in the oven is interfering with that."

Though the blood drained from Sheila's face and she looked at Elizabeth for support, she shook her head. "I won't be like Annie. I won't cry every night, wondering whether my baby was a girl or a boy. I didn't plan this, but I can't kill my baby. I'll find a way."

Elizabeth wished there were something she could do, but she knew the fallacy of believing she could solve every problem. This was between Phoebe and Sheila. She could only pray that they'd find a solution.

"I knew you were stubborn the first day I set eyes on you," Phoebe said, her lip curling in disgust. "You haven't changed a mite. If anything, you're worse." She tapped her crutch on the floor, then looked back at Sheila. "All right. Have your baby. You'll entertain the men as long as you can, and then you can work in the kitchen and mend clothing. But as soon as that baby's born, you're going back to work."

Sheila's eyes filled with tears. "Thank you, Phoebe. You won't regret this."

"I already do."

"So, tell me, Rose. What is your most favorite thing?"

Gwen tried not to stare. Elizabeth was so engrossed in reading a letter from one of her sisters that it appeared she hadn't noticed Harrison's unusual behavior. It had started at supper. He looked the same as ever, but he wasn't acting the same. While they'd eaten, he'd been uncharacteristically quiet, yet his expression had been thoughtful. Gwen had caught him staring at her, his eyes filled with something that looked a bit like longing, almost as if she were a fancy pastry that he wanted to sample but couldn't. That thought had brought a flush to her cheeks, causing her to look down at her plate, pretending to be entranced by the sight of roast beef and newly harvested carrots. Other times, she'd seen him studying Rose. Not once had his gaze moved to Elizabeth, though she'd been entertaining them with stories of her day. Now that the meal was over, he and Gwen were seated on the matching chairs in the parlor with Rose playing at their feet, while Elizabeth occupied the settee.

It was clear that something had changed, but Gwen couldn't imagine what it was. All she knew was that Harrison was acting like a different person. The glances were unusual enough, but this . . . It was the first time Gwen could recall Harrison asking Rose anything. In the past, he would speak to her, telling her things, almost as if he were lecturing her. He never asked her opinion. In fact, he never asked Rose anything. Until tonight.

If Rose recognized there was something different about tonight, she gave no sign of it. Instead, her face lit with enthusiasm as she uttered the word Gwen expected. "Horses!" she cried, clapping her hands. "I like horses."

Harrison chuckled, perhaps remembering that Gwen had had to restrain Rose to keep her from running into the street to join the Independence Day parade. The fascination with horses which Gwen had believed she'd outgrow had only increased, causing her daughter to plead for a horse of her own.

A smile softened Harrison's face as he leaned toward Rose. "You know what," he said in a conspiratorial tone so different from his normal blunt speech that Gwen's eyes widened in surprise, "so do I." Rose giggled, the wariness with which she normally regarded Harrison seemingly forgotten. He waggled his eyebrows at her. "Do you want to know a secret?"

Like any child, Rose could not resist that particular lure. She nodded and moved closer to him. "I like secrets," she admitted.

Though Harrison lowered his voice, Gwen had no trouble hearing him. "This is my secret. When I get the store built, I'm going to buy a ranch and raise horses right here in Wyoming."

"You are?" It was Rose who asked the question, but Gwen wanted to echo it. She'd thought that once the store was complete and Barrett and Charlotte returned to Cheyenne, Harrison would go back to his family home in Pennsylvania. That prospect had disturbed her more than she wanted to admit. Now it appeared he had other plans.

Gwen tried to quell the surge of optimism that started to flow through her veins. Just because Harrison might stay in Wyoming didn't mean she'd see him once he bought the ranch. He might as well be in Pennsylvania. After all, he'd have a new home, many new responsibilities, and no need to take meals with her and Rose. In all likelihood, the only time she'd see him would be if they had a chance encounter in Barrett's store.

Gwen took a deep breath, biting back her disappointment. Her ma had told her there was no point in borrowing trouble, and that's what she was doing. What she ought to be doing was enjoying the fact that Harrison had not frightened Rose tonight.

"Yep, I sure am gonna raise horses." Rather than his usual brusque tone, Harrison's voice remained soft, coaxing Rose closer. If she moved another couple inches, her head would be touching his.

"More than one horse?" Rose demanded.

"Lots more. I'll have black horses and chestnuts and grays . . ." Harrison let his voice trail off. Then, as if the thought had just occurred to him, he asked, "Would you like to visit them?"

There was no question of Rose's response. "Oh yes!" She clasped her hands together and looked up at Gwen. "Can I, Mama?"

The pleasure that Gwen had felt over Harrison's new gentleness toward her daughter evaporated, replaced by annoyance that he'd even mentioned the possibility. Harrison had no children, and so he didn't realize that Rose's sense of time was different from his. For her, a week was a long time, a month an eternity. It would be considerably longer than a month before Harrison had a horse ranch.

"It'll be a long time," Gwen cautioned.

"Maybe not as long as you think," he countered. "I've already started looking for the right place." He kept his gaze fixed on Gwen, his blue eyes sparkling as he asked, "Would you and Rose like to help me choose it?"

As the words registered, Gwen gasped. "I couldn't do that." Just the thought was preposterous. A woman, even a widow like Gwen, didn't accompany a man while he selected the site for his home. That was a privilege reserved for a fiancée or possibly a sister. Gwen was neither.

"Why not?" he demanded. "You know Wyoming better than I do. I'd like a woman's opinion." He paused for a second, never dropping his gaze from hers, and the expression in them sent color flooding to her cheeks again. "I'd like your opinion," he said. "Yours, Gwen."

"Please, Mama, please." Rose added her plea.

Wishing her face weren't so warm and hoping that Harrison didn't realize how flustered his words had made her, Gwen ducked her head. "We'll see."

Later when Harrison had left and Gwen was brushing her hair, she replayed the evening. Elizabeth might not agree, but Gwen had found it extraordinary. Tonight she'd seen a new side to Harrison, and she liked it. She liked it very much. She drew the brush through her hair, smiling when it sparked with electricity. Oh, why pretend? She had liked the old Harrison too, even though she'd worried about Rose's reaction to him. Harrison made her feel the way Mike had.

When she'd met Mike, Gwen had been a young girl, untutored in the ways of love. It had been first love for both of them, and their marriage had been happy. But Mike had died, and then there had been that awful time with the man she thought had loved her. Gwen thrust those memories aside. She had been deluded, but she was wiser now. Harrison was not at all like that man, and when she was with him, she was different from the woman who'd been so easy to fool.

When she was with Harrison, she felt like a young girl again. He was an attractive man, and though Gwen knew it wasn't true, when he smiled at her, she felt as if she were an attractive woman. It was foolish, of course, to entertain such thoughts. Harrison regarded her as a cook, nothing more.

Still . . . tonight had been different. Tonight it had seemed that Harrison was trying to win Rose's affection. He'd made a pretty good start too. And then there'd been that glint in his eye when he'd said he wanted Gwen's opinion. For a moment, it had seemed as if he cared about her as a woman. If only that were true. Gwen had no illusions. She knew that no man would find a woman like her attractive.

She sighed and laid the brush on the dresser before she began to braid her hair. It would be different if she were tall and slender like Elizabeth. Gwen's fingers moved swiftly, taming her hair into a plait. There was no point in wishing for things that could not be. She would never look like Elizabeth, and yet . . . She stared at her reflection, frowning at her plump cheeks. It was true that she couldn't change her height, but perhaps she could do something about her weight.

When she'd been at the market last week, she had heard two women talking about patent medicines. It seemed there was one for everything that ailed you, including extra pounds. The claims were amazing. Even if they were only half true, the potion would help her. Within a month, maybe sooner if the medicine worked the way it was supposed to, she would be as thin as Elizabeth.

Gwen nodded, her decision made. It was too late now, but tomorrow morning she'd buy a bottle. Maybe two.

"Good afternoon, Dr. Harding, or may I call you Elizabeth?"

Elizabeth hoped her surprise didn't show when she entered the waiting room and saw Tabitha Chadwick standing there. Impeccably groomed as always, the auburn-haired woman gave her a cool look that made the hair on the back of Elizabeth's neck rise. Of all the women she'd met at Miriam and Richard's party, Tabitha was the last one she would have expected to see in her office.

"If this is a social call, Elizabeth is fine," she told the woman who might or might not be a patient.

"It's not a social call. I'd like to see how you've set up your office, and then I need to consult you."

It was an unusual request, but Elizabeth saw no reason to refuse. "This is the infirmary," she said, leading Tabitha into the long narrow room that held a bed on wheels and a comfortable chair. A tall screen blocked one corner and would provide privacy for patients' personal needs.

"Only one bed?" Tabitha raised a perfectly shaped eyebrow.

"I hope I won't have to use it very often. My goal is to keep people healthy so they don't need the infirmary at all. And this," she said as she opened the door to the small kitchen, "needs no explanation."

An expression of feigned horror crossed Tabitha's face. "You cook?"

"Not well," Elizabeth admitted, "but if I do have patients in the infirmary, I want to be able to heat broth for them."

"I suppose."

Elizabeth crossed the hall. "As you can see, this room serves as my dispensary and office as well as an examining room." She gestured toward the chairs in front of her desk, taking her place behind the desk and pulling out a sheet of paper. As she dipped her pen into the inkwell, she raised her eyes to meet Tabitha's. "How can I help you?"

Tabitha's gaze moved to the tall cabinets that lined one wall, as if she were seeking a specific medicine. "I need a bottle of ergot."

Elizabeth's hand paused. Her instincts hadn't failed her. This was neither a social visit nor an ordinary office call. "Ergot is a very powerful medicine," she said firmly. "I don't dispense it or any medicine without assuring myself that the patient's condition warrants it."

Tabitha's green eyes narrowed, and her lips curled, leaving Elizabeth no doubt that this was not the response she had expected. "Dr. Worland used to."

Elizabeth noted Tabitha's use of the past tense. That explained her presence here today. For some reason, the older doctor had refused Tabitha's demand. "I am not Dr. Worland." The phrase was becoming a refrain. "I would be happy to help you with whatever is wrong, but first I need you to describe your symptoms."

Her right hand fluttering in what appeared to be a dismissive gesture, Tabitha spat the words, "Female problems."

That was a wide category. "What sort of female problems?"

"The kind that ergot helps."

Elizabeth knew of only two uses for the drug. Though some midwives employed it during childbirth to hasten delivery, that was obviously not the reason Tabitha wanted her to prescribe it. The second and more common use was as an abortifacient. Though she had no proof, Elizabeth suspected that was why Tabitha was here. The night of Miriam and Richard's party, Elizabeth had overheard a woman saying that Tabitha was loath to ruin her slender figure with pregnancy.

"I'll need to take your medical history and examine you before I can prescribe anything," she said, watching Tabitha's face closely.

The woman refused to meet her gaze. Instead, she stared at the wall behind Elizabeth. "You surprise me, Dr. Harding. I didn't think you'd turn away a patient. From what I've heard, your practice is small. Very small." Tabitha tapped her index finger on Elizabeth's desk. "I can help you, you know. Many women in Cheyenne listen to me."

It sounded more like a threat than a promise, and that raised Elizabeth's hackles. While she did not doubt Tabitha's influence, she did doubt her motives. Under no circumstances would she dispense ergot to this woman. "I'm sorry, but I cannot give you what you want."

Tabitha's laugh was as brittle as the smile that creased her face. "I suppose you've got scruples and principles. They're all fine and good, but they won't pay your rent or feed you." She rose and gathered her reticule. "I thought you'd understand that I wanted to help you, but I was obviously mistaken. I'll get the ergot from someone else."

Hours later, Elizabeth was still shaken by her encounter with the lovely woman. She stood in her waiting room, staring sightlessly out the window. How different Tabitha Chadwick was from Sheila Kerrigan! Tabitha was a wealthy woman with a husband who doted on her. Undoubtedly, she had servants who would care for a child, and yet she was so opposed to the idea of motherhood that she was prepared to abort her unborn baby. Sheila had no husband, doting or otherwise. She had no money, nor any servants to help her raise a child. She knew that motherhood would be a struggle, and yet she wouldn't consider giving up her baby.

"You look like you want to throttle someone."

Elizabeth's head jerked to the side and she stared at Jason. "I'm sorry. I didn't hear you come in."

He shrugged. "You were obviously lost in your thoughts. They didn't appear to be happy ones, either."

"They weren't."

"Can I help?"

"I don't know." Suddenly aware that her legs were tired from standing, she sank onto one of the chairs and offered Jason another.

"I can listen."

But she could not speak. Or could she? Though she could not divulge the details, there was no harm in discussing generalities. "I'm disturbed by some women's attitudes toward children. They don't seem to realize that they're gifts from God."

A smile crossed Jason's face. "The reverend used to say that."

"The reverend?"

"My father. Mrs. Moran always referred to him that way, so I called him the same thing. He seemed to like it."

Elizabeth could not imagine herself or her sisters calling their father anything other than Papa. "It sounds so formal."

"He was a formal man. I can't recall ever seeing him without his clerical collar. For him, being a minister was more than a calling. It was who he was." Jason chuckled. "I never could picture the reverend as a boy, and yet he was good with the children in the congregation. He didn't treat them as if they were too young to understand something."

Jason leaned forward, propping his elbows on his knees. "Sometimes he'd take me with him when he visited parishioners. Most times I'd just sit in the buggy, waiting for him to finish, but I remember one time when he was called to a family whose baby was close to death. That time he took me inside with him." Jason frowned at the memory. "The baby died almost as soon as we arrived. I'll never forget the reverend telling me that children were a gift from God, even if the family only had that gift for a moment."

As tears welled in her eyes, Elizabeth nodded. "Your father sounds like a remarkable man."

"He was." But Jason's expression told Elizabeth that had not been enough.

10

July slid into August, with each day a few degrees hotter than the previous one. Occasionally a late afternoon thunderstorm relieved the heat temporarily. That was cause for thanksgiving, as were the days when a storm was followed by a rainbow. Though fleeting, the brilliantly colored arcs never failed to boost Elizabeth's spirits, for they reminded her of her childhood and how her mother would stop whatever she was doing to gaze at a rainbow. "They're a gift from God," she told her daughters, "a sign of his unending faithfulness." The day Mama had died, there had been a rainbow, and though her grief had been overwhelming, Elizabeth had found herself smiling at the thought that God and his angels were welcoming Mama to heaven with one of her beloved rainbows.

Elizabeth capped the ink bottle as she finished the letter she had been writing to Charlotte. Though she was disappointed that Charlotte and Barrett would not be returning to Cheyenne as soon as they had expected, she understood that some things, including the schooling Charlotte was receiving, took longer than anticipated. "We'll be there by Christmas," Charlotte's last letter promised.

Christmas. Just the thought caused Elizabeth's smile to broaden. It would be wonderful to spend the holiday with her family, especially after several years of celebrating alone. That thought, like so many others, raised questions about Jason. How did he spend Christmas? How deep were the wounds Mrs. Moran had inflicted? And, perhaps most importantly, had his father given him tangible signs of his love? Elizabeth did not doubt that the reverend had loved his son, but she feared he'd never demonstrated that love.

Other than smiles and an occasional pat on the shoulder, Papa had not expressed his love. It had been Mama who'd dispensed hugs and kisses, telling her daughters with actions as well as words that they were loved. Without a mother, Jason might not have been so fortunate. His father had told him that children were a gift from God, but Elizabeth wondered if anyone he knew had described rainbows the way her mother had.

Rainbows were one of the few similarities between Cheyenne and the other places Elizabeth had lived. Though she missed the mature trees that lined many of the streets in both Vermont and New York, she had to admit that the Wyoming sky was beautiful. It seemed bluer, and perhaps because there were few trees to block the view, it seemed bigger. The heat was different too. Wyoming was drier, making the heat seem less oppressive than New York's. Equally important, the heat dissipated soon after nightfall rather than lingering all night. Though it had been difficult to sleep in New York during one of the summer heat waves, Elizabeth had had no trouble falling asleep and remaining asleep here.

While she couldn't say when it had occurred, Elizabeth felt as if contentment had settled over her like the woolen cloak Charlotte had given her for her last birthday, and like the cloak, it warmed her. There were many reasons to give thanks. It was true that patients were hardly stampeding to her door, but each week brought her one or two more, and it would soon be time to return to Phoebe's for the girls' monthly checkups and to remove Phoebe's cast.

Elizabeth was grateful for both her growing practice and the fact that Gwen seemed happier, perhaps because Rose had developed an attachment to Harrison. The little girl who'd once shied away from him now chattered about horses whenever she saw him, and every day she demanded to know whether he'd bought any. Elizabeth might have called Rose's behavior badgering, but Harrison didn't seem to mind. He just grinned, bestowing smiles on both Rose and her mother. In return, Gwen beamed with happiness whenever Harrison was around.

Elizabeth couldn't help wondering whether the plan to establish a horse ranch was a recent development, perhaps precipitated by Harrison's desire to spend more time with Gwen, or whether he'd had it in mind when he returned to Cheyenne to assist with the store renovations. Regardless of the reason, she imagined that Barrett would be glad to have one of his brothers living in Wyoming. Family was important.

Elizabeth leaned back in her chair and closed her eyes, sending a prayer of thanksgiving heavenward that by the end of the year she would be reunited with her sisters. When she opened her eyes again, she tried not to frown at the reminder that Jason had no family. One day when they'd been sharing another of Mr. Ellis's cakes, he'd told her that he had no aunts or uncles to give him cousins. He was alone in the world.

There had to be something she could do. Before she could complete her thought, Elizabeth heard a woman shouting.

"Dr. Harding! Dr. Harding!"

Elizabeth sprang to her feet and rushed into the waiting room. Her eyes widened in surprise when she realized that she knew this woman, though the voice was so distorted by panic that she hadn't recognized it. "What's wrong, Delia?"

When her maid's hand had become infected, Miriam had brought the young woman to Elizabeth's office. It had been simple enough to remove the splinter that had festered, more difficult to convince Delia that she needed to keep the hand bandaged for a week. Fortunately, when she had returned eight days later, Delia's face had been wreathed in a smile, and she'd admitted that the bandage hadn't curtailed her activities as much as she'd expected.

Delia was not smiling now.

"It's Miss Miriam." She paused, correcting herself. "Mrs. Eberhardt, that is. She's mighty sick and she needs you."

Seconds later, Elizabeth had her medical bag in her hand and was climbing into Miriam's carriage. "I'm glad you brought the buggy," she told Delia as she settled the bag at her feet.

"Me and Roscoe knew there was no time to waste," the young woman said, gesturing toward the driver. "Miss Miriam wants you, but Mr. Richard called Doc Worland."

Elizabeth tried not to frown at the prospect of once again locking horns with the older physician. Fortunately, he had not yet arrived at Maple Terrace. Elizabeth was surprised when there was no sign of Richard as she entered Miriam's room. She would have expected him to be at his bride's bedside. Keeping her expression even, though the sight of Miriam sent

158

waves of alarm pulsing through her body, Elizabeth greeted her patient. Her face was flushed, her eyes glassy. There was no doubt that Miriam was, as Delia had said, mighty sick.

"I'm glad you came." Miriam's voice was as weak as she appeared. "I feel awful." She laid her hand on her forehead. "I'm so hot. Oh, Doctor, I'm worried that I might hurt my baby."

One touch was enough to tell Elizabeth that Miriam had a dangerously high fever. "You do have a fever," she said, neglecting to add that she shared Miriam's concern that the elevated temperature might be harmful to her unborn child. There was nothing to be gained by adding to her patient's distress.

"Let's see what's causing that fever." Elizabeth slid the thermometer under Miriam's tongue and ran her hands along her patient's throat. What she found disturbed her as much as Miriam's fever.

"I'm so weak," Miriam cried when Elizabeth completed her palpation. Her green eyes were frantic with worry. "I tried to get out of bed, but my legs just collapsed. Oh, Doctor, I'm so afraid."

The symptoms were consistent with Elizabeth's tentative diagnosis. All she needed was one more confirmation. She touched Miriam's lips. "Open wide," she ordered. "I want to look at your throat." Miriam's throat revealed what she feared. Elizabeth took a deep breath, then laid her hand on Miriam's in what she hoped would be a comforting gesture. "There's no easy way to tell you this. You have diphtheria."

Miriam's reaction was instantaneous. As her eyes widened, she clasped her abdomen. "Will I die? Will my baby?" It was a valid fear, for diphtheria killed close to half those who contracted it.

"Not if I can help it." Elizabeth reached into her medical bag, pulled out two bottles, and uncorked the first. "I'm going to swab your throat with tincture of iodine, and I want you to gargle with this at least three times a day," she said, holding out the second bottle. "It's hydrogen peroxide," she told Delia, whom she'd summoned from her post by the door.

Elizabeth removed the swab from Miriam's throat and tossed it into the sack she had brought for that purpose as she heard Richard's voice. "Right this way, Doc."

Elizabeth's nemesis had arrived.

Miriam cringed and tugged the bedcovers over her head. "Don't let him use leeches," she pleaded.

"I'll do what I can." It was all she could promise. Straightening her shoulders and fixing a neutral expression on her face, Elizabeth took a step away from the bed as the two men entered the room.

"What are you doing here?" Though Richard's words could have been confrontational, he sounded confused rather than angry.

"I sent for her." Miriam lowered the covers and looked at her husband. "She's my doctor." Though her voice was weak, she sounded determined.

"Harrumph!" Dr. Worland made no effort to hide his displeasure at Elizabeth's presence. "A midwife at best."

Laying his hand on her forehead and stroking it gently, Richard addressed his wife. "Now, darling, I know you meant well. It's fine for Dr. Harding to attend you when the baby is born, but you need a real doctor now."

Though Elizabeth's blood boiled at the implication that she was not a true physician, she said nothing. There was naught to be gained by antagonizing either Richard or Dr.

160

Worland, and so she merely stood at the foot of Miriam's bed, ready to help if she were allowed.

Richard nodded at her. "I think it's best if you leave Dr. Worland with his patient."

"No!" Miriam clenched Richard's hand, her face flushing, her voice tremulous. "I want Dr. Harding. She'll save our baby."

Though Richard's eyes were tender, he shook his head. "Doc Worland will treat you." His voice brooked no argument, and Miriam slumped back on her pillows.

Elizabeth squeezed Miriam's hand, then gestured to Delia to follow her out of the room. "I'll be back later," she said softly. "Get her to gargle if you can," she said as she handed Delia the bottle of peroxide. "It will help." Though Elizabeth doubted Delia would be able to swab Miriam's throat without causing a gag reflex, she gave her the bottle of iodine and a handful of swabs.

"Thank you, Doctor," the young maid said. "I'll do my best."

Elizabeth was descending the stairs when she heard Dr. Worland emerge from Miriam's room after what must have been only a cursory examination. "It's what I thought," he said, addressing Richard. "She has scarlet fever. The only way to cure that is to bleed her." He paused for a second before adding, "I have leeches with me."

Scarlet fever! Leeches! Elizabeth shuddered at yet another example of the older doctor's incompetence. Spinning around, she raced back up the staircase. "You're mistaken, Dr. Worland," Elizabeth said when she reached him. "Mrs. Eberhardt does not have scarlet fever. There is no reddening of the tongue, but if you examined the back of her throat"—and

Elizabeth doubted he had, given the short time he'd spent with his patient—"you would have seen that the diphtheric membrane is enlarged."

The older physician took a step toward Elizabeth, his posture menacing. "Are you presuming to question my diagnosis?"

Under other circumstances, Elizabeth would have chosen a more private venue for this discussion. Medical etiquette decreed that one doctor did not challenge another in the presence of patients or family. But she doubted Richard would leave her alone with Dr. Worland.

"Yes, Doctor, I am questioning you. Mrs. Eberhardt has diphtheria. The symptoms are conclusive. This is diphtheria, not scarlet fever. Bleeding the patient would be the worst possible thing you could do for her and her baby." Elizabeth turned to Richard. Though she hoped he would support her, she knew it was unlikely. It was clear that Richard shared Dr. Worland's opinion of her abilities.

"My wife is afraid of leeches," he admitted. "Isn't there any other way to save her?"

"None. None at all." Dr. Worland glared at Richard. "If you're going to take this chit's word over mine, I'll wash my hands of you."

The threat met its mark. "Let's not be hasty." Richard gave Elizabeth a short nod. "I'm afraid you'll have to leave. Roscoe will drive you back to your office. Dr. Worland is in charge here."

Feeling beaten and defeated, Elizabeth descended the stairs.

Jason pulled the watch from his pocket and opened it. Two seventeen. The middle of the afternoon. That was what he thought, and it concerned him. He hadn't heard any sounds from Elizabeth's office since this morning when she'd left in Richard and Miriam's carriage. Jason had recognized the driver and had seen Elizabeth speaking with a young woman whose clothing announced that she was a servant. That had been hours ago. It was possible that nothing was wrong, that that had been nothing more than an ordinary house call, but Jason doubted it. Something was amiss. His intuition told him that.

Covering the distance from his office to his front door in a few long strides, Jason went outside and looked at Elizabeth's window. The sign still indicated that she was gone, so perhaps he was mistaken in believing she needed his help. And yet . . . Obeying an instinct he couldn't ignore, Jason turned the doorknob. To his surprise, it opened. That was odd, for Elizabeth was conscientious about locking the door whenever she left the office. "I have too many medicines here," she had explained when he'd commented on the fact that she secured it even if she was only coming next door to see him. "I can't risk someone helping themselves to the wrong one." But now, though the sign proclaimed that the doctor was gone, the door was unlocked.

Jason stepped inside. "Elizabeth!" There was no answer, and yet the office did not have that peculiar feeling a building did when it was empty. "Elizabeth!"

It took only seconds to cross her waiting room, but when he opened the door to her office, Jason stopped in his tracks. He'd been right. Something was wrong, for Elizabeth was slumped over her desk. She wasn't asleep. He knew that from the ragged breathing and the shudders that wracked her shoulders. "What's wrong?"

Slowly she raised her head from her folded arms, revealing a face that was swollen and blotchy, eyes and nose that were red from weeping. Gone was the confident woman he knew. In her place was one who appeared devastated by whatever life had sent her way.

"I failed," Elizabeth said, her voice distorted by tears. "No one would listen to me, and now Miriam may die." A broken sob escaped. "You were right when you told me people were not ready for a woman doctor. I should never have tried."

As his heart ached at the pain she was enduring, Jason searched for a way to help Elizabeth. There had to be something he could do. Words were fine, but she needed more. Though he'd never before done anything like it, Jason crossed the room, moving behind Elizabeth's desk. Before she could protest, he reached down and pulled her from her chair, wrapping his arms around her when she was upright. Her body stiffened for an instant, and he feared she would push him away, but then she relaxed and let herself lean against him.

He pulled her closer, hoping that his nearness would comfort her while he searched for words to ease her pain. Despite her final statement, questioning the wisdom of choosing this profession, Jason realized that Elizabeth's worries were not for herself. She was suffering because of her patient. "Tell me about Miriam," he said softly.

Elizabeth nestled closer to him, burying her face in his chest, her motion sending the sweet scent of lavender upward. Jason took a deep breath, knowing that from this day forward, lavender would always be linked to thoughts of Elizabeth and memories of his attempt to comfort her.

When she spoke, her words were so muffled that he had to strain to hear them. "I can't tell you anything more than that she's very ill and that I'm worried about her. I tried to tell Dr. Worland and Richard that, but they wouldn't listen to me. Richard just insisted I leave and let Dr. Worland take care of Miriam."

Jason thought quickly, hoping the idea that popped into his mind wouldn't offend Elizabeth. She might view it as undermining her authority, but it appeared that the situation was so dire that there were few alternatives. "Perhaps I could convince Richard to let you treat Miriam. He's a friend as well as a client. If I go there as a friend, he might listen to me."

Relief flowed through Jason as Elizabeth's expression changed from despairing to mildly hopeful. "Would you do that? I hate the idea that Richard doesn't trust me." Her voice broke again as she said, "He told Miriam I wasn't a real doctor."

And that hurt. Stroking her back in what he hoped was a comforting gesture, Jason murmured, "That's not true. You know that. Those were the words of a man who loves his wife and who feels powerless to help her. I'm not saying it's right, but I can understand that Richard might be afraid to trust anyone other than the doctor who's been in Cheyenne for decades."

Elizabeth nodded, and Jason hoped it wasn't simply his imagination that her eyes looked brighter. "It hurt my pride," she admitted, "but that's not important now. All that matters is Miriam's life."

Jason agreed. "I'll do whatever I can," he promised. For Miriam, but mostly for Elizabeth. The strong, independent woman who'd been so quick to defend herself and her gender had been battered, revealing an unexpected vulnerability. To Jason's amazement, he found that vulnerability endearing.

Perhaps it was nothing more than masculine pride or bravado, but his heart swelled at the thought that he might be the one person in Cheyenne who could help her. And suddenly nothing was more important than making Elizabeth smile again.

11

It was a week later, and Elizabeth was still worried about Miriam. Though she tried to concentrate on the article in Mr. Taggert's *Telegraph* while she waited for patients to arrive, her thoughts tumbled faster than the leaves that had torn from the trees during the last thunderstorm. If Miriam's case of diphtheria followed the normal pattern, she should have reached the crisis by now. The next few days would determine whether or not she lived. Elizabeth had gone to Maple Terrace two days after she had made her diagnosis, hoping to check on Miriam's condition, but Richard had announced that his wife was too ill to have visitors. The way he'd emphasized the word *visitor* had told Elizabeth that Jason's conversation with him had not changed Richard's mind. He still did not consider her a real doctor, and he was not about to let her treat his wife. Though that realization was painful, the memory of Jason's concern helped to mitigate it.

Elizabeth felt her lips begin to curve into a smile, and she laid the newspaper aside. Her eyes were reading words, but her brain was not registering their meaning. Instead, her thoughts focused on Jason and how he'd tried to help her. His concern had told her that he cared, and that had warmed her heart. But it wasn't simply Jason's concern that assuaged some of the pain of being rejected by both Richard and Dr. Worland. It was the way he'd demonstrated that concern.

He'd held her in his arms. It was the first time a man had done that, and it had felt so very good. Jason had given her comfort, but he'd given her so much more. Even now, when she closed her eyes, Elizabeth was filled with the memory of how wonderful it had felt to have his arms around her. Jason's strength had buoyed her. The steady beat of his heart had helped calm her ragged breathing. And when his heartbeat had accelerated, Elizabeth had felt an unexpected warmth flowing through her veins. She had no words to describe it. All she knew was that Jason was a special man. Somehow, just by drawing her into his arms, he had turned a truly horrible day into one that lingered in her memory and made her smile.

Elizabeth was still smiling when the doorbell tinkled. Rising quickly, she walked into the waiting room, where a woman and a small boy stood.

"Dr. Harding?"

As she had been trained, Elizabeth assessed the woman's health as she nodded. The potential patient was about Elizabeth's height, with brown hair and eyes, and she guessed she was a few years older. Elizabeth gave her a warm smile of greeting.

"I am Dr. Harding," she confirmed. "What can I do for you? Are you here for yourself or your son?"

The woman laid a comforting hand on the boy's head. His hair was lighter brown than his mother's, but there was an unmistakable resemblance. All except for body stature. The child, who appeared to be around four years old, was heavily built, while his mother was very thin.

"Both," the woman said, her eyes softening as she looked down at her son. "I hope that's all right. Louis is a little scared of Doc Worland. I thought you might be gentler with him."

"I will certainly try." Elizabeth's opinion of Dr. Worland sank to a new low. Though the man must surely have some good characteristics, she had not seen them. While she led her patients into her office, Elizabeth learned that the woman was Laura Seaman and that her son was indeed four years old. "What seems to be Louis's problem?" she asked as she lifted the child onto the examining table.

"It's his ear." Laura Seaman gestured toward the boy's right ear. "He keeps tugging on it. When I ask him why, he says it hurts. He won't let me touch it."

Elizabeth nodded, then turned her attention to Louis. "I bet you don't feel much like playing when your ear hurts, do you?"

He shook his head.

"Then let's see what we can do to fix it. Will you let me look inside your ear? I'll try very hard not to hurt you."

Louis stared at her for a moment before nodding. "Okay. I'm a big boy. I won't cry."

Elizabeth suppressed a smile, remembering how often she had told Charlotte and Abigail that she was a big girl, only to be informed that she was their little sister. "You are indeed a big boy. Now, let me see what I can find." It took only a few seconds to identify the cause of Louis's earache. "It's no wonder your ear hurts," she told the child. "You have a large pustule in it."

Though Laura Seaman gasped, as Elizabeth had hoped, Louis seemed impressed by the unfamiliar term and the fact that whatever it meant, he had a large one. Little boys, it seemed, were not that different from little girls, and at this age, bigger was better. "What's a pus . . . pust . . . whatever it was you said?"

Grabbing a piece of paper from her desk, Elizabeth made a quick sketch. Though she would win no awards for artistic ability, she suspected that Louis would be intrigued. "This is what your ear looks like." He nodded solemnly. Her pen moved again. "This is what a pustule looks like." When Louis nodded, Elizabeth tapped her pen against the drawing of his ear. "You have a pustule right here."

"Is it serious?" Laura had been silent while Elizabeth had examined her son, but now she could not conceal the worry in her voice.

"No," Elizabeth was quick to reassure the young mother. "It will probably drain on its own at some point, but Louis will be more comfortable if I lance it today. Is that all right with you?"

When Laura agreed, Elizabeth turned back to her patient. "I'd like to make this pustule go away. It may hurt a little. Do you think you can be brave?" His eyes widening with either anticipation or apprehension or perhaps a combination, Louis nodded. "All right. Let's get ready." Elizabeth drew a small scalpel and a piece of cotton batting from one of her drawers.

"I'd like you to hold your mother's hands." That would keep Louis steady. "When I tell you, take a deep breath and hold it until I tell you to release it." There was no medical reason for the child to do that, but it would give him something to think about other than the pain Elizabeth was about to inflict.

"Ready? Breathe in." Within seconds, she had lanced the boil. "You can breathe again," she told Louis, pleased that he had barely winced. When she'd cleaned his ear and applied salve to the small incision, she smiled at her patient. "You were the bravest patient I've ever had. Would you like a licorice stick as a reward?"

As the boy grinned and popped the end of the candy into his mouth, Elizabeth turned to his mother. "His ear should heal quickly. I'd like you wash it every morning and night. Just put a little warm water on a soft cloth and dribble it inside. That's all he needs."

Laura stroked her son's head. "Thank you, Doctor. Louis seems happier already."

Elizabeth gave her a crooked smile. "Licorice will do that."

"You're too modest. Doc would never have taken so much time with a little boy."

Though Elizabeth didn't want to talk about Dr. Worland, she couldn't ignore Laura's comment. "I believe all my patients deserve to be treated with dignity and respect. Age doesn't matter." She lifted the boy from the table, placing him on the floor. "You said you also wanted to consult me."

Laura looked at her son. "Louis, I want you to play in the other room so Mama can talk to the doctor. I'll be right in here, and you'll be able to see me."

"I'm a big boy," he announced as he took long strides toward the waiting room.

When he was seated on one of the benches, apparently content to munch his licorice, Laura turned to Elizabeth. "I didn't want him to overhear our conversation. I'm never sure how much he understands." She clasped her hands together and took a deep breath once she settled into a chair in front of Elizabeth's desk. "Dr. Harding, Louis is four years old. Lloyd and I want another child. We have ever since he was born, but it hasn't happened. I hoped you'd be able to help us."

Elizabeth reached for a clean sheet of paper and began to take notes. "Did you have trouble conceiving Louis?"

"Not at all. It happened the first month we were married."

Then it seemed logical that she would have had a second child or even more by now. "Was there anything unusual about your delivery?"

Laura inclined her head. "The midwife thought it was going too slowly, so she gave me something to strengthen the contractions. I can't remember what she called it."

"Ergot?" Even as she pronounced the word, Elizabeth hoped she was mistaken.

"That's it."

Laura's smile told Elizabeth she had no idea how dangerous the medication was. "Do you recall how much the midwife gave you?"

"A lot. She said it would help the baby come more quickly, so she gave it to me a few times then, and after he was born, she gave me more."

Trying to keep her expression impassive to avoid worrying her patient, Elizabeth said, "Some people believe it's helpful in delivering the afterbirth."

She must not have succeeded, for Laura raised an eyebrow. "But you don't?"

Elizabeth's chair creaked as she leaned forward. "It's a very powerful medicine. I prefer to use other methods." Ones that might not have such serious aftereffects. "Would you mind sitting on the table and removing your shoes and stockings? I'd like to examine your feet."

"All right," Laura said, her reluctance obvious, "but . . ."

Two minutes later, Elizabeth expelled a sigh of relief. "Everything's fine," she said, smiling when Laura giggled as she touched the inside of her arch. The fact that her feet were ticklish confirmed Elizabeth's opinion.

"What did you expect?"

There was no reason to dissemble. "I was concerned about how much ergot you were given. It can cause permanent damage to the extremeties. When I was studying to be a doctor, I had to amputate a woman's foot because she'd taken too much ergot."

Laura shuddered. "Do you think the ergot is the reason I haven't had another child?" she asked when Elizabeth completed her examination.

"I don't know. It would be unusual, but I can't rule it out. Everything else seems normal."

Squeezing her eyes closed to keep the tears from falling, Laura shook her head. "Oh, Doctor, Lloyd and I want another baby so badly."

"Have you considered adoption?" Just last Sunday the minister had announced that two little boys had been orphaned and had asked the congregation to pray for them.

Laura shook her head. "Lloyd won't agree. He says that if God wants us to have a baby, he'll give it to us." She blinked back tears. "There's got to be something we can do."

Elizabeth wished she could offer encouragement. Unfortunately, she could not. "I'll do what I can to help you, but I have to be honest. It may take a miracle."

Elizabeth was still thinking about Laura Seaman and wishing she had had better news for her when she heard the door open again. The softer footsteps told her her visitor was not Jason, and though she would have enjoyed seeing him, Elizabeth's spirits rose at the prospect of two patients in one morning. The rent for this office was far from exorbitant, almost covered by what Phoebe paid her, but an additional patient or two would make a difference.

A welcoming smile on her face, Elizabeth entered the waiting room, then felt her heart plummet when she recognized the woman who stood by the doorway. Delia. Elizabeth hadn't seen her since the day she had been practically evicted from Maple Terrace. By now Miriam's crisis should have passed. There should be no need for a doctor unless . . . Elizabeth didn't want to complete the sentence.

"Miss Miriam wants you to come." Delia's shy smile told Elizabeth her mistress was in no danger of dying. Whatever the reason for the summons, it was not for a final farewell.

"Does Richard know that you're here?" He'd been adamant that Elizabeth not return while Miriam was under Dr. Worland's care.

The young maid shook her head. "No, ma'am. He's gone right now."

Elizabeth felt the tension that had gripped her begin to subside. Richard's absence was another sign that Miriam must be on the mend. Elizabeth was certain he would not leave his wife if she were in danger.

"Miss Miriam said it was important," Delia continued. "She asked you to bring your bag with the listening thing."

"My stethoscope."

"That's it. Will you come?"

"Of course." Even if it meant defying Richard, Elizabeth would not ignore a patient's request. And, regardless of what he had said, Miriam was her patient.

It took only a few minutes to cover the distance between Elizabeth's office and Maple Terrace. Though Elizabeth plied Delia with questions about her mistress's condition, the young woman would only say that Miriam wanted to see her.

When they arrived, Delia left Elizabeth at the foot of the stairway, then descended to her own quarters in the basement. Though Elizabeth was tempted to take the stairs two at a time, she mounted them decorously, knocking before she opened the door to Miriam's room. To her relief, normal color had returned to Miriam's face, and while she appeared thinner than a week ago, she was smiling. There was no doubt that she had survived her bout of diphtheria.

"I'm glad you came." Miriam's voice was hoarse, undoubtedly the residual effect of the infection, but it was strong enough to dismiss Elizabeth's last concerns.

"You look much better," Elizabeth said after she'd offered a silent prayer of thanksgiving.

"That's thanks to you. Delia did everything you told her." Miriam's hand flew to her throat, and she sent Elizabeth a crooked smile. "It was no fun having her poking around inside my throat, but I'm convinced that's the reason I'm still alive." Her smile faded. "Doc Worland wasn't happy when I refused to let him bleed me. He told Richard it was your fault. I'm afraid you've made an enemy, and it's all my fault."

"Nonsense. Dr. Worland and I have had differences of opinion from the first time we met, but Cheyenne's big enough for both of us." Or so Elizabeth hoped. "What's important is that you're feeling better. May I look at your throat?"

"Of course." Miriam opened her mouth.

Elizabeth depressed Miriam's tongue and examined her throat. When she was finished, she smiled. "Perfect. The diphtheric membrane is normal." Laying a hand on Miriam's forehead, Elizabeth smiled again. "Your fever is gone too. Now all that remains is to regain your strength."

Miriam nodded. "I wanted to come to your office, but my legs won't cooperate. They're still awfully weak."

"That's normal. Diphtheria is a serious disease, and it takes several weeks to recuperate. Your baby should be all right too."

A smile wreathed Miriam's face. "That's why I asked you to come today. The most wonderful thing happened. I felt the baby move!"

The young mother-to-be's enthusiasm was infectious, and Elizabeth's lips curved upward. "That is definitely wonderful."

"I want you to listen." Miriam pointed to Elizabeth's medical bag. "I want to be sure the baby's fine."

When Elizabeth completed her examination, she smiled at Miriam. "As far as I can tell, your baby is perfectly healthy. I'll come back in a week, just to be sure. After that, you should be able to come to my office."

Laying a protective hand on her stomach, Miriam looked up at Elizabeth, her eyes glistening with unshed tears. "Thank you, Doctor. For everything."

Elizabeth was grinning as she descended the stairs. Miriam had survived. Her baby was well. This was why Elizabeth had become a doctor.

"I don't know how you get any work done here." Nelson shifted his chair so that he could glance out the window without twisting his neck. He'd already told Jason that Oscar had been placated by the prospect of receiving a quarter of the company shares in the event of Nelson's death and that Jason should proceed with the incorporation papers, but he showed no sign of wanting to leave.

"What do you mean?" Judging by the amount of time his client spent looking outside, Jason assumed the answer was there.

"If I had a beautiful woman next door, I'd be spending my time with her, not sitting here with old men and dusty law books."

"Ah, but those men and what's in the books pay for my food and lodging. No matter how beautiful she is, Elizabeth doesn't do that."

Nelson swiveled around and gave him an approving glance. "So it's Elizabeth, is it? Good for you. I'm glad to see you're getting acquainted."

"I'm just being neighborly." That was not completely true. While Jason believed in being friendly with his neighbors, he had not spent much time with the previous tenant. The grizzled man who'd run the barbershop hadn't welcomed visits unless they involved a transfer of money. There was no need to tell Nelson that, just as there was no need to tell him that Jason could not forget how good it had felt to hold Elizabeth in his arms. It shouldn't have mattered so much—after all, he had only wanted to comfort her—but his mind kept replaying the way she had looked at him, as if he were the hero of one of those storybooks the girls at school used to read. Her eyes had been red-rimmed with tears, but they'd sparkled by the time he left. If he closed his eyes, Jason could smell the faint scent of lavender that clung to her and feel the warmth of her arms as they'd circled his back. He could . . .

"Neighborly." Nelson's voice snapped Jason back to the present. "I see." The way his client waggled his eyebrows told Jason he didn't believe him. "It's a pity I'm in good health. I wouldn't mind spending some time with the pretty doctor." Nelson looked at his feet. His gaze moved to his arm. At last he touched his throat. "That's it. I'll pretend to have a sore throat. It'll give me an excuse to visit your neighbor." Nelson emphasized the last word. "I wouldn't mind having that pretty face close to mine."

Though he suspected that Nelson was teasing him, that he'd somehow realized Jason's thoughts of Elizabeth were more than neighborly, Jason wasn't certain. What he was certain was that he didn't like the idea of Nelson entertaining such thoughts of Elizabeth. "I doubt your wife would approve," he said as mildly as he could.

Nelson turned abruptly and looked Jason in the eye. "That's where you're wrong. Tabitha wouldn't care."

12

He had never felt so awful. Jason struggled to open his eyes, instantly regretting the action. Sunlight was flooding the room, its brightness making him wince with pain. But that was nothing compared to his throat. It ached. He closed his eyes and winced again, reflecting that whatever was wrong with his throat was also affecting his brain.

Jason made his living with words. Precise words. But this morning he could find none. Ache was far too mild for what he felt. His throat hurt so much that he could hardly swallow. Though he'd never done it, he suspected this was what it would feel like if he'd attempted to eat a flame. The constant burning sensation was bad enough, but when he tried to swallow, he felt as if there were a huge obstacle lodged at the back of his throat.

And then there was his head. Jason didn't need one of Elizabeth's fancy thermometers to tell him it was too hot. Worst of all were his legs. When he'd stumbled into bed last night, they'd felt as weak as overcooked noodles, and they'd only grown worse. Just the thought of trying to descend the stairs made him cringe, but there was no choice. Whatever was wrong was serious, and it wasn't going away. He needed help.

Forcing himself into a sitting position, Jason glanced around the room. He'd been too weak to remove his trousers before sleeping. At the time, he'd been annoyed. Now he was grateful, for it was one less hurdle to overcome. He was halfway decent. Still, he ought to put on a shirt. He stumbled the few feet to the chair where he'd dropped the shirt, sinking onto it as he grabbed the garment and attempted to dress himself. One sleeve. Good. The second. Excellent. When his fingers fumbled with the buttons, Jason gave up. At least he was covered. All but his feet. The effort of bending over to tug on boots was more than he wanted to attempt.

Slowly, painfully, he made his way to the door, pausing every few feet to catch his breath. When he closed the door behind him and regarded the exterior stairway, his heart sank. The seventeen steps had never been a challenge. Indeed, he'd often climbed them two at a time. Now just the thought of having to descend made him wonder if it might not be better to simply stay here.

No. He couldn't do that. He placed his right foot on the first step, then dragged the left next to it. Gripping the railing like the lifeline it was, he took another step. He was walking like a child, needing to have both feet flat on one step before he attempted the next.

One more. He could do that. Now the next. When he reached the street, Jason staggered to the front of the building, clutching the bricks for support as he made his way past the entrance to his own office. *It's only a few yards*, he told himself as he gripped the windowsill. *You can do it.*

He paused, trying to catch his breath while he grabbed the doorknob. *Please, let it be unlocked.* It was. A second later, he was inside.

"Elizabeth, help me!"

She was there almost before he finished his cry. "What's wrong?" The scent of lavender was stronger than normal, perhaps because it was early morning and she had just applied it. Jason inhaled deeply, regretting the action as his throat tightened.

"What's wrong?" she repeated. Her gaze moved swiftly from his unshaven face and half-buttoned shirt to his bare feet. Though she said nothing, Jason saw Elizabeth's lips tighten.

He kept his back against the wall, his last reserve of energy almost depleted, but something—perhaps foolish pride—made him grin at the woman he hoped could end the horrible burning in his throat and restore his legs to normalcy. "You're the doctor," Jason said with what he hoped looked like a smile. "You tell me."

He must look even worse than he felt, for Elizabeth did not smile. Instead, her eyes were somber as she said, "I'm glad to see you haven't lost your sense of humor. Can you make it into my office?"

Jason tried. He really did, but all he managed to do was stumble.

Swiftly, Elizabeth put her arm around his waist. "This is no time for pride," she announced in a tone that brooked no opposition. Not that Jason had any intention of objecting. "Lean on me."

Together, they shuffled into her office and somehow managed to hoist him onto the long table that formed the room's centerpiece. Gripping the table edge in an attempt to remain upright, Jason looked at her.

"Can you tell me what hurts?"

"Everything. My head, my throat, my legs."

If he hadn't hurt so much, Jason might have been amused by the change in her demeanor. Always in the past, when he'd seen Elizabeth, she'd been a woman who made little attempt to hide her emotions. But now, perhaps because he was seeing her as a doctor for the first time, her expression was inscrutable. Other than that momentary tightening of her lips when they'd stood in the hallway, she gave no sign of her feelings.

She laid a cool hand on his forehead, nodding as she said, "You have a fever. Let's learn why." Opening one of the drawers in the nearest tall cabinet, she pulled out a flat piece of wood. "I need you to open your mouth." When Jason did, she placed the wood on his tongue, depressing it. As the memory of his conversation with Nelson flitted through his mind, Jason wanted to tell his client he was wrong. It wasn't romantic at all, having Elizabeth examine his throat. It was uncomfortable. Downright uncomfortable. Of course, if his throat didn't hurt so much, he might feel differently.

"It's not good, is it?" he said when she'd completed her examination.

"No, it isn't." For the first time, Elizabeth's mask slipped a bit, and he saw worry reflected in her eyes. "You have diphtheria. Do you want me to get Dr. Worland for you?"

Jason looked into her eyes. "Why would I do that? You're a doctor."

Half an hour later, having assured herself that Jason was resting as comfortably as possible under the circumstances, Elizabeth locked the front door to her office and hurried home. Gwen needed to know what had happened and what the next week or so would be like, while Elizabeth needed to make preparations for an extended stay in her office. Her infirmary had its first patient, and she was determined that he would have the best care available in Cheyenne. Though her spirits were buoyed by Jason's faith in her, Elizabeth could not dismiss her worries about his condition. There was no doubt that he had diphtheria and little doubt that his case was more severe than Miriam's had been.

"What are you doing here now?" Gwen asked when Elizabeth opened the door to the apartment. Surely it was only Elizabeth's imagination that the words were uncharacteristically brusque and that Gwen did not want her to see the glass in her hand.

Dismissing her concerns, Elizabeth said, "I wanted to tell you that I won't be back for a few days, maybe a week or more. I have a patient in the infirmary." When she had designed the office, Elizabeth hadn't thought it would be occupied so soon, but Jason could not care for himself.

Gwen nodded as she carefully placed her half-filled glass in the dry sink. "I can bring you meals and something for the patient if you tell me what you need."

It had been Elizabeth's imagination that something was amiss, for this was the Gwen she knew, always thinking of ways to make life easier for others. "I hate to ask you to go to so much trouble, but it would help." Elizabeth headed toward her bedroom, planning to pack a change of clothing. "I'm worried about my patient. He has diphtheria."

"He?" Elizabeth turned as Gwen's voice rose an octave, a clear indication that she was more than startled. She appeared horrified.

"It's Jason."

This time there was no question of Gwen's opinion. She was astonished by the news and not in a positive way. "Is that proper, you being alone with him?"

Elizabeth blinked at the question. "I'm a doctor, Gwen. He's a patient. Of course it's proper."

"It wouldn't be proper." Harrison ran his hand through his hair as he was wont to do when disturbed. Though Gwen found the gesture endearing, she did not like the words that accompanied it. As soon as Elizabeth had returned to her office, Gwen had finished her morning dose of tonic, then rushed downstairs to tell Harrison the news. She had expected him to comment on the dubious propriety of Jason remaining in Elizabeth's infirmary, but she had not anticipated this.

"As much as I'll miss your cooking and your company," Harrison continued, leading Gwen further into the shop that was slowly taking shape, "I can't jeopardize your reputation. It wouldn't be proper for us to be alone in your apartment."

Gwen looked around, noticing that now that the demolition was complete and the two stores were combined into one large space, it was possible to imagine Barrett's dream of a large dry goods store becoming reality. While she had fond memories of shopping in what had been called Yates's Dry Goods—it was there she had met Charlotte, and her life had changed—the new store would be more attractive and could carry more merchandise. But that was in the future.

Gwen didn't want to think about the future and the prospect of Harrison's moving out of the city. She had told herself that she would enjoy every moment of the present. Now even the present looked bleak, for she would soon be deprived of Harrison's company.

Gwen could hardly disagree with his assertion that they'd be flouting propriety if he continued to dine with her. It would be hypocritical to do that after she'd tried to dissuade Elizabeth from spending her nights at the office while Jason was in the infirmary. And yet she wished Jason had gone to Doc Worland.

It was selfish. Gwen knew that. But she hated giving up her time with Harrison. Though she enjoyed Harrison's company every day, the evenings when he remained to talk to her while Elizabeth worked in the parlor were the most enjoyable. It was then that Gwen could pretend that they were a family: she, Harrison, and Rose. It wasn't true, of course, but there was nothing wrong with a little pretense. But now, for however long Jason was ill, she wouldn't have even that.

Gwen thought quickly, searching for a solution. "I'd be glad to bring your meals to you the way I did before Elizabeth arrived," she said, trying to disguise her excitement. If Harrison agreed, she'd be able to see him, if only for a few minutes. If not . . . Gwen didn't want to think about how lonely it would be with both Elizabeth and Harrison gone.

Harrison ran his hand through his hair again, his reluctance apparent. "I hate for you to go to all that extra effort. I know you'll be busy, trying to help Elizabeth, so I'll eat at one of the hotels. It won't be as good, but I can't burden you."

"You're not a burden," Gwen assured him. "Rose and I have to eat, and I'm planning to take food to Elizabeth, so I'll be cooking anyway."

A smile brightened Harrison's face. "In that case, I won't turn down the offer. Your meals are the highlights of my days."

They were pretty words, and they warmed Gwen's heart. Still, she couldn't help wishing Harrison had said that the time they spent together was the highlight of his days. It would be wonderful if he cared about her as well as her cooking. But he wouldn't, not until she was as thin as Elizabeth. That was why she drank Lady Meecham's tonic twice a day.

"I'm glad you enjoy the food," she told Harrison, smiling into those eyes that were so much darker blue than her own. "It's a pleasure to cook for a man again." Elizabeth and Charlotte had appreciated Gwen's meals, but there was nothing like a man's hearty appetite to make a cook feel good.

"The pleasure is mine." Harrison raised his voice slightly to be heard over the hammering. "I'm thirty-six years old, and you've given me the best meals of my life. I want to repay you."

"Nonsense!" She didn't want repayment. She wanted love. But she couldn't admit that. No lady would. "You're already paying for most of the food." When Gwen had invited him to take meals with her and Elizabeth, Harrison had insisted on contributing to their food budget. The amount he'd suggested had staggered Gwen, but he'd claimed it was no more than he would have had to spend if he'd eaten in restaurants.

"At least let me take the meals to Elizabeth. That way you won't have to worry about Rose while you're gone. Besides," he said, looking at the confusion that reigned inside the store, "I could use an occasional break from this."

It was an attractive offer, made all the more appealing by the fact that it would give Gwen another opportunity to see Harrison. "All right, if you're certain it won't be inconvenient."

"I'm certain." He gave her a smile so tender that it made Gwen want to weep from happiness. A second later, his face returned to its normal genial expression.

What a fool she was! There she was, harboring secret dreams that Harrison would view her as a woman, not just a cook. When he'd given her that look, for a second she had thought he might touch her cheek, but then his gaze had moved downward, and everything had changed. He'd seen her waist.

Gwen was huffing by the time she reached the top of the stairs. She knew she was heavy, but, oh, how it had hurt to see Harrison's expression sober when he'd seen the rolls of fat that even Charlotte's clever needle hadn't been able to hide. She had to—she absolutely had to—lose more weight.

Gwen hurried into the apartment and drew the blue bottle from the cabinet. She thought the bottles she had drunk of Lady Meecham's Celebrated Vegetable Compound were working. Surely it wasn't her imagination that her clothes felt looser, but even if that was true, it wasn't enough. She had to try harder.

Pouring a larger than normal dose into a glass, Gwen looked at the bottle. The label advised taking it twice a day. She would do better. She would take a double amount three times a day. Just to be certain, she would ensure that she ate no more than Rose. That would work. It had to. And then, when she was as thin as Elizabeth, maybe Harrison would smile at her again.

"This isn't good." It was the first time Harrison had been inside Elizabeth's office, and he was taking his time, looking around. He'd brought the basket that Gwen had filled with dinner, carrying it to the small kitchen at the rear of the building. Now, unbidden, he'd walked into the adjoining infirmary and was staring at Jason.

"Illness is never good, and diphtheria is particularly dangerous."

Harrison shook his head. "I wasn't referring to that. It's not good for you to be here alone with Jason."

Elizabeth tried not to bristle as she wondered whether Gwen had shared her concerns with this man. "Jason is my patient." A very ill patient.

"He's also a single man, and you're a single woman."

Elizabeth led Harrison out of the room before she responded. While it was true that she didn't want their voices to disturb Jason, she also needed to harness her temper. There was nothing to be gained by arguing with Harrison.

"Would you be having this conversation with Dr. Worland if he were treating me?" Elizabeth asked as calmly as she could.

"Of course not." Harrison's lip curled in scorn. "But this is different, and you know it."

"What I know is that Jason needs my care."

"That may be true, but people will talk. Back in Pennsylvania, the whole town would already know that he was in your infirmary."

Elizabeth doubted that news had spread that quickly here. Jason had entered her office early enough this morning that there had been few people on the street, and she'd had no patients since then.

"Cheyenne isn't a small town in Pennsylvania," she told Harrison. "It's a big city."

"But people are the same everywhere." Harrison's expression grew grave. "I don't want you hurt by gossip."

"I'm not worried." Nor was Jason. Though he'd warned her about malicious gossip when he advised her not to take Phoebe's girls as patients, Jason had willingly come to her office. That must mean that he had no qualms. Or that he was too weak to walk the extra block and a half to Dr. Worland's. Elizabeth tamped back that thought.

"Dr. Worland is not the best man to treat diphtheria." Though it would be unprofessional to tell Harrison of the older doctor's erroneous diagnosis of Miriam's illness and the dangerous treatment he had proposed, Jason knew of her concerns. Elizabeth suspected that that rather than mere proximity had figured into his decision to seek her assistance.

Harrison was silent for a moment, but though Elizabeth hoped he agreed with her, his frown said otherwise. "Regardless of Doc Worland's skills, you should be worried about your reputation. Once it's destroyed, you'll never be able to restore it." Harrison's expression softened. "Now, before you protest, let me tell you that I won't allow you to refuse what I'm going to offer. I've already told Gwen that I'll bring your meals to you. As long as I'm going to be here, I'll take that time to help Jason with his . . ." Harrison paused for a second, evidently searching for a word. "Shall we say his personal needs. That'll be one less reason for people to gossip."

Elizabeth couldn't disagree. "Thank you, Harrison. You're a good man."

He wasn't getting any better. As much as she hated to admit it, Elizabeth knew that was the case. Jason's fever had increased. That was alarming enough. Even worse was the condition of his throat. Though she had swabbed it with iodine six times a day and forced Jason to gargle with hydrogen peroxide almost as often, the diphtheric membrane continued to thicken. It was gray, slimy, and dangerous. While some doctors believed that diphtheria's fever caused its high mortality rate, Elizabeth had been taught that an enlarged membrane was even more deadly. If it continued to swell, the membrane would block Jason's throat so much that breathing would be impaired. It might even cause him to stop breathing. She couldn't let that happen. Jason had trusted her with his life. She could not fail him.

It had been four days since he had stumbled into her office, four days when Elizabeth had had little sleep. Though Harrison had offered to spell her, she had remained in the infirmary, sleeping fitfully while she sat in a hard-backed chair close to Jason. The comfortable chair that she had believed would be so useful had been moved to the corner of the infirmary when Elizabeth realized that it was far too easy to fall asleep in it. She dared not do that for fear of missing a change in her patient's condition. But she did need more sleep than the chair afforded, and so she had accepted Harrison's help. While she would not allow him to stay for extended periods lest there be problems at the store, during the two hours each day when he sat with Jason, Elizabeth was able to stretch out on the examining table in her office and sleep. It wasn't enough, but it would have to do.

Elizabeth managed a small smile as she realized that this was the first time she'd been grateful for not having patients. She was still smiling when she heard Jason stirring.

"How many days now?" It was the same question he asked

each time he opened his eyes. Though her medical books hadn't mentioned it, she suspected that the high fever somehow scrambled his brain, making him forgetful. Or perhaps it was only that the pain of his swollen throat kept him from focusing on anything else.

"Four," she said, trying to keep her expression calm.

Jason touched his throat and winced. "I'm not getting better, am I?" It was a measure of the disease that his voice was little more than a rasp.

She wouldn't lie. "Sometimes diphtheria takes this course."

"And then the patient dies." He completed the sentence.

Shaking her head, she positioned her stethoscope on Jason's chest. "I won't let you die," Elizabeth said when she'd assured herself that his heartbeat was still regular. "You can't die." With a forced lightness, she added, "If you did, who'd share Mr. Ellis's cakes with me? You know that even the smallest ones are too much for one person."

Though she'd thought he might laugh or at least smile, Jason's expression remained somber. "I'm not ready to die," he said. "There are so many things I still want to do."

"Like what?" She laid her stethoscope aside but did not reach for the iodine and swabs. They could wait. If there was one thing she had learned while studying to become a physician, it was that a focus on the future had therapeutic benefits. Patients with a strong will to live sometimes overcame what appeared to be insurmountable obstacles, while others with lesser ailments succumbed, simply because they gave up. Fortunately, Jason did not appear close to surrender. He was, however, very ill.

Jason looked at her, his eyes dull with pain. "I always thought I'd marry and have half a dozen children. That was the one promise the reverend extracted from me. He would have preferred that I follow in his footsteps and become a minister, but eventually he understood that that was not my calling, and he stopped trying to dissuade me. But even to the very end, he was adamant that the Nordling name had to continue, so I promised that I'd marry and do my best to sire the grandchildren he'd never see."

That was the longest speech Jason had made since entering her infirmary, and Elizabeth was certain it had taxed his throat and vocal cords. She ought to advise him to rest his throat, and yet she did not, for he'd piqued her curiosity.

"Why haven't you?" She was certain it wasn't for a lack of interested women. With his good looks and financial prospects, Jason must have had every single woman in Cheyenne vying for his attention when he first moved here.

"I never met a woman who . . ." He grimaced and touched his throat. "It hurts too much to talk."

It was silly to wonder what he had meant to say. She was Jason's physician and his friend, not a prospective bride.

"That's all right," she told him as she reached for the covered bowl that she'd placed on the table behind her. "There'll be time to talk later." Once the crisis passed. She had heard that some patients were filled with energy right before it occurred. Perhaps that was why Jason had been able to say so much. "Try drinking some of this broth," she urged him. "You need to keep your strength up."

Elizabeth held the bowl while Jason spooned some of the still-warm liquid into his mouth. Wincing as it slid down his inflamed throat, he shook his head. "Hurts too much."

Within minutes, Jason was once again asleep, but this time he seemed more restless than before, tossing from side to side, muttering in his sleep. The crisis was approaching. Elizabeth knew it, and with that knowledge came the realization that Jason might die, and that if he did, her life would be irrevocably changed. It wasn't just that he would be the first of her patients to die. That would be painful enough. But it would be even worse because she had violated one of the first precepts she had been taught: she had let her emotions become involved. Jason wasn't simply a patient. He was . . . Elizabeth paused, searching for the correct word, finally settling on *friend*. A very dear friend, and one who might die. She had exhausted her knowledge. There was nothing more she could do, nothing but ask for help from the One who gave life.

Kneeling on the floor, Elizabeth closed her eyes in prayer. "Dear Lord," she whispered, "I know you have a plan for Jason. I pray that that plan is for him to live. If it is, I ask that you show me the way to save him."

There was no answer, nothing but the feeling that she had forgotten something important. She rose and returned to her office to leaf through her medical books, searching for a treatment that she had missed. There was nothing. She was already doing everything recommended, but it wasn't enough. She knew that.

Returning to the infirmary, Elizabeth took Jason's hand between both of hers, hoping that the contact would comfort him. Touch, she had learned, had great powers. But though she stroked the back of his hand and murmured words of encouragement, he continued to groan with pain, and his fever continued to rise. There had to be something else she could do. When Jason turned away from her, Elizabeth released his hand and walked to the window. It was an uncharacteristically gloomy day, with clouds obscuring the sun, though no rain was falling. And yet, though the day was dismal, two men stood on the opposite side of the street, their heads tipping backward as they laughed.

She clenched her fists. It was illogical, but somehow it seemed wrong that these men were laughing when Jason neared death. She wanted to open the window and shout, telling them that a man's life hung in the balance, that they should be praying rather than laughing, but as she reached for the window sash, the sight of the men's laughing faces triggered a memory and Elizabeth stopped short.

It had been a winter day, snow swirling around the building, stinging her face as she walked to class. For reasons that she could no longer remember, she had been unhappy that day and had considered staying home. But something had driven her. Perhaps it was the realization that her classmates expected her to give up. She wouldn't give them that satisfaction. That was the day the professor had described diphtheria.

When he'd finished outlining the accepted treatment regimen, the professor had set the class to laughing with tales of primitive treatments. "No one would consider doing this," he told them as he mentioned the placement of leeches on the throat. "The outside, of course," he added. Just as primitive, he'd told them, was the use of a rose's thorny stem. "That was applied to the interior of the throat," he announced. "Naturally, it failed. You can't scrape the diphtheric membrane."

At the time, Elizabeth had agreed with her professor. That was before she had seen an actual case of diphtheria. Now, faced with the reality of Jason's situation, she wondered if the supposedly primitive technique might work. It couldn't be coincidence that she had remembered that particular lecture, not when she had just prayed for guidance. She wouldn't use a rose, of course, but she couldn't let the membrane continue to thicken.

After bringing a lamp to supplement the existing light, Elizabeth withdrew a scalpel from one of the drawers in her instrument cupboard. She was ready. Only one thing remained.

She touched Jason's shoulder, shaking him slightly. "You need to wake up," she told him. When he did, she asked him to open his mouth. As she had feared, the membrane was continuing its relentless course. Hoping the fever and pain did not prevent him from understanding what she was telling him, Elizabeth explained about the thickening membrane. "I'm afraid it will kill you," she said. "That's why I want to remove it."

Though his eyes were still dull, she saw the gleam of understanding. "Will that help?"

"I believe it will. I'll give you some laudanum to ease the pain."

Jason shook his head. "No. Had once." He grimaced, though Elizabeth did not know whether it was from the memory or the pain in his throat. "Bad reaction."

Elizabeth laid her hand on his. "It will be very painful without laudanum."

He nodded. "Worse with. Go ahead. I trust you."

And I trust that God will guide my hand. Elizabeth offered a short prayer before wielding her scalpel, then reached inside Jason's mouth. It had to hurt. She knew that, and yet the only sign he gave was to grip the side of the bed. She began slowly, cautiously scraping the outermost part of the membrane. But as his breathing seemed to improve, Elizabeth became bolder. When she finished, the slimy gray mass was gone. After she swabbed the area with iodine, she laid her hand on Jason's forehead.

"You can sleep now. Don't try to talk."

He nodded. For the next hour, Elizabeth did nothing but watch and listen. At first there was little change, but as the minutes passed, she knew it was not her imagination. Jason's breathing had improved, and he no longer seemed to have as much difficulty swallowing. The surgery was a success.

13

August became September. By the end of the first week of the new month, Jason felt well enough to return to his office. A rueful smile crossed his face as he descended the steps, recalling the last time he'd done that. That morning, he'd barely been able to keep his head upright. Today he felt like a new man. Elizabeth had warned him, but even so the recovery had taken far longer than Jason had expected.

Though he'd been able to swallow more easily within minutes of the surgery, he had required substantially more time to regain his strength. By the third day, he'd been fidgeting and griping so loudly that Harrison had hauled him upstairs, declaring that Elizabeth had no need of a quarrelsome patient. At the time, he'd been too weak to object, but now he knew Harrison had motives beyond sparing Elizabeth the sound of his complaints.

"You ought to marry the gal, you know," Harrison had

announced one morning when he'd come to help Jason bathe and shave.

"Elizabeth?" he asked, wondering why Harrison was mentioning her and marriage in the same sentence. When the older man confirmed that it was indeed Elizabeth he was discussing, Jason shook his head. Elizabeth was beautiful, she was talented, and he enjoyed her company more than any woman he'd ever met, but she was not the mother he wanted for his children. He didn't doubt that she would love them—the way she cared for Rose dispelled that concern—but a part-time mother wasn't enough, at least not for his children.

There was no reason to tell Harrison that. The man was in one of his cantankerous moods, and he'd only disagree. Instead Jason introduced an argument Harrison could not rebut. "Even if I were interested, Elizabeth isn't planning to marry. She's certain God intended healing people to be her whole life."

Jason had been surprised when she'd said that. It had been the day after she had scraped his throat. When she had announced that he would live to marry and have children, he'd turned the tables, asking her when she planned to marry. Though her response had not been the one he'd expected, it had confirmed what he already knew: that Elizabeth was no ordinary woman.

Harrison handed Jason a towel to wipe the residual shaving soap from his face. "That may have been her plan at one time, but she'll change her mind when she loses her patients. I doubt she'll have many left once folks hear how you spent a week in her infirmary."

Absurd! It was true that Jason had warned Elizabeth about

a potential backlash if she treated Phoebe's girls, but surely this was different. "I was ill. From what Elizabeth says, I was one step away from the pearly gates. How could anyone believe anything improper occurred? It's preposterous!"

Harrison's shrug was eloquent. "You've lived in small towns, Jason. You know that gossip is a major pastime."

"Cheyenne is not a small town."

"That's what Elizabeth said too. For both of your sakes, I hope you're right."

The memory of that conversation lingered. Jason shook his head as he unlocked his office door. It did more than linger. It haunted him. He would never have willingly done something to harm Elizabeth, but now the damage was done. All he could do was hope that no one learned he'd been her patient. That hope was soon dashed.

"I'm glad to see you're back in business," Richard said as he entered Jason's office and took his favorite seat in front of the desk. Pushing the chair back a few inches so he could stretch his legs, he added, "I was worried when I heard you'd caught diphtheria."

Jason managed a small nod. "As you can see, I survived." He wouldn't mention Elizabeth's role in his survival. Though he trusted Richard, the fewer people who knew, the better.

"I have to admit I was surprised when I heard you let Elizabeth treat you."

So much for secrecy. "How did you hear that?"

"When Miriam came for an appointment one day, she heard you and Harrison Landry talking and realized you were in the infirmary. She said he was insisting you had to get well in time for the grand opening."

Jason had no trouble recalling that conversation. Harrison

199

had just received a letter from Barrett, saying he and Charlotte were delayed and that Harrison should open the dry goods store without him. In typical Harrison fashion, the man was fuming . . . loudly. It was no wonder Miriam had heard him. Jason wouldn't have been surprised if passersby had heard the tirade about how Barrett's delay was putting a crimp in Harrison's plans. "I've got my eye on a piece of land that'll be perfect for horses, but I can't very well move out there if I have to run Barrett's store."

Jason had been sympathetic that day. Today he wished he'd told Harrison to keep his troubles to himself. "It's true," he admitted. "I was Dr. Harding's patient." Perhaps if he referred to her formally, Richard would understand that the time Jason had spent under Elizabeth's roof had been purely professional. "I would prefer that you not mention that to anyone, though."

"I understand." There was a brief silence, as if Richard were measuring his words. "No man would want it known that he went to a lady doctor. The way I figure it, you were too sick to get to Doc Worland's. But you needn't worry. I won't tell anyone."

"That's not the reason for silence. Elizabeth is a fine doctor. I doubt I'd be here if it weren't for her."

When Richard raised his eyebrows, Jason told him how Elizabeth had used a decidedly unconventional technique to clear his throat. "That's what saved me. I could feel the change immediately. You may not believe me, but I'm convinced that Doc Worland would never have tried that."

"You may be right," Richard said slowly. "Miriam claims it was Elizabeth's treatment that cured her and not anything that Doc Worland prescribed. It was only after she was on the mend that Miriam admitted she never drank any of the purgatives Doc gave her. It seems Elizabeth left some medicines of her own, and Delia made sure she followed Elizabeth's instructions." Richard crossed his ankles, uncrossing them a second later in an uncharacteristic sign of discomfort. "I guess I owe Elizabeth an apology."

"Or a thank-you."

"You're right. I also owe her payment for services rendered." Richard was silent for a moment. "I'm not sure I understand. If you're not ashamed that Elizabeth treated you, why are you concerned about secrecy?"

"It's Harrison. He thinks folks will be scandalized if they learn that I stayed in the infirmary."

His expression pensive, Richard inclined his head. "He could be right. A single man. A single woman. I can see how tongues might wag. It probably wouldn't hurt you, but Elizabeth's another story." He nodded briskly. "You don't need to worry about me. I won't say anything, and I'll make sure Miriam doesn't either. Your secret is safe."

Jason hoped he was right.

Elizabeth's step was jaunty as she headed for Phoebe's establishment. There were so many reasons to give thanks: the beautiful day with just a hint of autumn's cooling in the air, Gwen's cheerful mood, and most of all, Jason's recovery. His throat had healed properly, leaving him with no aftereffects from the disease. Truly, it was a day for rejoicing.

"I'm glad to see you again, Dr. Harding." Today, rather than its usual intricate arrangement of curls, Phoebe's light blonde hair was braided and arranged in a coronet. That and the purple gown were enough to give her a regal air, but what set her apart today was the imperious tilt to her head. Gone was the injured woman who'd leaned on Elizabeth. In her place was a self-sufficient female, a woman accustomed to having her word be law.

Elizabeth tried not to frown as she wondered what edict she would hear today. Each time she had visited her, Phoebe had insisted that Sheila was making a mistake in keeping her child. Perhaps today she was going to issue a royal proclamation, demanding that Elizabeth resolve the problem according to Phoebe's desires. No matter how it was phrased, Elizabeth's response would be the same.

"I won't say the girls are looking forward to your examination," Phoebe continued, "but at least they don't complain the way they did when Doc Worland came."

Although grudging, it was a compliment, and Elizabeth accepted it as such. "Shall I begin with you? You look like you're walking normally now that the cast is off, but I want to check your ankle again."

"Certainly." Phoebe led the way to her quarters. "Come on in, and be sure to come back when you're finished with the girls. We'll have a cup of coffee while we talk."

If Elizabeth had had any doubts that Phoebe was preparing to give her an ultimatum, the thinly veiled command to return and report, all under the guise of a friendly cup of coffee, would have quashed them.

When Phoebe had removed her slippers, Elizabeth examined the previously broken ankle, comparing it to its mate. Everything looked fine, but that didn't mean the healing was complete. The key was range and flexibility of motion. "Flex your toes," she directed, watching the movement carefully.

"All right. Twist your foot to the right. Now the left. Point your toes down." When Phoebe had completed the exercises, Elizabeth smiled. "It appears to have healed properly," she confirmed.

"I'm glad to hear that," Phoebe muttered as she slipped her shoes back on. She faced Elizabeth and added, "Wearing that cast put a crimp in my business. I don't entertain too many gentlemen callers, but I've got a few regulars. All except one declined the pleasure of my company while I had the cast."

That was more than Elizabeth needed to know. "You shouldn't have any residual effects," she told Phoebe, hoping that the time for embarrassing confidences was ended.

"Good." Phoebe narrowed her eyes, studying Elizabeth for a long moment. "You're a mighty fine doctor. Even though you and I don't always agree, I know that my girls and I are fortunate to have you, but I am puzzled about one thing. You seem to be what my mother would have called a gently reared lady. Don't you want a husband and children?"

It was the same question Jason had asked the day after she'd scraped his diphtheric membrane. At the time, she had given him the answer she gave everyone, that God had different plans for her, but ever since that day, the image of holding a baby with Jason's strong features and his dark hair kept flitting through Elizabeth's mind. The thought was tempting, so tempting, and yet she knew it could never be. Jason would not settle for a part-time wife and mother, and she could not abandon the gift God had given her and the life he had planned for her.

"Maybe someday," she conceded. It was possible that someday she might meet a man who could accept her calling and love her despite it. It was also possible that someday

God might tell her she had done enough healing. Until one of those seemingly unlikely possibilities occurred, Elizabeth would continue on her current path. "Right now my purpose in life is being a doctor."

"Can't you do both?" Phoebe seemed genuinely puzzled. Leaning back on the settee, she cupped her chin in her left hand and gave Elizabeth a slow appraisal.

"Only with a very special man." A man like Jason and yet not like him. Unwilling to continue the discussion, Elizabeth rose as she said, "I ought to see the girls."

She saved Sheila for the last, in part because she suspected that examination would take longer than the others. Sheila always seemed anxious to talk to Elizabeth, admitting that the subject of her unborn child was not one the other girls welcomed.

"Is she all right?" From the beginning, Sheila had insisted that her child would be a girl whom she would name Louella.

Elizabeth looked up from the notes she was making in her patient records. "Your baby seems to be healthy," she told the young mother-to-be, "but I'm concerned that she's not as big as she should be. Corsets aren't good for you or your baby. They don't give her enough room to move."

Elizabeth had had a long conversation with Charlotte over the subject of corsets when her sister and Barrett had stopped in New York on their way to Massachusetts. When Charlotte had claimed they were essential to give the gowns she created the right lines, Elizabeth had deplored their effect on women's lungs and ribs. It was true that Elizabeth wore a corset, but she kept it laced far looser than fashion dictated. Sheila's was cinched as tightly as it could be in an attempt to hide her pregnancy.

"You shouldn't be wearing a corset at all." Elizabeth made it a command rather than a suggestion.

Her lower lip trembling, Sheila shook her head. "Phoebe won't let me loosen them. She says men won't have nothin' to do with a girl who's in the family way."

Trying to keep her expression impassive, Elizabeth slid her patient notes into an envelope. "I thought you were working in the kitchen."

"Not yet." Sheila touched her midsection. Though her pregnancy was obvious when she wore no corset, the whale-bone-stiffened garment would hide it for another month or two, perhaps longer if she continued the tight lacing.

"I'll see what I can do about that." Descending the stairs, Elizabeth rapped on the door to Phoebe's suite, entering only when the older woman called to her. Suspecting that Phoebe might be more receptive to her concerns if she accepted the offer of coffee, Elizabeth waited until Phoebe had placed a cup and saucer in front of her before she introduced the subject of Sheila.

"It's time for her to stop entertaining men," Elizabeth said, nodding her appreciation of the well-brewed beverage.

"I can't do that." Phoebe smiled as if they were discussing nothing more serious than the weather. "Sheila's one of my best. Men like that dark Irish coloring and her lilt. They call her the Irish rose. Saturday nights, they line up for her."

Trying to block the images Phoebe's words conjured, Elizabeth said, "I understand your reasons, but if she continues, she may lose her baby."

Phoebe shrugged and took a deep swallow of coffee. "Contrary to what you may believe, I am not an unfeeling woman, Dr. Harding, but I do have a business to run. Sheila should have done what the others did and put an end to it. One or two good doses of ergot and the problem is gone."

Though it was not the most commonly prescribed medicine in a physician's pharmacopoeia, since she had come to Cheyenne Elizabeth had heard more references to ergot than she liked. Tabitha Chadwick had demanded a bottle; Laura Seaman was suffering from an overly liberal dosage; now Phoebe was advocating its use.

Elizabeth knew that Dr. Worland had dispensed it in the past, because Tabitha Chadwick had told her so, but Phoebe made it sound as if she had another source.

"Ergot is very dangerous," Elizabeth said, her voice as stern as an angry schoolmarm's. "Your girls should not be drinking it."

A small smile crossed Phoebe's face, making Elizabeth think she was pleased that she'd managed to anger her. "You're not going to stop them."

"Where do they get it? I've been to every drugstore in Cheyenne, and no one carries it."

The smile turned secretive. "Don't they? Sometimes you need to know how to ask for something. And you needn't ask me where I get it, because I'm not going to tell you. I've got to worry about my business."

Elizabeth felt as if she and Phoebe had engaged in a sparring match. At this point, there was no winner. Realizing she would learn nothing more today, she nodded. "I understand your concern about your business. I don't agree with you, but I won't argue." If she angered Phoebe too much, the woman might have Dr. Worland resume care of the girls, and that would not be good for either the girls or Elizabeth. "You should know, though, that ergot could kill one of your girls, and if Sheila continues to entertain in those corsets, you may lose her as well as her baby."

Phoebe was silent for a moment. Letting out a sigh, she looked Elizabeth in the eye. "All right, Dr. Harding. You've won this round."

"Mr. Nordling?"

Jason nodded at the man who'd entered his office. A couple inches over six feet, he had the broad shoulders and calloused hands of a man accustomed to hard labor. A rancher, Jason surmised. And though his dark brown hair was dusty, his clothing was relatively new and well-made. Unlike some of the farmers who barely survived, it appeared that this man had prospered.

"Call me Jason," he said as he ushered the man into his consulting room. His professors had stressed the importance of maintaining formality with clients, but they hadn't practiced law in Wyoming Territory. Life was less formal here. Furthermore, Jason had discovered that a more relaxed atmosphere fostered a greater level of trust, and that was something both he and his clients needed.

"What can I do for you?"

"Harrison Landry told me about you." As the man started to settle into a chair, he rose again and stuck out his hand. "I'm Kevin Granger, by the way." When the pleasantries were completed, he took his seat and gazed at Jason. "No point in beating around the bush. I need to make sure my girls are cared for if I die."

It wasn't uncommon for a man to ask Jason to prepare a will so that his wife and children would be protected, but this was the first time a man as young as Kevin Granger had been so blunt. "Are you ill?" There were no visible signs, but Jason knew that some diseases attacked from the inside and weren't evident until the end was near.

"No, sir," Kevin said, "but I can't take any chances. My wife wasn't ill either. She just dropped dead a month after the baby was born. No warning at all."

For a second, Jason was transported to the past and the day his father had died. There had been no warning then, either, at least none that Jason had seen. He wondered, though, whether the reverend had had a premonition, for it had been the previous night that he'd told Jason how important it was that the Nordling line continue.

"Lucky I was in the barn," Kevin continued, wrenching Jason back to the present and the realization that this man was in the same situation the reverend had been: widowed with children. "I heard Ruby scream. When I got there, she was clutching her chest."

Jason nodded as images of his father's final moments flooded through him. The reverend had gripped his head, his grimace leaving no doubt that he'd been in excruciating pain. Doc Rollins had claimed that something must have burst inside his brain. This was different. It sounded as if Ruby Granger's heart just gave out. Heart or brain, the result was the same.

"I'm sorry for your loss," Jason said. And he was. It had to be difficult to be a widower with more than one child, for Kevin had said girls, plural. But though he sympathized with the bereaved father, Jason's heart went out to the children who'd lost their mother. He could only pray that they were not being raised by someone like Mrs. Moran. Biting back his emotions, he nodded again. "What you need is a will."

"Yes, sir. I don't want there to be any question that my girls will get the ranch." Kevin scuffed the floor with the toe of one boot. "Not that it'll do 'em much good right now. They're too young."

"All right. Let's start at the beginning." Jason pulled out a clean sheet of paper and prepared to write. "Give me their names and ages." When he'd noted the information, Jason looked at the man who was trying to raise three girls under six years old. How did he manage?

"I've got a woman who cares for them during the day," Kevin explained. A housekeeper. Jason tried not to shudder. They weren't all like Mrs. Moran.

"An older woman, sort of a grandmother. She's not much of a cook, but she's gentle with the girls." Unlike Mrs. Moran, who'd delighted in twisting little boys' ears.

"I can protect the girls' inheritance," Jason assured Kevin. "The problem is, you'll need to appoint a guardian."

"What's that?"

"Someone to raise them. Usually it's a family member. Given their ages, I would recommend an aunt or uncle."

Kevin's scowl told Jason his opinion of that recommendation. "I wouldn't trust my family with them. We didn't part on the best of terms."

"What about close friends? Church members?"

Kevin shook his head. "I haven't been to church since Ruby died. I figured that if God loved me the way the preacher claimed, he wouldn't have taken her."

Jason knew that was a common reaction. He'd been with the reverend on more than one call when he'd tried to comfort bereaved spouses. "Sometimes it's difficult to understand God's ways," Jason said, paraphrasing his father's words.

"The Bible tells us that God promises to turn even bad to good for us, but it doesn't always happen the way we would like or as quickly as we think it should."

Kevin's scowl deepened. "No offense, sir, but I didn't come here for a sermon."

Jason knew when to stop. "That's true. You didn't. My father was a minister. I guess more of his preaching rubbed off on me than I realized." Jason cleared his throat, wishing there were something he could do to help this man and his motherless daughters. "As I said, I can draft a will to protect the assets, but you need to find someone you'd trust to care for your daughters. Most men would marry again."

"I've had a couple widows suggest that. I'll tell you what I told them: I won't marry unless I find a woman I love as much as I did Ruby."

"That's what my father said when I asked why I didn't have a stepmother. He told me the housekeeper he'd hired would take care of our needs. She didn't."

"I know." Kevin's expression was solemn. "That's why I spend every minute I can with the girls. I reckon I have to be both father and mother to them. That's what Ruby would have wanted."

Jason was still considering the subject when he ushered Kevin out of his office, promising to have the will drafted within three days. In one respect, he was more fortunate than Kevin, for he had friends here in Cheyenne. But love? Kevin had the advantage there, for he'd had his Ruby, the woman who'd given him three children and who'd filled his life with so much happiness that he wouldn't consider replacing her, even to make his daily life easier. It would be wonderful to have a wife like that.

As he closed the door, Elizabeth's face came to mind. Jason tried to brush it away. It was silly to be thinking about her, no matter how beautiful she was, no matter that her quick wit energized him, no matter that her smile made his heart beat faster. He couldn't marry Elizabeth, couldn't even consider it.

14

It would be childish to slam the door. Elizabeth knew that, and so she closed it carefully, refusing to give in to the temptation to vent her emotions on the front door to her office. She unpinned her hat and placed it on the rack before entering her examining room. She would file patient notes. That was the most boring task she had, and maybe, just maybe, it would release the tension that had been building since she spoke to Phoebe. The contentment Elizabeth had felt on her walk to Phoebe's was gone, shattered by the knowledge that though Phoebe claimed Elizabeth had won this round, the war still raged. Elizabeth had no doubt that Phoebe would be extra vigilant with her girls, ensuring that if another one developed what she called a "problem," she'd be given a massive dose of ergot before Elizabeth knew of her condition.

"You look as if you lost your best friend."

Elizabeth turned, startled to see Jason. Either she'd been so lost in her thoughts that she'd been unaware of his approach or his steps had been quieter than normal. It was unlike her to not hear either the doorbell or footsteps.

"I'm sorry. I'm a bit out of sorts today."

"Do you want to talk about whatever's bothering you?"

Elizabeth shook her head. "I can't." When Jason nodded, as if he understood, she added, "Let's just say that I'm concerned about some of my patients." Though she had tried to convince herself that the situation would have been no better—perhaps worse—if Dr. Worland were treating them, that knowledge did nothing to allay Elizabeth's concerns. It was unrealistic to think that she'd never lose a patient and that the ones she had would always follow her advice, and yet Elizabeth couldn't help wishing that were true.

Jason appeared to be studying her as intently as she did a new patient. Gesturing toward the door, he said, "What you need is a change of scenery." The smile he gave her was as warm as an August sun. "I'm willing to wager that you haven't left Cheyenne since you arrived."

Elizabeth was a physician. She knew that hearts weren't wounded by words or unkind acts and that they couldn't be mended with a smile, and yet she couldn't deny that she felt better simply because Jason was at her side. When she'd been a child, her sisters, especially Abigail, had been able to coax her out of a bad mood, but since she'd become an adult, there had been no one to lighten her spirits. No one until Jason. "You'd win that bet," she told him. "I haven't ventured outside the city limits." There were even parts of the city itself that she had not explored.

"Then it's time. Let's close up shop and go."

"Where?"

Jason shook his head. "It wouldn't be a surprise if I told

you. I'll be back in half an hour." Giving her clothing a quick glance, he said, "You might want a heavier coat. The weather can change quickly at this time of the year." Or at any time. Elizabeth had seen a sunny July day turn into a thunderstorm that had dropped buckets of rain. An hour later, the sun had returned, evaporating the water so quickly that she'd wondered if she had merely imagined the downpour.

"All right," she agreed. "Half an hour." Fortunately, she kept a warm cloak in her office, so there was no need to return to her apartment and explain to Gwen why she was playing hooky.

Twenty-eight minutes later, Elizabeth was seated in Jason's carriage, heading west on 15th Street.

"I thought we might be going to City Park," she said, "but it's the opposite direction."

A Cheshire grin lit Jason's face, as if he realized that she had spent the past half hour speculating on their destination. "The park is too civilized. Besides, it's inside the city, so it wouldn't accomplish my goal of getting you outside of Cheyenne." He gestured toward the mountains looming on the horizon southwest of the city. "I wish we had time to go there, but we don't."

Perhaps someday she would visit the Rockies. Though their snow caps had melted over the summer, Elizabeth knew it was only a matter of weeks—perhaps days—before the high country had its first snow and the mountains were once more white.

One evening when she'd been in a nostalgic mood, Gwen had regaled Elizabeth with stories of the time she and her husband had gone to the mountains. According to Gwen, they'd been such greenhorns that they hadn't realized they might suffer from the altitude. What was supposed to be a romantic interlude had turned into a nightmare filled with nausea and brutal headaches. "If you ever go there," she'd cautioned Elizabeth, "be sure to drink lots and lots of water. I've heard that that helps."

It was advice Elizabeth had followed during her first weeks in Cheyenne, for although the city wasn't nearly as high as the mountains, at over 6,000 feet above sea level, Cheyenne was still high enough to cause discomfort to travelers unaccustomed to the thinner air. When both Charlotte and Abigail had warned her of the dangers of altitude, Elizabeth had done some research and discovered a scholarly article touting the therapeutic effects of increased fluids and reduced physical exertion.

"I'd like to visit the mountains someday, but in the meantime, I'm enjoying the carriage ride. Even if we don't go any further," she said, gesturing as they passed the train depot, "it's been a nice break."

The beautiful red sandstone edifice that had been under construction for over a year appeared to be nearing completion. With its Romanesque arches, this depot was a far cry from the simple wooden building where she'd disembarked more than three months earlier. It was also a fitting companion to the capitol that was being erected eight blocks north. Though very different in both color and architectural styles, the two structures were designed to showcase Cheyenne's role as the largest city in the territory and one of the wealthiest cities in the country. Passengers leaving the depot would have a fine view of the light gray sandstone building that would boast columns and a dome when finished, and legislators departing the capitol would have no doubt of the railroad's importance in Cheyenne, for the Union Pacific depot would dominate their view.

"You need more than a break. You need a change of scenery."

Elizabeth looked down the street. If she craned her neck, she could see a small range of mountains to the northwest. Though less imposing than the Rockies themselves, they were still beautiful.

"Those mountains would also qualify as a change of scenery," she told Jason.

"I'm glad you think so, because you'll see them from where we're going today." Jason waved at Nelson Chadwick as they passed the lumberyard. "We don't have enough time to go all the way to the Laramies, but there won't be any clients or patients to interrupt us where we are headed."

There were none. Once they left the city, there was nothing to see but rolling prairie, the short grasses now golden with autumn's return, and the grayish-blue peaks of the Laramie Mountains on the horizon. Overhead, a hawk drifted on the air currents, perhaps looking for his next meal. Mindful of the danger, a prairie dog barked a warning, sending his neighbors scurrying into their burrows. And above them all was a sky so perfectly blue that it threatened to bring tears to Elizabeth's eyes.

"It's beautiful," she whispered, not wanting to spoil the moment with loud noises. "And so peaceful."

Jason stopped the carriage and turned toward her. "I agree. Michigan has its own kind of beauty. There's nothing quite like the sight or scent of an orchard in bloom. But once I saw Wyoming, I knew there was no other place for me." He wrinkled his nose. "Not everyone feels the same way. Look

216

around." Jason gestured expansively. "The treeless prairie can be intimidating, especially to Easterners. I've had some of them ask me where we hid the forests."

Elizabeth's smile turned into a grin. "That sounds like my sister Abigail. When she first came here, she thought the land was boring."

"But you said she plans to move back."

Elizabeth chuckled. "It didn't take her long to fall in love with both Wyoming and a special man."

The look Jason gave her made Elizabeth regret her choice of words. She hadn't meant to speak of love.

"What about you?"

Deliberately misunderstanding, she said, "I'll admit there are times when I miss the trees, but not today. The fresh air, the sunshine, and the sheer expanse are wonderful. I feel as if they're sweeping the cobwebs from my brain."

Jason's nod told her the danger had passed. There would be no discussion of love. "So this is what the doctor ordered?"

"It's what the doctor should have ordered," she amended, "only I didn't know it was what I needed."

"But now you're here." He helped her out of the carriage, and they walked silently for a few minutes, her hand on his arm. The grasses crunched underfoot, and when her skirt disturbed a sagebrush, the shrub gave off its distinctive scent, reminding Elizabeth of the stuffing Mama made for Thanksgiving turkeys. Jason was right. This was what Elizabeth had needed, this vast landscape filled with subtle beauty. Seeing the majesty of God's creation made her realize how small her problems were.

"Do you want to talk about what was wrong?" Jason asked when they turned to head back to the carriage. "The reverend used to claim that an important part of his ministry was getting people to open up."

"My father used to say the same thing. When I started to study medicine, I wondered whether talking was like lancing a boil, letting the poison out so that the healing could begin. I don't feel as if there's poison inside, and yet . . ." Elizabeth hesitated, knowing she could not breach her patients' confidentiality. She started to shake her head, then nodded as she rationalized that what she was going to say wouldn't violate her ethics. "I'm worried that so many of my patients are treating themselves."

Jason laid his hand on top of hers, his touch as warm as his voice. "People have been doing that forever."

"And they've been dying before their time too." That was the problem. Medicines—even ergot—could be therapeutic, but only if used judiciously. More often than Elizabeth wanted to accept, patients believed that if a little was good, more would be better, and despite repeated warnings, they took too much.

"You can't save everyone," Jason said, tightening his grip on her hand and slowing their pace until they were barely moving.

"I know that, but . . ."

"You want to."

He understood. The tone of his voice told her that, and it warmed her heart another few degrees. Even her sisters hadn't completely understood what had driven her to become a doctor.

"Yes. Is that wrong?"

"Of course not. It's what you must do, at least for now." He stopped and turned so that he was facing her, his expression enigmatic. Perhaps she'd been mistaken. Perhaps he did not understand.

"You sound as though you don't believe I'll be a doctor ten or twenty years from now."

"People change." Though Jason's eyes were warm as they gazed into hers, his words sent a sudden chill down Elizabeth's spine, making her wish she could shut her ears to whatever he intended to say. "You might decide you want a more settled life, perhaps a husband and children."

She shouldn't listen, for his words stirred up emotions best left alone. "Have you been talking to Phoebe?"

"No." Jason's reply was instantaneous. "I don't frequent her establishment, and she's not a client, so I have no reason to speak with her. Why did you think I did?"

"Because she said almost the same thing this morning."

Jason was silent for a moment, but his gaze never left Elizabeth's. "Is that one of the reasons you were upset when you returned?"

"No." Elizabeth paused, considering the question, not liking the answer that echoed through her brain. "I don't think so."

"I want to have a party," Tabitha Chadwick told her husband. Nelson had just arrived home from the lumberyard and was changing into the formal attire that she insisted on for dinner. This was the one time of the day when she knew she would have his almost undivided attention. "I want a party that will make everyone forget that soiree Miriam and Richard hosted." It had been downright annoying the way people kept talking about that evening. Oh, it was true that the Taggerts' mansion was even larger than Tabitha's, and the music had been pleasant, but surely Cheyenne's society matrons knew that she was a more accomplished hostess.

It hadn't been easy, living next door to Amelia Taggert. Though the woman had never actually snubbed her, Tabitha had the feeling she was looking down that aristocratic nose of hers. The old cow. She was probably worried that her husband would take more than a neighborly interest in Tabitha. As if she'd be interested! If there was one thing Tabitha had learned in the years she'd been married to Nelson, it was that she'd never again look at an older man.

"Will a party make you happy, my dear?" Nelson slid a cuff link into his shirt.

The only thing that would make her truly happy would be if he died, leaving her a wealthy widow, but the party would be an amusement. "Of course, darling." Though she forced a sweet tone to her voice, inside Tabitha was shrieking a denial. She should not have married Nelson. It had been more difficult than she had expected, pretending even the slightest affection for this old man. But the deed was done. Now she had to make the best she could of it, and that included showing everyone who mattered that she was the city's premier hostess. By the time Tabitha was done, Amelia Taggert would be green with envy.

"We'll invite Richard and Miriam and her parents," she said while Nelson tugged on his waistcoat. The man had developed a bit of a paunch, and it was decidedly unattractive. "We'll show them what a real party is. And," she added as if it were an afterthought, "I suppose we should invite Oscar and Jason." Just because she was tied to Nelson didn't mean she couldn't surround herself with young, attractive men. Oscar and Jason weren't merely attractive; they were downright handsome. Even after the Adam Bennett debacle, Jason was still one of Cheyenne's most sought-after guests, second only to Oscar.

Tabitha smiled. Jason had refused many invitations, but he wouldn't refuse Nelson. His presence alone would cement Tabitha's reputation. By now the old biddies would have forgotten about the Adam Bennett affair; all they'd remember was that Jason was one of the city's most handsome bachelors. Tabitha's smile broadened as she thought about the seating arrangement. She'd place them next to her at dinner. If anyone asked, she would claim it was because Oscar was Nelson's most trusted employee and Jason his attorney. The truth was, she wanted virile men near her, if only for the length of a meal.

The expression Nelson gave her made Tabitha think he had read her thoughts. Absurd! The man saw only what he wanted to see, and that was a devoted wife.

"If you invite Jason, you'd better invite Dr. Harding too."

"Why on earth would I do that?" Not only was the woman almost as beautiful as Tabitha, but Jason had driven the meddling doctor home from Richard and Miriam's party, and he'd accompanied her to the Cheyenne Club's celebration. It hadn't meant anything, of course. He was merely being polite. Still, Tabitha had no intention of seeing Jason and Elizabeth together, much less being the reason they were in the same room.

Nelson's eyes narrowed, and once again Tabitha had the unsettling feeling that he knew what she had been thinking.

"They seem to be spending a lot of time together," he said, never letting his gaze stray from her face. "I saw them riding in Jason's carriage earlier today."

It had to have been business. Tabitha couldn't imagine that Jason found anything attractive about that lady doctor. She was pretty enough, but once she opened her mouth, vinegar spilled out. Jason couldn't like that.

Knowing better than to argue with her husband, Tabitha nodded and said sweetly, "Whatever you say, darling." In the meantime, she'd learn what she could about Jason and the doctor. If there was anything to the story of their being together, she would discover it, and then she'd find a way to destroy their relationship. Jason deserved better than Elizabeth Harding.

When dinner was over and Nelson had retired to his smoking room, Tabitha summoned her maid.

"Camille, I want you to find out everything you can about Dr. Harding. Tell me everything you learn, no matter how insignificant it may seem."

The maid nodded. "Yes, ma'am."

The only good thing he could say about this party was that Elizabeth was here. Jason frowned as he looked around the ballroom, waiting for the interlude before the dancing began to finally end. He hadn't wanted to come and had in fact penned his regret, but when Elizabeth had mentioned receiving an invitation, he'd torn up his note and sent Tabitha Chadwick a brief message, saying he would be pleased to attend. That might have been true if he were spending the evening with Elizabeth. When he'd offered to drive her to the Chadwick mansion, he'd thought they would remain together. That hadn't happened.

For some reason, Oscar Miller seemed determined to

monopolize her. The instant they'd set foot inside the huge parlor that had been turned into a ballroom, Oscar had insisted he would be Elizabeth's partner for the first dance. Jason had thought he'd share that with her, but when he started to protest, Elizabeth had told him he could have the last. The way her eyes had sparkled when she'd said that told him she thought there was something special about the last dance. Jason had never put any special significance to the evening's finale, but if that was the way Elizabeth felt, he'd make certain the dance was special. Very special.

"We need to talk." Richard gestured toward the currently unoccupied dining room. "Let's go there." When they were far enough inside that their voices would not be overheard, Richard made his announcement.

"You ought to marry her."

Jason stared. His friend sounded like Harrison Landry, perhaps taking his place, since Harrison was not among the list of attendees at Nelson and Tabitha's gathering.

"She's not interested." There was no point in feigning ignorance of the object of Richard's suggestion.

Richard's narrow face seemed even thinner than usual as he frowned. "The rumors have started," he said, keeping his voice low. "I don't know how it happened, but I overheard Oscar telling a couple of his cronies that Dr. Harding was no better than she needed to be."

Clenching his fists, Jason wished he didn't know what Oscar meant by that particular phrase. It wasn't true. He knew it. Just as he knew that he would bash in the man's face if he dared to repeat such a vile rumor.

"He didn't mention your name specifically," Richard continued, "but he left enough hints that anyone could guess."

"That's ridiculous, and you know it."

"I know what really happened—or, in this case, what didn't happen. So do you, so does Elizabeth. Unfortunately, what matters is what everyone else believes. Truth doesn't necessarily play any part in that."

The anger that flared through him startled Jason with its intensity. How dare someone impugn Elizabeth's honor? That was bad enough, but the scurrilous nature of the attack was even worse. A true man would have confronted her, not filled the room with insinuations.

"I'll make him retract it. And then I'll give him a thrashing he won't forget."

Richard grabbed his arm and pulled him back. "You can't do that, Jason. Don't you see, that's what he's counting on, that someone will tell you and you'll react. If you do, it'll only confirm Oscar's story. That would hurt Elizabeth even more."

Jason hated the fact that Richard was correct. "It's not fair. Elizabeth's a good doctor and an honorable woman."

"I agree, but as I told you before, what you and I know isn't as important as what others believe."

"So, what can I do other than smash every bone in Oscar Miller's body?"

The orchestra had ceased its endless tuning and had begun the first dance, the dance that Elizabeth would share with that despicable cur. Jason wanted to rush into the parlor and pull her away from Oscar, but Richard was right. That would play into Oscar's hands.

Richard's expression remained solemn. "If you want to help, you can marry Elizabeth or at least court her for a while. That'll give the gossips something else to chew on. You know there's nothing they like as much as a romance."

224

"Marriage?" He couldn't marry Elizabeth. She wasn't ready to give up her practice, and he couldn't—wouldn't—marry a woman who would be only a part-time mother.

"Or courtship."

Jason took a deep breath, willing his anger at Oscar to subside as he considered Richard's suggestion. The thought of courtship—a temporary courtship until the nasty rumors had subsided and Cheyenne's gossips found other grist for their mill—was oddly appealing. Elizabeth was beautiful, intelligent, and fun to be with. She challenged him in ways no other woman had ever dared, and though it wasn't always comfortable to be on the receiving end of her criticism, she was equally lavish with her praise.

Elizabeth was unlike any woman Jason had met. If circumstances were different, if she weren't wedded to her profession, he might court her in truth. But for a while at least, he would take Richard's advice. He would do what he could to deflect rumors.

As he felt the anger drain from him, Jason smiled. Courting Elizabeth wouldn't be so bad. As for marriage . . . there was no need to rush into that.

The man was disgusting. He was wearing some kind of cologne that made Elizabeth's eyes water. That was bad enough. Even worse was the way he held her too close. Worst of all was the way he leered at her. Her gown was not provocative. The neckline was demure; gloves covered her hands and most of her arms. There was no reason he should be staring at her as if he were a starving man and she a roast chicken. Would this dance never end?

Though it was probably only a few minutes, it felt like hours later when Elizabeth heard the final strains of the waltz. At last! She prepared to get as far from Oscar Miller as she could. The instant he released her, she would escape. But as the music died, instead of lowering his arms, he drew her closer, propelling her into the hallway.

"I thought the dance would never end," he said, his hazel eyes glinting with an expression that made Elizabeth's skin crawl. "I've never met a woman who could flirt with just her eyes the way you do. Yours told me you want this as much as I do." Before Elizabeth could respond, he lowered his head, his pursed lips leaving no doubt that he intended to kiss her.

"No!" She broke away from him. Though the temptation to run was strong, Elizabeth's instincts told her he would consider that part of the game. Instead she forced herself to look him in the eye as she said, "You are sadly mistaken if you believe that I would welcome a kiss or any form of attention from you. I don't know what other women have told you, but I find you repulsive."

"Aw, c'mon, sweetheart." He grasped her arm, preventing her from fleeing. "All I want is what you've been giving to the others."

As the implication of his words registered, Elizabeth felt bile mingle with the anger that was coursing through her. "That insinuation is not worthy of a reply."

Wrenching her arm from his grip, she spun on her heel. It would have been a more effective gesture, Elizabeth reflected five minutes later as she sat in the ladies' retiring room, a needle and thread in her hand, if she'd been a bit more graceful. That impetuous spin had resulted in her catching her heel on her skirt and ripping the ruffle.

"There you are." Miriam's face brightened as she entered the room and saw Elizabeth. "I wondered where you'd gone."

Elizabeth pointed to the ruffle she was attempting to re-attach to one of Charlotte's masterpieces. "My skirt needed a minor repair." And she had needed the time to let her anger subside.

"I saw you dancing with Oscar." Miriam gave her a questioning look.

"I'd appreciate it if you wouldn't mention that man's name in my hearing."

A chuckle greeted her words. "He is a loathsome creature, isn't he? I don't understand it. Nelson's the finest man you could hope to meet—other than Richard and my father, of course. I can't imagine why he chose Oscar as his foreman."

Elizabeth didn't know, and she didn't care. All she cared about was staying as far away from Oscar Miller as possible.

"There were rumors that Tabitha insisted on it," Miriam said, her voice thoughtful.

After she secured the final stitch, Elizabeth looked up. "I don't put much stock in rumors."

Miriam raised an eyebrow. "Perhaps you should. Rumor has it that Oscar plans to court you."

15

"How could you do it?" Tabitha glared at the man who sat next to her, a plate heaped with scrambled eggs, bacon, and freshly baked biscuits in front of him. Oscar had joined her and Nelson for what had become a weekly tradition of sharing a leisurely Sunday breakfast. Today, however, Nelson had left after eating only a few bites. Though she doubted it was possible that he'd read her mind and known that she wanted time alone with Oscar, she was grateful for her husband's departure. Now she could tell Oscar everything that had been simmering in her mind since the previous evening's party.

"You were practically drooling over her," she said, her voice harsh with the memory. "I've never seen such a disgusting sight."

Apparently unfazed by her anger, Oscar took another bite of bacon, chewing carefully before he replied. "What's the matter, Tabitha? If I didn't know better, I would think you were jealous. But why would you be? You got what you wanted." He gestured at the breakfast room with its imported wallpaper and the furniture that had once graced a French chateau. "You're Mrs. Nelson Chadwick, one of Cheyenne's most illustrious society matrons."

Tabitha started to choke on her coffee. When she'd managed to swallow it, she turned back to Oscar. "You make that sound like a disease."

"Perhaps it is. It doesn't seem to make you happy." Oscar split a biscuit, then dabbed a heaping spoonful of jam on one half. "You're not the fun-loving girl you were before you married Nelson." Stuffing the biscuit into his mouth, he stared at Tabitha while he chewed. "Do you ever wonder what it would have been like if you'd married me?" he asked when he'd swallowed the last bite.

Every day, but that was something she had no intention of admitting. "There's no need to wonder," Tabitha said, keeping her voice as cool as ice. "I know exactly what it would be like. We'd both still be poor." And that was unthinkable.

Oscar's eyebrows rose, as if he had read her mind. "I won't deny that rich is better than poor, but I miss your kisses."

And she missed kissing him. Oh, how she missed that. "You can still have them. You don't have to chase after the doctor."

"I'm afraid not." Though she read the regret in his eyes, Oscar's tone was steely. "I may not have the highest scruples in the world—I proved that when I took the job you arranged for me—but I won't stoop so low as to dally with another man's wife." Oscar took another sip of coffee. "You don't need to worry about the doctor, though. She was just a diversion. I thought it would be entertaining to see how you and Jason Nordling reacted. Now I know. You're both jealous."

"Of course I am. You're mine." Oscar was the only man

Tabitha had ever loved. It was true that Jason was handsome, but he didn't make her heart race the way Oscar did.

He shook his head. "That's where you're wrong. You made your choice, and now you belong to Nelson. My boss." Oscar practically spat the words. "I won't dishonor him."

Clenching her fork, Tabitha stared at Oscar, searching for a way to convince him. "Why not? It's not as if Nelson would care. He has no compunction about breaking his wedding vows."

Oscar blinked, his surprise evident. "Nelson? Never!"

Tabitha started to laugh until she remembered that what Oscar hated most was to be ridiculed. She curled her lip and hoped he would realize the scorn was directed at her husband. "You think Nelson's some kind of saint? Hah! He visits a whore at least once a week, sometimes more often. I wouldn't be surprised if that's where he is right now."

Though he'd appeared to be enjoying his meal, Oscar pushed the plate aside as if he'd lost his appetite. "I can't believe it. Who is she?"

"I don't know, and I don't care." Oscar's expression said he didn't believe her. "Why should I care? Nelson is giving me what I want—money and a respected position in society. If you weren't so prudish, you could give me love."

Heedless of the fact that etiquette demanded he wait for her to rise, Oscar pushed back his chair and got to his feet. "I'm sorry to disappoint you, Tabitha. Regardless of how Nelson may or may not be spending his evenings, there will be nothing other than simple friendship between you and me so long as you're Nelson's wife."

Tabitha rose. Placing her hand on Oscar's arm and giving him her warmest smile, she looked up at him. "You'll change your mind," she said, stroking his arm. "I can make you change your mind."

He pulled his arm from her grip and shook his head. "No, you can't."

"Are you heading home?"

Elizabeth turned, her hand still on the doorknob. "Yes." It was a few minutes earlier than usual, but she'd had no patients this afternoon, so there seemed little reason to linger. She had planned to stick her head inside Jason's office to tell him she was leaving, but now there was no need. He was standing next to her door.

"I thought you might enjoy some company on your walk. May I come along?"

Trying to mask her surprise, Elizabeth nodded. "Certainly." Though she and Jason spent at least a few minutes together each day that Elizabeth had office hours, he'd never accompanied her home. Why today? She couldn't point to anything specific, but Jason had seemed different ever since the Chadwicks' party. Perhaps he had heard the rumor that Oscar Miller planned to court her, and his visits were designed to protect her from unwanted advances. Elizabeth did not believe there was any truth to the rumors. Surely no man would pursue a woman who had called him repulsive. Besides, she had seen the way Oscar's gaze followed Tabitha Chadwick. If she were inclined to bet, Elizabeth would wager that Oscar harbored tender feelings for his employer's wife.

Dismissing thoughts of Oscar and Tabitha, Elizabeth smiled at Jason. He crooked his arm and waited until she placed her hand on it, then returned her smile. "Which way shall we go?"

Elizabeth looked north. "I usually take 17th over to Ferguson."

"Then let's go another direction. It's not much farther to head down 16th. Besides, it's a nice day for a stroll with a beautiful woman."

Elizabeth could feel her face flushing. Though she'd never thought Jason was given to flattery, he was mistaken in calling her beautiful. She wasn't. Far from it. She looked across the street, pretending to focus on a mother who was trying to corral two rambunctious children, while she waited for her cheeks to cool.

"What's the matter, Elizabeth? Hasn't anyone told you you're beautiful?"

She turned back to Jason and shook her head. "Charlotte's the beautiful one." Both Mama and Papa had said that. Each of their daughters, they claimed, had her own talents. Charlotte was beautiful and a gifted seamstress. Abigail was adventuresome and a wonderful teacher. Elizabeth was kindhearted and a skilled healer. She knew better than to delude herself about any claim to beauty.

"There I beg to differ. I never met your sister, but I saw her one day when she was inspecting your office. She's pretty enough, and Barrett certainly seemed besotted with her, but she can't hold a candle to you."

The flush deepened. "You're making me uncomfortable," Elizabeth admitted. Although there was something reassuring about Jason's compliments. Unlike Oscar Miller's leering and crude innuendos, Jason's words seemed sincere. Unfortunately, they also reminded her of what she'd forsaken when she'd decided to study medicine. "I'm a doctor," she said firmly.

"But you're also a woman."

Though she couldn't deny that, this was one conversation Elizabeth did not want to continue. It sounded almost like the prelude to courtship, and while she knew that couldn't be the case, for she was the last person Jason would consider wooing, Elizabeth did not like the feeling those thoughts aroused.

"It seemed as if you had more clients than normal today." This was safer ground.

"I've been busy the last few days," he agreed.

"I'm happy for you. I wish I could say the same thing, but I haven't had any new patients all week." Not only that, but two women had missed their scheduled appointments.

Jason's glance slid from hers, but not before Elizabeth noticed his discomfort. "That'll change," he said, his words at odds with his expression. "I imagine medical needs are similar to legal problems: cyclical. I can never predict whether I'll be busy or not. Now, tell me," he said, "what you think of your first autumn in Wyoming."

The forced gaiety in Jason's voice told Elizabeth he was as uncomfortable discussing her practice as she was talking about love and marriage. If they did not find a neutral subject, it would be a long, silent walk—very different from the easy camaraderie they usually shared.

As they crossed Capitol Avenue, Elizabeth pointed at the building that dominated the northwest corner. Three stories tall, with arched windows and a wrought-iron railing on the balcony over the main entrance, it was an impressive sight. Surely it would be a noncontroversial topic of discussion.

"The InterOcean's a beautiful hotel," she said. "Charlotte mentioned that the owner is a former slave."

Jason nodded, his expression once more relaxed. "That's right. Barney Ford. He's turned it into the city's finest hotel.

I've been told that all the traveling dignitaries stay there, even Sarah Bernhardt." Jason smiled as he looked down at Elizabeth, and she knew he'd welcomed her change of subject. "It's a shame you didn't arrive in Cheyenne in time to see her performance in *Fédora*. Even I, who don't speak a word of French, can't forget the way Miss Bernhardt portrayed that poor, doomed princess."

Though Elizabeth had heard of the actress's skill and knew that she'd been in Cheyenne in early June, just a few weeks before Calamity Jane had visited the city, she was unfamiliar with the plot of *Fédora* and told Jason so. "All I know is that Sarah Bernhardt entranced audiences from New York to Cheyenne when she played that role."

"I'll tell you the whole story some other time. The plot is complicated and some critics call it melodramatic, but that didn't stop anyone from enjoying it." Jason tipped his head back toward the hotel that they'd just passed. "Have you eaten at the InterOcean?"

Elizabeth shook her head.

"We'll have to remedy that. The dining room is excellent. When it opened, guests were offered a choice of twenty entrees and more than fifty kinds of desserts." Jason shrugged. "There's a smaller selection now, but everything is delicious. I don't eat there very often, especially since you and I discovered Mr. Ellis's cakes, but whenever I go, I enjoy it." The earlier constraint had vanished as quickly as morning dew under an August sky. Jason gave Elizabeth a smile that warmed her all the way to her toes. "Have I convinced you? Will you be my guest for dinner at the InterOcean next week?"

She nodded, surprised at how much the prospect pleased her. "I'd like that." She wouldn't tell Jason that this would be the first time she'd dined with a man in a public place. That might make him feel awkward, and that was not her intent. Undoubtedly he'd invited her because he found dining alone boring. Perhaps she could return the favor.

"I hate to think of you always eating alone. I wish I could invite you to stay for supper tonight, but I'm not sure Gwen has enough food for an extra person. Perhaps another time?"

The sparkle in Jason's eyes confirmed that Elizabeth had been right in her assumption that he was lonely. "I don't want to impose."

"It's no imposition. Gwen likes to cook, and even more, she loves having people appreciate her food. I'll see if she can be ready tomorrow."

An hour later, with the meal complete and Harrison back in his own apartment, Elizabeth asked Gwen about inviting Jason for supper the next day. Rose was playing quietly in the corner of the parlor while Elizabeth and Gwen enjoyed one last cup of coffee at the dining room table.

Gwen's eyes lit, and she nodded enthusiastically. "He's perfect for you, you know."

Though she was tempted to protest, Elizabeth knew the futility of it. "I won't deny that I enjoy Jason's company," she admitted, "but we're simply friends. I'm not ready for marriage, and Jason . . ." Elizabeth paused, searching for the right words. While she wanted to discourage Gwen's speculation, she did not want to reveal the details of Jason's childhood. She settled for saying, "Jason's not interested in a woman like me."

A knowing smile greeted her words. "You can say that if you like, but I know romance when I see it. I was right about Charlotte and Barrett, and I know I'm right about you and

Jason." Gwen started humming Mendelssohn's "Wedding March."

Realizing there was nothing to be gained by arguing, Elizabeth decided to turn the tables. After draining her cup, she looked at her friend. "What about you and Harrison?" Elizabeth had seen the glances the two gave each other when they thought no one was watching. Gwen looked as if the sun rose and set on Harrison, and he appeared equally smitten with her. Though neither one had mentioned the word love, it shone from their eyes.

"Harrison is the most wonderful man I've met since Mike died. He's warm and caring and he's even managed to win Rose over." A deep sigh accompanied Gwen's admission. "The problem is, he sees me as just a friend. I don't know what to do."

Jason was whistling as he walked toward the livery. Though he'd considered taking the carriage, he'd decided to ride today. It would be faster, and he knew he'd enjoy the time on horseback.

His whistling became more melodic as he reflected on the past few days. This courtship business was easier and more pleasant than he'd expected. For three days now, he'd walked home with Elizabeth. Each day they took a different route, even though that meant traversing a greater distance. Elizabeth didn't seem to mind, and Jason most definitely did not, for each day he learned something new about her.

Something about walking seemed to loosen her tongue. Or perhaps it was only the invigorating fall air. Whatever the reason, Elizabeth seemed more open and—dare he say it?—happier. Jason was happier too, for according to Richard, the ugly rumors Oscar had tried to spread appeared to have died, and at least so far, no one had begun speculating on the reason Jason was spending more time with Elizabeth. That would change once they'd dined at the InterOcean. In the meantime, he would enjoy learning more about Cheyenne's newest physician.

The day he'd told her the story of *Fédora's* tragic ending, Jason had seen Elizabeth's lips droop into a frown, and he'd realized that she was more sentimental than she might admit. Supper with Gwen, Rose, and Harrison had revealed a different facet to Elizabeth. Watching the gentle way she talked to Rose and the affectionate gestures she gave the little girl told Jason that whether or not she would admit it to herself, Elizabeth loved children, and not just as a doctor, a friend, or even an aunt. There was something distinctly maternal about the way she watched Rose, and—to Jason's surprise—seeing her tenderness toward the child touched something deep inside him. Perhaps a husband and children weren't as far from Elizabeth's mind as she claimed.

He took a deep breath as he headed out of the city, reveling in the fresh air and the open spaces. Though tumbleweeds danced across the prairie, causing his horse to shy when one came too close, Jason's grin only grew. For him there was nothing as beautiful as the vast expanse of Wyoming. It was no wonder men like Kevin Granger stayed, even though tragedy might have sent him back East. Farming in a settled area would have been easier than raising sheep in Wyoming, particularly with the increasing hostility between the cattle ranchers and sheep men, but Kevin had told Jason he was determined to raise his daughters here, on the land he and his beloved Ruby had chosen.

That was why Jason was on horseback today. He'd finished drafting the will, all except for the name of the guardian, and though he could have waited for Kevin to return to his office, he'd decided to save the man a trip into town. But the more important reason for his ride was to view the land Kevin treasured.

Jason tugged the reins when he saw wagon ruts leading to the left. Although no sign marked the entrance, he was certain this was the Granger ranch, Kevin and Ruby's special place. Jason looked around as he approached the farmhouse. To his eyes, there was nothing distinctive about the land. It looked like the rest of the prairie he'd traversed. And yet Kevin claimed there was no place on Earth more beautiful.

The small house was pleasant. Only one story high, perhaps in deference to the strong winds that swept across the land most of the year, it appeared to have two additions to the rear. The chimney on one suggested it was a kitchen, while Jason suspected that the other provided expanded sleeping quarters. A family with three children needed more space than the original building afforded.

Hitching his horse to the railing, Jason admired the porch that lined the front of the house. Though not deep, it held two full-sized rocking chairs and three smaller ones. A pang of regret stabbed Jason when he realized that one of those rockers would remain empty, for he could not imagine Kevin sitting there with his daughters, accompanied by their housekeeper.

Jason gave the front door a brisk knock. "Mr. Granger. Kevin. It's Jason Nordling," he called when there was no answer.

A few seconds later, heavy footsteps followed by softer ones announced the approach of Kevin and at least one of his daughters. "Come in." Kevin swung the door open and ushered Jason into his house. As Jason had surmised, one of the girls stood at her father's side, her eyes wide with curiosity. Jason tried to mask his own curiosity at Kevin's attire. Though the man wore his normal work pants and shirt, he had a ruffled apron tied around his middle.

Kevin shrugged, as if he'd noticed the direction of Jason's glance. "As you can see, I'm fixing dinner for the girls and me. There's plenty if you'd care to join us."

Though Jason hadn't intended to do more than deliver the will, his stomach growled, reminding him that it had been hours since he'd eaten. "Something smells delicious."

Kevin led the way through the front room, which apparently doubled as parlor and dining room, to the kitchen where a pot, redolent with some kind of spices, was simmering. Jason's stomach grumbled again. Judging from the aroma, the stew promised to be as good as Gwen's, and the smell of baking bread caused his mouth to water.

"You look surprised." Kevin offered a crooked grin as he introduced his daughters to Jason. Rachel, the one who'd accompanied Kevin to the door, appeared shy, but her older sister Rebecca greeted Jason solemnly, while baby Ruby banged a wooden spoon against the tray of her high chair. All three girls shared their father's dark brown hair and brown eyes, and Jason suspected they'd inherited their snub noses from their mother.

"Actually, I am surprised," he admitted. "I thought you had a housekeeper."

Kevin shrugged. "I did, but it turned out that three young girls were too much for her. They put up a big fuss every time I left, crying to beat the band. The housekeeper got so frazzled she left, and the next two didn't last a week. That's why we're muddling along by ourselves now." When Jason raised an eyebrow, wondering how a rancher managed to work with three children nearby, Kevin continued. "They stay in the corral while I'm working close in. When I have to go any distance, I take the wagon instead of riding, and they sit in the back. It's not perfect, but it's better than worrying about what's happening when I'm gone."

Jason couldn't help wondering what his life would have been like if his father had done something similar. The times the reverend had let Jason accompany him had been special, but they'd also been rare.

"I think you made the right decision," he told the rancher. Then, not wanting to continue that discussion, he sniffed appreciatively and asked Kevin who had taught him to cook. "I never learned how," Jason admitted. "Both my father and the housekeeper claimed it was women's work."

Kevin shrugged as he pulled four plates from one of the open shelves, directing the two older girls to carry only one at a time. The baby gurgled contentedly from her perch in the high chair. "Work is work. When Ruby and I were first married, before the babies arrived, we used to do most things together. She'd help me with the sheep, and I'd lend a hand around the house. Cooking and cleaning go a lot faster when there are two of you."

Jason had never thought of it that way. There had never been any suggestion that he or his father would assist Mrs. Moran with chores like cooking and cleaning. Jason had helped in the stable, mucking out stalls and grooming the horse, but Mrs. Moran had milked the cow, gathered the eggs, and done all the household work.

"The way you and Ruby worked together sounds a bit like a partnership."

Kevin nodded. "That's the way we figured it. It was a mighty fine way to live, because it gave us more time together. Of course, it's not so good when one of the partners is gone." Sorrow filled his eyes as he gestured toward the stove. "I keep remembering how we used to cook together. Ruby taught me everything I know about cooking, and I taught her how to shear a sheep."

Jason tried to picture Elizabeth shearing a sheep. Although the image of what her first attempts would be like was amusing, he suspected that if she set her mind to it, she would become a proficient shearer.

"Was Ruby good at it?" he asked.

Kevin shrugged. "Not really, but that didn't stop her from trying. I know she tried just so we could be together. That made it special, even if the sheep got a few more nicks than they should have." He stared out the window. "You probably don't think much of this place. It probably looks like an ordinary ranch to you, but this is the place where Ruby and I lived and loved. That makes it beautiful to me."

"Don't you find it painful, being here without her?" Jason regretted his words the instant they were spoken. What kind of a man was he, reminding another of his loss?

"It is," Kevin admitted, "but don't get me wrong. Even though Ruby and I had a lot less time together than we'd expected, I wouldn't have traded what we had for anything. She was one special lady."

Like Elizabeth.

16

G wen."

She turned, so startled by the sound of his voice that her knife slipped, gouging the cake she'd been frosting. Her heart pounding, Gwen stared at Harrison. "What's wrong?" Normally she would have heard the sound of footsteps on the stairs or the door opening, but somehow she'd been so preoccupied that she had been unaware of his approach. Harrison stood just inside the kitchen door, a perplexed expression on his face.

He shook his head, perhaps at Gwen's question, perhaps at the mess she'd made of their dessert. "You certainly know how to take a man down a peg. Do you think the only reason I come here is to eat or carry bad tidings?"

Though she hadn't expected it, his blue eyes reflected something that could have been pain. "I didn't mean to insult you." Far from that. The hours Gwen spent with Harrison were the highlight of her days. Usually her time with him was limited to meals, but today for some reason, Harrison was here barely an hour after noon.

"Shall we start over?" As a smile crossed his face, Gwen returned it, pleased to see the pain—if that's what it was— fading. "Good afternoon, Harrison. It's a pleasure to see you." And it was. He looked different today. His hair was freshly cut, and that was a new shirt he was wearing. If she hadn't known better, Gwen would have thought today was a special day.

His smile broadened as he took another step into the apartment. "That's better. It's a pleasure to see you too." He looked around, his eyes skimming over the small room. "Where's Rose?"

"Taking a nap. She rarely does that, but she seemed more tired than usual today, so I put her to bed." That had given Gwen the unexpected opportunity to frost a cake without Rose's constant pleas for a taste.

"Then perhaps my plan should be postponed." Harrison fixed his gaze on Gwen. "I have a favor to ask of you—a big favor."

Gwen swirled the frosting, trying to hide the gouge she'd made, then laid the knife down, resisting the urge to lick it. The cake wasn't perfect, but it would have to do.

"I'll help you any way I can." Though she couldn't imagine what possible assistance she could provide, she'd never refuse him.

"You know I was looking for a ranch where I could raise horses." When she nodded, Harrison continued. "I found one that looks promising, but before I buy it, I wondered if you and Rose would visit it. I'd like your opinion."

Gwen's heart began to pound at the thought that this man,

this wonderful man, wanted her opinion. "Today? What about the store?" It had been only a few weeks since Landry Dry Goods had opened, and Harrison had reported that the early surge of customers continued.

"Daniel can take care of it. I really want you and Rose to see the ranch today."

He sounded sincere, and that made Gwen's pulse surge. "I don't know a lot about ranches," she cautioned him.

"But you do know about houses. That's where I need help."

Gwen glanced at the parlor clock. "Rose should be waking any minute." It had already been half an hour, and that was usually the limit of her daughter's naps.

As if on cue, Rose emerged from the room they shared, rubbing sleep from her eyes. "Mama, why is Mr. Landry here? It's not suppertime yet."

"No, it's not. He wants to take us on a ride. Would you like that?" It was a rhetorical question, for Rose would do anything to be close to a horse.

"Oh yes!" She flashed Harrison her brightest smile. "Let's go now."

"I hope you won't regret this. My daughter can be a bit rambunctious," Gwen said as she gathered coats and bonnets for herself and Rose. Though the October sun was bright, the air would cool quickly as the afternoon progressed.

"I don't mind." While Rose scampered down the stairs, Harrison and Gwen followed more slowly. "I thought we'd take the wagon," he said, pointing toward the street where his horse was hitched. "The ranch is about three quarters of an hour from here. I figured Rose would be happier in the back."

She was. Rose had insisted on bringing her doll with her and spent the time pointing out sights to the doll while Gwen simply enjoyed being with Harrison. "Tell me about the ranch," she said when they'd left the city, headed east. For a second as they'd driven south on Ferguson, she'd feared that the ranch Harrison wanted to buy was the one where she'd spent the worst night of her life. When he turned east, the sickening dread had drained away. That ranch had been west of the city. She would never have to see it again.

"It's not big, at least not by Wyoming standards," Harrison said with a self-deprecating smile. "Only forty acres, but the grass looks rich, and there's a small creek. The owner said it has water all year." The enthusiasm in Harrison's voice left no doubt that he was excited about the prospect of the ranch. "The house is smaller than I would have liked, but I can always add to it."

"How much space does one man need?" she asked. Harrison had told Gwen that he didn't intend to hire help, that he would raise only as many horses as he could handle by himself.

His jaw tightened and he looked away for a moment. When his eyes met Gwen's again, his expression was hooded, and his voice sounded almost strangled as he said, "I was hoping I wouldn't be living there alone."

"Of course." No wonder Harrison was so ill at ease. It had to be awkward for him to refer to a future wife in front of another woman. It was more than awkward for Gwen. It was painful. And so she turned toward the back of the wagon under the guise of checking on Rose.

When she had regained her composure, Gwen asked Harrison about the breeds of horses he planned to raise. The conversation remained on safe ground until they arrived at the ranch. Other than the small house and a couple outbuildings, there was no sign of habitation. Though the sole spindly tree near the house had lost its leaves, the row of cottonwoods whose presence marked the banks of the stream had a few leaves clinging to their gnarled branches.

"The owners moved back East," Harrison said as he helped Gwen down from the wagon, "but they left most of their furnishings." He looked at Rose, who was racing toward the outbuildings, her feet churning up dust. "Is it all right to leave her outside while we go in?"

Gwen nodded as she studied the house that Harrison planned to share with his bride. Though it had once been white, the sun and wind had taken their toll on the modest structure, leaving it in need of at least one coat of paint. Had it been her home, Gwen would have added a porch on the east side. Protected from the wind, it would be a pleasant spot to linger after supper, talking about the day that had just passed, making plans for the next.

"What do you think?" To Gwen's surprise, Harrison sounded almost nervous.

Unsure of what to say, she told him the truth. "It needs a porch."

"A porch?"

"Yes. With a swing." Gwen's eyes narrowed as she envisioned herself sitting on that swing. It wouldn't happen, but it didn't hurt to dream.

Harrison inclined his head. "I like that idea. A porch swing makes a house a home."

It was silly to feel so elated, simply because he shared her opinion, but Gwen's spirits rose and she was smiling as they entered the house. Though not much larger than the apartment she shared with Elizabeth, it felt more spacious, perhaps because the walls were whitewashed rather than being papered. The interior consisted of one large room that served as a parlor and dining room, with a medium-sized bedroom on one side and a kitchen grafted onto the back.

Looking at the scarred table and chairs and the straight-backed upholstered chairs that created a sitting area in the parlor, Gwen wondered about the people who had lived here. What dreams had brought them here, and why had they left? Though there was something sad about the half-furnished house, the rooms also seemed filled with possibility. Perhaps that was what had attracted Harrison.

"It's very nice," she said honestly. "All you need are some curtains and rugs and it'll feel like home." As she pronounced the words, Gwen's mind conjured the picture of red gingham curtains and a braided rag rug in the dining area, solid red curtains and a hooked rug in the parlor. A couple soft pillows would transform the uncomfortable-looking upholstered chairs into a pleasant sitting area, while a brightly colored quilt would enliven the bedroom. It wouldn't take much to turn this into a real home.

Her mind whirled with the image of herself hanging those curtains, then laughing when Harrison didn't notice the difference. Mike hadn't cared how she decorated their house, and she suspected Harrison would be no different. *Silly girl*, she chastised herself. *There's no point in dreaming about things that will never happen.* "It's a nice house," she said after she cleared her throat.

Harrison pursed his lips. "There's no room for children, though."

Children. Of course. He would want children as well as a wife. "You'll have plenty of time before a baby arrives," Gwen said as calmly as she could, while all the while her stomach roiled. She gestured toward the south wall. "You can put a door there. Once you open the wall, the room can be as big as you want. You could even have two rooms if you have a lot of children." She absolutely would not picture Harrison holding an infant in his arms, smiling at the baby, then giving the child's mother a loving look.

Oblivious to her inner distress, Harrison seemed to relax. "So you like it? Would you be comfortable living here?"

It was a rhetorical question. Gwen wouldn't delude herself into thinking he meant anything special by it. She'd made that mistake before, believing that a man cared for her and wanted to marry her. She wouldn't fall into that trap again.

"It's a lovely home, Harrison." By some miracle, her voice sounded bright and cheerful. "Any woman would be happy to live here."

Though she'd thought she had managed to allay his fears, he still looked dubious. "Mrs. Rodgers wasn't. That's why they moved back East. She hated the wind and being so far from town."

"That's unfortunate for her and her husband, although it's good for you, isn't it?" Gwen walked to the west window to check on Rose. As she'd expected, her daughter was walking more slowly now, but she appeared to be studying everything about the ranch. Gwen wouldn't be surprised to learn that Rose was counting blades of grass. Of course, she couldn't count very high, so that pastime was often a frustrating one.

Gwen turned around and smiled at Harrison. "It's amazing how different we all are. I grew up on a farm. I was so used to open spaces that it was an adjustment when Mike and I lived at Fort Russell. I wasn't comfortable having so many people so close, but I adjusted. I'm sure your wife will too." Gwen wouldn't think about how often she'd dreamed about being that woman. No matter how deeply she cared about him, she knew that a man like Harrison Landry would never marry a woman like her. "I'd better check on Rose," she said, though there was no need.

Deliberately pushing thoughts of Harrison's wife aside, Gwen resolved to enjoy the rest of the afternoon, and she did. Rose was happier than Gwen had seen her in months. Just running from the barn to the house to the chicken coop seemed to thrill her, and when Harrison showed her where he planned to locate the corral, she was ecstatic, begging him to bring her back when the horses arrived. The sparkle in Rose's eyes and the color in her cheeks told Gwen that her daughter loved the outdoors. If this were their home, Rose would thrive here. But it wasn't, and Gwen had to remember that.

She looked at Harrison. He'd lifted Rose onto his shoulders when the child had, in typical Rose fashion, declared that the view would be better if she were taller. Once perched on his shoulders, in another change of mood so characteristic of Rose, she had decided that Harrison was a horse and that he should take her for a ride. He'd acceded to her demand, trotting around the house once. Now he placed her back on the ground, saying firmly, "That's enough for today. This is an old horse."

While Rose scampered off to the chicken coop, Gwen darted a glance at Harrison. Perhaps it was her imagination, but he still seemed nervous. He'd been his old self while he was playing with Rose, but now that he was alone with Gwen, he seemed ill at ease. That was unlike Harrison, but today was unlike any other time they had spent together. He must have felt as uncomfortable talking about his future wife as Gwen had knowing she was passing judgment on another woman's home. No way around it, it was an awkward situation.

Though he hadn't mentioned her before, Harrison's prospective bride must be someone from his home in Pennsylvania. If she had been a local resident, he would have brought her out to see the ranch. Gwen sighed at the realization that the only reason he'd asked for her opinion was that he wanted a woman—any woman—to see the house and land before he bought it.

And yet, hours later, Gwen could not forget how beautiful the ranch had been. Others might claim that it was simply a piece of land and a small house, but it had seemed like so much more. When she'd been there, Gwen had felt as if she'd come home. The ranch would be the perfect place for both Rose and her. If only . . .

Though she knew that it was probably too late, that any changes she might make were futile, for Harrison had already chosen his bride, Gwen reached for the bottle. Perhaps if she took another dose of the medicine, that ugly lump of fat around her waist would go away and Harrison would see her for what she was: the woman who loved him.

No matter how often she told herself to be calm, Elizabeth could not recall the last time she'd looked forward to anything as much as she was dinner tonight. She smiled as she gazed at the pale blue silk gown that lay across her bed, waiting for her to don it. With its matching gloves and the ribbon that she'd threaded through her hair, it was an ensemble fit for a princess. Thanks to Charlotte, Elizabeth would be well-dressed for her dinner at the InterOcean. Thanks to Jason, she had the excitement of anticipating her first public meal with a man.

Elizabeth picked up the gown and began to step into the skirt, trying to chase away the memory of the last time she'd seen Miriam. Though Miriam had come to the office for an official visit, conversation had turned to personal matters.

"He's courting you," Elizabeth's patient and friend had said with a knowing smile when she mentioned the invitation to dinner.

Fortunately, Elizabeth had been reaching for her stethoscope when Miriam had made that pronouncement. Her bent head kept Miriam from seeing the blush that stained her cheeks. "Jason isn't courting me any more than Oscar Miller was. Your problem is that you see romance everywhere you look."

Miriam chuckled. "I don't have to look very hard to see you and Jason together. I've seen you walking past Maple Terrace at least three times in the past week."

"It's true that Jason walks home with me every day," Elizabeth admitted, "but I wouldn't call that courting."

"Just what would you call it?"

"Friendship."

Miriam's laugh left no doubt of her opinion. "When a man looks at a woman the way Jason looks at you, friendship is not what's on his mind."

Placing the stethoscope on Miriam's belly to listen to the baby's heartbeat, Elizabeth shook her head. "Jason's a friend. A good friend, but that's all."

"If you say so." And Miriam had laughed again.

The memory of Miriam's laughter still echoing through

her brain, Elizabeth called to Gwen. "I'm ready for you." Though she could manage the skirt without assistance, the bodice was another story. Elizabeth stretched her arms out as far as she could so that Gwen could slide the bodice on. With her corset laced as tight as it had to be for this gown, Elizabeth could not easily complete the rest of her toilette.

She took a shallow breath, her thoughts wandering to Sheila and her unborn child. Though she hoped the woman had put her corsets aside, Elizabeth doubted that was likely, but she hoped Sheila was at least loosening the laces. Charlotte's claim that gowns like this made a woman appear beautiful was correct. They did. The question was, at what cost? Elizabeth knew she would suffer no permanent harm from having her ribs constricted for an evening, but many women, including Sheila, wore their corsets both night and day, believing that a tiny waist was worth any price.

As she stood next in front of the mirror, assuring herself that everything was perfect, Elizabeth caught a glimpse of Gwen's profile. Surely it wasn't her imagination that the woman who shared her apartment was thinner.

"Have you tightened your laces?" she asked.

Gwen shook her head. "Why do you ask?"

"You look thinner."

The smile that lit Gwen's face told Elizabeth she had said precisely the right thing. "And you look beautiful."

Jason echoed Gwen's sentiments when he arrived. Giving a soft whistle, he grinned at Elizabeth. "You look more beautiful than ever tonight."

Elizabeth shook her head. The one who was beautiful was Jason, though she doubted he'd appreciate her telling him that. It wasn't the first time she'd seen him in formal clothing, but Elizabeth never failed to be impressed by how distinguished he looked in his tailcoat and black waistcoat. Though some men appeared uncomfortable in stiff-bosomed shirts, Jason gave no sign of discomfort. To the contrary, his elegant clothing seemed to fit him as well as his more casual daily wear did. Perhaps it was simply that he was comfortable with himself, and clothing was of little importance.

"Beautiful," he said, contradicting her silent protest.

"That's what I told her, but she wouldn't believe me," Gwen chimed in.

Rose tugged on her mother's skirts. "Aunt Elizabeth is pretty."

"See, it's unanimous."

Elizabeth conceded defeat. "Thank you all," she said with a small curtsey. "Charlotte's gowns are designed to make the wearer look beautiful."

Gwen rolled her eyes and turned to Jason. "She's hopeless."

"But beautiful." Jason smoothed the cape over Elizabeth's shoulders and opened the door for her. As they descended the steps, he added, "You're not just beautiful. You're a fine doctor too."

"You're going to turn my head." During the years that she'd been studying medicine, Elizabeth had learned to ignore jeers and insults, but she'd had no experience with compliments, and so they left her feeling slightly disoriented. Still, she couldn't deny that it felt good to be the object of a man's admiration.

Elizabeth smiled as she and Jason were ushered into the InterOcean's dining room. Looking around as the waiter showed them to their table, she noted that the room was as elegant as the exterior of the building had led her to expect.

Highly polished dark paneling covered the lower half of the walls, and the ceiling was coffered with the same wood. Snowy white table linens and shiny wallpaper lightened what could have been an almost depressingly dark room, turning it into a luxurious space that somehow managed to feel intimate, despite its size. It was no wonder this was one of Cheyenne's most popular dining spots.

"The chef is famous for his wild game dishes," Jason told Elizabeth after the waiter presented them with menus.

She wrinkled her nose. "No venison for me tonight," she said, her eyes darting to the upper wall where an impressive ten point buck's head looked down on the diners. "I don't think I'd enjoy a single bite."

"I'm not so squeamish." Jason matched his actions to his words and ordered the roast venison while Elizabeth contented herself with baked trout.

It was the finest meal Elizabeth had ever eaten, made so by a combination of faultless service and exquisitely prepared food. But what set the evening apart was sharing it with Jason. Unlike the first day he'd accompanied her on her walk home, when Elizabeth had found herself searching for a neutral topic, tonight it seemed as if they had an inexhaustible supply of subjects to discuss, everything from music and books to Harrison's plans to start a horse ranch.

"Gwen said the site is beautiful," Elizabeth told Jason.

He nodded as he chewed a bite of the perfectly roasted potatoes that had accompanied both of their entrees. "If she approved it, I imagine Harrison will proceed with the purchase. I know he wanted her and Rose to see it before he signed the agreement." Jason cut another piece of venison, then laid his knife back on the plate. "It's amazing what two people can do with a plot of land out here. I visited one of my clients a few days ago. He raises sheep," Jason explained, "even though a number of people advised him not to. Despite everything, he's prospering. The ranch isn't huge, but what impressed me was that he and his wife built everything themselves. Most folks hire help."

"You sound surprised." The surprise, Elizabeth was willing to bet, was that the client's wife had had such an active role.

"I was. I never really thought of women doing things like roofing a barn."

Had another man made the same comment, Elizabeth might have taken offense, but this was Jason, and she knew he was simply being honest. "Be careful." Her tone was light, almost mocking, as she cautioned him. "You're starting to sound like Doc Worland. Next thing I know, you'll refer to us as the weaker sex. Women are stronger than you realize."

Jason shook his head. "You don't need to convince me. You've shown me that a woman—at least one woman—can do anything she sets her mind to. I think what surprised me was that a woman would want to haul around lumber and nail on a roof."

Though his confidence in her was appealing, Elizabeth couldn't let Jason continue to believe she was a paragon of skills. She wasn't. The truth was, she was lacking in what many men would consider basic womanly talents. Her sewing consisted of the ability to do basic mending, nothing more. As for cooking . . . "I've never hauled lumber or laid a roof. I never had the need, but I suspect it would be easier than learning to cook. I'm a dismal failure at that."

Jason blinked in surprise. "You can't cook?"

"Not well. I can make staples like oatmeal, and I can stew

a chicken, but I seem to burn every roast I put in a pan, and my biscuits and bread verge on inedible."

"You're joking."

"You wouldn't say that if you'd eaten one of my meals. There's a reason my sister convinced Gwen to stay in the apartment. Charlotte didn't want me to starve."

Elizabeth watched Jason closely, wondering how he would react to her revelation. She doubted it was what he'd expected. Most men seemed to think that girls were born knowing how to cook, clean, sew, and raise children. He gave her a long look, his expression as solemn as if he were facing a jury. And then he laughed.

"At last!" There was an unmistakable note of triumph in his voice. "I found something you can't do perfectly." Jason's grin broadened. "You don't know how that reassures me. Everyone needs to have failings."

He'd reacted more positively than Elizabeth had expected. "Cooking is a big failing. If I ever have a house of my own, I won't be able to invite guests for dinner."

"You'd find a way."

Jason's assurance warmed her. "I suppose I could hire a cook." That was what Miriam had done.

"Or maybe your husband would help." Jason chuckled at the sight of her disbelief. "Don't look so surprised. The same client shocked me when he came to the door wearing an apron. He's a widower now, but he said he used to help his wife cook and clean and do laundry. He called their marriage a partnership."

"What an intriguing idea. My parents' marriage was a happy one, but it wasn't like that. They each had their own responsibilities. I can't ever recall Papa being in the kitchen, and Mama would never have presumed to help him with his sermons."

"It was a new concept for me too, but I have to admit that Kevin's stories got me thinking."

"And what do you think?"

Jason wrinkled his nose. "That I'd hate doing laundry."

All too soon, the evening was over, and Elizabeth was back in her room, brushing her hair and preparing for sleep. She had told Gwen about the meal and about the people who'd stopped by their table to greet Jason. What she hadn't told Gwen was that she had added tonight to the images she'd been collecting.

Her mother had had a memory box, a small cedar box that housed mementos. Mama had treasured locks of her daughters' hair, a seashell she had found on the beach the one time Papa had taken her to the ocean, a pressed flower from her wedding bouquet. Elizabeth's treasures were less tangible. She collected memories. Memories of walking with Jason, riding with Jason, sharing one of Mr. Ellis's cakes with Jason. Tonight she'd added the memory of sharing a meal, of laughing at the smell of lye soap, of discussing marriage as a partnership. It was an evening Elizabeth knew she'd never forget. But then she couldn't forget Jason.

She cherished the memory of his hand on hers while they walked, the warmth of his arm next to hers as they rode in his carriage, and the butterfly-light brush of his fingers across her cheek when he'd settled her cloak over her shoulders.

Never before had a man captured her thoughts the way

Jason had. What she felt for him was bright and new, as shiny as freshly fallen snow, as beautiful as a sunrise. How fortunate she was that Jason Nordling was part of her life.

"I heard you're courting Elizabeth." Harrison settled into one of the chairs in front of Jason's desk, making himself comfortable while he waited for Jason's response. Though he had ostensibly come to review the terms of the ranch purchase, it was clear he had other things on his mind.

Jason gave a noncommittal shrug. "Could be." Inside, he rejoiced at the fact that the ugly rumors about Elizabeth had been replaced with more acceptable ones. Richard had been right. This temporary courtship was a good idea. It was protecting Elizabeth, and it had added a new dimension to Jason's life. The time he spent with Elizabeth had quickly become the highlight of his days.

Harrison let out a sigh. "I figured I'd be a bachelor all my life. Now all I can think about is marriage."

"Have you told her how you feel?"

Harrison crossed his ankles, then uncrossed them, putting his feet flat on the floor. A second later, he stretched his legs out again, crossing the ankles. No doubt about it, the man was nervous.

"I'm scared," Harrison admitted. "What will I do if she refuses me?"

"She won't." Gwen would be crazy if she did. It was clear that Harrison was hat over boots in love with her, and the looks she had given Harrison the night Jason had joined them for supper told him the feelings were reciprocated. Even Rose had seemed to approve of Harrison. There was absolutely no reason Jason could imagine that Gwen would refuse Harrison's offer of marriage.

"I wish I were that confident. I tell you, Jason, I've never felt like this before. I can talk a customer into buying things he didn't even know he needed, but I can't figure out how to tell Gwen that I want to marry her."

"You ought to court her. What do you think about a picnic in Minnehaha Park with Elizabeth and me?"

Harrison looked thoughtful. "It would be a treat for Gwen if she didn't have to cook."

"And Rose would have a place to play . . ."

Harrison grinned. "While I sweet-talked her ma. Perfect. You're a genius, Jason."

Or a man searching for ways to spend more time with Cheyenne's lady doctor.

17

I can't go on this way any longer."

Phoebe lowered her eyes, trying to mask the emotions that Nelson's declaration evoked. He was seated next to her on the settee in her boudoir, his hands clasped in his lap. Her own hands threatened to tremble, but she willed them to remain steady as she forced a calm expression onto her face. Despite her determination to keep everything businesslike, Nelson had managed to slip beneath her armor, and somehow during the two years since his first visit he'd developed into more than a paying customer. Phoebe welcomed his visits, not simply because of the generous gifts that he gave her in addition to her normal fee. Over the course of the years, he'd become, first a pleasant companion, next a friend, then the one man who touched her heart. But now that she had finally admitted to herself how deeply she cared for him, he was leaving.

"I'm sorry," she said, proud that her voice did not quaver. "I'll miss our times together, but I understand your reasons."

Tabitha must have learned about his visits and objected to them. Phoebe had no illusions about her importance in Nelson's life. She was a diversion, nothing more. Some wives might turn a blind eye, pretending they didn't know where their husbands spent their evenings, but from what Phoebe had heard, Tabitha Chadwick was not one to forgive a peccadillo. Another man might insist that he had a right to physical pleasure, but not Nelson. He would do anything to placate his young wife.

"I'm sorry." Phoebe repeated the words that only hinted at her true feelings.

To her surprise, Nelson's brown eyes glinted with what appeared to be gratitude. "So you do care—at least a little. I always wondered whether it was all pretense."

Of course it had been pretense at the beginning, but Phoebe wouldn't tell him that. No man wanted to hear that a woman cared only for the money he gave her. A good whore knew that and made each man feel special, pretending that her heart was engaged, when reality was, all she cared about were the coins she would earn. Phoebe couldn't explain why or even when her feelings had changed, but they had. Nelson was no longer simply a customer.

She gave him a gentle smile as she said, "You wouldn't be here if I didn't care for you . . . at least a little." Unwilling to reveal her true feelings, Phoebe forced her smile to turn mocking as she repeated his words. "Very few men have ever entered this suite, and you're the only one who has a key." She extended her left hand, palm up. "Under the circumstances, you'd best return it. You wouldn't want your wife to find it and ask awkward questions."

"Tabitha wouldn't care." Bitterness tinged Nelson's voice.

261

"Furthermore, I don't care if she learns about my visits here. In a few months, she'll have no reason to complain." Phoebe's expression must have revealed her confusion, for Nelson let out a short mirthless laugh. "I can see that you don't understand. I'm not proposing to end my time with you. What I am going to end is my marriage. I can't bear it any longer."

Phoebe didn't bother to hide her shock. Men in Nelson's position did not leave their young and beautiful wives. "You're going to divorce your wife?" Phoebe's voice rose with disbelief. "Do you have grounds?"

As Nelson shook his head, Phoebe noticed that he needed a haircut. If she'd had any doubt how disturbed he was, that would have quenched it. The Nelson she knew was always impeccably groomed.

"I have no proof that Tabitha's been unfaithful, but it's no secret that she's unhappy. If I offer her enough money, she'll agree to a divorce. That's all she ever wanted: my money."

Though Phoebe suspected that Tabitha had also been attracted by Nelson's social standing, now was not the time to mention that. "Are you certain you want to do this?" Phoebe had long thought Nelson would be happier if he hadn't married Tabitha, but she'd never considered that he would reach this point.

He turned so that he was facing her, and his eyes filled with pain. "Why wouldn't I? I'm not happy, and neither is Tabitha. Just being with her is turning into an ordeal. The only things she wants to talk about are clothes and jewelry. If I mention the company, all she wants to know is how much profit I'm making." Nelson let out a sigh. "You're the only one who listens to me."

Phoebe recalled the nights when he had sat right here, his arm wrapped around her shoulders as he spoke of plans for his lumber company. He'd been in no hurry to enter her bedroom but had insisted on spending his time talking. Those were the nights Phoebe cherished. Nelson might not remember it, but it was after the first of those nights that she had given him the key to her suite.

She cared for this man. Oh yes, she did. And because she cared, she had to do what was best for him, regardless of how it affected her.

"Have you told Tabitha you're unhappy?" When Nelson gave her a look that suggested he'd rather be flayed alive than admit his vulnerability to his wife, Phoebe continued, "Marriage vows are sacred. You can't just walk away."

His jaw dropped in astonishment. "I don't believe you're saying that."

"Why? Because I run a bordello?" Of course he would think that a woman who sold her own and other women's bodies would have no regard for marriage vows. That wasn't the case. When she'd moved to Cheyenne and opened her establishment, Phoebe had decided that no one needed to know what had brought her here. As far as anyone in Wyoming was concerned, she was a single girl, planning to make her fortune by trading on men's desires. Though she referred to herself as Mrs. Simcoe, most people assumed it was a courtesy title, and Phoebe didn't bother to enlighten them. There was no reason to reveal her past tonight, and yet this was Nelson, the man she cared for, more than just a little.

"I was married once," she said slowly. "I would still be married, only he died and left me penniless."

Nelson leaned back and studied her, as if trying to determine whether she was telling the truth. "Surely you could have married again."

"There were plenty of men who asked," Phoebe agreed. "The problem was, I didn't love them. I figured marrying one of them would be no better than selling myself, so I did exactly that. This way I have more money than I would as a wife, and I'm not beholden to any man." She had not let another man into her heart since Philip died. Until Nelson.

"Be careful, Nelson," she said, laying her hand on top of his. "You don't want to turn your wife into an enemy."

Elizabeth took in a deep breath, reveling in the glorious day. Though not as bright a blue as it had been in August, the October sky was beautiful. Yesterday's wind had subsided, leaving today calm and warmer than normal. It had been the perfect day to walk to church, and now it was the perfect day for a picnic.

"Did you order this weather?" she asked Jason as they descended the stairs. Both he and Harrison had come to the apartment. Though it seemed unnecessary, Jason had admitted he and Harrison had been unable to decide which of them would escort the women downstairs. Eventually, they'd realized that the best solution was for both of them to do it.

Jason looked as if the thought of placing an order for weather amused him. "Not exactly, but I did tell God I'd be grateful for a nice, warm, calm day."

"I asked for the blue sky," Harrison chimed in from behind them.

"Then we thank you both." An uncharacteristic giggle accompanied Gwen's words. Elizabeth smiled. Her friend was more excited today than she'd ever seen her, and the excitement appeared contagious, for Rose had dashed down the steps and was racing back and forth along the boardwalk, her impatience with the adults visible.

"Horses!" Rose crowed. "Two horses!"

And two carriages. Elizabeth raised an eyebrow as she looked at Jason. "You each brought a carriage?"

He shrugged as if it were of no account. "There's too much food to fit into one."

"I doubt that." Either one of the carriages could transport several large trunks. A single meal for four adults and a child would not require more space than that. There had to be another reason why Jason and Harrison had decided to bring separate conveyances. An ulterior motive.

"Are you questioning my veracity?" Jason asked, feigning indignation.

"I suspect you might have stretched the truth a bit."

Gwen and Rose waved at Elizabeth once they were settled in the first buggy. A few seconds later, Harrison flicked the reins, and they headed south on Ferguson, leaving Elizabeth standing next to Jason.

"The unstretched truth," he said as he handed her into his carriage, "is that I wanted the pleasure of your company . . . alone."

"Oh!" Elizabeth felt warmth rush through her veins. There was no way to respond to a comment like that without blushing, and so she simply smiled.

"I'm glad you were able to come," Jason said as he turned onto 17th Street, apparently taking the concept of privacy to a new level. Since Harrison had continued to 16th, Jason and Elizabeth would not see their friends until they all arrived at the park. "I worried that one of your patients would have an emergency and you'd be with her."

Though that had yet to happen, emergency calls were part of a physician's life, just as they were for a minister. Undoubtedly Jason had memories similar to Elizabeth's of meals and sleep and family activities being disturbed by a parishioner's needs. Those memories combined with being raised by a housekeeper had formed Jason's view of marriage and child rearing. They were the reason he would never be more than her friend.

Pushing aside those thoughts, Elizabeth gave herself up to the pleasure of riding to the park. Minnehaha, Jason explained, was the city's newest park, a mere five years old. "Of course," he said with a laugh, "the city is only twenty years old." Those twenty years had wrought many changes in Cheyenne. As a result of its growth, the city planners had decided there should be a park on the eastern edge and had piped water from Sloan's Lake to create Minnehaha Lake and the lagoons that were now a popular spot for boating.

"It needs trees," Elizabeth announced when they arrived at the park. Though they'd left a minute or so before her and Jason, there was no sign of Gwen and Harrison. Elizabeth suspected that Rose had seen something, perhaps a train, and had wanted to watch it.

Jason shrugged. "The city needed trees too, when it was founded. There wasn't a single one on the prairie when the railroad crew came through. Every one you see now had to be planted and nurtured. And, as you'll discover this winter, that wasn't easy. I'm still amazed that trees survive the winds. Some of the gusts practically knock me over, and I'm a lot sturdier than a sapling." He helped Elizabeth descend from the carriage.

"The trees must be resilient." Though she couldn't explain why, the word *resilient* made Elizabeth's thoughts turn to Sheila. As happened so often, particularly when she was dressing herself, she pictured the young woman and hoped she had followed Elizabeth's advice to put away her corsets. The baby in Sheila's womb would have trouble developing normally if it was constrained by whalebone and metal.

"What's wrong?" Jason's eyes reflected concern.

"I was just thinking about one of my patients and hoping she's all right."

As Harrison's carriage approached, Jason's expression remained solemn. "It's hard to let go, isn't it? There are times when I worry about my clients, especially those I know are in difficult circumstances. Let's try to put them aside today, though. I want this to be a special day." As he pronounced the final words, Jason's lips curved into a smile so genuine that Elizabeth could not help returning it.

Her smile broadened as she watched Rose insisting on being the first out of the carriage. As soon as she was on the ground, the little girl raced to the horse that was still hitched to Jason's carriage and began speaking to it. Gwen and Harrison followed at a more decorous pace, but the flush on Gwen's cheeks left no doubt that she was as excited as her daughter.

"Well, ladies, what would you like to do first?" Jason said, addressing Elizabeth and Gwen. "It's your day. Harrison and I are here to make your every wish come true."

"Eat! I wanna eat!" Though she'd been yards away, apparently intent on her conversation with the horse, Rose had heard Jason's question.

Gwen gave her daughter a fond smile. "I guess you've got your answer."

"And I've got the perfect place." Harrison pulled a blanket from the back of his carriage and spread it on the ground near the lake. Though a number of other families were taking advantage of the warm Sunday afternoon and were strolling around the lagoons and lake that were the park's primary attraction, no one else seemed to be picnicking here.

Harrison gestured at the blanket. "If you ladies would like to sit, Jason and I'll get the food."

"Are you sure I can't help?" Gwen's question left no doubt that she was uncomfortable being waited upon.

"You're our guests," Harrison insisted.

Rose, who'd been watching the exchange intently, tugged on his pant leg. "I can help."

"You're a guest too."

When Rose wrinkled her nose, Harrison relented. "All right." His hand snaked out, as if he were going to pat Rose's head. At the last second, he drew back and laid his hand on her shoulder. "You'll be a big help," he told the little girl.

"Rose seems to have lost her fear of Harrison," Elizabeth said as she arranged her skirts around her legs. Though her family had had occasional picnics in Vermont, it had been a long time since she'd sat on the ground.

"It's wonderful, isn't it?" Gwen straightened a wrinkle from the blanket before she settled onto it. "Sometimes Harrison seems like a different man from the one who visited Barrett last year. That one was gruff, and every time he looked at me, I felt his disapproval."

This was the first time Gwen had said anything like that. "You must have been imagining it. Why would he disapprove?"

"I don't know, but I'm glad it's over."

"I haven't seen anything that resembles disapproval," Elizabeth told her friend. "To the contrary, it appears to me that he's attracted to you."

Gwen stared at the lake, her expression wistful. "I wish that were true, but I don't think it is. He . . ."

Before she could complete her sentence, Rose arrived, holding a plate in each hand. 'Look, Mama. They let me carry the plates."

"I see. That's because you're a big girl." As Rose preened, Gwen held out her hands "Now, give them to Mama."

When Rose had complied, she scampered back to the men.

"Are you certain we can't help?" Elizabeth called out when she saw both Jason and Harrison apparently rummaging in the back of their carriages.

Jason turned. Placing his hand on his hip, as if he were annoyed, he asked, "Aren't we moving fast enough for you? Patience is a virtue, you know."

"It's not that." Although it was true that patience was not her dominant virtue. "I ust thought you might like some assistance."

"Harrison already told you that you're guests, and guests don't work. Besides, we're almost ready."

Matching his actions to his words, Jason hauled a basket from the carriage and brought it to the blanket. Harrison followed with another equally large basket. As they unpacked the bounty, Elizabeth stared in amazement. Fried chicken, baked beans, yeast rolls, apple butter, jars of cool tea and water, and two delicious-looking pies. There was a seemingly endless supply of food.

"Which of you is responsible for this feast?" she asked, her gaze moving from Jason to Harrison and then back.

The two men shared a conspiratorial smile before Jason said, "Both of us."

"You both cooked?" Gwen couldn't hide her surprise.

"Who said anything about cooking?" Jason demanded. "You asked who was responsible. I arranged for one of my clients' wives to prepare the chicken and beans."

"And I recruited the daughter of one of the men who worked on the store to bake."

"Clever!" Elizabeth admired their ingenuity.

"And delicious too," Gwen added. But though she appeared to enjoy the food, Elizabeth noticed that she took no more than a bite of each dish.

"Are you feeling all right?" Elizabeth's voice was little more than a whisper, for she did not want either the men or Rose to overhear her question.

"Of course. Why did you ask?"

"You're not eating much."

"I'm not hungry." The words came out louder than Gwen had probably intended, for Harrison frowned in apparent response and stared at Gwen's plate with its barely touched food.

"I am!" Rose started to reach for another piece of chicken, then stopped to look at Gwen for approval. When Gwen nodded, she grabbed the meat and began to gnaw on it as if she'd been starving.

Elizabeth took another spoonful of beans, smiling when she saw Gwen cut a piece of chicken and place it in her mouth. She must have been mistaken. It was only Elizabeth's imagination that Gwen's appetite seemed diminished, for she accepted a small slice of apple pie and ate every bit.

When the meal was completed and the remains stowed in

the carriages, Harrison suggested a walk. He helped Gwen rise, while Jason extended the same courtesy to Elizabeth. It was nothing more than a polite gesture, and yet the touch of Jason's hand on hers made Elizabeth's pulse accelerate, and the smile he gave her sent waves of warmth flowing through her veins.

Apparently unaffected by their proximity, Jason turned to Rose, who'd started to grab her mother's hand. "Would you like to walk with Aunt Elizabeth and me?"

Harrison shot Jason a grateful smile as Rose shrieked, "Yes!" While her mother and Harrison headed out on one of the paths that ringed the lake, Rose looked longingly at the water. "Can we go in a boat?"

Elizabeth shook her head. "Not today. The water's too cold." Though she'd seen a few boats on the lake, the occupants had been adults, not active children like Rose who'd want to lean over the side and might tumble into the water.

"Is not!" As if to prove it, Rose raced to the edge of the lake and thrust both hands into the water. "It's warm," she insisted. "Please, Mr. Nordling, can we go?"

Jason gave Elizabeth a look that said he was unaccustomed to dealing with a dynamo like Rose. "It's your decision," he told Elizabeth. "Would you like to go boating?" As if on cue, two boats approached, and one looked as if it were going to be docked.

"I don't know how to row," Elizabeth admitted. There was no reason to confide that she'd never been in a boat.

"Then let's remedy that gap in your education." Jason strode toward the water and engaged in a brief conversation with a couple who were in the process of docking their small rowboat. When the man nodded, Jason returned to Elizabeth and Rose. "These nice people have agreed to let us use their boat for a few minutes." He lifted Rose and placed her on the middle bench. "You need to sit quietly. Don't stand up, or you'll rock the boat. Aunt Elizabeth might fall in," he said with an exaggerated frown. "We wouldn't want that, would we?"

"No, sir." She attempted to match his frown but wound up giggling.

A minute later, Elizabeth was seated in the front of the boat facing backward, while Jason plied the oars from the other end. Rowing was quieter than she'd expected. Although there was a rhythmic creak as the oars moved in their locks, the boat made little noise as it glided through the water. Even normally garrulous Rose was silent, as if awed by the fact that she was moving across the lake.

At first it had seemed strange, riding backward and seeing the surroundings only after she'd passed them, but Elizabeth soon discovered there was an advantage to her position: she could watch Jason. He'd removed his coat, and as he rowed, she could see that his arms were well-muscled. It was true that she'd seen his bare arms and chest when he'd been her patient, but this was different. Today she was seeing Jason as a man, a handsome, virile man.

"Do you want to try rowing?" he asked when they'd completed two circuits of the lake and had ventured into one of the lagoons.

Though she was tempted, Elizabeth shook her head. "Another time." Enraptured by the boat, Rose had been remarkably calm, but Elizabeth recognized the signs of impatience returning. It was time for the girl to be on dry land, running.

The middle-aged couple who had lent them the boat

were waiting as Jason docked it. Both were well-dressed, the woman in a gown that bore Charlotte's distinctive double box pleating, the man in a perfectly tailored suit. Both had kind faces, but what drew Elizabeth's attention was the man's moustache. It was longer and more elaborately curled and waxed than any she had seen. She only hoped that Rose, who was notoriously outspoken, would say nothing embarrassing.

Jason took the man aside, and the woman approached Elizabeth, a welcoming smile on her face. "Your daughter appears to like boating." The smile lines that had formed at the corners of the woman's mouth deepened. "I remember when our Anna was that age. She wouldn't have sat still for so long."

"I probably shouldn't admit it, but Rose surprised me. She's not always that well-behaved," Elizabeth said. "She's also not my daughter."

"I wondered. She doesn't resemble either of you."

"Rose is the daughter of a good friend. We gave her mother a short break."

The woman chuckled. "I wish I'd had a friend like you when Anna was three or four."

Rose, who'd been bouncing up and down next to Elizabeth but who'd been surprisingly quiet, spied her mother rounding a corner of the path. "Mama, Mama!" she shrieked as she raced toward her. "Aunt Elizabeth and Mr. Nordling took me on a boat! It was fun." She tugged on Gwen's hand. "You gotta come see it."

"You were a lucky girl, weren't you?" Gwen's voice floated across the still air.

"Come, Mama. You gotta go on the boat too."

Elizabeth smiled at the woman. "That's the real Rose,

lovable but lively." She extended her hand. "I want to thank you for lending us your boat. As you can see, Rose enjoyed it, and so did I."

"Make that unanimous. We all did," Jason said as he and the mustached man approached Elizabeth. Jason smiled at the woman. "Did Elizabeth introduce herself?" When she shook her head, he continued. "Mrs. Mullen, this is Dr. Harding."

"The lady doctor I've heard so much about?" Mrs. Mullen shook Elizabeth's hand. "I'm pleased to meet you, more than you might guess." She gave Jason a quick look. "I'm glad to see that the nicer rumors are true." Turning back to Elizabeth she said, "Our Anna's sixteen now, and she's put up a big fuss about going to the doctor. Horace and I want her to see one, but she refuses." Mrs. Mullen's expression became determined. "Anna and I will be in to see you next week."

As the Mullens left, Jason grinned. "That worked out well, didn't it?"

"Mr. and Mrs. Mullen seemed very pleasant," Elizabeth agreed, "and of course I'm happy about the prospect of two new patients."

"It's my first time meeting them, but your brother-in-law liked Mr. Mullen well enough. He bought Charlotte's ring from him."

Elizabeth's eyes widened as she realized what Jason had said. "He's that Mr. Mullen?" When she had admired one of Miriam's brooches, Miriam had said it had come from Mr. Mullen's shop.

"Indeed. Horace Mullen is one of the city's finest jewelers. If his wife is satisfied with your care, you'll probably get more patients."

"I can't have too many of them." Elizabeth's practice had

been slow, particularly the last few weeks, but that was a thought she did not want to entertain today. Instead, she turned to look at Rose, who'd grabbed her mother's hand and led her to the lake's edge, perhaps to demonstrate that the water was not too cold for boating. Gwen shook her head and said something to Harrison. A minute later, they were standing next to Elizabeth and Jason.

"I'd better get her home. Rose will never admit it, but she's tired."

Lifting Rose onto his shoulders, Harrison turned to Jason. "There's no need for you to leave. I've heard that sunset's pretty here."

Though she wasn't certain this was the best place in the city to view the sunset, Elizabeth wasn't about to argue, not when it gave her an excuse to spend more time with Jason. It had been a wonderful day so far, one that she would add to her memory box, and she wasn't ready for it to end.

"I'm in no hurry to get home," she told Jason when he asked whether she wanted to walk around the lake. Strolling in the park with him would be like walking home from her office. But it wasn't.

Elizabeth wasn't certain how long they walked. She wasn't certain what they discussed. At the time, it seemed like everything and nothing. What she knew was that nothing had ever felt so good—so right—as strolling around this small lake, her hand tucked in the crook of Jason's arm. As they walked, he'd look down at her and smile, his eyes sparkling when his gaze met hers, and she'd smile in return. There was no need for words when a smile conveyed her contentment at being here with this very special man.

The first time they circled the lake, Elizabeth saw a few

families enjoying the scenery, but as they completed their second circuit, the others were gone. Minnehaha Lake had become a private sanctuary for her and Jason. And then the sun began to set, turning the sky a brilliant orange as it descended below the horizon. The clouds that had been snowy white became a vibrant reddish orange with slender fingers of yellow emerging from their bases, while the tops turned as dark as charcoal. Elizabeth stared, enraptured by the beauty, not daring to take her eyes from the sky, for it seemed to change with each second. More quickly than she had thought possible, the orange faded to pink, then blue, until finally the sky was gray. Night had fallen.

"It's lovely," Elizabeth said, smiling up at Jason.

"So are you."

He stared at her for a moment, his eyes solemn, as if he were asking a question. Then, without a word being spoken, he lowered his lips to hers.

18

Elizabeth laid her fingers on her lips. It had been two days since that magical kiss in the park. She sighed as she tried to concentrate on the newspaper in front of her. It was no use. No matter what she did, her thoughts returned to the time she'd spent with Jason. The whole day had been perfect. She'd enjoyed the picnic and her first boat ride, but nothing could compare to the sunset and what had accompanied it. Elizabeth knew that even if she wanted to, she would never regard a sunset in the same way. Forevermore sunsets would be linked to the wonder of Jason's kiss.

Her first kiss! As a child, Elizabeth had heard her sisters discussing what it might feel like to be kissed. Charlotte and Abigail had giggled uncontrollably at the prospect, while Elizabeth had wondered if anyone would want to kiss her . . . and whether she would want to be kissed. Not once had she dreamt that a kiss could be so glorious. When Jason's lips had touched hers, shivers of delight had spiraled down her spine. Every nerve ending had tingled with pleasure. Her toes had curled inside her high-buttoned boots, and for a second, she could have sworn that she was floating. She wasn't, of course, and yet even now, almost forty-eight hours later, she could not forget how good it had felt to stand in the circle of Jason's arms, his lips pressed to hers.

That was one memory she hoped would never, ever fade. And even though it distracted her at the most awkward times, like when Harrison had asked her to pass the potatoes and she'd been so lost in reverie that he'd had to repeat his request three times, she wouldn't have changed one second of it.

As the front doorbell tinkled, Elizabeth rose and entered the waiting room, smiling when she saw the patients who awaited her. Memories were wonderful, but patients paid the rent.

"Good afternoon, Mrs. Seaman. Hello, Louis." A quick appraisal told Elizabeth that the reason for their call was not acute.

The thin woman whose son had needed her care on their last visit managed a smile, although it seemed forced. Perhaps Elizabeth's assessment had been faulty and one of the Seamans was more ill than she'd believed. "Call me Laura, please."

"Certainly."

"I'm glad to see you're still here."

Elizabeth knew her expression revealed her surprise. "Why wouldn't I be?"

A flush rose to Laura Seaman's cheeks. "I know it's wrong to listen to gossip, but I heard some ladies at church saying that Mr. Nordling is courting you and before we know it, you'll be married."

Elizabeth shook her head. "I'm not planning to marry, but even if I were, I'd still be a doctor. My patients are important to me."

"Then Mr. Nordling isn't courting you." Laura appeared almost disappointed.

Elizabeth shook her head again. "We're friends."

As Louis started to fidget, his mother laid a cautionary hand on his head. She lowered her voice, as if whatever she was about to say was confidential. "Doc Worland is wrong."

Elizabeth refused to ask what the other doctor had said, but she had no need, for Laura continued her story. "He said it was only a matter of time until you killed a patient and were run out of town."

Elizabeth took a deep breath, exhaling slowly as she tried to control her anger. She shouldn't have been surprised by Dr. Worland's comments. She'd known that he considered her an enemy. But his claim that she would kill a patient set her blood to boiling. There was a huge distinction between failing to save a patient and killing one. The former happened to every doctor at one time or another, despite their best efforts.

"I have not lost any patients," Elizabeth told Laura Seaman, "and if I do, it will not be for lack of trying to save them. But, tell me why you're here today."

"It's Louis."

Bending down to his level, Elizabeth spoke to the boy. "How is your ear?"

"Good." He tugged on both earlobes, as if assuring himself that they were still attached.

"It's not his ear," Laura explained with a worried look at her son. "His throat seems to hurt. I'm worried that he might have diphtheria."

Though the number of cases had not become an epidemic and had, in fact, subsided over the past month, Elizabeth would not discount a mother's instinct that something was wrong with her child.

"Let's take a look." She led Laura and Louis into her examining room. "You remember my table, don't you, Louis?"

"Yes, ma'am."

"Let's get you up there." As she lifted the child onto the table, she couldn't help hoping that Laura did not have to carry him often, for the boy was heavy for his age. A woman as thin as Laura should not be lifting so much weight.

"I need you to open your mouth as wide as you can," she told Louis. The boy complied, revealing a throat that bore no sign of illness. Elizabeth saw no redness, nor was the diphtheric membrane swollen or irritated. She laid her hand on Louis's forehead, checking for fever, but found none. "I'm going to listen to your heart and lungs," she told him as she pulled her stethoscope from a drawer and inserted the plugs into her ears. A minute later, she turned to Laura. "I wish all my patients were as healthy as your son."

"Are you sure?" Though Elizabeth had expected relief, she was faced with disbelief. "I know something is wrong. Louis was rubbing his throat yesterday. I was sure it was diphtheria."

"Would you tip your head back, Louis?" Elizabeth demonstrated the position she wanted. When he did, she pointed to a small scratch on the boy's neck. "Perhaps that's why he was rubbing it. It may have hurt or itched, but now it's almost healed."

Laura flushed. "Lloyd was right. I'm being silly to worry so much. It's just that Louis is our only child." As Louis took the candy Elizabeth offered him and scampered into the waiting room, Laura shook her head slowly. "Oh, Doctor, I wish I could have another baby."

He couldn't stop thinking about her. She'd been foremost in his mind for weeks, ever since he'd decided to begin the temporary courtship, but the kiss they'd shared had changed everything. He shouldn't have done it. It hadn't been part of the plan, but when they'd stood side by side watching the sunset, Elizabeth had been so beautiful, her smile so sweet, that he hadn't been able to resist the allure of her lips. And now . . . Sunrise, sunset, and all the hours in between, he couldn't stop thinking about Elizabeth and how soft and sweet her lips had been, how right it had felt to hold her in his arms.

This was a temporary courtship, Jason reminded himself sternly, its only purpose to protect Elizabeth. It wasn't as if she were eager to marry. She'd made it clear that she was not. It wasn't as if she were the kind of woman he intended to marry. She was not. And yet, there were times—more times than he could count—when he wondered whether he'd made a mistake. Not the kiss. He'd never call those moments when their lips had met a mistake. No, if there was a mistake, it was in believing that a temporary courtship was a good idea.

When he heard the office door open, Jason felt excitement course through his veins at the prospect of a visit by Elizabeth. But the heavy footsteps told him he was mistaken, and he bit back his disappointment when he realized that his visitor was Nelson Chadwick.

"Good afternoon, Nelson." Though he was tempted to murmur the platitude that it was good to see him, Jason did not, for his normally calm client appeared anxious. Nelson's face was pale, almost gray, and his hands were clenched.

"This is not a social call," the owner of the lumberyard

said as Jason ushered him into his office. "I need your legal expertise."

"That's my specialty." When his attempt at levity failed to rouse even a hint of a smile, Jason's concerns deepened. This was not like Nelson. Jason waited until his client was seated before he pulled out a piece of paper and a pen. "What can I do for you?"

"I want to divorce Tabitha."

No preamble. No explanation. Just the bleak statement. Jason was not surprised by either the curt delivery or Nelson's intentions. There had been numerous signs that the Chadwicks' marriage was in trouble. While Jason didn't know all the details, he surmised that Nelson had been blinded by Tabitha's youth and beauty and was now paying the price. It was an unfortunate situation, for marriage, Jason's father had insisted, was sacred, ending only with death.

Jason tried not to sigh at the realization that the reverend would not have been pleased that Jason was about to help Nelson sunder ties forged before God.

Keeping his voice as even as if he were discussing nothing more important than the color of Nelson's shirt, Jason asked, "Is your wife aware of your plans?"

"Not yet." Nelson twisted his hands together, his distress evident. "I want the papers drawn up before I talk to her."

Unspoken was the fact that Nelson was dreading that particular discussion. It must be horribly painful to contemplate ending a marriage. Jason couldn't imagine voluntarily leaving Elizabeth. He blinked at the thought that had popped into his brain, then forced his attention back to Nelson. "What are you prepared to offer her?" As Nelson spoke, Jason took notes. At least while he was writing, his mind did not wander.

When he finished, Nelson summarized, "Tabitha will have enough money to live on."

"But she won't be wealthy." Jason had handled only one other divorce, that of a cattle baron from his wife, and that settlement had been considerably more generous. Nelson had never struck him as a stingy man, but perhaps the obvious pain Tabitha had inflicted had left him disinclined to offer a liberal settlement. It was Jason's responsibility to caution him. "Since you're the one asking for the divorce, your wife may demand more."

Nelson appeared surprised. "Like what?"

"The house." The Chadwick mansion was worth a considerable sum, even this year when the cattle barons' fortunes had plummeted and several had been forced to sell their homes for less than they'd paid to build them.

Though Jason had thought Nelson might protest, he reacted as if Jason had suggested he cut out his heart and hand it to Tabitha on a platter. "Never! She can't have the house. That's where I plan to live with my next wife."

"You intend to remarry?" Though he tried, Jason knew he had not succeeded in masking his surprise. He'd thought Nelson would be gun-shy after one failed marriage.

"That's what this is all about." Nelson leaned forward, bracing his arms on Jason's desk. "I want a wife who values me for myself, not the money I lavish on her. I want a wife who loves me." He looked Jason in the eye as he asked, "Is that too much to expect?"

"No." It was no more than any man would want, no more than Jason himself wanted. "You sound as if you've found that woman."

"I have." For the first time since he'd entered the office,

Nelson's face relaxed, and his eyes shone with happiness. "She's not like Tabitha. She's honest and caring."

"Do I know her?"

Nelson chuckled as he shook his head. "Probably not, but you will, once we're married." He leaned back in his chair, apparently once more relaxed. "I may even ask you to be my best man."

Jason was intrigued as much by the change in Nelson's demeanor as by the mysterious woman's identity. When he'd entered Jason's office, Nelson had appeared downtrodden, but now his face had regained its normal ruddy hue, and his head was once more held high. Whoever she was, the woman appeared to have Nelson under a spell. "So, who is she?"

"You'll just have to wait and see. She doesn't know I'm planning this. It didn't seem right to say anything until I was free. That's why I'm in a hurry." Nelson leaned forward. "I'll pay you extra to rush the divorce." He looked like a young boy, counting the days until school ended.

Jason shook his head. "There's no extra charge. I'll have the draft for you at the beginning of next week."

And maybe then he'd learn who'd caught Nelson's eye. Jason could only hope that it wasn't another young woman who cared more for Nelson's money than for him.

"I'm home, Gwen." Elizabeth smiled as she hung her cloak on a hook near the doorway. As usual, Jason had accompanied her from her office. It had become part of their daily routine, and though she couldn't speak for Jason, it was the best part of Elizabeth's day. They'd walk and talk and enjoy their time together. One day when it had rained, he'd held an umbrella over them both. It was a simple act, nothing more than a courteous gesture, but it had made her feel cherished and protected. And that feeling, that wonderful feeling, had turned an ordinary day into something extraordinary.

It wasn't courtship, though. Elizabeth knew that. If Jason had wanted to court her, he would have told her of his intentions, asking her permission. But he had not. That meant it was something else. For want of a better word, she continued to call it friendship. An unusual friendship, to be sure. A friendship that included kisses and touches.

Today Jason had come to her office a few minutes earlier than usual and had helped her don her cloak. A month ago Elizabeth might have thought it was her imagination, but there was no doubt. His fingers had lingered on her face, caressing her cheek. The memory of the warmth they'd engendered still coursed through her veins, raising the question of his intentions. If he wasn't courting her—and she did not believe he was—why was he so attentive, so loving?

"Gwen?" Elizabeth dragged her thoughts back to the present. If Charlotte or Abigail were here, she might have asked them, but there was only Gwen, and Elizabeth already knew Gwen's views on the subject. The woman heard wedding bells every time the wind blew.

Where was she? Though Rose was playing in the parlor, Gwen was not in the kitchen, and there were no signs of supper preparations.

Looking up from the doll she'd been dressing, Rose said, "Mama's in the bedroom. I think she's sick."

Gwen was never ill. At least she hadn't been since Elizabeth had moved into the apartment. When Elizabeth had arrived, Gwen had welcomed her as both a friend and a doctor, though she'd boasted that she rarely needed the latter. Today was different. Concerned that her friend might have contracted something serious, Elizabeth rushed to the room Gwen shared with her daughter.

Elizabeth's worries increased when she saw that Gwen lay on the bed, fully clothed. She hadn't even removed her shoes, though the blacking would stain the quilt. That alone was cause for alarm, but there was also the stench. If she hadn't known better, Elizabeth would have said that Gwen had been drinking whiskey. That was improbable. There were no strong spirits in the apartment, and even if there were, Gwen would not have drunk them. She'd once told Elizabeth that liquor would never cross her lips. There had to be another explanation for the sour smell.

"What's wrong, Gwen? Are you ill?" Elizabeth approached the bed, recoiling slightly when she realized that the foul odor was emanating from her friend.

Gwen placed her hands on the bed and struggled to a sitting position. Her head lolled to one side before she made a visible effort to straighten it. "Nothin's wrong. I jush . . . just," she corrected herself, "took a little nap." There was no ignoring the fact that Gwen's words were slurred. "My head felt like it was going to esplode." She shook her head, wincing at the motion. "No, that's not right. Esp . . . exp. That's it. Explode." The silly smile that accompanied her word erased the last fragment of doubt. Gwen was drunk.

"What happened, Gwen? Where did you get the whiskey?" *And why did you drink it?* Elizabeth wouldn't ask that now. First she needed Gwen to be sober.

"Whiskey? I don't drink whiskey. You know that." The words were so slurred that Elizabeth could barely understand them.

"Then what have you been drinking?"

"Jush my medicine." Gwen waved a hand toward her bureau. Elizabeth's heart sank when she saw three blue bottles lying on their sides, two standing next to them. Though the labels looked familiar, she walked to the bureau to confirm what she feared.

"Patent medicine." And one of the worst. On the day when he'd delivered a diatribe about the potential dangers of patent medicine, Elizabeth's professor had used Lady Meecham's Celebrated Vegetable Compound as an example. "It does no good," he'd declared, "but it can do definite harm, especially if ingested in any quantity." Judging from the empty bottles and her condition, Gwen had done that.

"Oh, Gwen, why did you drink it?"

Gwen held her head in both hands, her lips twisted into a grimace. "I'm fat," she said. "No man would ever look at a ball of lard like me. I had to do shom . . . something."

Elizabeth wondered how long her friend had been trying to lose weight. The only time Elizabeth had been aware of Gwen eating less had been the picnic at Minnehaha Park, but it was unlikely that had been the beginning. She must have been clever and had reduced the size of her portions at home. Though she never finished before Elizabeth and Harrison, Gwen could have been eating slowly. There would have been no reason for Elizabeth to notice that, just as she had not noticed smaller serving sizes.

Elizabeth sighed. The combination of little food and an increased dose of patent medicine with its high alcohol content would explain Gwen's current state.

"You've got to stop," she said firmly. "Don't you know, patent medicines can kill you?"

Gwen looked up, her expression as contrite as a naughty child's. "Truly?"

"Truly. It's dangerous."

"But it sheems . . . seems to be working. My clothes are looser." Gwen tugged on her waistband, showing Elizabeth that it was no longer straining at the buttons.

"That's because you're eating less, not because of that awful concoction." Elizabeth shuddered at the thought of what Gwen had ingested. "You need to trust me, Gwen. You should not be drinking Lady Meecham's or any other tonic."

"Could it really kill me?" Though her eyes were bleary, there was no disguising the fear in them.

"It could."

There was a moment of silence as the words penetrated Gwen's clouded brain. "If I died, what would Rose do?" Gwen began to sob. "I can't leave my baby all alone."

"That's why I'm going to throw the rest of these away." Elizabeth picked up the two unopened bottles. "Rose needs you, and so do I."

Though Gwen gasped, perhaps appalled by the thought of the money she'd wasted, she nodded. "All right. I'll find another way to be thin."

"I'll help you," Elizabeth promised. She would do more than that. She would watch Gwen carefully. Some doctor she'd proven to be! She hadn't even noticed potentially dangerous changes in her friend's behavior. She'd been so caught up in her own life, in the wonder of Jason, that she had paid scant attention to Gwen. That would stop. Immediately.

19

Elizabeth quickened her pace, knowing she was a few minutes later than normal this morning. For the first time since she'd arrived in Cheyenne, she had made breakfast. Gwen had offered to do it, but Elizabeth hadn't needed a medical degree to see that her friend was in no condition to cook. Gwen admitted that her head hurt, and she complained of her stomach feeling queasy. Both were understandable, considering the quantity of alcohol she had consumed. What concerned Elizabeth more was Gwen's mood. Though she clung to Rose and refused to let her out of her sight, she would barely look at Elizabeth. If Elizabeth had had to diagnose the cause, she would have said shame. And that shame, she suspected, was greater because Elizabeth was her friend as well as her doctor.

Elizabeth's professors had warned their students about the dangers of physicians treating their own family, pointing out that it was difficult to maintain objectivity when dealing

289

with loved ones. They had not, however, mentioned patients' potential reaction.

Elizabeth shook her head as she crossed Capitol Avenue. One more block, and she'd be at her office. And, if her prayers were answered, Gwen would realize that she didn't need Lady Meecham's or any other tonic.

Her fear that Harrison did not find her attractive had no foundation. Every time he looked at Gwen, the man appeared smitten, but either Gwen did not notice his occasionally love-lorn expression or she refused to believe that she was the object. Harrison had obviously wanted time alone with Gwen at the park, but it appeared that whatever they had discussed while they'd strolled around the lake had not allayed Gwen's worries. If only those two would admit their feelings. Surely that would resolve Gwen's concerns and keep her from buying another bottle of tonic.

Gwen had vowed that she wouldn't drink anymore, and Elizabeth knew she was serious when she made that resolution, but whether she could adhere to it was questionable. The manufacturers were clever when they concocted their so-called remedies. The high alcohol content dulled pain and created the illusion that the medicine was healing the patient's ailment. That very same high alcohol content also encouraged dependence. That was good for sales of the patent medicine, but it was most definitely not good for those duped into drinking it. Though Elizabeth hoped Gwen would be strong enough to withstand the siren's call of the bottle, she was realistic enough to know that she could not stop her friend. All she could do was pray that Gwen had the strength she needed.

Elizabeth smiled as she rounded the corner onto Central,

knowing the buildings would block the wind for the final yards to her office. She could tell that a few tendrils of hair had come loose, but a minute in front of the mirror she kept in her kitchen would remedy that. By the time her first patient arrived, she would once more be well-groomed.

Elizabeth raised her eyebrow at the sight of a carriage parked in front of her office. When she recognized it, her pulse accelerated. There was no mistaking the Eberhardts' buggy, but Miriam wasn't scheduled for an appointment this morning. Elizabeth practically ran the short distance to the carriage.

"You've got to come." Delia leaned out, her lips pursed with worry. "Miss Miriam needs you."

"What's wrong?"

"She's bleeding, Doctor. I'm mighty worried."

So was Elizabeth. Bleeding was never a good sign, and it was particularly worrisome during pregnancy. Miriam's baby wasn't due for more than two months. If she delivered now, chances of the infant's survival were not good. "When did the bleeding start?"

"Less than an hour ago."

At least Miriam hadn't been losing blood all night. As quickly as she could, Elizabeth unlocked the door to her office. When she had packed everything she might need for a delivery, she returned to the carriage and climbed in next to Delia. "You could have gone to my home. That would have saved a few minutes."

"I did," Delia replied. "You'd already left. Mrs. Amos wasn't sure which way you were walking, so I had Roscoe bring me right here. When I saw that your door was still locked, I checked with Mr. Nordling. He said you were usually in your office by now."

Most days she was, but today Elizabeth's worries about Gwen had kept her home later than normal. She could only hope that the delay had not harmed Miriam.

Within minutes, Roscoe had parked the buggy in front of Maple Terrace and ushered Elizabeth inside. As she hurried up the stairs to Miriam's room, Elizabeth couldn't help remembering the first time she'd been summoned here. Then her patient had had diphtheria. Today could be equally dangerous.

Elizabeth gave a perfunctory knock on the door before entering. When she was inside, she kept her expression calm.

"What's this I hear about bleeding?"

"Oh, Doctor, I'm so scared." Miriam's pallor and the trembling of her hands underscored her fears.

"It may not be serious. Some women experience this occasionally." But a quick examination revealed that Elizabeth's optimism was misplaced. Miriam's bleeding was cause for concern, particularly when Elizabeth could not find the source. With nothing to clamp or suture, all she could do was try to stanch the flow.

"My baby. Is my baby going to be all right?"

Though she wanted to assure the expectant mother that everything would be fine, Elizabeth could not. She settled for telling her the truth. "I'll do my best. I'm encouraged by the fact that you're not having contractions. The longer your baby remains in the womb, the better for both of you." Miriam's pulse was thready, but that was to be expected, given the loss of blood and her fears. "Your baby's heartbeat is regular." Elizabeth wouldn't mention that it was fainter than she would have liked. "Now all we have to worry about is stopping the bleeding."

It took longer than Elizabeth had hoped, but eventually the flow ceased.

"What caused it?" Miriam asked when Elizabeth assured her that she and the baby were no longer in danger.

"I'm not sure." How Elizabeth hated admitting that! "There's still much we don't know about the human body, especially women's bodies. What I do know is that you've lost a lot of blood. You need to regain your strength." Miriam nodded slowly, her green eyes solemn as she regarded Elizabeth. "I want you to stay in bed until the baby is born," Elizabeth continued. When Miriam started to protest, Elizabeth held up her hand. "I know you've probably planned to attend parties and other gatherings, particularly as we get closer to Christmas, but I'm afraid they'd be dangerous. You should not exert yourself at all, and you most definitely should not climb stairs."

Miriam closed her eyes for a second, making Elizabeth wonder if she was trying to stop tears from falling. "My parents will be upset," she said. "Their Christmas Eve party is the highlight of the season, and I know they wanted Richard and me to be there. I hate disappointing them."

Elizabeth suspected it was Amelia Taggert's disappointment and possible disapproval that Miriam feared. The few times she'd met him, Cyrus Taggert had impressed Elizabeth as a rational man and a doting father who'd put his daughter's health above all else.

"Your baby's life and yours are at stake," Elizabeth said firmly. "Surely that's more important than a party."

"You're right." Nodding slowly, Miriam extended her hand. "Thank you, Doctor. I'll do as you said."

Jason was whistling when he left Mr. Ellis's shop. Though he had had little opportunity to sample the confections that were reputed to be as delicious as the baked goods he and Elizabeth enjoyed, Jason had just purchased a box of candy for her. He smiled as he looked down at the box with its jaunty ribbon, hoping Elizabeth would be pleased by the gift. Flowers, books, and candy, he'd been told, were suitable items for a man to give the woman he was courting.

There were few flowers in Cheyenne at this season, and Jason knew Elizabeth had little time to read. That left him with one choice: candy. And, judging from the relish with which she ate dessert, he suspected it would be a welcome gift. Though he was tempted to take it to her right now, Jason had decided not to give it to her at the office. Perhaps it was foolish, but the candy wasn't for Elizabeth the doctor. He'd bought it for Elizabeth the woman. While he wasn't certain she saw the distinction, he did. Though he'd begun this temporary courtship to help Elizabeth the doctor, it had been Elizabeth the woman he'd kissed, and it was Elizabeth the woman who haunted his thoughts.

Half an hour later Kevin Granger's voice interrupted Jason's perusal of the divorce papers he was drafting for Nelson Chadwick.

"Do you have a moment, Jason?"

"I always have time for you," he answered with a broad smile. The widower was one of Jason's favorite clients, a man he wouldn't mind having as a friend. "Come in."

Kevin stretched his long legs out in front of him as he settled into the chair Jason had indicated. "I was in town getting some supplies and I figured I should let you know that I've been thinking about what you said. It was good advice."

"What advice was that?" Though they'd discussed a wide range of subjects in the two times they'd met, the only advice Jason could recall offering was that Kevin should name a guardian for his daughters.

"You told me children need two parents and that house-keepers are poor substitutes for a mother."

Jason nodded as he remembered how didactic he'd been that day. "I didn't mean to preach at you."

"I reckon you come by that naturally." Kevin shot a wry smile at Jason. "I don't mind admitting that at first I was kinda riled by the idea of marrying again. No one can take Ruby's place, and it irked me that you'd suggest it. But then I realized you weren't saying that I should replace her. A new woman—a new wife—wouldn't take Ruby's spot in my heart. She'd have her own."

That was what he had meant, though Jason wasn't certain his words had been as eloquent. As he recalled, he'd been a bit pompous, certain he knew better than Kevin how children should be raised. The day he'd gone to the ranch had shown Jason just how wrong he'd been. Kevin knew far more than he did about what children needed, and—more importantly—he was giving it to them. Jason doubted any of Kevin's daughters would ever question her father's love. "It sounds like you've got it all worked out."

Kevin shrugged. "The first steps, anyway. I hired a man to help with the sheep so I'd have more time with the girls, and I took them to church on Sunday. You were right again. Folks welcomed us." Kevin grinned at the memory. "A couple of the ladies were especially welcoming. One of them, a widow lady with a boy of her own, invited us to supper this week. She's watching the girls right now."

It was a beginning. A good beginning. The fact that Kevin had opened his heart and mind to the idea of a second wife so quickly was more than Jason had hoped for. "I'm glad for all of you."

"There's no tellin' how it'll work out, but it's a start. I'm mighty obliged to you for the advice."

"I'm glad I could help." The truth was, all he'd done was plant seeds. Kevin had nurtured them.

Kevin leaned forward, his smile turning into a conspiratorial grin. "I'm gonna give you some advice in return. You oughta find yourself a gal of your own. There's nothing like the love of a good woman to make a man's life complete."

Jason was still thinking about Kevin's advice as he approached Elizabeth's house that evening. He hadn't spoken to her all day. In the morning, she'd rushed off to the Eberhardt house before he could greet her, and he hadn't seen her return. She must have, for she'd left him a note, probably while Kevin was in his office, saying she had to make a house call and would go home from there.

A full day without Elizabeth. Jason hadn't realized how much he looked forward to the time they spent together until it had been taken from him. Without Elizabeth, today had seemed like a stew without seasoning. While it might provide sustenance, there was little flavor and no pleasure in tasting it. Fortunately, he had a way to add savor to his day. The candy gave him an excuse to see Elizabeth.

"Good evening, Jason." Gwen smiled as she opened the door. "Elizabeth didn't mention that she was expecting you."

"She wasn't." He looked around, surprised when he didn't

see her. She had told him that normally she spent the hours between supper and bedtime in the parlor. "Is she home?"

"Yes." Gwen nodded at her daughter, who was playing with her doll. "Tell Aunt Elizabeth that Mr. Nordling is here."

Rose scampered off to do her mother's bidding, and a few minutes later Elizabeth emerged from her room. Surely it wasn't his imagination that she looked different, that her shoulders were slumped and her smile a bit forced.

"Is something wrong?" Elizabeth's eyes were troubled, as if she were expecting bad news.

"No," Jason was quick to assure her. "I just wanted to see you. Would you like to take a short walk?" Though the night was cool, the wind had diminished enough that they could walk and talk. In private. It was probably foolish, but Jason wanted to be alone with Elizabeth when he gave her the candy.

For a second, he thought she would refuse, but she did not. "That sounds wonderful." she said softly. As she reached for her cloak, she turned to Gwen. "I won't be long."

Jason waited until they reached the bottom of the stairway before he spoke. "I missed you." He crooked his arm so that Elizabeth could rest her hand on it.

"I missed you too. It was a difficult day."

He'd guessed that much from the almost haunted expression in her eyes. "Do you want to talk about it?"

"I can't." He heard the regret in her voice. "You know I can't discuss my patients any more than you can tell me about your clients."

But she wanted to. He took comfort from that realization. Perhaps Elizabeth the doctor and Elizabeth the woman weren't as far apart as he'd feared. Perhaps one day she'd recognize that she was a woman first, a doctor second. But that day, Jason knew, was not today.

Sensing that she needed cheering, he stopped and looked down at her, hoping she'd see the amusement in his eyes. "You'll never guess what happened to me today," he said in an overly melodramatic tone. "One of my clients shocked me."

"What did he do?"

"I'm not sure you're ready for this revelation. You'd better hold on to my arm." When she tightened her grip, he pretended to frown. "Are you ready?" She nodded. "All right. Here it is: he took my advice."

Elizabeth placed her free hand on her chest and feigned astonishment. "You're right. That is shocking. Truly shocking." Amusement colored her voice as she said, "I do hope you didn't admit that to him."

"Of course not. I had to be professional."

Her expression sobered again. "That's what's been worrying me."

"You don't think I'm professional?" Jason surmised that she meant nothing of the sort, but he had to do his best to cheer her.

"It's not you. I'm worried that I'm not as professional as I ought to be. I try not to, but I'm afraid that I'm making a classic mistake and am becoming emotionally involved with my patients."

Miriam Eberhardt. Though Elizabeth had mentioned no names, Jason was confident that it was Miriam's case that worried her today. Or maybe not. There had been something unusual in Elizabeth's expression when she'd spoken to Gwen. Though the woman did not appear to be ill, Elizabeth had seemed worried about her.

"I imagine it's difficult not to become involved," he said slowly. "The reason you became a doctor was to help people. You care about them."

"Perhaps too much. In school they warned us about the dangers of becoming too close to our patients. The professors told us to keep a balance, that we couldn't let our patients become part of our lives. They said we must separate our personal feelings from our responsibilities as physicians." Elizabeth looked up, the confusion evident in her blue eyes. "I'm not sure I know the difference anymore. I'm a doctor, but I'm also a woman. I don't know where one stops and the other begins."

To Jason the distinction was simple. Being a doctor was nothing more than Elizabeth's profession. Just as he would still be a man even if he did not practice law, Elizabeth would be a woman even if she never treated another patient. The problem was, she was so tightly focused on her career that she didn't seem to realize that.

They'd been walking steadily north and were now opposite Barrett Landry's mansion, the house where Elizabeth's sister Charlotte and her son would live when she and Barrett returned from the East. Jason guided Elizabeth across the street, stopping in front of the handsome three-story brick building.

"Perhaps I can help." He pulled the box of candy from his pocket and offered it to her. "This is for Elizabeth the woman."

Her eyes widened in apparent pleasure when she read Mr. Ellis's name on the cover. "Oh, Jason!" Elizabeth untied the cord and gave the chocolates an exaggerated sniff. "Do you know, this is the first time anyone's given me candy?"

He tried not to let his surprise show. Surely someone had given this beautiful woman chocolates, and yet the fact that no one had could be the reason why she had so much trouble separating her profession from herself. It appeared that no one had treated Elizabeth like a woman.

That part of her life had just ended.

❧ 20 ❧

She hated November. If her mother were still alive, she would say it was foolish to hate a month, but Tabitha knew better. November was the most boring month of the year. The wind had begun to howl. It snowed occasionally. Worst of all, there were fewer parties than during any other month. Tabitha could not think of a single good thing about November. And that idea of setting aside a special day to give thanks was downright ridiculous. There was no reason to thank God or anyone else for the things she'd received, when they were the result of her own cleverness.

Tabitha looked around the room she had designed as her private retreat, her eyes lighting on the elaborate mantel. Not only had the marble been brought all the way from Italy, but Nelson had even hired Italian craftsmen to carve it. This room was beautiful. No one in Cheyenne would deny that the whole house was magnificent. Tabitha's clothes were some of the finest in the city, her collection of expensive jewels unsurpassed. But all that beauty had come at a price.

For once the splendor of her royal purple and gold room failed to soothe her, and Tabitha frowned as she admitted that the price she'd paid was more than she had bargained for. Living with Nelson had been worse than she'd imagined. At first he'd been a cheerful, easily biddable man, but now he was as gloomy as a November day. He refused to discuss anything that interested her, and he seemed annoyed when she didn't care about the latest order that the lumber company had received. Why would she care about pieces of wood? The only thing that mattered was how much money he was making from selling that wood. It was no fun, no fun at all, being married to Nelson Chadwick, especially in November.

Tabitha leaned back on the chaise longue that had come from Paris, stroking the purple satin covering. If her life wasn't what she'd dreamed it would be—and it wasn't—there was only one person who could change it. She'd done it before, exchanging a humdrum existence as a shopgirl for the glittering world of Cheyenne's high society. She could do it again. She'd find a way.

Tabitha closed her eyes for a second, then smiled. A party. That was the answer. Hosting the city's elite and showing off her beautiful home never failed to boost her spirits. So what if others didn't hold parties this month. She would. And every important person in the city would come. By the time Thanksgiving Day arrived, they'd have a new reason to give thanks, for her gala would chase away everyone's doldrums. Perfect.

She was still smiling ten minutes later when Nelson entered the room.

"We need to talk," he announced.

Tabitha looked up, surprised to see her husband in the room that he had declared ostentatious. It had been months, perhaps even longer, since he'd crossed this threshold, but here he was. Her eyes narrowed, considering the man who'd been the object of her thoughts. It wasn't like Nelson to be so abrupt, and it definitely was not like him to have that odd expression on his face. If Tabitha didn't know better, she would have said that he'd just eaten something sour, but Nelson ate only at prescribed times.

"Certainly," she said, smiling as sweetly as she could. Her smiles were practically guaranteed to improve Nelson's mood. The silly man was drawn to them like bees to lilacs. "I wanted to talk to you too, sweetheart." The endearment was his favorite, the one that never failed to put a smile on his face. Oddly, he did not smile today. "It's time we host another party. I was thinking about inviting—"

"I'm afraid not," he said, refusing to let her finish her sentence. His voice was harsh, his expression unyielding. Something was wrong, but for the life of her, Tabitha could not imagine what it was. "There will be no more parties," he continued in that strangely cold tone. "There will be no more 'we.' It's over."

Tabitha shook her head, trying to clear her brain. Nelson was making no sense. It was almost as if a stranger had taken residence in his body. "What do you mean?"

He took a step closer, those brown eyes that had once sparkled when he looked at her now cold. "Exactly what I said. It's over. Our marriage is over. I'm going to divorce you."

Tabitha felt the blood drain from her face as the word registered. Nelson couldn't be serious. This must be some sort of nightmare. If she waited a minute, she'd waken, and everything would be back to normal. She gripped the edge of the chaise in an effort to force herself awake, but it did no good. She was already awake, and Nelson was still standing there, that peculiar expression on his face.

"You can't divorce me," she said, blurting out her first thoughts. "I've given you no reason."

"Don't be so certain of that." This time there was no doubt about it. Nelson was smirking, almost as if he were enjoying her discomfort. "You've refused to give me a child. That's a mighty good reason for a divorce."

Tabitha thought quickly. She couldn't let Nelson divorce her. If he did, she'd be the laughingstock of Cheyenne. She knew people had laughed at Nelson when he'd married her, calling him an old fool. Tabitha hadn't minded that. He had been a fool if he'd believed her protestations of love. But she would not let anyone laugh at her. There had to be a way to change his mind.

"You'll never prove that was my fault." The only person who knew about the ergot she'd taken the four times she'd found herself carrying Nelson's child was her maid, and she would never divulge her mistress's secret. Camille knew that Tabitha had not been joking when she'd said that the consequences of betrayal would be severe. Very severe.

"Won't I?" Nelson's lips twisted into a snarl. "Don't underestimate my power or my determination. Marrying you was the biggest mistake of my life, but staying with you would be even worse."

Tabitha rose, moving slowly and seductively toward her husband. "You don't mean that, sweetheart. I know you love me." She laid her hand on his cheek.

"Stop it, Tabitha." Nelson brushed her hand away, then took a step backward. "Nothing you do will change my mind. This farce of a marriage is over."

Tabitha stared at the man who'd promised to love and cherish her. There was only one possible reason that he was speaking such nonsense. "Who is she?"

As the long case clock in the hallway chimed the quarter hour, Tabitha watched Nelson carefully. She was right. Though he tried to hide it, the tightening of his lips and the downcast eyes betrayed his guilt.

"Who is who?" he demanded, his voice steely.

"The girl who's caught your eye. That's the reason you're saying those things." It was the only possible reason. "You've found someone younger than me. Tell me, Nelson, who is she?" It wasn't anyone in society. Camille would have heard the rumors if that were the case. It must be another shopgirl. No matter. When she discovered her rival's identity, Tabitha would make certain the woman understood that she would never, ever become Mrs. Nelson Chadwick. That was Tabitha's name. She'd worked hard for it, and she wasn't going to share it or the money it represented with anyone.

"There is no one." Though his words were brave, Nelson still refused to meet her gaze.

"You're lying."

Half an hour later, Tabitha banged on Oscar's front door.

"Let me in," she shouted when he opened it. The fool had left her standing on the stoop for the better part of a minute. Didn't he know that a lady's reputation could be ruined for lesser offenses than calling on a single man? If the situation hadn't been so dire, she wouldn't have come, but there was no one else she could trust, and she couldn't summon him to her house when Nelson was there.

"What are you doing here?" Oscar asked as he ushered her into his parlor.

Tabitha took a deep breath, forming her words. She hadn't wanted to waste time having her carriage brought around, so she'd practically run the three blocks to Oscar's home. Now that she was here, she wondered if she'd made a tactical mistake. Perhaps she should have summoned him, after all. It was too late for that. She was inside the modest building that Oscar called home. Though Nelson paid him a good wage, it didn't compare to the profits Nelson took from the company. Oscar lived in a house a quarter the size of Tabitha's and had no servants other than a woman who cooked, cleaned, and took care of the laundry.

Tabitha perched on the edge of a horsehair couch, patting the spot next to her. When Oscar was seated, she answered his question. "Nelson has gone crazy." As she spoke, Tabitha watched Oscar's expression. A feeling of relief rushed through her when he raised his eyebrows. It appeared that Nelson hadn't confided his plans to Oscar. Perhaps he wasn't serious. Perhaps there was still a way to change his mind. "He wants to divorce me."

Oscar's eyebrows rose another inch, his skepticism evident. "That doesn't sound like Nelson. He loves you."

Tabitha tried to control her exasperation. "Oh, Oscar, don't be a fool. Nelson never loved me. He wanted me just like he wanted a fancy house and servants. Now he thinks he wants someone else."

"Are you sure? The Nelson I know would never look at another woman."

Hah! "I'm as sure as a woman can be. I told you before that he was seeing another woman. I thought it was a whore, but it appears that I was wrong. We need to find out who the woman is. Then we can plot our strategy."

She hadn't planned to say "we," but when the word slipped out, Tabitha knew it was a stroke of brilliance, for Oscar's expression changed. Instead of disbelief, she saw sympathy, and for the first time since Nelson had made his declaration, she realized that a divorce might not be a tragedy. Nelson would pay well for the privilege of divorcing her, and once he did, she'd be free. Free to convince Oscar they belonged together.

Tabitha smiled. Perhaps November wasn't so bad after all.

She was tired. Bone tired. Elizabeth had heard that expression, but she had never before experienced the deep-seated ache that affected every part of her body. It had been a difficult two days as she found herself ministering more to her patients' spirits than their bodies. The first day, Miriam had been so worried that her baby was no longer moving that she had sent Delia for Elizabeth. Even though the child was simply sleeping, Miriam had not believed Elizabeth's reassurances and had insisted that she remain with her until she felt the baby move again. It had been then that Elizabeth had realized that bed rest, while essential for Miriam's well-being, was giving her patient too much time to worry, and so she had agreed to pay a house call every day.

Next Louis Seaman had somehow climbed the ladder into the barn loft and had fallen out, breaking his arm. Though it was a simple fracture, Laura had been too distressed by her son's injury to drive the wagon into town, and Lloyd had been working at the other side of the ranch. A neighbor had summoned Elizabeth. Even though it had been a pleasant day for a ride to the Seaman ranch, between the distraught mother and the injured son, Elizabeth had found herself with two patients, and she'd spent more hours than a broken arm should have required, simply because she needed to assure Laura that she was not responsible for her son's accident.

"Children are curious," she told the sobbing mother. "They like to climb and explore, and they don't yet realize the consequences of things like hanging too far over the edge." Elizabeth had had her own childhood experience with a barn loft. Lured there by the plaintive cry of a kitten, she'd fallen off the platform. Fortunately for her, she had landed in a pile of hay and had suffered nothing more than a few scratches.

She had returned from the Seaman ranch, intending to climb into bed as soon as supper was finished, but while she was eating, Kevin Granger's hired man had knocked on the door. It seemed that all three girls were ill, and Kevin was at his wit's end. And so Elizabeth found herself in the Granger girls' bedrooms, trying to determine what ailed them. She felt heads, peered at throats, listened to heartbeats, and when she was done, her diagnosis was nothing more than three upset stomachs.

"Have they eaten anything unusual recently?" Leaving the girls alone for a moment, Elizabeth returned to the kitchen to question the young rancher, who was trying to be both father and mother to his daughters.

He shook his head. "Nothing. In fact, they ate less than normal at dinner today. They said they weren't hungry. That was part of what worried me. My girls are always hungry, and then when they started clutching their stomachs and vomiting . . . Well, Doctor, I don't mind telling you, I was mighty concerned." Kevin was silent for a moment, thinking. "It makes no sense, unless . . ." He opened a cupboard door and frowned. "That's it. I didn't think they saw me put it there, but it's gone."

"What's gone?" He wasn't making a lot of sense.

"The candy. I bought a bag of candy. It was supposed to be a treat for them, but it looks as if they ate it all."

Elizabeth knew better than to laugh, even though the girls' gluttony was a simpler problem to cure than an infectious disease. "Do you think Rebecca and Rachel gave the baby some too?" she asked.

Kevin nodded. "I'd be surprised if they didn't. Ruby is starting to eat solid food, and she tries to imitate the others whenever she can."

"Then I think it's safe to say there's nothing more wrong with them than too much candy."

"I'm sorry to have called you all the way out here for that."

Elizabeth gave him a smile. "I'm glad you did. At least now we know what caused the problem, and I've had a chance to meet your daughters. If something more serious happens, I won't be a stranger to them."

His relief evident in the color that had returned to his face, Kevin nodded. "How much longer will they be sick?"

"The discomfort will take another few hours to subside," Elizabeth told him. "If you like, I can stay until they're all sleeping again."

The man's grateful expression told her he would not argue, and so Elizabeth gathered baby Ruby into her arms, intending to rock her until she fell asleep, while Kevin headed to the girls' room to read bedtime stories to the older two.

Pacing slowly from one side of the kitchen to the other, Elizabeth crooned to the baby. "You'll be all right, sweetie," she murmured. And so would Elizabeth, once she got some sleep. She shouldn't complain, and she wasn't, for this was what she wanted to be doing. From the beginning Elizabeth had known that her schedule would be unpredictable and that her patients' well-being came before everything else. Perhaps it was only because she was so tired that her thoughts veered into a different direction, but as she cradled Ruby in her arms, a desperate longing to have a child of her own lodged itself deep inside her.

Was it possible? When she'd told her parents of her intention to become a physician, they'd warned her that pursuing her dream would exact a high price and that she might never have what other women would consider a normal life. They had asked whether Elizabeth was willing to forgo having a husband and children of her own. At the time, she hadn't believed it would matter. She had believed that being a doctor would be her whole life. Now she wasn't so certain. Now she wondered whether there might be more to her life than simply healing others.

If only there were someone she could ask, but no one—not even her sisters—had been in this situation. Abigail had given up teaching when she married Ethan, and there'd been no question of Charlotte's continuing to make dresses once she became Mrs. Barrett Landry. It was true that Charlotte was going to open a school for special children, but that was different. Barrett had been part of the plan from the beginning, and they'd both agreed it was the best way to give Charlotte's son a close-to-normal future. For her part, Elizabeth had gone to medical school, intending to be a physician for the rest of her life.

Would she feel different if she had a child of her own?

Would healing others become less important? Elizabeth didn't know. All she knew was that there was a void deep inside her begging to be filled.

Help me, Lord, she prayed as she stroked Ruby's head. *Show me your plan.*

She was the stupidest woman ever born. Gwen felt the tears begin to trickle down her cheeks. Soon they'd become a torrent. It had happened each night since Elizabeth had told her how dangerous the tonic was, but for some reason tonight was the worst. Perhaps it was because Elizabeth was on a house call and Rose had fallen asleep sooner than normal, leaving Gwen alone with her thoughts. Though those thoughts circled like a swarm of angry wasps, they centered on one thing: her stupidity. How could she have been so dumb? She had thought only of herself, never considering that the medicine that promised almost miraculous results might have harmed her, might even have killed her. If she'd died, Rose would have been alone. Her poor baby would have been an orphan, all because Gwen had been stupid.

She pressed her fist to her lips, trying to contain the sobs, but it was to no avail. Her sobs turned into wails as she berated herself for her mistakes. Gwen leaned against the wall that separated her apartment from Harrison's as she looked down at her sleeping child. Rose was the most important part of her life. She'd known that, but still she'd jeopardized her daughter's happiness. Stupid!

Tears bathed Gwen's face as she tried to control her sobs. She couldn't waken Rose. Her darling wouldn't understand why Mama was crying. She shouldn't even be in this room, and yet she found herself unable to move, unable to take her eyes from her daughter. Precious Rose.

As if from a distance, Gwen heard the sound of a door banging against the frame, followed by heavy footsteps.

"Gwen! Where are you, Gwen? What's wrong? Is Rose ill?" Harrison barged into the bedroom, stopping short when the light from the kerosene lamp illuminated Gwen's face.

She cringed. She hadn't thought the day could get worse, but it had. Now Harrison would know how stupid she'd been.

"Rose is fine, but I don't want to waken her." Thanks to all the tears she'd shed, Gwen's voice was barely recognizable. "Let's go into the kitchen." When she started to move, her legs began to buckle. Almost as if he'd anticipated that, Harrison crossed the room in three swift strides and wrapped his arm around her waist, steadying her. It was the first time he'd touched her like that, and though Gwen knew he meant to provide nothing more than support, the warmth and strength of his arm was comforting, helping to dispel the anguish that had filled her heart. She leaned on him as they walked the short distance through the parlor to the kitchen, and with each step Gwen felt her heart lighten. For the moment, instead of being alone, she was with the man she loved so dearly.

"What's wrong?" Harrison asked again after he'd pulled out a chair and seated her at the table, treating her like a piece of fragile crystal rather than the lump of lard she knew herself to be. "Don't try to say there's nothing wrong. I heard you crying."

That explained why he had come. When she'd succumbed to her misery, Gwen hadn't considered that Harrison might be in his bedchamber this early and that he might hear her. Another stupid mistake. She covered her face with her hands.

She couldn't admit her stupidity. She couldn't. And yet she needed to. Deep inside, Gwen knew that she owed Harrison an explanation. He'd cared enough to come here to learn what was wrong, and he'd tried to comfort her. He deserved the truth, even though it would reveal her foolishness. Resolutely, she lowered her hands and turned to face him.

Harrison had taken the chair next to her but hadn't slid it under the table. Instead, he'd angled it so he could see her without twisting. His blue eyes were solemn, but there was no sign of condemnation. There would be, once he learned what Gwen had done.

"Oh, Harrison, I'm so ashamed. You'll despise me when you learn how foolish I've been." And that hurt more than anything except the knowledge that Rose might have suffered from her stupidity.

Harrison shook his head. "I doubt that. You're a good woman, Gwen Amos. Whatever you think you've done can't be as bad as you're imagining."

He was wrong. "You've never been as weak as I am. You've never risked your child's future."

Harrison shook his head again. "You're speaking nonsense. I know you. You would never hurt Rose."

"But I almost did. I drank bottle after bottle of a tonic that Elizabeth says could have killed me."

"What tonic?" For the first time, Gwen thought she heard censure in his voice. It was as she had feared. He would scorn her once he learned the truth.

"Lady Meecham's Celebrated Vegetable Compound."

His eyes bright with recognition, Harrison leaned forward, narrowing the space between them. "A traveling peddler tried to get my parents to stock that in their store. He claimed

313

Lady Meecham was a genuine English lady, married to some hobnobbing member of high society. Pa didn't believe that. Turns out there is no such person as Lady Meecham. The person responsible for the stuff is a former farmer from Virginia who saw a quick way to get rich. As for the stuff inside those pretty bottles, the so-called vegetable compound is nothing more than a few drops of carrot juice mixed with distilled alcohol."

Harrison's explanation only deepened Gwen's shame. She'd considered buying Lydia Pinkham's compound but had been impressed with the idea of having a tonic an English lady had developed. What a fool she'd been!

"So, why did you drink it?" Harrison wasn't going to stop until he'd uncovered the full extent of her shame.

Gwen took a deep breath, wishing she were somewhere— anywhere—else. And yet that wasn't completely true, for it had felt so good having Harrison's arm around her waist, and the concern that she saw reflected from his eyes ignited the hope that he might not laugh when he heard the reasons for her foolishness.

"Why? Because I'm fat and ugly and stupid and no one would ever love me the way I was. Mike was the only man who could love me, and he's gone." She hadn't intended to admit all that, but when she'd opened her mouth, planning to say nothing more than, "I wanted to be thin," the words had come out faster than a mountain waterfall in spring.

Harrison reached forward and took her hands in his. For a second, he said nothing, merely stared at her with an expression so intense that it made her wonder what he could possibly be thinking. He didn't look as if he disapproved. To the contrary, it almost seemed as if he wanted to smile at her. But he couldn't. No one could smile once he'd learned what she'd done.

"You're wrong, Gwen. Someone could love you. Someone *does* love you. I do."

He was being kind. That was Harrison, a kind man. "You don't have to say that just because you know I'm upset."

"It's the truth." Harrison tightened the grip on her hands and looked into her eyes. Gwen saw nothing but sincerity there, and it made her breath catch. "I think I fell in love with you when I was here last year." His lips curved into a sweet smile. "You believe you were foolish. I should win an award for stupidity, because I didn't recognize my feelings as love. I wasn't sure why I felt the way I did, but I knew one thing for certain: I was destined to remain a bachelor." Harrison chuckled. "Boy, was I stupid. All I could think about was you. I knew someone was courting you, and I couldn't stop myself from wishing I was that man."

Gwen's eyes widened at the notion that this wonderful man loved her. She couldn't claim that she'd spent months thinking about Harrison while he was gone. The truth was, after the man she believed loved her proved to be untrustworthy, she hadn't thought about any man, at least not in a romantic sense. She'd been so convinced that she was unworthy of love that she'd deliberately blocked all thoughts of love and marriage. But then Harrison had returned, and everything had changed.

Harrison smiled, as if he'd read her thoughts. "When Barrett asked me to come back to supervise the building, I thought it would give me a chance to get over my infatuation, and so I jumped at the opportunity. But I was wrong. When I got here, I realized that what I felt for you wasn't infatuation. It was love, and it grew each time I saw you."

315

Just as her feelings for him had grown with each hour that they spent together. Gwen had long since admitted to herself that she loved Harrison. That was the reason she'd drunk all those bottles of Lady Meecham's vile compound: she'd wanted to be beautiful for him, or if not beautiful, at least less ugly.

"Are you sure?" Though every fiber of her being wanted to, she still could not quite believe that Harrison loved her.

He nodded and tightened the grip on her hands. "I'm more certain of this than anything I've felt in my thirty-six years. I love you, Gwen. I want to marry you and be a father to Rose. And, if we're blessed, I want us to have other children—half a dozen or so."

Gwen couldn't help smiling at the thought of seven children running around the ranch, each one wanting to be the first to ride a new colt, but the thought that made her breathless was the picture of sharing a life with Harrison. Together they would turn the ranch house into a home, a home filled with love.

Harrison pulled her to her feet. Looking down at her, his eyes reflecting the love she knew he saw in hers, he asked, "Will you marry me and be the mother of my children?"

Gwen wrenched her hands from his and threw her arms around his neck. "Yes, oh yes!"

21

W e should make it a double wedding." Gwen glowed with happiness, her round face beaming, her eyes sparkling as she washed the last of the breakfast dishes. She'd stayed in the parlor, waiting for the hired man to bring Elizabeth home from the Grangers', and though Elizabeth had been exhausted when she'd arrived, sleep was soon the last thing on her mind. Gwen's news was truly the answer to prayers.

"He told me he loved me, even when my face was blotchy from crying," Gwen had said, her voice filled with wonder. "He wants to marry me."

"Of course he does. He couldn't find a better wife than you if he spent the rest of his life searching." Though she'd miss Gwen's company, Elizabeth knew that marriage to Harrison would bring both Gwen and Rose the family and home they deserved. Barrett would be pleased. The brothers would be reunited, and Elizabeth would have both of her sisters close by. But, while the new year would bring many good things, a double wedding was not one of them.

"I'm afraid not," Elizabeth told Gwen. After she'd offered prayers of thanksgiving for Gwen's happiness, Elizabeth had repeated her pleas for guidance. There had been no voices from burning bushes, no words written on stone tablets, but when she awoke, it was with the conviction that God intended her to be a doctor. Not just for a few months or even a few years, but for her entire life. And though the image of holding a baby with Jason's brown eyes and square chin refused to fade, Elizabeth could not envision that ever becoming reality.

"Why not?" For a second, Elizabeth feared Gwen had read her thoughts, but then she realized Gwen was still talking about the double wedding. "Harrison wants to wait to be married until Barrett and Charlotte return. If we wait a bit longer, Abigail and Ethan will be here. You could have both your sisters as your attendants."

Elizabeth tried not to sigh at the thought of having her sisters with her on such a joyous occasion. They'd all been together for Charlotte's first wedding, and Charlotte had witnessed Abigail's marriage to Ethan, but when Charlotte and Barrett had wed, there had been no family members present.

"It's a lovely idea, Gwen, and it was generous of you to suggest it, but there are two problems." When wrinkles formed between Gwen's eyes, Elizabeth continued her explanation. "A wedding is a special day. I don't want you to share yours with anyone."

Gwen smiled as she hung the dish towel to dry. "I wouldn't mind, and I'm sure Harrison wouldn't, either."

"Rose might." Gwen had told Elizabeth that she was going to have her daughter walk down the aisle with her and stand at her side as she and Harrison exchanged vows. "She's old enough to remember the day, and I don't want her confused about whose wedding it is."

Gwen's pursed lips told Elizabeth she was considering that argument but wasn't convinced. "You said there were two problems. What's the other one?"

It was simple. "No one has asked me to be his wife."

Smiling once more, Gwen shook her head. "That won't be a problem," she predicted. "I know you deny it, but everyone knows Jason's courting you."

Was he? Elizabeth asked herself as she headed toward Phoebe's establishment. It was true that even though he had never announced his intention or asked for her approval, many of Jason's actions resembled traditional courting. They spent a lot of time together. Then there were the dinners they'd shared, the candy he'd brought her, the book he'd given her only yesterday. And of course there was the kiss. That wonderful, toe-tingling, unforgettable kiss. The kiss that had not been repeated.

Of course Jason hadn't repeated it, for he wasn't courting her. Elizabeth was not the woman of his dreams. No matter how much time they spent together and how congenial that time seemed, she was not the kind of mother he wanted for his children. Jason wanted a woman who'd spend all her time raising her children, giving them the maternal love he'd never known.

She couldn't fault him for wanting that, even though she could not be that woman. Though her will had faltered last night, dawn had brought the realization that she could not give up her practice, not even for Jason. Doing that would mean abandoning more than her dreams. Elizabeth would also be straying from the path she believed God had established for her, and that was one thing she would not do.

"How much longer will it be before Sheila's brat is born?" Phoebe demanded an hour later when Elizabeth had finished her monthly visit. Following the custom that she and Phoebe had established the first time she'd come to the bordello, Elizabeth's last stop was Phoebe's apartment. There they'd share a cup of coffee and a few minutes of conversation.

"Another month," she said, replacing the delicate china cup on its saucer. Like the building's furnishings and the girls' clothing, the china was of the finest quality. Phoebe spared no expense on the business that bore her name.

Inclining her pale blonde head in a gesture that was almost regal, the madam smiled. "So she'll be able to entertain customers by Christmas."

"I'm afraid not." Elizabeth refused the plate of cinnamon rolls that Phoebe offered. "Sheila will need at least six weeks after giving birth before she can . . ." Elizabeth paused, then chose Phoebe's euphemism. "Entertain."

"Such foolishness!" Phoebe spat the words. A second later she shrugged her shoulders in apparent resignation. "I'm not sure who's the bigger fool—Sheila for getting trapped like that or me for not throwing her out when she refused to get rid of the brat."

Elizabeth took another sip of coffee, considering the woman who sat in the chair opposite her. Her words were harsh, but the softening in her eyes told Elizabeth Phoebe was more bluster than bite. "You're an intriguing woman, Phoebe Simcoe," she said softly. "I'd like to think that even though you try to pretend otherwise, underneath it all, you have a kind heart."

"Who, me? Never! Now finish that coffee and get out of here before I decide to turn my business back to Dr. Worland."

"You wouldn't do that."

Phoebe raised an eyebrow, then nodded. "You're right. I wouldn't, but don't press your luck, thinking I'm kind. You've got enough kindness for both of us."

Elizabeth was frowning as she walked back to her office, and it had nothing to do with Phoebe or her girls. Though she couldn't explain why, her thoughts kept returning to the Granger girls. There was no cause for worry. Elizabeth was certain of her diagnosis, and that diagnosis meant that by now they were fully recovered from last night's illness. And yet she could not stop thinking of them.

By midafternoon, when thoughts of the girls still tumbled through her mind, she admitted defeat. "I'm leaving early today," she told Jason.

He nodded, as if her leaving several hours early was a routine occurrence, when it was not. "Let me get my coat. I'll go with you."

Elizabeth shook her head. "I'm not going home." The only reason she'd come to Jason's office was to keep him from worrying when she didn't return by her normal quitting time. "I want to check on some patients." She glanced at the window. Though thick clouds obscured the sun, the predicted snow had not begun. "It's a bit of a ride, and I want to be back by nightfall. I'm not used to driving in the dark."

Jason slid his arms into the sleeves of his overcoat and grabbed his hat. "I'll be glad to drive you wherever you're going. That way if your call takes more time than you expect, it won't be a problem. Unlike you, I've had plenty of experience driving a team after dark."

Elizabeth's heart accelerated at the thought of spending more time with Jason. They'd talk and laugh, and the miles would pass quickly. It was tempting, and yet . . . "Thank you, but I can't impose. It would be boring for you, just waiting while I make my house call."

After settling his hat on his head, Jason reached for his gloves, apparently dismissing Elizabeth's protests. "It will be no more boring than sitting here, and this way I'll have the pleasure of your company on the ride. It'll be like my childhood when I accompanied the reverend on his calls." Jason grinned. "Of course, a few things will be different. I'll be the one who's driving. More importantly, the company will be much more attractive."

Elizabeth felt the color rise to her cheeks. "You're sure it won't be a bother?"

"I'm sure. Now, where are we going?"

"The Granger ranch."

Jason's face lit with enthusiasm. "Great! Kevin started as one of my clients, but I now consider him a friend. I can visit with him while you give his girls a checkup."

As Elizabeth had known would be the case, the ride was pleasant. She and Jason spoke of everything from Gwen and Harrison's engagement to their own plans for Thanksgiving, and as they did, Elizabeth's concerns over the Granger girls subsided, replaced by the delight of being with Jason. The way she felt today, she could spend the rest of her life riding with him, if only the wind would stop. Out on the open prairie, it seemed colder and fiercer than it had in town, easily penetrating her woolen coat, and though she had a thick blanket wrapped around her legs, Elizabeth could not help shivering.

"You're cold." Jason turned to look at her, shaking his head slightly as he said, "I should have hired a closed carriage." He stretched out his arm, wrapping it around her shoulders, and drew her closer. "The least I can do is share some of my warmth with you."

Perhaps she shouldn't have accepted the invitation. Mama would have been scandalized by the thought of her unmarried daughter sitting so close to a single man. But Mama had never experienced Wyoming's cold wind, and Mama had never met Jason. Elizabeth would be perfectly safe with him. Moreover, she might be warmer.

Nestling close to Jason, Elizabeth laid her head against his chest. It was only her imagination that she heard his heart beating. With the layers of clothing that separated them, not to mention the wind, she could hear nothing more than the sound of her own heartbeat, and that had accelerated the instant Jason had put his arm around her shoulders. Still, she could not deny the fact that she was warmer and that being here with Jason made her heart sing. It felt so good, so right, sitting close to him, traveling together to check on her patients. How wonderful it would be if they could do it again, if Jason were a permanent part of her life. But that was only a dream.

When they reached the ranch, Kevin Granger emerged from the farmhouse, his expression a mélange of curiosity and pleasure. "Jason, Dr. Harding. I wasn't expecting either of you."

From the man's carefree smile, it appeared that Elizabeth's fears had been for naught. "I was concerned about your daughters," she admitted. "I wanted to be certain their illness was nothing more serious than too much candy."

Jason shot Kevin an amused look. "You fed the girls candy? Even I know better than that."

"I didn't exactly feed them." As he ushered them into the house, Kevin explained what had happened. "I hope they learned their lesson."

"If they're like me, it'll take more than one sore stomach." Jason punctuated his statement with a chuckle. "Candy's an irresistible lure."

Apparently attracted by the sound of voices, the two older girls burst from their room, skidding to a stop in front of Elizabeth and Jason. "I remember you." Rebecca pointed at Elizabeth.

"You held my head when I was sick," her younger sister announced. "I'm better now."

Elizabeth nodded. "I can see that, but I'd still like to make sure you and Ruby are all right."

"We are," Rebecca announced. "We promised Pa that we wouldn't eat any more candy." When Jason gave Kevin a smile that said he suspected that promise would be broken more than once, Rebecca tugged on Elizabeth's skirt. "Can you play with us?"

Elizabeth raised an eyebrow as she looked at Jason. A quick nod told her he didn't mind the delay. "Maybe for a few minutes." Though playing games with children wasn't an official part of being a physician, the additional time with the girls would give Elizabeth the opportunity to observe them more closely.

"Why don't you stay for supper?" Though Kevin addressed the question to Elizabeth, he clapped Jason on the shoulder.

"Your plan seems to be working. I've never seen so much food. It appears that every young woman in the congregation has brought me at least one huge meal. I may be able to hang up my apron soon."

Bemused by the image of the tall rancher in a ruffled apron, Elizabeth did not respond. Jason did. "A home-cooked meal is one invitation I won't refuse, but it's up to the doctor." He turned to Elizabeth. "Can you stay?"

"Please. You'd be doing me a favor." Kevin added his encouragement.

"Thank you. I'd enjoy that." While Elizabeth examined the girls and satisfied their curiosity about her stethoscope, the sound of pans rattling and the aromas of food warming came from the kitchen. Though it was a bit earlier than she was accustomed to eating, the delicious smells made Elizabeth's stomach growl, provoking another peal of laughter from the girls. Their idea of playing, it seemed, involved inspecting the contents of Elizabeth's medical bag and listening to each other's heartbeats.

"Supper's ready," Kevin called before the novelty of playing doctor wore off.

"Come, girls." Elizabeth gathered the baby into her arms and nodded to Rebecca and Rachel. "We need to wash our hands before we eat."

Within minutes, they were all seated. Kevin indicated that Elizabeth should take the place at the foot of the table opposite him, with Jason and the baby in her highchair on one long side, the two older girls on the other. Though Elizabeth wondered whether the girls were disturbed by another woman in their mother's chair, no one seemed to place any significance on it.

After Kevin offered thanks for the food, Rachel looked from Elizabeth to Jason. "Is he your pa?"

Jason sputtered and plunked the platter that he'd been holding for Elizabeth back onto the table.

"My pa?" Elizabeth was almost as amused at the idea of Jason being her father as he was and started to laugh. Her amusement faded a second later.

"She means your husband," Kevin explained.

Her husband. Only in her dreams. Hoping no one noticed the flush that had colored her cheeks, Elizabeth turned toward the little girl. "Mr. Nordling is my friend, Rachel. I'm not married."

"How come?" Rebecca demanded.

His lips twisted in a smile, Kevin turned to Jason. "How come? Seems to me you're old enough to be married and have children of your own. Even if they do sneak candy, I wouldn't trade mine for anything."

Kevin gave his daughters a fond glance while Elizabeth tried to cool her cheeks by taking a sip of water. Though she knew the girls meant no harm, she hated the thought that Jason might be as embarrassed as she. The sooner they put this subject to bed, the better. Elizabeth looked from Rebecca to Rachel, keeping her voice neutral as she said, "I'm not married because I'm a doctor."

Apparently content with the explanation, Rebecca nodded. "Oh, all right."

Of course it was all right. There was no reason why Elizabeth should feel so empty inside, no reason why she wished she had a house, a husband, and children of her own. No reason at all.

Where was he? Tabitha arranged her skirts as she reclined on the chaise longue, trying not to frown at the realization that he was late. Though Oscar had once told her she looked seductive on the chaise, she was certain he would not find a frown appealing. Oscar liked women who smiled.

It wasn't difficult to smile whenever he was near. He was young and handsome and, before she married Nelson, had made no secret of the fact that he found Tabitha attractive. Today there was an additional reason to smile. Oscar had sent a message, saying he had the answer she sought. Ten minutes later a discreet knock sounded on the door to her sitting room.

"Mr. Miller is here to see you, ma'am." Tabitha's butler inclined his head as he'd been taught. She hadn't been able to convince him that he should click his heels the way she'd heard German butlers did, but other than that, he was the ideal servant. Tall, distinguished-looking, and obsequious.

"Show him in." When the door closed behind Oscar, Tabitha extended her arm, expecting him to kiss her hand. He did not.

"I have good news," he announced, taking the chair across from her rather than perching on the side of the chaise as she'd expected. Tabitha refused to be annoyed by his stand-offishness. Oscar had brought good news. That was what was important.

"You discovered who she is." She made it a statement, not a question.

He nodded. "I did, and you have no need to worry. Nelson will never marry her."

Oscar must be mistaken. The only reason Nelson would have demanded a divorce was that he wanted to marry some other woman. "Why not? Is she already married?"

"Hardly." Oscar's lip curled with disdain, and for an instant, he was less than handsome. Tabitha would have to advise him not to curl his lips like that. Not today, though. There'd be time for that later, once they were married.

"So, who is she?"

Oscar curled his lip again. "She's a madam. The woman Nelson spends his nights with is Phoebe Simcoe."

"Phoebe!" Tabitha took a deep breath, trying to control her alarm. Of course she'd heard of Phoebe Simcoe. Who in Cheyenne hadn't? Everyone knew that Phoebe ran the most exclusive bordello in the city, catering to the wealthiest men in town. Men like Nelson.

Phoebe was almost as young as Tabitha, and she was pretty enough, if you liked light blonde hair and blue eyes. Tabitha did not, but she had once heard Nelson say that blue-eyed blondes always made him think of angels. Phoebe Simcoe was no angel. That was certain. But if the rumors were accurate, she knew exactly how to please a man.

Oscar leaned forward, propping his elbows on his knees. "I don't understand why you seem surprised. You once told me you thought Nelson was visiting a whore."

"That's true, but I didn't realize it was Phoebe."

"What's the difference? A whore is a whore. Nelson will never marry one."

Even if he didn't, once his connection with Phoebe became common knowledge, Tabitha would die of embarrassment. Tabitha Chadwick thrown over for a whore! It was one thing for him to visit Phoebe while he was married to Tabitha. He wasn't the only man in Cheyenne who paid for pleasure. But to divorce Tabitha and still continue to patronize Phoebe—that was unacceptable. Tabitha would never recover from that disgrace. She'd become the laughingstock of the city. She couldn't let that happen. She *wouldn't* let that happen.

"Your baby's fine, and so are you." Elizabeth folded the stethoscope and placed it back in her bag, saying a silent prayer of thanksgiving that she could give Miriam the continued good news.

"Does that mean I can get out of bed?" Miriam sat up, her back propped by several pillows, and fussed with the bow on her mint-green bed jacket.

Though she would have liked to agree, Elizabeth knew she could not. "Not until you deliver. The good news is that remaining in bed has prevented more bleeding or other complications. If you continue taking care of yourself, you should have a healthy baby."

Miriam nodded. "That's what Richard and I want. It's just so boring, staying here all the time. Mama and my friends visit, and they do their best to entertain me. Mama keeps bringing me new bed jackets." Miriam fingered the one she was wearing. "She thinks they'll make me happy, but all I want is to be out and about like you." Miriam narrowed her eyes slightly. "I heard you and Jason went for a ride yesterday."

It was clear there were no secrets in Cheyenne, not that there was any reason to keep the ride a secret. "He took me to call on some patients," Elizabeth explained. "It turned out that the man was one of Jason's friends, so we stayed for supper."

Miriam nodded again, as if she'd heard that part of the story. "I'll say one thing for Jason. He's taking this courtship business more seriously than I thought he would."

Closing her bag, Elizabeth looked steadily at Miriam. "He's not courting me."

"I know." Miriam reached for the glass of water she kept on her bedside table and took a sip before she continued. "I told Richard you knew that Jason was only trying to protect your reputation."

Though she'd been ready to leave, Elizabeth stopped in midstride. "What do you mean?"

To her surprise, a flush colored Miriam's cheeks. "Nothing." She reached for the glass again.

Elizabeth shook her head. "It's not nothing. What do you mean about my reputation?"

"I thought you knew. I thought you agreed that it was the only thing to do."

Though Miriam was forming complete sentences, they made no sense to Elizabeth. "Start at the beginning," she said firmly.

Clearly uncomfortable, Miriam shrugged her shoulders. "I don't know how it got started, but there was a lot of gossip after Jason spent a week in your infirmary."

"He had diphtheria."

"You and I know that, but the gossipmongers claimed it was just an excuse, that all kinds of illicit things were going on."

"That's absurd! No one would believe that." But as memories of the Chadwick party and Oscar's advances resurfaced, Elizabeth realized that at least one person had believed the vile rumors.

"Women were saying they didn't want a doctor with low morals." Miriam's green eyes darkened with regret as she continued the story.

So that was why appointments had been canceled soon after the party. At the time, Elizabeth had been puzzled, but she'd thought it might have been pure coincidence that half a dozen women had broken their appointments. Now she knew the truth.

Miriam fiddled with her bow again, perhaps to avoid having to meet Elizabeth's gaze. "Richard told Jason the only way to stop the gossip was to have everyone believe you were in love. If they were gossiping about your courtship, they'd forget about the time Jason spent in your infirmary. Folks will forgive almost anything in the name of love."

Elizabeth stared at her patient, wishing the conversation had never begun, yet knowing that she would have learned the truth at some point. "So it was all a game." No wonder Jason had never asked permission to court her. No wonder he had not tried to kiss her a second time. He wasn't courting her. He was simply protecting her. "A game." Elizabeth repeated the word, hating the very idea.

"That's one way of looking at it," Miriam agreed. "I'd say it was awfully nice of Jason to help you. But don't worry. He knows how important your practice is. No harm was done."

"No, none," Elizabeth agreed. At least none that she would ever admit. It was her own fault that she felt so empty inside. Though her heart ached as if she'd been betrayed, she knew that wasn't the case. Jason had done nothing wrong. He'd never misled her. It was only her imagination that had transformed simple friendship and kindness into something more, something that had tempted her into wishing her life could be different.

She had asked God for a sign, and now she had it. There was no question of what her future would be. She would be a doctor. Nothing more, nothing less.

And yet, though Elizabeth told herself that it wasn't Jason's fault that she felt as if she had just lost something infinitely precious, anger bubbled up inside her, propelling her back to her office in record time. She heard her feet clacking as her heels hit the sidewalk, and her breathing was ragged by the time she opened Jason's office door. Anger had turned to fury, and while most of it was directed at herself, part of her blamed Jason.

"Are you ready to go home?" he asked and started to reach for his coat.

She shook her head, refusing to leave the hallway to enter his office. That was the place where they'd shared cakes and cookies and conversation. If she proceeded, memories of the happy times they'd known might overwhelm her. She couldn't let that happen.

"There's no need to continue the pretense." Elizabeth kept her voice as even as she could, but there was no ignoring the anger that bubbled just below the surface. "Tell me, Jason. When were you going to admit the truth?"

He stared at her as if she were spouting nonsense. "What are you talking about?"

"The charade, the game, the ruse."

Jason's eyes narrowed, and he took a step closer to her, his motion releasing the scent of soap and starch. Elizabeth wondered whether she would ever be able to smell that particular combination of scents without being reminded of Jason. He looked at her, his expression earnest as he said, "You'll have to be more specific. I don't know what you mean."

For a second, Elizabeth considered the possibility that Jason was telling the truth, that Miriam had been mistaken. But that couldn't be. There was no reason for Richard and

Miriam to concoct a story of a sham courtship. Furthermore, the evidence all pointed to the truth of Miriam's tale. Elizabeth drew herself up to her full height and stared at Jason, willing him to back down. "Did you or did you not agree to pretend to court me in an attempt to salvage my reputation?"

The blood drained from his face, leaving him deathly pale. "Yes, but . . ."

Elizabeth spun around to grab the door handle. "That's all I wanted to know." She swiveled her head, giving him a brief glance. "I suppose I should thank you for your kindness. Thank you, Mr. Nordling. Your services are no longer required."

22

Elizabeth tried not to shudder as she looked at her patient. She had wanted something to take her mind off Jason, but not this. Never this. When she had learned of Jason's deception, she had been hurt. Now she recognized her feelings for what they were—pure selfishness. She should have been grateful for Jason's friendship and concern, especially since they both knew they had no future together. Instead, Elizabeth had reacted with anger, lashing out at Jason, when he'd done nothing to deserve it. If she'd needed further proof of how wrong she'd been, it was in this room. Elizabeth's feelings weren't important. What was important were her patients. She was a doctor, and though she'd done her best, she had failed. If only . . .

But there were no second chances for Sheila.

Elizabeth washed her hands in the basin of warm water that someone—perhaps Katie—had placed on the bureau. They'd used bucket after bucket of water, yard after yard of cloth, trying to prevent the inevitable. Now all that remained was the final cleansing.

Elizabeth bit back a sob. If she gave in to it, she'd soon be wailing, and that would accomplish nothing. She needed to devote every bit of skill she possessed to her remaining patient. She wouldn't think about the one she'd lost. Not now.

"How is she?" Phoebe stood in the doorway, her royal blue gown with its pale gray fur trim looking incongruous in the room that had seen so much suffering over the past hour. This was a room of red and white, the red of blood, the white of skin now drained of its life-giving fluid.

"Sheila's dead." Oh, how Elizabeth hated pronouncing those words. Though she'd seen people die when she was training, this was the first time she had lost one of her patients, and it hurt more than she had believed possible. "By the time you called me, there was nothing I could do for her." She'd found Sheila lying in a pool of blood, her heart barely beating. When she had realized Sheila would be unable to deliver her baby, Elizabeth had performed her first emergency Caesarian section, and though her heart ached, she had smiled when she'd seen that Sheila had been right. She had been carrying a daughter.

Elizabeth nodded toward the woman who stood next to the bed, a warm cloth and a tiny form in her arms. After she'd brought Elizabeth to the bordello, Katie had volunteered to assist Elizabeth, saying she'd helped her mother deliver her last three children. Now Katie held the infant whose birth had cost Sheila her life.

"Louella is so small, I'm not certain she'll survive," Elizabeth told Phoebe. Though her limbs were perfectly formed, Louella hadn't taken a breath when she was pulled from the womb. Even the traditional swat on the buttocks had provoked no response. In desperation, Elizabeth had dipped the infant into a bucket of cold water, feeling an enormous rush of relief when the baby had howled her annoyance. Since then, though her breaths were shallow, they continued, and the ominous blue tinge had left her fingers and toes.

"Louella?" Phoebe raised one perfectly shaped eyebrow.

"That's the name Sheila chose. She was certain she would have a daughter, and she was right." But Sheila had never imagined that she would not survive to raise her child.

"I washed her the way you said, Doctor." Katie held the infant out for inspection. When Elizabeth nodded, Katie swaddled Louella in a clean cloth.

"Thank you." Elizabeth turned back to Phoebe. "The baby needs constant care if she's going to live. I'm going to take her to my infirmary." And, God willing, Louella would survive.

"What'll you do after that?" To Elizabeth's surprise, there was a hint of concern in Phoebe's voice. She might pretend to have no tender emotions, but the sight of Sheila's baby had softened her expression.

"I don't know."

"She can't come back here." Though Phoebe's voice was stern, she gave the baby a long look, almost as if she were apologizing. "There's no one here who can care for her."

"I know." Elizabeth nodded at Phoebe. The bordello was no place for a motherless child to be raised. "I'll worry about that once Louella's out of danger. Meanwhile, I've plenty to do." It wasn't simply the oath she had taken when she'd become a physician. Elizabeth also felt an obligation to Sheila. The woman had given her life for her baby. Elizabeth would do what she could to preserve that child's life.

When Phoebe had descended the stairs, Katie turned to Elizabeth. "I wanted to call you sooner, but Sheila said not to bother you. She figured it was too early for the baby to be coming. By her reckoning, it would be at least three more weeks."

Elizabeth looked down at the tiny, dark-haired baby. "Babies come on their own schedule. Louella should be bigger, though. If I didn't know better, I'd say Sheila kept wearing her corsets."

"She did."

The pain Elizabeth had felt at Sheila's death deepened. "I warned her about the dangers." She'd told both Sheila and Phoebe that tightly laced corsets gave the baby too little room to move and that they could endanger the mother as well. While Elizabeth couldn't say that Sheila had died because she'd laced her corsets, she had no doubt that they had been a contributing factor.

"Phoebe insisted. She wanted Sheila to sing for the men, even if she couldn't entertain them any other way."

And the men who visited Phoebe's bordello would not want to see a woman great with child. Elizabeth knew that. "She never told me."

Katie's lips turned down. "Phoebe woulda thrown her out if she didn't sing."

"I see." Though it was too late to save Sheila, it was important that Phoebe understand the consequences of her demands. But that discussion could wait. Right now, Elizabeth's most important responsibility was to ensure that Sheila's daughter lived. Taking a sheet of paper from her bag, she wrote a brief note to Gwen, telling her she would not be home tonight and perhaps not for the next few days. Phoebe's driver could deliver the note once he'd taken Elizabeth and Louella to her office.

The ride took no more than five minutes, but throughout it, Elizabeth kept her eyes focused on the baby. Swaddled in the soft clothes that Sheila had sewn for her and wrapped in a warm blanket, little Louella should have no difficulty with the brief time outdoors, and yet Elizabeth could not help worrying. This mite of a child had already suffered more than an infant should.

As soon as she entered her office, Elizabeth hurried to the small kitchen that adjoined her infirmary. Switching on the light, she found a box that would serve as Louella's cradle. Lined with flannel, it would protect her and help keep her body warmth contained.

After laying the baby inside her new bed and placing it on the table, Elizabeth turned to the stove. Though Louella had not complained, it was time for her to begin eating. Elizabeth warmed milk, testing the temperature by flicking a drop on her wrist. When she was convinced that it would not burn the baby's delicate mouth, Elizabeth soaked a rag in the warm liquid. Though she'd considered using a dropper, she knew that babies had a strong need to suck.

"Open up," Elizabeth said as she softly tickled the skin under Louella's chin. When the child complied, she placed the dripping rag into her mouth. At first, Louella did not react, other than to open her eyes and stare at Elizabeth, as if puzzled by the foreign object in her mouth. Then she began to suckle.

"Good girl." When Louella drifted back to sleep, obviously sated, Elizabeth smiled. The first hurdle had been crossed.

What a fool he'd been! Only a fool would have agreed to the courtship pretense, and only a bigger fool would have not told Elizabeth the truth when he'd realized that he wanted it to be a genuine courtship.

Jason stared at the plate of pork chops and mashed potatoes that he'd brought home when he realized he was such poor company that he shouldn't spend time in a restaurant where people might expect him to be sociable. The food was delicious. It was only his thoughts that soured his stomach.

When had it happened? Racking his brain, Jason tried to pinpoint the hour, even the day, when his feelings for Elizabeth had changed. It might have been the Sunday at the park when he'd watched her pleasure over nothing more special than a boat ride. Perhaps that had been the reason he'd kissed her. Jason wasn't certain. It might have been the day Kevin Granger had described his life with Ruby. That had been the first time Jason had realized there might be a future for him and Elizabeth. It might have been even earlier than that.

Jason cut another piece of meat, chewing slowly while he tried to marshal his memories. He was an attorney, a man accustomed to identifying facts and placing events in a logical sequence, but when it came to Elizabeth, logic went out the window. All he knew was that at some point, his feelings had changed. He still felt a desire to protect her, but it was no longer enough to defend her reputation as a physician. Now Jason wanted to protect Elizabeth the woman.

He should have been honest with her, but he had not. He had remained silent and was reaping the consequences of his foolishness. Elizabeth was so angry that she wouldn't listen to him. She had closed the door in his face when he had tried to apologize, and when he'd attempted to walk home with her, she'd crossed to the opposite side of the street. Even if she did let him speak, it was unlikely she'd believe him. Jason couldn't blame her. No woman liked being duped. He shook his head, correcting himself. No one—man or woman—liked that. Elizabeth must feel the way he had when he'd discovered that Adam Bennett had lied to him.

He pushed the plate aside, his appetite destroyed by the thought of Elizabeth's anger. There had to be a way to convince her of his sincerity, but, though he'd wrestled with the problem for days, he had yet to find an answer. Deep in thought, Jason walked slowly to the front window, his eyes widening in surprise when he saw Elizabeth alighting from an unfamiliar carriage. The presence of a horse and buggy was strange enough. What was even odder was the timing. Though Richard and Miriam occasionally lent her their carriage, at this time of the evening Elizabeth should be going home, not to her office. The few times she'd returned here after dark, she'd been alone, not carrying something in her arms.

Though he was curious, Jason waited half an hour before he descended the steps, wanting Elizabeth to be settled before he intruded. Rather than enter her office by the front door, he walked to the rear of the building. There was no point in provoking more gossip by having someone observe him going into Elizabeth's office at night. That was how he'd gotten into the mess of a make-believe courtship. Even though he desperately wanted it to become a real one, he wouldn't repeat his mistake.

Rapping on the door, Jason waited for what seemed like an eternity before Elizabeth cracked it open. The light from the hallway spilled out, revealing the surprise on her face.

Though those blue eyes that figured in so many of his dreams were serious, he saw no anger. If he'd been asked, he would have said it was sorrow he saw reflected in them.

"What are you doing here?" It wasn't Jason's imagination. Elizabeth's voice held a hint of sadness.

"I came to ask you the same question." Now that he saw her, new questions filled his mind. Why was she sad? Did she regret the way they'd parted as much as he did? He wouldn't ask those questions yet. Instead, he said, "It's unusual for you to be in your office so late. I wanted to be certain you were all right."

Shivering slightly from the cold breeze that blew into the building, Elizabeth beckoned him inside. "I have a patient in the infirmary." The unmistakable sound of a child crying punctuated her words.

"A baby?"

She nodded. "One of Phoebe's girls gave birth this afternoon." There was something about the way Elizabeth pronounced the words that told Jason there was more to this story than she was admitting. And that story, he surmised, was the reason for her sorrow.

"Is the mother here too?" Though he believed he knew the answer, Jason did not want to make any assumptions.

The spasm of pain that crossed Elizabeth's face was all the answer he needed. As the baby wailed again, she hurried into the infirmary, lifting the infant into her arms.

"Sheila died," she said softly as she tried to comfort her patient. To Jason's amazement, even wrapped in a blanket, the baby appeared almost impossibly tiny. "By the time I got there," Elizabeth continued, "it was too late. All I can do now is hope Louella survives." She walked back into the kitchen and reached for what appeared to be a piece of cloth. As the child began to suckle, Elizabeth placed her into a flannel-lined box.

"How can I help you?" Jason didn't know much about babies, but there had to be something he could do.

Elizabeth lit the stove and placed a saucepan over the flame before turning to look at Jason. "Why would you want to do anything?"

It was a fair question. What he didn't know was whether or not she would believe his answer. "Because I care about you." There. The words he'd longed to say were out in the open.

The blood drained from Elizabeth's face, and she stared at him, her expression one of pure astonishment. "What did you say?"

"I care about you." Though he wanted nothing more than to take her into his arms, Jason remained standing where he was. "This is not the way I had planned to tell you, but I want our courtship to be a genuine one." His smile was rueful as he looked at the small kitchen. Elizabeth stood there, her eyes moving from the temporarily contented baby to him, while behind her, a pan of milk was heating. If there was a less romantic spot, Jason would have been hard-pressed to find it.

"I doubt any woman dreams of a setting like this, but it's true. That's what I tried to tell you the day you discovered Richard's plan. The courtship may have started as nothing more than a way to preserve your reputation and keep your practice from dwindling, but I soon realized that what I feel is more than friendship. I hope you feel the same way, because I want us to have a real courtship so we can discover whether we have a future together."

Elizabeth was still staring at him, but her eyes had softened. As she started to say something, the baby's arms flailed. Elizabeth lifted the infant into her arms and began to croon.

The sight of Elizabeth cuddling the baby made Jason catch his breath. He swallowed deeply before he spoke. "I want to fill your life with happiness. What can I do?"

A soft gurgle followed by the sound of liquid hitting the floor was his answer. "Would you hand me the towel?" Elizabeth asked. Her patient had spit up.

Elizabeth laughed, a shaky laugh that sounded closer to a cry than an expression of mirth. "I'm not laughing at you, Jason," she assured him. "I'd never do that. I'm laughing at Louella. Babies have terrible timing, don't they?"

That was one way of describing it. If he were a superstitious man, which he was not, he might have thought it was an unfavorable omen. But Jason knew better. "I meant what I said. I want to help you, so tell me what I can do."

Elizabeth dipped her fingertip into the milk that was warming, the slight shake of her head announcing that it wasn't yet the correct temperature for the baby. "I want to believe you," she said softly, her blue eyes shining with something that he desperately wanted to believe was love. "I want to be courted by you, but look around." She inclined her chin in the direction of the stove. "This is my life. I have a newborn baby who has no one but me to keep her alive." Leaning forward, she pressed a kiss on the infant's forehead, then looked up, her eyes meeting his. "I'm scared, Jason. I don't know whether I can be both a doctor and a good wife and mother. What if I fail?"

That was the real issue: Elizabeth blamed herself for the death of the baby's mother, and that made her fear that she would fail at everything. Jason had experienced those same

343

fears when he'd learned the truth about Adam Bennett. Gradually, though, the pain had faded, and as it did, his confidence had returned. Perhaps he could hasten the healing process for Elizabeth.

"You did the best you could for Sheila, just as you will for her baby, but ultimately life and death are in God's hands."

"I know," she said, her voice cracking with emotion, "but it hurts so much to lose a patient. Sheila was the first." Still clutching the baby to her chest, Elizabeth began to sob.

Gently, Jason pried the infant from her arms and laid her in the makeshift cradle. The little girl remained silent as Jason wrapped his arms around Elizabeth and drew her head to his chest.

"I wish I could have spared you the pain of losing a patient, but I can't. All I can do is be here now. No matter what happens, I want you to know one thing: you're not alone."

Jason's words echoed through Elizabeth's brain for the next four days as she kept her vigil over Sheila's daughter. She wasn't alone, and that made what could have been an ordeal much easier. As Elizabeth had feared, Louella showed signs of suffering from her premature birth. There had been several times when she'd stopped breathing the first day, her fingers and toes turning blue, her face contorting in what appeared to be pain. Each time, Elizabeth had revived her with cold water. The first time, the application of a cloth to her face had not been sufficient, and she'd had to immerse little Louella in a bucket of cold water, but by the third occurrence, simply placing the cold compress on her forehead had been enough to shock her back to breathing. That had been the final episode. Now, although she seemed to be hungry again almost as soon as she'd finished feeding, Louella's color was good. Sheila's daughter was a small but otherwise perfect baby girl.

"What are you going to do with her?" True to his word, Jason had spent most of his time with Elizabeth, providing whatever assistance he could. The first day, he'd found a bottle that Elizabeth could use to feed the baby, and to her surprise, he'd proven adept at convincing the little girl to drink. Other times, he watched over the baby while Elizabeth stole a few hours of sleep. Throughout it all, Jason was unfailingly cheerful, assuring her that no one could provide better care for Louella than Elizabeth. If this was courtship, it was a decidedly unconventional one, and yet it brought smiles of pleasure to Elizabeth's face.

"I don't know what to do with Louella," she told Jason. "I thought about adopting her myself, but the answer to that was very clear. I'm not the mother God intended for Louella, nor are my sisters." That had been a disappointment, for, though she knew she shouldn't, Elizabeth had become attached to the tiny infant. There were times when she held Louella in her arms and imagined this was her daughter and that she and Jason were raising her. At those times, she tried to picture what Louella would look like as she grew. It would be a joy, having a child like this. But God had other ideas. The disquiet that Elizabeth felt each time she considered making Louella hers told her that.

"There must be someone who'll care for her," Jason said.

He'd no sooner spoken than the doorbell tinkled, announcing someone's arrival. "I'll watch Louella while you see your patient," he told Elizabeth.

Carefully closing the infirmary door behind her, Elizabeth

walked into the waiting room, smiling when she recognized Laura Seaman. For the first time, she did not have Louis with her. Though she returned Elizabeth's smile, Laura twisted the strings of her reticule, as if she were nervous, and her face was paler than usual. Elizabeth hoped whatever was bothering her patient was not serious.

"Come in," she said, gesturing toward her consulting room. When they were both seated, she asked, "What brings you here today?"

Laura gripped the chair arms, her eyes searching the room before she looked at Elizabeth. "Is it true that you have a baby in your infirmary?"

It was far from the response Elizabeth had expected, but there was no reason to deny the truth. "Yes. I've been caring for Louella since her birth."

Though she hadn't thought it possible, Laura's pallor increased. "Her name is Louella?" she asked, her voice shaky. Her eyelids closed and her lips moved without making a sound, as if she were praying.

"That's the name her mother gave her." Elizabeth watched her patient, waiting until Laura opened her eyes again before she spoke. "If you know she's here, you probably also know that Louella's mother died in childbirth."

"I do." Lacing her fingers together, Laura leaned forward. "Oh, Doctor, I've prayed and prayed about this, and I believe that Louella is the answer to my prayers. You know how much I want another child. Please, let me have this one."

Elizabeth kept her expression emotionless as she considered the woman's plea. If this truly was God's will, it could indeed be the answer to prayers, both hers and Laura's. "I thought you and your husband were opposed to adoption."

Laura nodded. "We were, but it's different this time. No matter what I did, I couldn't stop thinking about this little girl ever since I heard about her." Louella must have wakened, for a faint cry penetrated the closed door. At the sound, Laura turned abruptly, color staining her cheeks. "When you told me her name was Louella, I knew she was the one God meant for us. You see, that was my mother's name. Lloyd and I always said we'd name our first daughter after Ma." Laura placed her folded hands on Elizabeth's desk and fixed her gaze on her. "Is it possible? Could we adopt her?"

There was no doubting the woman's sincerity or the fact that Louella needed a home. "Are you both certain this is what you want?" Elizabeth had never met Lloyd Seaman, but she'd heard that he was a good man. A bit stern, perhaps, but basically a loving father.

"Yes." Laura dropped her eyes. "At first Lloyd objected. He didn't approve of the mother's profession, but eventually he agreed with me. A baby's a baby, and this may be our only chance to give Louis a sister."

The feeling of peace that settled over Elizabeth told her this was indeed God's will. "I can't think of anyone who'd be a better mother than you. Would you like to see Louella now?" Elizabeth raised her voice slightly so that Jason would hear her.

"Oh yes!"

When she heard the back door close and knew that Jason had left rather than provoke more gossip, Elizabeth rose and took a step toward the hallway. "Come with me."

When they reached the infirmary, the baby was stirring. Elizabeth drew Louella out of the makeshift cradle and handed her to Laura, watching the thin woman beam with happiness as she held the child.

"She's beautiful." Laura traced the outline of Louella's face with one finger, as if memorizing it. "Can I take her home today?"

Though Elizabeth wished she could agree, she could not. "Louella had some problems breathing at the beginning. I believe she's fine now, but I want her to stay here for a few more days." Seeing the woman's disappointment, she added, "You and Lloyd and Louis are welcome to spend as much time as you like with her. In fact, it would be a big help to me if you'd take over Louella's care."

Tears of joy filled Laura's eyes. "You don't know what this means to me, Doctor. Thanks to you, my dreams are coming true." She pressed a kiss on the baby's forehead before looking back at Elizabeth. "There's no way I can repay you, but if there's anything I can do for you—anything at all—all you have to do is ask."

23

She had never had a favorite month, never even thought about it, but this year November was turning into the most wonderful month Elizabeth could imagine. Other than Sheila's death, it had been filled with happiness. Louella had gained weight more quickly than Elizabeth had expected, perhaps as a result of Laura's constant attention and love, and so Elizabeth had released the baby to Laura and Lloyd's care only four days after Laura had asked to adopt her. Jason had agreed to handle the paperwork, but even before the adoption became official, it was clear that Louella was thriving in her new home. Even Phoebe, who'd expressed surprise that anyone would want Sheila's baby, admitted that everything was turning out well for the orphaned girl.

And, to Elizabeth's surprise, when she had confronted Phoebe about Sheila's corsets and the probability that they had contributed to her death, Phoebe had admitted that she'd made a mistake. "It won't happen again," she promised. "And there will be no more ergot, either."

Elizabeth had left the bordello with a grin as wide as Wyoming Territory on her face, thrilled by Phoebe's concessions.

Just as wonderful, both of her sisters now had firm dates for their return to Wyoming. Charlotte's training would conclude on the first of December, which meant that she, Barrett, and David, the precious nephew Elizabeth had met only once, would arrive by the middle of the month. Abigail and Ethan would be a bit later, but they would be in Cheyenne before Christmas.

That was cause for rejoicing, but there was more. Elizabeth touched the edge of the curling iron, testing the temperature before she reached for another lock of hair. Though she normally wore her hair in a simpler style, Gwen had convinced her that an evening at the Opera House was special enough to warrant curls. Even if Elizabeth didn't agree with Gwen's assertion that Jason intended to propose marriage tonight, the midnight blue silk gown she was wearing demanded a more intricate hairstyle.

She glanced at the mirror, admiring the result. The gown, one of Charlotte's creations, was magnificent, and the curls added softness to Elizabeth's face. But it wasn't the finery that made her eyes sparkle. It was the thought of her official courtship. Though it had been only a little more than two weeks, they had been the most memorable of Elizabeth's life. She and Jason had done the same things they'd done before. They'd shared cakes in the afternoons, occasional suppers at night, and he walked home with her every day. It was different this time, though, for they talked—they really talked.

Instead of trivialities, they shared their hopes and dreams. Elizabeth learned that, although he would handle all kinds of law, Jason wanted to specialize as a defense attorney, ensuring that falsely accused citizens received justice. She told him of her desire to uncover more of the mysteries of women's bodies so that her patients could live longer, healthier lives. They both spoke of their desire for children, with Jason admitting that he still believed children needed a full-time mother. And through it all, Elizabeth's regard for Jason grew. He was kind; he was thoughtful; he was everything she could ask for in a man. Jason was the man of her dreams. What she did not know was whether he loved her enough to accept the fact that she was not the kind of wife and mother he had once dreamt of.

Anticipation surged through Jason's veins as he turned the carriage onto 17th Street. Tonight would be a once-in-a-lifetime event. Tonight was the night he would ask the woman he loved to marry him. He'd visited Mr. Mullen's store this morning and had found Elizabeth's ring. Though he'd gone with no preconceived ideas of style, when the jeweler had shown him a tray of diamond rings, Jason's eye had lit on one, and he'd known it was the right one for Elizabeth. It wasn't the largest or the most expensive, but the instant he saw it, Jason could picture it on Elizabeth's hand. A modest center diamond was circled by a row of smaller ones, and as he turned it, the stones caught the light, reflecting rainbows of color.

"A wise choice." Mr. Mullen fingered his moustache when he saw Jason's interest in that particular ring. "It will be beautiful on your lady's long fingers."

For a second, Jason was confused, wondering how the jeweler knew that Elizabeth had long, slender fingers. Then he recalled the day he'd borrowed the Mullenses' boat. Mr. Mullen had met Elizabeth that day, and—just as Elizabeth admitted she looked at even strangers as potential patients, searching their expression and their demeanor for signs of illness—Mr. Mullen had undoubtedly given Elizabeth's hands a more than cursory glance.

"You're right," Jason told the jeweler as he paid for the ring. "This is perfect for Elizabeth."

Now, approaching her home, he smiled at the thought of placing that ring on Elizabeth's finger. Normally she wore no jewelry other than the watch that she kept pinned to her bodice, but after tonight, he hoped she'd wear his rings. First this one, the symbol of the future they would share, and then the wedding band that would mark their union.

It couldn't have been a more perfect evening. Though the weather was cold, the sky was clear, highlighted by a sliver of a moon and thousands of twinkling stars. It was the perfect evening for a concert at the Opera House, and when that was over, it would be the perfect evening for a drive through the park.

Jason had it all planned. After he claimed the night was too beautiful to waste, he'd take Elizabeth to City Park. Once they were there, he'd tell her how much he loved her and that he wanted to spend the rest of his life showing her just how deep that love was. He would ask her to be his wife, and when she said yes, he would slide the ring onto her finger. And then . . . then he would press his lips to hers.

Jason's smile broadened at the thought of their embrace. He'd wanted, oh, how he'd wanted to kiss her again, but every time he'd come close to pulling Elizabeth into his arms, something deep inside him had told him to wait. It was right

352

that the next kiss they shared would be that of a betrothed couple.

Looping the reins over one of the hitching posts in front of the new Landry Dry Goods store, Jason grinned at the sight of Rose peeking out of a second-story window. Gwen's daughter would announce his arrival by racing around the apartment. At least that's what she'd done the last time, working herself into a frenzy, or so Harrison had claimed. But his friend would not be there tonight. He'd told Jason that he had been banished so that Gwen could fuss over Elizabeth. She had no need for fussing. Even when she'd been exhausted from her vigil over Louella, her hair coming undone, her dress bearing stains from the baby's tendency to spit up the last ounce of milk, Elizabeth had been beautiful.

"You're here!" Rose opened the door and tugged on his hand. "Come see Aunt Elizabeth. She's bootiful tonight."

And she was. Jason stood in the doorway, his pulse racing at the sight of the woman he loved dressed in a magnificent gown of dark blue silk. Though the bodice was modestly cut, the rich color highlighted the creaminess of her skin, skin that he knew was softer than the silk. Elizabeth had been beautiful before, but tonight her beauty surpassed everything in Jason's experience.

He cleared his throat as he tried to form words. "An attorney's never supposed to be speechless," he told Elizabeth, "but I don't know what to say. You're more beautiful than ever."

The color that rose to her cheeks only enhanced that beauty. "Thank you. It's the magic of Charlotte's gown." She gestured toward the blue silk, as if she truly believed it was the source of her beauty.

"I won't get into that argument again. Just let me say that you're the most beautiful woman I've ever seen." And if the evening ended the way he hoped, that beautiful woman would soon be his betrothed. Jason reached for Elizabeth's cloak and settled it over her shoulders. "Shall we go? I wouldn't want us to be late and disappoint the other concertgoers."

"What do you mean?" It was Gwen who asked the question. Jason gave her a quick glance, noting that she looked prettier than he recalled. While no one could compare to Elizabeth, ever since Harrison had asked her to marry him, Gwen had blossomed.

"Elizabeth and I have seats in one of the boxes." Jason smiled at the woman he loved. "You and your gown will be on display."

"A box at the opera house!" Gwen laid her hand on Elizabeth's arm. "You'd better hurry, and make sure you remember every detail so you can tell me. I imagine it will be very different from my evening at the Opera House." Gwen wrinkled her nose. "When your sister and I went there, we sat in the last row. That was all I could afford."

The box might seem like an extravagance to some, but Jason hadn't minded the cost. He'd chosen box seating deliberately, wanting Elizabeth to have no doubts about his sincerity. He was proud to be in her company, and he wanted all of Cheyenne to know it.

"You're spoiling me," she said as they descended the steps.

"That is my intention."

When they reached the street, Jason helped Elizabeth into the carriage, then climbed into the driver's seat. As he flicked the reins, another coach barreled down Ferguson, headed toward them. It wasn't unusual to see other carriages on the street, but this one's speed was unexpected. Moreover, it should have been on the opposite side of the road.

"That's Phoebe's landau." Elizabeth laid a restraining hand on Jason's arm. "I wonder why she's here."

A second later, the carriage lurched to a stop, and a girl leaned out.

"Dr. Harding," she cried, her voice shrill with emotion, "you've got to come. Something horrible happened."

"You don't need to come in with me," Elizabeth said as she and Jason approached Phoebe's bordello. When she'd heard Katie's plea, Elizabeth had rushed back into the apartment to grab her medical bag; then she and Jason had followed Katie and Phoebe's driver back to 15th Street, racing as if it were a matter of life and death. Perhaps it was. Katie would say nothing more than that Elizabeth was needed in Phoebe's suite, repeating the word "horrible" several times.

When they arrived, the girl who'd summoned Elizabeth to Sheila's side only a few weeks before leapt from the landau and hurried to Jason's carriage. "Come, Doctor. Around the back. That's where I heard the noise. I was too scared to go in."

Elizabeth nodded. No wonder Katie had been unable to give her details of what had occurred.

"I'll be fine," Elizabeth assured Jason with false bravado as he helped her out of the carriage. The truth was, she was concerned about whatever had spooked Katie. The girl had always seemed sensible. Even when Sheila had been dying, Katie had remained calm, but tonight she seemed close to panic.

Jason shook his head. "I'm not going to let you go in there alone. We don't know what happened." He handed Elizabeth her medical bag, then put his arm around her shoulders, drawing her close for a second. "You can send me away once I see that you're safe inside. I'll wait in the carriage until you're ready to leave. You won't be alone." He repeated the words that had comforted Elizabeth when she was struggling to keep Louella alive.

"Thank you." Though she hadn't wanted to ask Jason to accompany her, believing it would be an imposition and yet another reminder that her profession was interfering with his plans for the evening, Elizabeth felt a sense of relief that she would not be alone when she faced the cause of Katie's panic. Perhaps Katie was mistaken. Perhaps whatever had happened was not serious, and Elizabeth and Jason would be able to reach the Opera House before the concert began.

Elizabeth shivered as they rounded the corner and approached the back of Phoebe's house, apprehension mingling with the cool November air.

"This way, Doctor." Katie pointed toward the outside entrance to Phoebe's apartment.

To Elizabeth's surprise, the door was ajar, and though the breeze was carrying most of it away, there was no mistaking the smell of blood. Katie had been right to believe something was wrong. Her heart sinking at the realization that she might be too late to help, Elizabeth approached Phoebe's parlor.

"Someone has lost a lot of blood," she said softly, in case Jason did not recognize the smell.

He nodded, then pushed the door open for Elizabeth. She entered the room, trying not to recoil at the sight. A lamp cast its warm yellow glow over the room, revealing a crystal decanter and two glasses set on a low table in front of the tapestry-covered settee. A potted plant with a few blossoms decorated a tall plant stand. Everything seemed normal, so long as Elizabeth did not permit her gaze to move to the floor. She had feared death, but it was worse than she had expected, for not one but two bodies were sprawled there.

Nelson Chadwick lay in the center of the room, his legs bent at an awkward angle, his sightless eyes staring at the ceiling. He had been dead for a few minutes. Elizabeth knew that instantly, just as she knew that the cause of death was the stab wounds he'd sustained to his chest. The slit shirt and the bloodstains on its previously snowy front told her that. Though there was no sign of the weapon, Elizabeth suspected a knife.

"Poor Nelson. He didn't deserve that."

Jason was right. Knowing there was nothing she could do for Nelson, Elizabeth turned toward the second body, dreading what she would find. Like Nelson, Phoebe did not deserve violent death. No one did. The blonde-haired woman who'd proudly placed her name on this building lay facedown a few feet away from Nelson, a pool of blood spreading beneath her.

There was no way of telling whether she was still alive, but Elizabeth said a brief prayer as she knelt next to Phoebe, carefully turning her over. *Oh, Phoebe!* Elizabeth shuddered at the sight of the pale face and closed eyes. The knife embedded in Phoebe's chest left no question about the source of the blood.

"She killed him! She killed Mr. Chadwick!"

Elizabeth turned, startled by the shrieking. Though she had thought Katie had remained outside, it appeared that she had entered the room behind Elizabeth and Jason. "I heard voices," Katie screeched. "I heard arguing. Then someone fell."

Elizabeth gave Jason an imploring look as she placed her stethoscope on Phoebe's chest, hoping against hope that the woman was still alive. She did not need a frantic woman shouting while she tried to treat a patient.

Jason grabbed Katie's arm. "Dr. Harding and I will take care of this," he said sternly as he marched Katie through the interior doorway and into the hall. "You go back to whatever you were doing. And don't say anything to anyone until the sheriff arrives. He'll want to talk to you."

It was a futile request. Elizabeth knew that, but she didn't care. What mattered now was saving Phoebe. For, though she had lost a large quantity of blood, she still clung to life. Her breathing was so shallow that her chest barely moved with each inspiration, but so long as she breathed, Elizabeth had hope.

"I think the knife may have punctured a lung," she told Jason when he returned.

Though his face whitened at the implication, he nodded. "Do you need help?"

She shook her head. She had handled knife wounds as part of her training, although this was the first time the victim had been a woman.

"Then I'd better get the sheriff before he hears a distorted view of what happened. Are you sure you'll be all right until I return?" Jason asked, inclining his head toward Nelson's body.

Elizabeth nodded. "It's not my first experience with death." Although it was the first time she'd encountered violent death. Moving as quickly as she could, Elizabeth cut away Phoebe's gown and corset before removing the knife. The gush of blood that she'd feared did not happen, but the wound was deep and would need to be sutured. And then there was the blood loss. Elizabeth had seen patients die after losing less than Phoebe had.

Saying a silent prayer as she kept her eyes focused on Phoebe, Elizabeth cleansed the wound site and began to suture the gash. Fortunately for Phoebe, the knife appeared to have missed her heart, though Elizabeth's first diagnosis had been accurate and Phoebe's left lung had been punctured.

"Oh, Phoebe, what happened?" Elizabeth murmured as she took tiny, careful stitches to close the wound. There was no answer, but she hadn't expected one. Phoebe was so near death that she was unable to speak, and as far as Elizabeth could tell, she was unaware of her surroundings. Given the amount of blood she'd lost and the seriousness of her condition, that was a mercy.

While her fingers moved mechanically, suturing the layers of skin and tissue, Elizabeth's brain continued to whirl. The girls had told her that while Phoebe rarely entertained men, there were one or two special customers who were admitted to her suite. Nelson must have been one of them. But if that was true, Elizabeth could not imagine why Phoebe had killed him. Though she didn't know Nelson well, he had always struck Elizabeth as a peaceful man. And though Phoebe had a quick temper, Elizabeth had never seen any signs of violence. Phoebe tended to be more bluster than bite.

Elizabeth tied a suture and clipped the end. It could have been a lovers' quarrel. She'd heard tales of them. But though that was possible, something still did not feel right. Elizabeth simply could not imagine Phoebe killing a man and then trying to take her own life.

"In here, sheriff."

Elizabeth turned at the sound of Jason's voice. He ushered a tall, very thin man with graying brown hair and shrewd brown eyes into the room. After he'd acknowledged Jason's introductions, the sheriff walked around the room, his expression grave. Though he did not touch either body, Elizabeth had the impression that his eyes were cataloging everything.

"It looks pretty cut and dried," he said at last. "Phoebe killed Nelson and tried to kill herself."

There was nothing Elizabeth could say, no way to refute the sheriff's allegations, even though she believed them to be false. She, Jason, and the sheriff were all missing a clue, for the Phoebe Elizabeth knew would not have killed a man she'd obviously favored, and she was an unlikely candidate for suicide. Phoebe enjoyed life too much to deprive herself of a single minute.

The sheriff looked down at Elizabeth as she bandaged Phoebe's wound. "You could save the Territory the expense of a trial by just letting her die now. I sure do hate to hang women, even when they deserve it the way she does."

Anger, sharp and fierce, flared inside Elizabeth. Even if the sheriff was correct and Phoebe had killed Nelson, she could not be left to die. Elizabeth rose. There was nothing more she could do for Phoebe here. The wound was closed, and Phoebe's breathing, though shallow, was improving. Once the sheriff left, Elizabeth would ask Jason to help her take Phoebe to her infirmary. She could keep a vigil there, but first she owed the sheriff a response. Looking him in the eye, Elizabeth said, "I will not let her die. I took an oath to save lives, and that's exactly what I plan to do. If Phoebe survives, she can stand trial."

The sheriff shrugged. "It won't be easy, finding someone to defend her. Lots of folks liked Nelson."

"Would you defend her?" Elizabeth asked Jason an hour later. They were sitting in the kitchen that adjoined her infirmary, sipping coffee that Jason had made while Elizabeth tended to her patient. Elizabeth gave a silent prayer of thanks that Phoebe had survived the short ride from her bordello to the infirmary and that her condition appeared stable, though she had not regained consciousness. While Phoebe's loss of blood might have been the reason for the unconsciousness, Elizabeth was inclined to blame the large bump on the back of Phoebe's head. She hadn't seen it at first, but when she'd helped lift Phoebe into the carriage, a few of Phoebe's intricate curls had come undone and Elizabeth had discovered the lump.

Jason drained his cup and poured another before he answered. "I know that everyone deserves a defense, but I can't afford Phoebe. I don't mean financially, either. People are starting to forget Adam Bennett. If I took on the case of another brutal murder, I doubt I'd have any clients left." Elizabeth heard the regret in Jason's voice and suspected what he regretted was disappointing her, not leaving Phoebe with no defense. "Besides," he added after he'd taken a large swallow of coffee, "Nelson was my client. If anything, I ought to be prosecuting his murderer."

"What if Phoebe isn't the murderer?"

"She is. The evidence is clear."

Though it had appeared that way, Elizabeth was not convinced. "I know Phoebe. She's a hard woman in some respects—she'd have to be to live the way she does—but I don't believe she's capable of murder."

Jason's grip on the mug told Elizabeth he disagreed. Though he'd only defended one murderer, he had undoubtedly studied numerous cases of homicide in law school and was more familiar with murderers' actions than Elizabeth. Like the sheriff, he believed Phoebe was guilty.

"People lie." Jason's voice was low but filled with pain. "They show you the sides of themselves they want you to see. That's what Adam Bennett did. He pretended to be a bereaved husband when he was really a violent killer."

Elizabeth cocked her head, wondering whether she had heard a sound coming from the infirmary. It might have been her imagination, for the only things she heard were the ordinary sounds of her breathing and Jason's, the ticking of the clock, and the clinking of the mug when Jason placed it on the table.

"I know what happened in the Bennett case and how painful that was to you. The problem is, I don't think this is the same. Even if Phoebe killed Nelson—and I can't believe that she did—why would she try to kill herself?"

"Remorse." Though his voice remained firm, Jason's shrug said he wasn't as certain as he sounded. "Maybe in her own way Phoebe cared about Nelson. Something angered her, and she lashed out, killing him, then regretted it."

The coffee was strong and hot, just what Elizabeth needed to clear the cobwebs that had taken residence in her brain. Unfortunately, though the coffee was good, the cobwebs remained. What Jason said made sense, and yet . . .

"I understand why you're such a successful attorney. You almost convinced me. Almost. I still don't believe Phoebe's a murderer."

Jason merely shrugged, indicating that nothing Elizabeth said would change his mind. They were at an impasse. Elizabeth glanced at the clock hanging over the table. "The concert must have ended by now."

"And no one got to see your gown."

She gave her dress a rueful smile. "It's ruined. I'll never get the bloodstains out." Elizabeth fingered the silk, carefully skirting the patches that were stiffened with blood. "Charlotte will claim she doesn't mind, but I know this was one of her favorite gowns. I hate the fact that I ruined it."

More than the gown had been destroyed by the events surrounding Nelson Chadwick's murder. Jason's plans for the evening had been ruined. He'd gone to so much trouble and expense, even arranging for box seats, and then Elizabeth's responsibilities as a physician had interfered. "I'm sorry, Jason."

He shook his head. "Don't be. I know you didn't plan this. You did what you had to do, and I . . ." He broke off and cleared his throat. "If you're going to stay here with Phoebe, why don't I ask Gwen to give me some fresh clothes for you?"

It wasn't what he had planned to say. Elizabeth knew that. The solemn expression in Jason's eyes told her she wasn't ready to hear the rest of his incomplete sentence. Not tonight. Tomorrow would be soon enough to listen to him admit that their courtship must end, that he was not willing to marry a woman who could not promise him more than a portion of her heart.

Forcing a smile, Elizabeth said, "That would be wonderful. Would you also tell Gwen that I may not be home for a few days? I don't want her to worry."

Gwen might not worry, but Elizabeth did. She worried about

Jason. She worried about what her life would be like when he was no longer a part of it. Most of all, she worried about Phoebe. Though she knew the sheriff and Jason were convinced otherwise, Elizabeth could not picture Phoebe killing Nelson.

"Why won't you wake up, Phoebe?" she asked as she checked on her patient. "I need you to tell me what really happened." That was the only chance Phoebe had of clearing her reputation.

Once again, there was no answer. Until Phoebe regained consciousness, there was nothing Elizabeth could do other than pray that her wounds would heal. Pulling back the sheet she'd placed over Phoebe, Elizabeth checked the bandages, nodding when she saw little seepage. The bleeding had stopped, and though it might be her imagination, Phoebe's breathing seemed a bit stronger.

Gently, Elizabeth turned Phoebe's head to the side so she could examine the contusion. Though the skin was not broken, Phoebe had an egg-sized bump. How had she sustained that injury? Elizabeth wouldn't have been surprised if Nelson had had a similar lump on his head. He had landed on his back. But she had found Phoebe facedown. It made no sense. As another thought teased her brain, Elizabeth pulled back the sheet and looked at the bandages again. Exultation raced through her veins.

She was right.

"Phoebe didn't do it," Elizabeth announced the minute Jason returned. While she was grateful to see that Gwen had sent several complete outfits and enough food for both Elizabeth and Jason to have breakfast, she was barely able to contain her excitement over what she'd discovered. That was far more important than food or clothing.

AMANDA CABOT

"Did she waken and tell you that?" Jason asked, his skepticism evident in his raised eyebrows and the tone of his voice.

"No, but I know it. Something felt wrong about the whole scene in Phoebe's sitting room, but I couldn't figure out what it was. Now I know." Elizabeth pulled out a chair and seated herself at the table, waiting until Jason took the other one before she continued. She wanted his undivided attention. "The bump on Phoebe's head has been bothering me. I couldn't figure out how she got it. I kept thinking that we were missing something and that there had to have been a third person in the room. Now I know I was right. Phoebe couldn't have stabbed herself."

Cautious curiosity colored Jason's expression. "Why is that?"

"Because she's left-handed. Look, Jason." Elizabeth extended her left hand, fisting it as if she were holding a knife. "If I were going to stab myself, here's where I'd do it." Her fist moved naturally toward the right side of her chest. "The wounds were on the other side, which would make sense if they'd been inflicted by a right-handed person. But it would have been awkward for Phoebe. The angle's all wrong."

As Jason repeated the exercise, Elizabeth watched the skepticism drain from his face. "You could be right," he admitted.

"I am, Jason. I know I am. It also explains the blow to her head." Elizabeth had thought of little else since she'd had the revelation. "I think there was a third person in that room. That person hit Phoebe on the head, knocking her unconscious, maybe so she wouldn't struggle. That same person killed Nelson, then stuck the knife into Phoebe, planning to kill her and make it appear to be a murder-suicide."

Jason nodded slowly. "That sounds plausible, but there are

365

still some inconsistencies. Why was Phoebe facedown? I can understand that she would have fallen that way if she was hit from behind, but the killer had to have turned her over to stab her. It would have been easier to just leave her that way."

"I agree." Elizabeth nodded. "I think the knife hit one of the stays in Phoebe's corset." When she'd pulled the knife out, Elizabeth had noticed that it had gone in at an oblique angle. Later, when she'd removed Phoebe's corset, she'd seen that the stays were steel rather than whalebone and that the corset cover had been ripped, as if the knife had twisted. "If the killer was in a hurry, the easiest way to kill Phoebe was to turn her over and let her body's weight impale her on the knife." It was a grisly thought, but Elizabeth could find no other reason for the change of position.

Jason was silent for a moment, considering Elizabeth's hypothesis. "It's possible," he admitted. "Of course, that raises another question. If Phoebe wasn't the killer, who was?"

24

S o, who did kill Nelson?"

Jason laid a hot towel on his face, the first step in his shaving process. He hadn't planned to tell anyone that Phoebe was still alive and that he and Elizabeth doubted she was a murderer, but as Mrs. Moran would have said, the cat was already out of the bag. When Richard had entered Elizabeth's office, intending to drive her to her appointment with Miriam since his coachman was indisposed, he'd seen Gwen and Rose emerging from the doctor's kitchen and had discovered that Elizabeth had a patient in her infirmary. It hadn't taken the skills of a detective to realize that the patient was none other than Phoebe Simcoe, the woman most of Cheyenne believed had died of self-inflicted wounds after murdering Nelson Chadwick. As soon as he'd delivered Elizabeth, Richard had returned to Central Avenue and had knocked on the door to Jason's private quarters.

"I wish I knew," Jason said, his voice muffled by the towel. Removing it and beginning to brush on a generous coating of soap foam, he continued. "The sheriff is convinced Phoebe was responsible. I think he's still hoping she'll die, and that's the reason he hasn't contradicted his initial report. He looked almost annoyed when I explained that Phoebe was left-handed and couldn't have stabbed herself." Jason picked up his razor and prepared to shave. "I thought the sheriff would listen to me, but he dismissed Elizabeth's theory, claiming that Phoebe must be ambidextrous."

"That doesn't sound like the sheriff. I always thought he was fair." Richard frowned. "Of course, I've never met the woman, so I can't say whether his claim is valid."

"Elizabeth's met her many times, and she says that's hogwash. Phoebe had trouble with crutches when she broke her ankle, because her right hand isn't as strong or flexible as the left one." As he scraped the whiskers from his cheek, Jason tried not to frown. "Phoebe is not ambidextrous, but even if she survives, I'm not sure she'll get a fair trial. As the sheriff said, no one will want to defend her."

"Including you."

"Well . . ."

Richard had been heading toward the window, but he spun on his heel and faced Jason. "Is that hesitation I hear in your voice?"

Jason gave a small shrug. "I have to admit that I'm reconsidering."

"Love will do that to a man." Satisfaction rang from Richard's voice. "I told Miriam no matter how it started, eventually that courtship of yours would become real when you realized that you loved Elizabeth."

Richard was far too astute. It would be easy to admit that his friend was right, but Jason had no intention of doing that. Elizabeth would be the first to hear his declaration of love.

"Love? We're talking about defending a woman, nothing more."

"Surely you're not going to deny that you love Elizabeth. It's plain as can be that you do. And since you love her, it only makes sense that you'd want to prove her theory."

Jason rinsed the razor, then began to shave his other cheek. "The only reason I'm considering taking Phoebe's case is that I owe it to Nelson to make sure his murderer is punished." And that brought Jason full circle, wondering who could have killed his client.

Who had killed Nelson? The question reverberated through Elizabeth's brain. She was seated in Miriam's bedchamber, sipping a cup of coffee. Though she had hated to leave Phoebe, she and Jason had agreed that it was best that Elizabeth maintain her regular schedule. She would make her daily call on Miriam and keep the office open for other patients. With Phoebe still in a coma, there would be no sounds to announce the presence of a patient in the infirmary. Unfortunately, Richard's arrival for a meeting with Jason had been unexpected, and he had seen Gwen and Rose entering Elizabeth's office. With typical childish candor, Rose had announced that Aunt Elizabeth had a lady sleeping in her office. Fortunately, Richard could be trusted to keep Phoebe's presence secret. Elizabeth could not say the same of his mother-in-law.

When she'd arrived at Maple Terrace, Elizabeth had found Miriam's mother with her, and judging from the questions Miriam had asked during her examination, the primary topic of conversation had been Nelson's murder. Now, once Elizabeth had pronounced Miriam and her baby in good condition, Mrs. Taggert was back in the room, pouring coffee for the three of them and talking about the scandal. According to her, the city was buzzing with the news that Phoebe Simcoe had killed Nelson, then stabbed herself with the same knife.

"I just came from the Chadwick house, and Tabitha's heartbroken," Amelia Taggert said as she stirred sugar into her beverage. "I've never seen a woman cry so much."

"Death is never easy for the survivors." And that included Phoebe. When she emerged from the coma—Elizabeth refused to consider the possibility that she would not—Elizabeth would have to tell her about Nelson.

"Poor Tabitha said her only consolation was that woman was dead."

Elizabeth bit her tongue. Though Richard now knew that Phoebe had survived the knife wounds, she had asked him to say nothing to anyone other than Miriam. The fewer people who knew that Phoebe was in her infirmary, the better. Elizabeth had enough to contend with, trying to keep her patient comfortable, without worrying about a lynch mob storming the office.

"It's a shame, a downright shame," Amelia continued, "that we allow women like Phoebe Simcoe in Cheyenne. We ought to have run them all out of town. Their very presence taints honest people."

Though she suspected she would gain nothing by objecting, Elizabeth could not remain silent. "Our Lord associated with prostitutes."

Amelia sniffed. "That was different."

A jury would probably agree with Amelia. Elizabeth took

another sip of coffee, trying to hide her expression. The only way to save Phoebe was to identify the real killer.

When she returned to her office, Gwen was in the kitchen with Rose, who was sitting on the floor, playing with her doll.

"What happened to her?" Elizabeth asked, gesturing toward the doll's bandaged head.

"Dolly's sick," Rose explained. She pointed toward Elizabeth's medical bag. "I need to listen to her." The child had been fascinated by the stethoscope from the first time she'd seen it.

"All right, but first I need to check on my patient."

"She's been very quiet," Gwen told her.

There appeared to be no change in Phoebe's condition. She lay on her back, her eyes closed, her expression as peaceful as if she were sleeping. But this was no natural sleep. Elizabeth knew that. She had been taught that a coma was one way the body healed itself and that the patient would regain consciousness when the healing was complete, but she could not repress the fear that Phoebe might never emerge from the coma. All Elizabeth could do was continue to pray.

Returning to the kitchen, she placed the ends of the stethoscope into Rose's ears, then laid the diaphragm on the doll's chest. "Do you hear anything?"

Rose nodded solemnly. "She sounds healthy. I think she wants me to take the bandages off."

"Are you certain she's fully healed?" Elizabeth played along with the child. "Sometimes patients are in a rush."

"I'm sure. Dolly is healed." She unwound the bandages, then lifted the doll and smiled. "All better."

"You've got a new admirer," Gwen told Elizabeth as she helped Rose button her coat. It was time for them to go home.

"While we were coming here, Rose told me that she wants to be a doctor like you when she grows up."

Elizabeth heard the concern in her friend's voice. "She'll outgrow it," she assured Gwen, "especially when she has horses to ride. Once you and Harrison are married and living on the ranch, Rose won't have time to think about anything other than how much she loves horses."

"I hope you're right. I probably shouldn't say this, but I want Rose to have an easier life than you."

As Rose squirmed and headed toward the door, murmuring "horses," Elizabeth smiled. "See? She's already forgotten. You can stop worrying, Gwen. The truth is, being a doctor is not for everyone, but it has its rewards. I was able to save Phoebe's life."

Gwen's lips twisted into a frown. "I'm not sure you did her a favor."

Elizabeth refused to believe that. Life was precious. All life.

That afternoon, she poured herself yet another cup of coffee in an attempt to stay awake. The long, sleepless night had taken its toll on her, and her eyes wanted nothing more than to close. But she could not, for she had a patient in the next room. She took another sip of the strong brew, savoring its flavor. And then she heard it. Elizabeth laid the cup on the table and rushed into the infirmary, hoping she had not been mistaken, that she had indeed heard Phoebe stirring. Though the woman's eyes were still closed, her position had shifted.

"No, Nelson." The words came out as little more than a whisper. "Not right. Can't marry."

It hadn't been Elizabeth's imagination. Phoebe's condition was changing. "I'm here, Phoebe. It's Dr. Harding. You're in my office." Elizabeth knew patients might be disoriented when a coma ended and that it was important they be told their surroundings. Though she repeated her explanation and watched Phoebe carefully, the woman gave no sign that she heard. Once more Phoebe lay silent and unmoving. But she had spoken. That was important.

Not bothering with a coat, Elizabeth rushed next door. "Can you come?" she asked when she saw that Jason was alone. "I don't want to leave Phoebe, but I need to talk to you."

When Elizabeth returned to the infirmary, Phoebe's coma appeared to be as deep as it had been all night. The only evidence that something had occurred was the fact that she was no longer in the center of the bed.

"She was delirious," Elizabeth explained to Jason. He stood at her side, looking down at her patient. "What she said didn't make a lot of sense, but I couldn't ignore it." Elizabeth told Jason what Phoebe had said. "I wonder what she meant."

"Perhaps nothing." Though his tone was matter-of-fact, Jason's expression belied the phrase.

Elizabeth took a deep breath, thankful that the scent of Jason's soap counteracted the odor of the salve she'd used on Phoebe's wound. "You don't believe that."

"No, I don't," he admitted. "I think it might be a clue, but . . ." He hesitated, and Elizabeth saw the conflict in his eyes as he weighed his words. "I shouldn't tell you this, because I was told it in confidence." Jason paused again, his gaze returning to Phoebe. "If Phoebe meant what I think she did, I don't believe he'd want me to remain silent."

Though Jason had mentioned no names, there was little question who he meant. "Nelson?" Jason nodded. No wonder he was reluctant to say more. Whatever he had been told was protected by client confidentiality.

Jason gestured toward the kitchen and waited until he and Elizabeth were seated before he spoke again. "You know Nelson was my client. What you don't know is that he asked me to draft a divorce for him. He also told me he planned to marry again."

Elizabeth was not surprised by the first part of Jason's revelation, but the second part gave her pause. "And you think Phoebe might be the woman Nelson intended to make his second wife?"

"He wouldn't divulge her name, but it would appear so. I can't imagine any other reason why Phoebe would have said what she did."

Elizabeth considered the significance of Jason's revelation. "If Tabitha knew about his plans . . ."

"She might have killed Nelson to prevent it." Jason completed Elizabeth's sentence.

"And then she would be a wealthy widow instead of a humiliated divorcee." Though Elizabeth did not know Tabitha Chadwick well, she could not imagine that the woman would have relished the thought of Nelson marrying a prostitute. No matter how high-class Phoebe's establishment was, there was no ignoring the fact that it was a house of ill repute.

"That's possible," Jason said, nodding his head, "but without proof, it's only speculation."

And that was the problem. "The sheriff won't believe it. He'll probably say I imagined it. You know how he dismissed my story of Phoebe being left-handed." Elizabeth clenched her fists, remembering that the sheriff had suggested she let Phoebe die. "In his mind, he's already tried and convicted her."

Jason reached for Elizabeth's hands and unfurled her fin-

374

gers. "We won't give up. All we need to do is find a way to prove that he's wrong."

Elizabeth smiled at the way Jason made it sound easy. Though the situation was deplorable, she could not deny that she was pleased by the way she and Jason were handling it, the way each of them seemed to understand what the other was saying.

Her smile broadened. "What if we . . . ?"

It was only four blocks. He could have walked, but Jason suspected Tabitha Chadwick's butler or maid or whoever opened the door would be more likely to admit him if he came in a carriage, and so he'd rushed to the livery for his. He'd also taken the time to change into his Sunday suit, suspecting that Tabitha would be favorably impressed. Jason was leaving nothing to chance. One way or another, he was determined to see the grieving widow before she learned that Phoebe was still alive.

As he flicked the reins and headed east on 15th Street, Jason felt excitement rush through his veins. It was true that he had been sorely disappointed that yesterday evening had not proceeded according to his plans. It had been tragic that Nelson had been killed, and yet something good had come from it. Jason smiled, recalling how often the reverend had reminded his parishioners that God had the power to turn evil to good. That had happened for Jason.

The time he had spent with Elizabeth in the aftermath of Nelson's death had erased Jason's last doubts. For the first time, he truly understood what Kevin Granger had meant when he'd spoken of his life with Ruby as a partnership.

Jason's hours with Elizabeth had been exhilarating. Never before had he felt as if he'd been united with the other half of himself. He hadn't known what had been missing until he found it, but now that he had, nothing would ever convince him to give it up. Elizabeth might have responsibilities in addition to being his wife and the mother of his children. She might not always be at home. But Jason knew beyond the shadow of a doubt that the time they spent together would be so wonderful that nothing else mattered.

Last night and today had been like that. He and Elizabeth had worked together, devising a plan to determine whether Tabitha had killed her husband. Jason shook his head. *Work* was the wrong word. That made it sound like a chore, when in fact, it had been as close to pleasure as was possible, given the fact that they were dealing with murder. He and Elizabeth had completed each other's sentences, almost as if their thoughts had been aligned. She would say one thing, and that would trigger a new idea in his brain. Together they were stronger and smarter than either one was alone. It truly felt as if they were partners in the highest sense of the word, two people working together for a common goal.

Jason grinned as he turned onto Warren. The feelings he had for Elizabeth—oh, why mince words?—the *love* he had for her had deepened as they'd put their heads together, literally as well as figuratively, to devise a way to prove Phoebe's innocence. There was nothing he had wanted more than to declare his love and place the ring that he still carried in his pocket on Elizabeth's left hand, but that would have to wait until they'd found Nelson's killer. That was why Jason was in front of Tabitha Chadwick's house. The first step was his. If it succeeded, Elizabeth would take the next.

Though his instincts urged him to race up the front stairs of the Chadwick mansion, Jason forced himself to move at a decorous pace. He was, after all, supposed to be paying a condolence call. That demanded slow and deliberate movements.

"Would you tell Mrs. Chadwick that Jason Nordling has come on a matter of some urgency," he said when a neatly uniformed maid opened the door. Though the maid appeared startled by the presence of a single man, Jason suspected that Tabitha was not as devastated by her widowhood as Miriam's mother had claimed and that she would welcome a male visitor, especially one with whom she'd flirted as blatantly as she had with Jason.

His theory was confirmed when the maid returned only seconds later and ushered him into a small sitting room. There he found Tabitha reclining on what he had been told was a fainting couch. Though she was dressed in unrelieved black as befitted a widow, Jason noticed that the neckline of her dress was far lower than most widows would have deemed respectable, and her face bore no sign of tears or grief.

He gave her a short bow, then fixed his gaze on her as he said, "I came to extend my condolences. Nelson was a fine man."

"Indeed he was." Tabitha extended her hand, gesturing toward a chair a mere foot from her couch. Curiosity shone from her green eyes, giving Jason the impression that she wondered whether he'd come to express more than sympathy. Surely the woman did not believe he'd court her so soon after her husband's death. But, Jason reminded himself, Tabitha might have killed Nelson not only to avoid potential shame but to free herself to marry again.

"I don't know how I'll survive without Nelson." Tabitha's words were expected. Only the tone rang false.

Jason said nothing, simply inclined his head to encourage her to continue. It was a technique that had worked well with witnesses, rarely failing to elicit more information. It did not fail today.

"That woman robbed me of the only man I've ever loved." Jason was certain it was not his imagination that the words sounded rehearsed. Tabitha Chadwick was a clever woman. She knew visitors would expect her to express her grief, and so she had prepared her speech as carefully as a politician. "My only consolation is that that woman paid the price for her wickedness."

Keeping his expression impassive, Jason exulted in the fact that Tabitha had not heard the whole story. It was what he had been counting on, that he would have the element of surprise. He wanted to see Tabitha's reaction when she learned that Phoebe was not in fact dead.

"I don't understand," Jason said softly. "What do you mean, paid the price?"

Tabitha's lip curled in scorn. "That woman—that whore—killed Nelson and then she killed herself. She was a wicked, wicked woman, and she deserves to rot in hell." Tabitha began to sob, but Jason noticed that there were no real tears, only what seemed like practiced sounds.

He waited until the forced sobs subsided before he said, "I'm afraid you're mistaken. Mrs. Simcoe is still alive. Dr. Harding arrived in time to save her."

Tabitha's head, which had been bent in feigned sorrow, jerked up. The blood drained from her face, leaving her green eyes startlingly bright against pale cheeks. "That can't be.

I . . ." She hesitated for a second too long. "I heard she was dead. The sheriff said she was dead."

If he had been a betting man, Jason would have bet a sizable sum on the fact that Tabitha had started to say, "I killed her." Tabitha was guilty. Guilty as sin. She murdered Nelson and tried to kill Phoebe. Jason was certain of it. All he had to do was prove it.

When Tabitha laid an imploring hand on his arm, he tried to hide his revulsion. Though he wanted to fling her hand away, he did not. Instead, he spoke softly. "Mrs. Simcoe was close to death when the sheriff saw her. He may have believed that she would succumb to her wounds within a few hours."

"But she's alive?" Fear mingled with shock, leaving Tabitha vulnerable and coloring her voice with genuine emotion.

"Barely so. Dr. Harding is keeping a vigil over her. She only leaves the infirmary for a brief evening meal." As Jason watched, a calculating gleam filled Tabitha's eyes. "The doctor is hopeful, though, that Mrs. Simcoe will recover enough to stand trial. A jury will decide her punishment once they hear her testimony."

"Testimony?" The word came out as little more than a squeak.

"Her version of what happened last night."

Tabitha was silent for a moment. "Yes, of course." Her eyes narrowed slightly, and Jason could practically hear the thoughts racing through her brain.

The trap was baited.

25

It couldn't be! Tabitha stomped her foot in frustration. Phoebe Simcoe could not have survived a knife slicing into her chest. No one could. But it appeared that evil woman, the one who had bewitched Nelson, was stronger than Nelson. He'd been easy to kill.

Tabitha stomped her foot again. It might be childish, but she didn't care. She had to do something to relieve the tension that had been building up inside her ever since Jason had announced that Phoebe had survived the attack.

He didn't know who'd been responsible for the Simcoe woman's wounds. There was no way he could know that. He'd merely come to express his condolences and to remind Tabitha of his interest in her. Jason didn't know the truth. There were only two people who did, and by the time today ended, that number would be reduced to one. Tabitha would not fail this time.

She stared sightlessly out the window as she considered the possibilities. Jason had said that Elizabeth went home for supper. If the gossipmongers were accurate, he would accompany her. Phoebe would be alone. But what if she were not? What if Jason remained or the doctor asked someone else to watch over her patient? Tabitha could not afford to take any chances. Her plan must be foolproof.

She clenched the windowsill, then spun around when she realized what she would do.

"Camille!" she shouted. "Come here."

"Are you certain this is all I can do for you?" Laura Seaman asked as she slid Elizabeth's cloak over her shoulders.

Elizabeth nodded. So far everything was going as planned. The weather had even cooperated. The evening was cold, giving Laura a reason to use the hood. Though she was the same height as Elizabeth, and the bulky cloak would disguise her thinness, the streetlights would have revealed the difference in their hair colors, for Laura's was many shades lighter than Elizabeth's. This way, all anyone would see was Jason walking with a woman, and since it was common knowledge that he normally accompanied Elizabeth, there would be no reason to suspect that his companion was anyone other than the doctor.

Though Jason had protested initially, declaring he did not want to leave Elizabeth alone, she had pointed out that Tabitha might become suspicious if they deviated from their routine. Both of them suspected Tabitha would be watching Elizabeth's office, waiting for her to leave.

"Besides," Elizabeth had reasoned, "I won't be alone. The sheriff will be here."

He hadn't come. Telling Jason that he and Elizabeth were

engaged in a wild goose chase, the sheriff had claimed he had more important ways to spend his time than waiting for a phantom murderer to appear. Eventually, faced with Jason's persistence, he had relented and sent his deputy. The man was even now seated in the infirmary, waiting for Elizabeth to return to her patient's bedside.

Laura gestured toward the cloak that made her resemble Elizabeth. "This seems like nothing at all compared to what you gave me. It's a miracle, having Louella." Laura's brown eyes softened as she smiled. "Louis is excited about being a big brother, and Lloyd and I . . ." She paused, clearing her throat. "There aren't enough words to tell you how happy we are."

Though her mind whirled with thoughts of what was to come, Elizabeth smiled at her patient. "I'm happy for all of you," she said. "I know you'll give Louella the love she deserves."

"That we will." Laura clasped her gloved hands together. "What do I do next?"

Elizabeth handed her the now-empty medical bag. "You and Jason will go out the front door, then walk as quickly as you can to my home. Don't run, but I want anyone who might be watching to think you're in a hurry." As Laura inclined her head in agreement, Elizabeth continued. "Gwen will be expecting you. I don't know how long we'll be here, but Jason will come back to take you home as soon as he can." He'd been the one who'd delivered the message to Laura and who'd brought her in through Elizabeth's back door an hour earlier. Though they both thought it unlikely that anyone was keeping the office under surveillance before dark, extra precautions couldn't hurt.

"Thank you again," Elizabeth said as Laura walked toward

the front door, her head held high in an imitation of Elizabeth herself.

Once she heard the door close, Elizabeth returned to the infirmary, where a small lamp burned. It was the same lamp that she'd lit at Phoebe's arrival. Though she extinguished it during the day, as the sun began to set, she'd lit it again, just as she would have if Phoebe were still in the room. Though, like many of the buildings in Cheyenne, her office had electricity, Elizabeth preferred the softer light of a lamp in the infirmary.

"They're gone," Elizabeth said as she slipped her arms into a nightshirt and reached for the wide white bandage she'd laid out earlier.

"And now we wait." Unlike the skeptical sheriff, the deputy seemed excited about his assignment, admitting this would be his first chance to apprehend a murderer. His eyes widened as he watched Elizabeth wind the bandage around her head. "If you don't mind my saying so, Doctor, that's a most unusual hat."

"But a necessary one. If Mrs. Chadwick comes, she'll expect to see Mrs. Simcoe, not a woman with brown hair." Elizabeth tucked in the end of the bandage, securing it. "This hat, as you call it, will keep her from realizing that the patient in that bed is not the woman she tried to kill."

Earlier that day, Elizabeth and Jason had moved Phoebe into Elizabeth's office. Fortunately, the infirmary bed had wheels, allowing them to push it with only a modicum of difficulty.

Elizabeth climbed onto the cot that Jason had found for her and pulled the sheets up to her neck. "I'm ready."

The deputy nodded and moved behind a large dressing

screen that Jason had positioned in the far corner of the room. "And now we wait to see if she comes."

Though she understood the deputy's skepticism, Elizabeth refused to entertain the idea of failure. If Tabitha had killed her husband—and Elizabeth believed she had—she would want to ensure that Phoebe did not live to testify against her.

"She'll come."

It felt strange, walking to Elizabeth's home with a woman who wasn't Elizabeth. On another occasion, Jason might have enjoyed Laura Seaman's company. Tonight, though, the thought that was foremost in his mind was whether Elizabeth might even now be confronting a murderer.

She wasn't alone. He reminded himself of that. The deputy was there. He would protect Elizabeth if Tabitha arrived before Jason could return to the infirmary. Elizabeth would be safe, and soon Tabitha Chadwick would be in custody.

"I think I felt a snowflake."

It would take more than a tiny piece of frozen water to distract Jason. He and Mrs. Seaman were almost at the corner of 17th and Ferguson. In less than five minutes, he'd have delivered her to Gwen, and then he'd be on his way back to Elizabeth.

As they turned the corner, Jason saw a carriage stopped in front of the apartment Elizabeth shared with Gwen. The dry goods store had closed for the day, so it couldn't be a customer. A feeling of apprehension slithered down Jason's spine. There was no reason to worry, and yet this was the first time someone had parked there.

"Doctor! Doctor!" A young woman leaned out the carriage window. "Come quickly. Mrs. Chadwick needs you."

How much time had passed? It felt like eons, but Elizabeth suspected it had been only a few minutes. Jason and Laura would not have had enough time to reach the apartment. It was merely the anxiety that welled deep inside her that made Elizabeth tremble. There was no reason to be afraid. The deputy was here.

She lay motionless, wishing she could talk but knowing that even a whispered conversation might keep them from hearing the door open. They must remain alert.

Another eon passed before a scream rent the night.

"Help me!" a woman cried. "Help me! He's killing me!"

The screams were close, coming from the alley behind Elizabeth's office. Elizabeth sat up and swung her legs over the side of the bed, but before she could do more, the deputy rushed from behind the screen, his revolver drawn.

"You need to stay here, Doctor. I'll call you if I need you."

The next sounds she heard were a thud and footsteps.

Mrs. Seaman looked at Jason, confusion evident in her brown eyes. "What should I do?"

Jason thought quickly. Though he was almost certain this was some kind of ruse, he could not risk anyone's life, not even Tabitha Chadwick's. If she really did need a physician's care, Jason would find a way to get it to her, but he would do nothing to endanger Mrs. Seaman.

"Go upstairs," he said softly, pointing to the outdoor staircase that led to Elizabeth's apartment. "I'll come for you later." As she turned, Jason approached the carriage. "What's wrong?" he asked. "The doctor's gone to fetch some supplies."

The woman in the carriage frowned, as if she hadn't expected that and wasn't certain how to respond. "Mrs. Chadwick collapsed," she said. "She went to the lumber company, and she was so upset that she collapsed."

It was a ruse, an attempt to keep Elizabeth away from her office. Jason was certain of that. Not only was it implausible that Tabitha would have gone to Nelson's place of work at night, but the woman's speech sounded as rehearsed as Tabitha's declaration of sorrow had.

Jason climbed into the carriage and faced the woman. "Where is she? Where is Tabitha?" he demanded.

Cringing, the woman repeated her earlier lies. "I told you. She's at the lumber company. She collapsed."

"Try again." Jason adopted the menacing tone one of his professors had claimed would elicit the truth from even a hardened criminal. "I don't believe you."

The woman shrank against the seatback. "I don't know. She didn't tell me. All she said was I was supposed to take you and the doctor to the lumberyard."

She was telling the truth. The woman might not be innocent, but she was ignorant of Tabitha's plans. Jason would learn nothing more from her. He leaned out and called to the coachman. "Take me to Dr. Harding's office. As fast as those horses will go."

Elizabeth needed him.

They were a woman's footsteps, and though the person who had entered her office through the rear door said nothing, Elizabeth knew those footsteps belonged to Tabitha. She had come to kill Phoebe. Elizabeth had expected that; however, she had not expected that neither Jason nor the deputy would be here when Tabitha arrived. Their plan had unraveled, and there was no one to help Elizabeth.

She retrieved one item from her instrument drawer, then settled on the cot, pulling up the sheets and turning on her side so that she faced the wall. Tabitha would expect Phoebe to be the occupant of the bed, and while most people saw what they expected, Elizabeth would take no chances. When she entered the infirmary, Tabitha would see only the back of a woman with a bandaged head.

Firm footsteps announced the visitor's arrival. For a second, there was no sound other than the two women's breathing. Then Tabitha laughed, a sound so devoid of mirth that it sent a shiver down Elizabeth's spine.

"There you are." There was no mistaking Tabitha Chadwick's voice. "You thought you were so smart, didn't you, trying to steal my husband? You were wrong, Phoebe. I gave up more than you can possibly imagine to become Nelson's wife, and I have no intention of being humiliated by a whore like you." Her voice filled with venom, Tabitha fairly spat the words. "You should have died the first time, but don't worry. You'll die tonight."

This was the confession Elizabeth and Jason had hoped to elicit. The problem was, there was no one but Elizabeth to hear it. She could only pray that the deputy would regain consciousness—for surely Tabitha had not killed him when she'd lured him outside with her false cries for help—in time to apprehend Tabitha.

Elizabeth lay quietly, wondering what Tabitha would do next. The woman seemed to have exhausted her supply of vitriol.

Elizabeth heard the swishing of something soft, perhaps a scarf, and guessed that Tabitha intended to strangle Phoebe. Moving so swiftly that Tabitha had no way of anticipating it, Elizabeth rolled onto her other side and sat up, facing Tabitha.

"Killing me won't accomplish anything. The sheriff knows that you murdered your husband and tried to kill Phoebe."

For a second, Tabitha stared at Elizabeth, confusion evident in her expression.

"Dr. Harding? What are you doing here? You're supposed to be . . ." Tabitha looked around the infirmary, clearly searching for signs of Phoebe. When her gaze returned to Elizabeth, Tabitha's green eyes filled with malevolence. "Where is she?"

Elizabeth kept her eyes fixed on Tabitha, refusing to even glance in the direction of her examination room, where Phoebe lay. "Safe," she said, keeping the scalpel that she held in her right hand hidden from Tabitha's view. It wasn't much of a weapon, but when she realized she was alone, Elizabeth had wanted some way to defend herself.

Tabitha shook her head. "She's here. I know she is." Pulling a pistol from her pocket, she pointed it at Elizabeth. "Come along, Doctor. We're going to find your patient, and when we do, you're going to kill her."

The woman was mad. That was the only explanation Elizabeth could find. Tabitha's anger and hatred had grown to monstrous proportions. She knew that Elizabeth would never kill a patient, and yet she seemed to believe it was a reasonable demand.

Elizabeth clutched the scalpel, wondering how she could use it to disarm Tabitha. She couldn't let her harm Phoebe, and yet there seemed no way to keep Tabitha from finding her. If Elizabeth refused to tell her where Phoebe was, Tabitha would simply shoot her and then search the office until she found Phoebe. Phoebe's only hope was for Elizabeth to stall Tabitha until Jason returned. *Please, Lord, make it soon.*

"There's no reason to kill Phoebe," Elizabeth said, keeping her voice as calm as she could. "She can't hurt you."

Tabitha's lip curled in disgust. "She bewitched Nelson. She deserves to die. Now, show me where she is."

Elizabeth slid the scalpel under her skirt, then began to unwind the bandage she'd wrapped around her head. Tabitha watched, almost as if she were mesmerized. "Why were you wearing that?"

"I wanted you to think I was Phoebe. I knew you'd try to kill her again, but I couldn't let that happen." Elizabeth folded the bandage, moving slowly and deliberately, as if there was nothing more important than having a precisely folded piece of cloth. When she finished, she removed the nightshirt she'd used to cover her own dress.

"How did you know I was the one?" Tabitha demanded. "I didn't leave any clues. I know I didn't."

Elizabeth lifted her left hand and mimicked a stabbing motion. "Phoebe is left-handed. She couldn't have inflicted those wounds herself."

For the first time, Elizabeth saw hesitation in Tabitha's expression, but it was only momentary. "Stop stalling," she said. "I want to see that woman."

See, not kill. Perhaps there was hope. Elizabeth stood and moved toward the door leading to the hallway. Taking Tabitha through the waiting room would require more time than going through the kitchen and across the hall to the examination room.

The waiting room was dark. Though Elizabeth knew she

could find her way without switching on the lights, she stopped and pretended to fumble with the switch. Light flooded the room.

"Of course she's not here. This is the waiting room." Tabitha sounded annoyed, and she jabbed the barrel of her gun into Elizabeth's back. "Where is she? Where is that harlot?"

Where was Jason? Elizabeth couldn't let Tabitha come any closer to Phoebe. She had to do something to stop the woman from killing again. Gripping the scalpel firmly, Elizabeth spun around and held it to Tabitha's throat.

"You can kill me if you want, but you'll die too. A woman who's been shot still has enough strength to cut your jugular vein."

Tabitha blinked but pressed the gun against Elizabeth's chest. "You wouldn't."

"Are you willing to risk your life?"

"Faster." Though the carriage careened around the corner, it wasn't fast enough for Jason. He had to reach Elizabeth. He had to know that she was safe and that the deputy had Tabitha in custody. There was no reason to worry, he told himself, and yet he did. As the buggy approached Elizabeth's office, Jason's sense of foreboding grew. Though the waiting room shades were drawn, light seeped around the edges. Why? No one should be there, and Elizabeth was far too frugal to light a room unnecessarily.

Leaping down from the carriage, Jason sprinted to the front door. As his hand touched the knob, he heard a small voice deep inside himself say, "Quietly." And so he opened the door as gently as he could and entered the hallway, every movement stealthy.

It was only a few steps to the waiting room. Jason reached the doorway, his breath catching and dread filling his heart when he saw them. The two women stood face-to-face, only inches apart. Elizabeth held a knife to Tabitha's throat, while the woman who had already killed at least one person had a gun in her hand, a gun that was pointed at Elizabeth's heart.

He would have only one chance. Jason knew that as surely as he knew that Elizabeth would never use that knife for harm. He took two long strides into the room, and then, heedless of the noise, leapt forward and knocked Tabitha to the floor.

The gunshot was deafening.

Shaking her head in a vain effort to stop her ears from ringing, Elizabeth knelt on the floor next to Jason and Tabitha. It had all happened so fast that she hadn't been able to see what occurred. One second Tabitha was pointing the gun at her. The next, both she and Jason were lying on the ground. And sometime—before, during, or after the fall, Elizabeth wasn't certain when—Tabitha's gun had gone off. Though she saw no blood, Elizabeth couldn't stop her heart from pounding with fear at the thought that Jason might have been wounded. Or worse.

Slowly, Jason shifted his weight and sat up, apparently unharmed. *Thank you, Lord.*

"Are you all right?" Elizabeth asked.

"Yes, and so is Tabitha. She's just stunned." Jason gestured toward the wall that separated the waiting and examination rooms. "Your wall wasn't so lucky."

A nervous laugh escaped from Elizabeth. That and the fact that her limbs were trembling like leaves in a thunderstorm were the natural aftermath of the ordeal she'd endured. She would be light-headed, even a little dizzy, for a few minutes, but then the effects would subside. She was safe. Even more importantly, so was Phoebe.

"Where's the deputy?"

It was Tabitha who answered Jason's question. "At the back door, out cold. The man was so worried about answering my cry for help that he didn't notice I was waiting for him with a brick in my hands." Once again Tabitha's laugh held no mirth.

Elizabeth scrambled to her feet. "I'd better check on him." The man would need a physician.

"Could you give me some bandages first?"

Feeling the blood drain from her face, Elizabeth stared at Jason. "I thought you were unharmed."

"I am, but I want to tie Tabitha's hands and feet. Then she's going to take a trip to the sheriff."

As Elizabeth watched, a calculating gleam filled Tabitha's eyes.

"You'll help me, won't you?" she asked Jason. "Help me like you did Adam Bennett. I'm no guiltier than he was."

Jason stared at her, his expression mirroring his incredulity. "That will never happen," he said, his voice steely with resolve. "If the sheriff agrees, I'll be the prosecuting attorney. I intend to see that you pay for everything you've done. It's the least I can do for Nelson and Elizabeth."

"Would you have used the scalpel?"

It was two hours later. The deputy had regained consciousness, and after he'd heard Elizabeth and Jason's story and the venom spewing from Tabitha's mouth, he'd announced that Tabitha would be spending tonight and all the nights until her trial in jail. When the deputy and his prisoner had left, Jason had helped Elizabeth wheel Phoebe back into the infirmary, then left to take Laura Seaman home. Now he was back, sitting at the kitchen table with Elizabeth.

"I don't know," she said in response to Jason's question. "I know I couldn't have killed Tabitha, but I also knew I couldn't let her hurt Phoebe. I kept stalling, and all the while I prayed that God would send you back in time. He did."

Jason's eyes glistened with an emotion Elizabeth could not identify. "He did more than that. He warned me to be quiet when I came inside. That way Tabitha didn't know I was there."

"I didn't, either." There had been a moment of confusion when Tabitha fell and the gun went off, but it had been followed by overwhelming relief that no one had died.

"Did you tell Laura what happened?"

Jason nodded. "I also stopped at the Taggerts' house. Cyrus is going to print a special edition of the paper, revealing the truth about what happened in Phoebe's parlor."

"I'm glad." Though Elizabeth could not condone Phoebe's way of life, the woman did not deserve to be blamed for a crime she did not commit. "Thank you."

Jason's lips curved into a smile. "Were the thanks for talking to Cyrus or getting the gun away from Tabitha?"

"Both. And many more things. Without you, I would not have been able to trap Tabitha. I wouldn't have been sure she was Nelson's murderer."

Jason's smile turned into a full-fledged grin. "We make

good partners." His voice deepened as he pronounced the last word. With a rueful glance at the stove and small dry sink, he stretched out his hands, capturing Elizabeth's. "This isn't the place I would have chosen," he said, his blue eyes fixed on hers, "but I don't want to waste another minute. Seeing how fast life can end made me realize that each moment is precious." He swallowed deeply, then tightened his grip on Elizabeth's hands. "I meant what I said about us being good partners. I don't want that to end. Will you be my partner for life? Will you marry me?"

He wanted to marry her! Elizabeth's heart soared, then sank as she recalled their conversations and the doubts Jason had shared with her. She closed her eyes, searching for the right words. "I want to," she said softly as she once again gazed at him. "But I'm afraid."

Jason laughed. "You? The woman who volunteered to be a decoy, the same woman who faced a gun without flinching, is afraid?" She must have winced, for she saw contrition in Jason's eyes. He raised her hands to his lips and pressed a kiss on them. "I'm sorry. I shouldn't have laughed. What do you fear? Is it me?"

She shook her head, then nodded. "I'm afraid of disappointing you. I'm afraid that after the initial . . ." She stumbled over the word "love." Jason had never used it, and she would not be the one to introduce it. Instead, she settled for saying "feelings." "I'm afraid they will fade and that you'll regret our marriage. You've told me what your childhood was like and how much you missed having a mother's influence on your life." Jason nodded slowly, encouraging her to continue. It had been a night of drama, and though she had faced the possibility of dying, somehow that seemed less frightening than watching the man she loved discover she was not the woman of his dreams.

"I know you want children. I do too, but I'm a doctor, Jason. I can't give that up, even for you."

He met her gaze, his eyes solemn as he said, "I wouldn't ask you to."

His words were brave, and yet she wondered if he truly understood just how difficult living with a doctor could be. "You've seen what my life is like. I never know when I'll be called away. I might miss our children's birthdays or Christmas, and there'll be times when I'm gone for days on end."

"I know that." Jason tightened the grip on her hands, as if he were afraid she might try to flee. "Believe me, Elizabeth, I've thought about that. I can't count the number of times I've asked myself if that was the life I wanted, and the answer was always the same. I'd rather have a few hours a day with you than all twenty-four with another woman."

Elizabeth's heart began to pound at the sincerity she heard in his voice, the emotion she saw in his eyes. Maybe, just maybe, they'd have the happily-ever-after they both wanted.

"At first, our lives won't be much different during the day," Jason continued. "I'm used to your having office hours. And if you're called out at night, I could go with you. I could drive the buggy and wait for you. Heaven knows, I had plenty of practice waiting for the reverend." Jason's lips curved upward again. "It wasn't bad then, but it'll be much better when I know that the waiting will end with us going home together. You can't imagine how often I've thought about that."

As she had. Only she had tried to deny it.

As if he understood, Jason gave her a crooked smile. "When the children arrive, we'll figure out the best way to raise them.

Together. That's what I want. I want us to be partners for the rest of our lives."

He paused, and as he did, Elizabeth felt the warmth from his hands spread up her arms, melting her last doubts. Jason did understand what their life would be like, and he was ready to do everything he could to make their marriage a success. He was right. They were partners. They worked well together. They completed each other's sentences. And yet what they shared was more, much more than partnership. They shared love.

Jason was the man Elizabeth loved, the one she wanted to spend the rest of her life with. And, though he hadn't said the words, she knew he returned that love. His expression, his actions, everything about him told her that. She knew it, and yet, though perhaps it was foolish, she longed for the words. Three simple words. Eight letters.

"Jason, I—"

He shook his head. "Please, let me continue." He released Elizabeth's hands and reached into his pocket, pulling out a square box that could hold only one thing. Elizabeth caught her breath, her heart leaping with joy at the proof that Jason's proposal was not a hasty one. He had done more than think about marriage; he had acted to make it reality.

His expression once more solemn, as if he were uncertain of her response, Jason said, "I had hoped to give you this last night after the concert." He opened the box, revealing the most beautiful ring Elizabeth had ever seen. Unlike her sisters, she had never fantasized about engagement rings, for she'd never believed that she would marry. But as she gazed at the round diamond surrounded by dozens of tiny ones, Elizabeth knew that if she had dreamt of rings, this would have been the one she would have chosen.

Jason removed the ring from the box and extended it toward Elizabeth. "Will you wear my ring? Will you take my name? If God grants them to us, will you bear my children?"

The smile he gave her was so filled with love that Elizabeth could hardly breathe. She should never have doubted him. Jason had given her many beautiful words. He'd done more than that. Every action had shown his love. There was no need for him to pronounce those three special words. Elizabeth took a breath, but before she could speak, Jason continued. "I love you, Elizabeth. Will you marry me?"

Somehow this wonderful man must have seen deep into her heart and realized how much she longed to hear those words. Her heart overflowing with happiness, Elizabeth gazed into Jason's eyes and smiled. "There is nothing I want more."

As he slid the ring onto her finger, tears of joy pricked her eyes. "I love you, Jason. I think I have from the very beginning. Yes, my dearest, I will be your wife."

Epilogue

You've outdone yourself, Charlotte." Elizabeth smiled as her sister Abigail gestured toward the white velvet creation that had taken Charlotte the better part of two weeks to complete, seemingly oblivious to the fact that Elizabeth was in the same room and was wearing the dress that had garnered Abigail's praise. "This is the most beautiful wedding gown I've ever seen." Abigail let out a little chuckle. "Jason won't be able to take his eyes off Elizabeth."

"In case you haven't noticed," Charlotte retorted, "when our little sister is around, Jason wouldn't notice if a bison strolled through the door."

This was vintage Harding sisters. Though Abigail and her husband had arrived only ten days before, reuniting the three sisters for the first time in almost four years, she and Charlotte had fallen into old patterns, frequently acting as if Elizabeth were not present. Elizabeth didn't mind, for it gave her a chance to observe her sisters, reassuring herself

399

that they were as happy as they'd appeared when they arrived in Cheyenne.

Charlotte and Barrett had exclaimed in delight when they'd disembarked at the new train depot, describing the red sandstone building that had been open only a few weeks to David, despite the fact that the two-year-old seemed more interested in the smells from a passing mule train.

The scene had been repeated three weeks later when Abigail and Ethan arrived, accompanied by Puddles, their now fully grown dog. Though Abigail had claimed that he was no longer as frisky as he'd been as a puppy, Elizabeth wasn't sure. Whether it was the presence of David, who'd attached himself to Puddles like a tumbleweed to a skirt, or simply the fact that he'd been released from the confinement of the train, Puddles seemed as rambunctious as any puppy Elizabeth had seen.

Christmas had been the most joyous holiday she had spent in many years. Not only had she and her siblings been together, but Harrison and Gwen had joined the festivities at Barrett's mansion. While the adults enjoyed a sumptuous dinner, Barrett's cook and butler had taken Rose, David, and Puddles to the smaller parlor for a celebration that had provoked barks, shrieks, and an ominous crash. Barrett had only shrugged, pointing out that once Charlotte opened her school for blind children, crashes would become a regular occurrence until the pupils learned the location of each piece of furniture.

Though it had been a wonderful Christmas, nothing could compare to today. Today was Elizabeth's wedding day. Soon the wait would be over and she would be Jason's wife. In the meantime, she was surrounded by her sisters, one of whom was discussing bison.

"Far be it from me to correct my elders," Elizabeth said, emphasizing the last word, "but bison do not stroll. They lumber, they charge, but they do not stroll."

One eyebrow raised in feigned amazement. Abigail turned to Charlotte. "You'll notice that she didn't try to deny that Jason's smitten."

"As if your husbands aren't." Gazing into the long mirror that Charlotte had set up in her former bedroom, Elizabeth could watch both sisters. "Mama and Papa would be so happy if they could see us today—all of us happy and married." She wrinkled her nose. "Well, almost married." In little more than an hour, Elizabeth and Jason would be man and wife. Then the three Harding daughters would be living the lives Mama and Papa had wished for them.

"Stop wiggling. I've got four more buttons to fasten," Charlotte groused. "Honestly, Elizabeth, you squirm as much as David. In fact, I think you taught him how to squirm. He was a lot calmer before he met you."

Elizabeth suspected that Puddles was the real cause of David's activity. Abigail and Ethan were living with Charlotte and Barrett until they found the right location for their ranch, and David and the dog had become inseparable. Though now was not the time to mention it, Elizabeth would not be surprised if Charlotte and Barrett added a puppy to their household.

She wouldn't deny that she doted on David. "Can I help it if I spoil him? He's my only nephew." Elizabeth had been amazed at how much the two-year-old was able to do, despite being blind. There were times when, if she hadn't known otherwise, she would have thought him a perfectly sighted child. And, if she spoiled him, wasn't that an aunt's prerogative, practically her duty?

"I hope you'll dote on my child as much as you do Charlotte's." Abigail's words were muffled as she bent to straighten Elizabeth's train, and for a second, Elizabeth wasn't certain she'd heard correctly.

"Your child?" she cried at the same time as Charlotte.

Abigail nodded, her cheeks a rosy red that might have been caused by embarrassment. "I hadn't meant to let it slip out." She gave Elizabeth a rueful smile. "Today's supposed to be your day, little sister. But, yes, I believe I'll be having a baby in about seven months."

Heedless of the wrinkles she might put in her gown, Elizabeth hugged her sister. "Oh, how wonderful! That's the best wedding present you could have given me." She turned to Charlotte, who remained uncharacteristically silent. "It's grand news, isn't it?"

Though Charlotte nodded, her expression was enigmatic. "Of course it is," she said, giving Abigail a quick hug. "It's just that I have some news of my own. Barrett and I are also expecting a baby in about seven months."

"I don't believe it!" Abigail threw her arms around Charlotte, then opened one and drew Elizabeth into the embrace. "When we were growing up, I always wanted cousins. Now my baby will have at least two." Shooting Elizabeth another smile, she added, "You and Jason better hurry so they can all be playmates."

"Let's get her married first." Charlotte straightened an imaginary wrinkle before pronouncing Elizabeth ready to head for the church.

Half an hour later, as the organ played the processional, Elizabeth placed her hand on Harrison's arm and began the slow walk down the aisle behind her sisters. It was a walk that would change her life forever, uniting Elizabeth with the man she loved so dearly.

She smiled at the guests, some her patients, others Jason's clients, still others friends they'd both made. In the almost two months since Tabitha Chadwick had been arrested for her husband's murder, both Elizabeth's practice and Jason's had grown. Though she would never have chosen it as a way to gain acceptance, the tragedy of Nelson's death and Elizabeth and Jason's role in uncovering his killer seemed to have brought the city together in support of them. Today Cheyenne's residents were here to celebrate their marriage. Only Miriam and Richard were absent, for even though Miriam had pleaded, Elizabeth had not wanted her out of bed for an extended period. The baby was almost due, and Elizabeth would take no chances.

Her smile broadened when she reached the front pew. Gwen stood there, Rose and David at her side, her eyes glistening with tears of happiness. Elizabeth suspected she was recalling her own wedding, less than a month earlier. Since then, other than Christmas Day, Elizabeth had seen Gwen only briefly, but each time, she'd been struck by the pure joy that radiated from her. Gwen had found the love of her life, and though it was too soon to know for certain, Elizabeth suspected that Rose would have a little sister or brother by next Christmas.

Thoughts of Gwen vanished as Elizabeth focused on the man waiting for her, his face wreathed in the sweetest smile she had ever seen. This was the man she loved, the man who returned her love, the man who wanted to share her life, no matter how unpredictable it might be.

"Dearly beloved." The minister intoned the familiar words. When Jason tightened his grip on her hand, Elizabeth's smile widened. How could she have ever doubted that this was what God had intended for her?

"I now pronounce you man and wife."

As the minister's words faded, Jason's lips curved. "I love you," he whispered as he pressed his lips to hers. "I love you, Mrs. Nordling." It was a brief kiss, as befitted the surroundings, but it was so filled with tenderness and love that Elizabeth knew she would remember it for the rest of her life.

"And I—"

Before she could complete her sentence, the church door banged open. "You gotta come!" Delia shouted. "Miss Miriam's having her baby."

Jason's laugh echoed through the sanctuary. A second later, he grabbed Elizabeth's hand. As they raced down the aisle, ignoring the guests' shocked expressions, he laughed again. "Come on, Dr. Nordling. We've got work to do."

Dear Reader,

We've reached the end of another series, and as was the case when I finished Texas Dreams, I'm filled with mixed emotions. There's satisfaction at typing the final words of a trilogy, but I'm going to miss sharing my days with one of the Harding sisters. It was such fun bringing them to life for you.

The good news is that, although Westward Winds has ended, a new series is starting. For this one, I'm taking you to a very different time and place: a resort in the modern-day Texas Hill Country. Here's a peek at what's coming.

Nestled in the middle of the Hill Country, Rainbow's End was a premier resort in its heyday. Unfortunately, that heyday is long past, and it's now little more than a collection of dilapidated buildings set in the midst of some spectacularly beautiful scenery. Unless a miracle occurs, the resort will close at the end of the season.

Advertising maven Kate Sherwood has her life all planned, and that plan doesn't include spending a month at Rainbow's End. But family ties bring her to Texas, where she soon discovers that nothing—including the handsome handyman—is what she expected. I hope you'll join me for Kate's story, which will be available this fall.

While you're waiting for that, I'm delighted to tell you that I'm part of Revell's first novella collection, *Sincerely Yours*. In this collection of stories by four different authors, four young women find their lives changed after each receives a letter that sets her on a new path toward a changed life—and perhaps lifelong love. *Sincerely Yours* will be released this April.

If *With Autumn's Return* was your first Westward Winds book, I urge you to pick up a copy of the others. *Summer of Promise* is the story of Abigail, who's convinced that Wyoming is the most boring place on earth until stagecoach bandits, a handsome Army lieutenant, and a mischievous puppy change her mind. *Summer of Promise* also introduces Charlotte, whose story continues in *Waiting for Spring*. You know that she marries Barrett, but I assure you that the road to happily-ever-after wasn't an easy one for her.

I also hope you'll visit my website (www.amandacabot. com) and sign up for my newsletter. I don't issue them too often, but they're my way of telling readers about new books and other good news. My email address and the link to my Facebook and blog pages are there too. I truly love hearing from you, so don't be shy.

Blessings,
Amanda Cabot

Dreams have always been an important part of **Amanda Cabot**'s life. For almost as long as she can remember, she dreamt of being an author. Fortunately for the world, her grade-school attempts as a playwright were not successful, and she turned her attention to writing novels. Her dream of selling a book before her thirtieth birthday came true, and she's been spinning tales ever since. She now has more than twenty-five novels to her credit under a variety of pseudonyms.

Her books have been finalists for the ACFW Carol award as well as the Booksellers Best and have appeared on the CBA bestseller list.

A popular speaker, Amanda is a member of ACFW and a charter member of Romance Writers of America. She married her high school sweetheart, who shares her love of travel and who's driven thousands of miles to help her research her books. After years as Easterners, they fulfilled a longtime dream and are now living in the American West.

Meet
Amanda Cabot
at www.AmandaCabot.com

Sign up for her newsletter and
learn fun facts about Amanda and her books

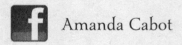 Amanda Cabot

"She creates characters that tug at my heartstrings, storylines that make my heart smile, and spiritual lessons that do my heart good."

—Kim Vogel Sawyer, bestselling author of *My Heart Remembers*

"There is romance, mystery, and the satisfaction of beating the odds to overcome the past and succeed at having love and happiness."

—*RT Book Reviews,* ★★★★

Don't Miss
Amanda Cabot's
NEW Contemporary Romance Series,
Releasing Fall 2014!

• • •

Visit AmandaCabot.com and sign up
for her newsletter to learn more